TOR BOOKS BY J. A. PITTS

Black Blade Blues
Honeyed Words
Forged in Fire

Black Blade Blues

J. A. Pitts

A TOM DOHERTY ASSOCIATES BOOK
NEW YORK

This is a work of fiction. All of the characters, organizations, and events portrayed in this novel are either products of the author's imagination or are used fictitiously.

BLACK BLADE BLUES

Copyright © 2010 by John A. Pitts

All rights reserved.

A Tor Book
Published by Tom Doherty Associates, LLC
175 Fifth Avenue
New York, NY 10010

www.tor-forge.com

Tor® is a registered trademark of Tom Doherty Associates, LLC.

ISBN 978-0-7653-6409-8

First Edition: May 2010
First Mass Market Edition: April 2011

Printed in the United States of America

0 9 8 7 6 5 4 3

This novel is dedicated to the three most important people in my life.

My wonderful wife, Kathleen, who has made my life a joy. I cannot imagine this journey without you at my side.

My son, John Patrick, who has grown to be a man of integrity and honor. You continue to amaze me with your wit and keen insight into the world.

And finally, my daughter, Emily Ann, who races through life with passion and a love of adventure. Don't grow up too fast. We have so many more books to share.

Acknowledgments

This book would not have been possible without the patience, encouragement, and support of a wide variety of people, some who will likely never know of their influence.

First of all, I need to thank the fine folks of Fairwood Writers Group who pushed me to be a better writer when I was unclear exactly what that meant—Renee Stern, Brenda Cooper, Patrick Swenson, Darragh Metzger, Leslie Clark, David Addleman, Allan Rousselle, Harold Gross, David Silas, Erin Tidwell, Janna Silverstein, Melissa Shaw, and Paul Melko.

First readers provide an immeasurable service to us poor writers, and I can't imagine succeeding without them. Thanks to Jen and Dan Berg, Rob Scott, Alecia Bolton, Chelsea and Owen Wessling, Cynthia and Jeff Wessling, Brenda Cooper, and Jay Lake for their insightful commentary.

Special thanks to Denise Little for buying the short story this novel is based on and including it in the anthology *Swordplay*, which came out in 2009. Also, Kris Rusch and Dean Smith, who showed me the possibilities and introduced me to Oregon Writers Network folks who have supported me so well over the last five years.

Of those who helped this become a reality, I'd like to express my utmost gratitude to my agent, Cameron McClure, who has done an excellent job keeping me informed and sane. Thanks to Claire Eddy for taking a chance on a newbie and being so excited about my work, and to Kristin Sevick for helping wrangle things in such a fine manner. And I would be remiss if I did not mention Irene Gallo and Dan Dos Santos for providing such an outstanding cover. I remain amazed at my good fortune.

Ken Scholes, my best writing buddy, and excellent friend. Jay Lake, mentor and guide on the road of my chosen career. Thanks to you both for sharing the campfires and braving the dragons on this adventure.

Finally, I'd like to acknowledge all the strong women who have influenced my life—from my great-aunt Dottie Buffin, who taught me to love science fiction, to Jules Unsel, who taught me the importance of seeing beyond my particular little corner of the world. These women have opened my eyes and filled my life with wonder.

Black Blade Blues

One

THE WARRIOR KING stood atop the hill, the light of a
new dawn cresting behind him. His pompadour, tall and
proud as a cockscomb, blocked the sun, casting his face
in shadow. Tiny shafts of light sprayed from the crystals
adorning his glowing white armor. The ebony blade he
held above his head drank in the light, casting a halo
around his upraised hands.

"I declare this land free from oppression," he called.
His voice rang. "I claim this, my birthright: this sword,
made from the shattered horn of Memphisto, and handed
down to me from my father, and from his father before
him. With this I cast the goblins from this land."

He swung the sword to drag it across the rocky crag
and shower sparks down upon the goblin horde at his
feet.

Instead, I watched the sword strike the ferrocrete stage
and snap. Fully one-third of the blade ricocheted toward
the goblins, who scattered, squealing.

Actors are so stupid—it was not supposed to actually
hit the stage. That's what special effects are for.

"Cut!" Carl called. Carl was the director.

JJ flung the sword to the ground, sending the goblins
into full retreat. "Stupid, useless props!"

The overhead lights came up, and the soundstage appeared, shattering the image of a vengeful King of Rock
and Roll and his mighty sword of doom.

I love my job.

"Everybody take fifteen," Carl said into his megaphone. "Sarah, do not kill the actors."

Several of the stagehands chuckled and cast sideways glances my way. I counted to ten. Honest I did. At least seven, I'm almost positive.

Seventeen extras in horrid rubber goblin suits began to waddle out to the lot, lighting cigarettes, their large costume heads under their arms.

I stormed over to JJ. "You idiot! You aren't supposed to actually hit the stage."

"Damn thing's too freaking heavy," he whined. "Can't we use a lighter prop? Maybe one that doesn't break?"

I knelt down, looking at the pieces. For a moment, I wanted to pummel JJ with the flat of the blade. I'd only likely bruise him. *Likely.*

Behind me, Carl sighed. "Do we have another black sword?"

"No," I said. Here goes a second career down the toilet.

"Well, it's too damn heavy," JJ groused. "Maybe you can make one out of Styrofoam or something."

I just stared at the back of his sweaty, overstyled head as he sauntered toward the gaggle of women waiting along the back of the soundstage.

With a sigh, I picked the sword up firmly by the handle. The broken blade lay forlornly on the rocks. It was a bad break, snapping midway to the tip. Be a bitch to repair this one. Reforging a sword was tricky business.

I do the blacksmithing thing for a living, so I had some idea what I was talking about. Being prop manager here was my night gig.

Not like I'd planned this life. I took welding in high school, and loved working with metal. I went to college to get away from my family—well, mainly my father—but didn't find any satisfaction in it. Da was convinced I'd come home after college and fit the mold he wanted.

The blacksmithing school I went to saved my life,

frankly. My father wanted me to get married and squeeze out half a dozen puppies, be a good homemaker, adore my husband, go to church. . . . I'd rather gouge my eyes out.

My farrier school gave me a reference to Julie Hendrickson, the blacksmith master I work for. She's supercool, but the pay doesn't cover all my bills. Student loans really add up.

I found the movie gig by accident. Carl hassled me at a local science fiction convention. He thought it was cool I was a blacksmith. We chatted—ended up he made movies, needed someone who was creative at making things, and here I am.

My two careers meshed together pretty well. Julie had no problem letting me use the forge after hours as long as I covered the expenses and cleaned up when I was done. Tonight's wages would cover fixing the black blade, and maybe help me afford to make a few more for the upcoming conventions.

Cons were a good place to sell weapons. Everyone who showed up wanted to be a hero, or be rescued by one. I was only too obliged to support the fantasy. Whatever made people happy, ya know? Of course, I'd be on my own for this effort. Julie was a farrier, and a good teacher, but her weapon skills sucked.

Which was a shame, actually. You could make a decent amount of scratch if you had made good weapons or armor. There was always someone willing to buy a cheap sword, but the real money was in the collectors and the cosplay folks. They liked the real thing. Costume players—cosplay. Anyway. They wanted to look the coolest, have the best accessories. I did my level best to fill that niche. Most shows had crappy knockoff weapons made in Pakistan, so I had a market.

But this sword, my black beauty, she was a special blade, not some beater we used in the Society or used to play dress-up. The Society for Creative Anachronism folks would never risk their precious weapons like this. Reenactors were crazy authentic, and treated their gear better than their spouses in some cases. The group I ran with— Black Briar—they were on the normal end of loony. Still, they thought I was nuts to risk a blade of this quality on a movie shoot.

Maybe they were right. I never should've risked the black sword here with ham-fisted JJ.

I carried the broken blade into the props cage and gently placed the pieces into the crushed velvet nest I'd hand-built for it. Who knew the case was better constructed than the blade?

"We won't need that sword again for a few days," Carl said, walking up behind me. "Why don't you take tomorrow off, see if you can repair it?"

Closing the case, I snapped the latches and hefted it up by the handle. "I'll do what I can," I said, smiling at him. "Plus, there's an antique auction in Seattle tomorrow. I'm hoping to get over and see if they have anything interesting."

Carl laughed. "You're quite the weapons nerd, Beauhall."

I stuck my chin up, tilting my head to the side. "You making fun of me, boss?"

He stepped back, hands in front of him, palms out, laughing. "God, no. I would never tease a blacksmith. I mean, with arms like yours . . ." He trailed off. "And any woman who collects swords, no chance." He gave me his best Boy Scout grin. "Too many sharp pointy things to be concerned about."

I smiled. He was cute, in a baby-faced sort of way. Not a bad director, either. More Ed Wood than Woody Allen, but his films didn't make me want to hurl. "All right, boss. I'll see you on Wednesday then?"

"You'll be bringing me a new ebony blade?"

"We're still doing wide-angle shots?"

"Yes, close-up shots aren't until next weekend."

"Okay, I'll have something you can use."

He grinned, but said nothing further.

I gave him a moment. "So, I'm not fired?"

"Not today."

"Great," I said. "We'll see how Tuesday goes."

Jennifer, the DP, came over shaking her head, complaining about the lighting. She was one of those high-maintenance photography directors who was worth every minute of time she sucked out of Carl. She'd have him tied up forever. The hangdog look on his face as I snuck away almost made me feel sorry for him.

Thing about Carl's films: most of the shoots happened after hours because nearly everyone had a day job, just to make ends meet. Tonight's was no exception. I had arrived here in Everett's industrial area, north of Seattle, around six forty after a hard day at the smithy. A quick shower at home, some decent clothes that didn't smell like smoke, and a drive-thru meal in me—I was good to go.

Carl worked a deal with the city to keep costs low so we shot from seven until midnight on good nights. Tonight was not a good night.

Two

IT WAS TWO thirty in the morning by the time I walked across the parking lot under sodium lights. As I was loading the case into my Civic, one of the goblins, a rather tall guy, black hair and beard, broke away from the smokers and sidled toward me. I didn't recognize him, but extras came and went with some regularity.

"Excuse me, miss," he said in a heavy Nordic accent.

"Something I can do for you?"

"I'd like to ask you about your sword," he said, speaking to my face instead of staring at my breasts. Just made eye contact. It was refreshing.

I closed the hatchback, gripping the car keys in my left hand. "She's a beauty," I said, and meant it. I liked that damn blade. But the craftsmanship left a lot to be desired.

"She?" he asked, taken aback. "You believe the sword to be female?"

"Oh, are you of the camp that all swords are phallic because of the sheath thing?" I asked him.

"I . . . Well . . ." He blinked furiously. "I just wanted to know where you got it."

Ah, a groupie. "I bought it in an estate sale, a couple years ago."

"Sweden?" he asked.

I laughed. Like I could afford to travel. "Why Sweden?"

"Because, you realize, the blade is Swedish."

Gotcha. I loved meeting other weapon geeks, but especially loved when they got things wrong. "It's Scandinavian. And I bought it in Seattle. There is a rather large Scandinavian population here."

"Well." He smiled. "I see how you Americans would mix up the lot of us—Swedes, Nords—Vikings all."

"Actually, Beauhall is Swedish, so I get the connections."

"My error," he said. "I was led to believe you were Celtic."

"I get that a lot."

I stood there, holding my keys, waiting for this to go . . . well, anywhere. He fidgeted a bit, scuffing his boots on the blacktop.

"Well, nice to have met you," I said finally, and walked around to the driver's side door.

"Why do you degrade it so?" he blurted out.

I looked back at him, standing in the circle of light cast by the streetlamp. He was gawkish and his skin almost glowed it was so white. Black beard, black hair. Something about him struck me as odd.

"Degrade what?" I asked.

"Fafnir's Bane."

A song ran through my head. It was one my girlfriend Katie sings sometimes at those science fiction conventions we attend.

> *I met a Swedish guy in Dublin*
> *who was going to school in France*
> *said he'd show me Odin's Gungnir*
> *if he could get inside my pants.*

"Fafnir's Bane?" I asked. Seriously? Norse myths and fairy tales? "You mean Gram, Sigurd's blade?"

I smelled stone then, like a gravel road when it first starts raining. I'll never forget that. The guy stepped toward me, keeping on the other side of the car, his eyes huge, drinking in the light. "Yes," he hissed. "You have become the caretaker, the guardian. Of those who have held that sword, I would expect you to be different." He paused, drawing in a rattling breath. "I can smell the forge on you."

Now I was insulted. I'd showered and everything. "Look, I'm exhausted. I'd be happy to talk swords with you after I've had some sleep. You could come by the shop one day this week, if you like—"

I fumbled in my wallet and pulled out a slightly bent business card.

"—and discuss it further." I held out the card.

He straightened, ran his thick fingers through his hair. "I sleep during the day. Work nights."

Yeah, I bet he did. This was annoying. "I gotta go."

I took a step back, and he reached for the card. He had big hands, rough from hard work. When his fingers touched mine, I caught a flash of heat and the distinct smell of hot metal.

The contact was brief, but for a split second there was a connection. Forge and hearth, hammers and tongs. This man worked metal, worked it with his body and his soul. It gave me a chill.

Under that funky costume, I bet he had shoulders like an ox.

"Good night, Ms. Beauhall." He nodded once, stepping back from me. "I'll be in touch."

I watched him as I ducked into the car.

I backed out of the space, keeping him in my mirror until the last moment. He stood there, staring at me with his hands tucked inside the rubber goblin head.

Big hands, thick fingers—connection with the forge and fire. Something about all that reminded me of the things Katie sang. She was always going on about elves and dwarves, magic stuff—myths and legends. I needed to call her to ask some questions.

I stopped at the shop. I kept the good swords in a safe there. Julie wouldn't be in until nine the next day.

I opened the safe and looked at my collection. There were some old blades in there. Some really old, but the black beauty was my favorite.

I was too tired to work, but I really wanted to fix the sword. Maybe tomorrow after we got the order out for Broken Switch Farm, I'd talk to Julie about me repairing this one.

The shop was strange at night, cold with the forge banked and the industrial ventilation turned off. I could smell sweat and smoke baked into the timbers of the place. Julie would be up in her trailer on the back of the lot, but the forge faced the main road. I wasn't exactly isolated, but for a moment, the emptiness scared me.

I placed the two halves of Gram on the anvil—funny how the name filled the blank spot in my brain. It felt right. I leaned against the rain barrel we used to cool horseshoes and studied the broken blade.

Another of Katie's songs swam in my head. Something about a dwarf from Dover and bending over . . . her lyrics trended toward raunchiness. But the line about the Dwarvish lover with big hands and their trysts in the dead of night made me think of the Swedish guy back in the parking lot.

Gram ended up in the safe with the rest of my treasures, and I slunk home, exhausted, and praying for sleep.

Three

KATIE MET ME at Monkey Shines for coffee before the auction. She was stunning in her teacher outfit—black mid-length skirt and white short-sleeved top. Hell, she was stunning in nothing at all, but that's beside the point.

Seeing her took the edge off my rocky morning. I'd slept poorly, with nightmares of ogres and trolls.

She kissed me while we were waiting for our drinks and the last of the night's stress melted away.

When I described the events of the night before, she got really excited.

"He's definitely a dwarf," she said over her mocha latte.

Katie lived the fantasy shit like no one else I knew. She spoke Elvish and even some Dwarvish from Tolkien, followed jousting troops like pro sports teams, and delved into myth and legend like most young women followed movie stars or rock bands.

"He's an extra on the *Elvis Versus the Goblins* thing I'm doing up at Carl's," I said, toying with my chocolate croissant. "I highly doubt a dwarf would be in Seattle, working on a low-budget movie. Besides, aren't dwarves short? This guy was easily six foot."

Katie waved a hand in my direction, like she was shooing flies. "You are so naïve. This isn't Disney." She leaned toward me. "Norse dwarves are as tall as normal people. They just can't be out in the daylight. It'll kill them."

I could tell she was getting excited, but come on. This was too much.

"If you have *the* Gram—"

She was practically bouncing in her seat.

"—a real magic sword . . . and this dude is a dwarf, maybe he'll help you reforge it. Give you some tips."

"You know this isn't real, right? He's just a guy and the sword is just metal. No magic, no gods. Just a steel blade that was flawed."

"Think of the possibilities," Katie rolled on. "If this is the sword Odin gave to the Volsung clan, can you imagine the possibilities?"

What could I say to that? Volsungs? Come on. A long-dead Scandinavian clan? And Odin? Norse gods were in comic books and dragons were in role-playing games. As far as I was concerned, it was all fairy tales.

"This is nuts, you know?"

She ignored me. "Wait until I tell Jimmy. He'll have tons of questions."

I winced. "Can we keep your brother out of it?" I asked. "It's hard enough with him being the leader of Black Briar, and me dating you." I sighed.

Her eyes took on that twinkle I loved and feared. "He knows we're sleeping together," she said with a wicked grin. "I told him it's none of his business who I fuck."

Great. I looked around the coffee shop. "I don't think the people in the drive-thru heard you."

She raised her eyebrows. "Don't make me stand on the table and sing it to the whole joint."

I rolled my eyes. "Fine, be that way." She made to stand and I slid down in the seat, covering my face with my hands.

She laughed. "Relax, Beauhall. I won't make a scene."

I moved my hand, looking at her.

"This time," she said, winking.

Oh, lord. She was so damn cute, but what had I gotten myself into?

I sat up straighter when I realized she was teasing me. I wish I was as free about all this as she was. Me, I tried not to think about it too much. The voices in my head were too loud, too judgmental. You can take the girl out of the hard-core religious lifestyle, but you can't make her . . . oh, to hell with it.

"Dwarf or no dwarf, I'm gonna fix the blade tonight, after Julie knocks off for the day."

"Oooh," she said, clapping her hands together. "Can I come?"

I rolled my eyes. She'd bring her guitar and sing while I worked. It was cute, and somewhat annoying. "Fine, but you need to bring the beer for after."

She sat back, a twinkle in her eye. "No drinking while you are working hot metal," she said. "I'll bring something special for after."

The auction was a bust. There were two hunting knives and a commemorative sword celebrating the end of the Spanish-American War. Nice stuff, but too young for my tastes.

Four

KATIE WATCHED SARAH walk across the parking lot toward her car. She put her hands-free set on and dialed her sister-in-law.

"Hey, Deidre."

Deidre and Jimmy had been married for about forever, and she was a huge help after Katie's parents died. "How was the auction?"

"Good. Sarah is like a kid at those things. Wants to touch everything."

Deidre laughed. "Did she buy anything?"

Sarah waved as she drove out of the lot, and Katie blew her a kiss. "Nothing today, but I get to watch her fix a blade tonight at the smithy."

"Ooh, lovely. Things going well with you two?"

Katie thought about it, started her car, and pulled out of the lot. "You know she's sexy as hell. I love how strong she is, physically and mentally."

"She's a good fighter. Everyone in Black Briar seems to like her well enough."

Katie smiled. "True. She's got horrible self-esteem, but when she's not dwelling on it, she's dreamy." When she wasn't worrying how fat she was. Katie hadn't met anyone in better shape in her life, and that included the SCA folks she knew.

"But . . . ?"

That's the thing, she thought. Is there a downside? "We've been together a while now, but she's still too uptight about it, you know?"

Katie could hear Deidre scheming. "We'll have to get together and strategize on it."

"Excellent," Katie said, laughing. "Is my lazy, no-good brother around? I have something he needs to hear."

"This about Sarah?"

"Yes, and about Black Briar inner-circle stuff."

"Okay," Deidre said. "You know these phones are not secure."

"Yes, Mom," Katie said with a laugh. "I'll be brief and vague."

"Good, hang on—"

Katie heard her put the phone down.

"—Jim, it's Katie."

Now to convince him that sitting on the sidelines wasn't working any longer—no matter what promise he made to Mom and Dad before they disappeared. Besides, they'd been looking for something big their whole adult lives. Maybe this was it. Maybe this was the real Gram and the cycle had begun anew.

Five

I MADE IT back to the smithy by one o'clock and helped Julie pack up for our trek out to Broken Switch Farm. They had seven horses and a pony, so it was after dark by the time we got back to the forge.

"Katie's coming over tonight while I reforge the black sword," I said as Julie filled out the deposit ticket to take the day's earnings to the bank. "I need to fix it before the shoot tomorrow night. Carl needs it."

She looked up at me, her half-moon glasses hovering near the tip of her nose. The cowboy hat she normally wore hung off a wrought-iron coatrack I'd made her as one of my first projects. She ran her hand through her burgundy hair, pushing it off her forehead. Her complexion was ruddy from working over the fire for all these years. But she had an incredible body for someone in her forties. I hoped I looked as good when I was her age. As it was, being twenty-six was no great shakes. My arms were great, but I felt a little dumpy.

"Make sure the tools are put away, and keep track of the propane."

"I thought I might use the Centaur forge tonight." I think I was bouncing at that moment, but I wouldn't admit it.

"The propane would be cheaper," she said, shaking her head. "But I know how you are. Just keep track of how much coal you use. We're running low."

"You got it, boss."

I returned to sweeping down the shop. I loved starting a new project.

And, I'd be seeing Katie. There may have been a part of me that wanted to show off for my girlfriend. Is that so wrong?

So what if I changed into a sleeveless T-shirt—it was hot. Besides, it was nice to have her watch me—see the hunger in her eyes, know that she wants me. And hang my father. He wouldn't understand no matter what. Lust was a sin. Hell, with him everything was sin.

I stopped and closed my eyes. This was not his space. He held no power here. After three long, cleansing breaths I began arranging the forge, straightening tools, making things nice. Working with fire took order, control. Katie saw passion as the opposite—wild and abandoned. I needed to work on separating the two in my mind. Fire . . . passion . . . each burned, each consumed.

Julie smiled at me as she left the shop. "Be careful," was all she said as she walked out.

By the time I heard the crunch of Katie's tires on the gravel drive, I had already carried buckets of coal from the dwindling supply out back into the building and started the Centaur forge. I needed a good thirty minutes or more to get the coals heating evenly.

Katie respected places of power. She entered the shop quietly, head bowed, so as not to disturb the fey she was sure were always present at a working forge.

She was dressed in a brown and gold peasant skirt with tiny bells sewn all around the hem. That's what she'd worn the first time we'd met and it was what I slid off of her the first time we'd made love. God, that was almost a year ago.

My heart was pounding in my chest. I watched her place her guitar and cooler against the wall by one of the cleared worktables, thinking back to the first time I'd watched her.

Six

WE WERE BOTH at a renaissance faire over on the Olympic Peninsula. I had just finished farrier school and was doing double duty. I hadn't started with Julie yet, even.

The ren faire gig had me spending the majority of my time manning a rough smithy, putting on a show for the paying guests. On top of that, I was temping with an equestrian group, keeping their horses in shape for the five three-day weekends in a row.

I was checking out a statuesque black Friesian named Pericles, owned by a strapping young knight in the group. He went by Sir Wenceslas, if you can believe it. He had a penchant for strutting around in a sleeveless cuirass so he could show off his bulging biceps.

I was pretty sure I could take him.

Despite a poor education in the classics and history in general, he had no problem attracting oodles of women.

Most women, and here's the crux of the tale.

I was busy, making sure a rock hadn't bruised yon knight's ride, when he muttered, "Holy mother, look at her."

This lovely young woman walked by in a plain white cotton top, and a brown and gold peasant skirt. The bells on the hem jangled when she walked, drawing attention to her strut.

I lowered the Friesian's leg and stepped to the fence, leaning beside him, catching a very nice view of her walking away. It wasn't hard to admire her contours.

"Callipygian," I said.

Sir Wencesloser looked over at me with a very puzzled look.

"Greek for nice ass," I said, punching him in the arm and turning back to the horse.

"Greek, huh?" he asked, leaning way over the fence to continue watching her. "They had a thing for asses."

"Present company excluded, I'm sure," I muttered.

I ignored the wolf whistle our young mister ripped out of the smithy and finished with Pericles, who proved to be a kind and patient animal. I suspected he had to be in order to put up with Lover Boy.

When I was done, I grabbed an apple from my kit, pulled out my pocket knife, and fed several slices to my patient. "You are amazing," I said, rubbing his nose.

"Thanks," Wenceslas muttered, watching the crowd. "I think I may have found a young maiden to rescue."

I walked over, looking for his obvious target, when the gorgeous girl walked by again.

"This is her fourth time walking past," he said, turning to the side and flexing his biceps at the world. "She has a thing for me."

She passed us, her walk just as enticing as last time, but she did not look our way.

He seemed to deflate a bit, lowering his arms. "She's playing coy."

"Yeah. That's it," I said, patting him on his shoulder. "Maybe you should take Pericles here back to camp and get him some water."

He glanced back at me, calculating. "Isn't that what you're getting paid for?"

See. Now he'd pissed in my Wheaties. Of course, I liked this gig. Paid really well. But there was a line he was approaching quickly.

"Sure thing," I said, unwinding Pericles' lead from the fence. "I'll be back in a few minutes. Think you can watch my gear?"

He was too good for the hirelings, I guess. He waved a hand at me, not even bothering to turn around. "Yeah, okay."

Pericles followed me without as much as a snort. Smart fella. We cut across the market square, between the funnel cake stand and the roasted cashews. I loved the way he walked, the clip-clop of his hooves as we crossed the footbridge near the spot where the pickle man kept his barrels cooling in the stream.

Up the hill a ways was the encampment of the knight's group. ORDER OF THE LEAF read the sign over their main tent. Marijuana leaf was my bet. Several young men lounged about, polishing armor and drinking large cans of overly caffeinated beverages. It was early, around two in the afternoon, and I knew they had shows at six and seven. They'd hit the hard stuff after that.

"You guys seen Sir Wenceslas's squire around?" I asked.

One of the guys belched and the other three laughed.

"How dare you speak to one of my station," the belching knight said.

I could learn to hate these playacting clowns.

I bowed, bending one knee and dipping my head. "Pardon, good knight. I am on an errand for your brother, Sir Wenceslas. Might I inquire to the location of his good squire?"

One of them pointed past a row of sleeping tents to the lot where the horse trailers were parked. "He's in the back, you'll recognize the crest on the horse trailer." One of them winked, and another made some gesture I didn't catch. "Be sure and announce yourself."

I nodded and led Pericles away. Idiots.

Okay, eagle on a banner—that's Wenceslas's symbol. Hope these guys knew something about it.

I found the trailer, fourth from the end. They had a dozen horses and kept them in good shape, or I wouldn't have been here. They just partied too much to be jousting, in my humble opinion.

As I approached the trailer, I heard giggling and stopped. This I did not need.

I banged on the side of the trailer and a young woman in a barmaid's outfit scrambled out, tucking her rather large breasts back into her top. She winked at me as she went past. Ren faire folk are all in collusion, that's the general understanding.

A young man of about seventeen came out after her, buckling his pants—obviously frustrated by the interruption.

When he saw it was me, his look of embarrassment and shame switched to lurid bravado.

"Well, hello," he leered, leaning against the side of the trailer and letting his belt fall, untended.

He topped six feet, but was about as wide as a ruler. "Willowy" came to mind. "Your master bids you take possession of his steed."

Maybe he was nineteen, but he looked me up and

down, pausing at my breasts and really not leaving that point.

"You are a comely lass. Perhaps you'd like to . . ." He wiggled his eyebrows at me. "Since you ran Gwendolyn off and all."

I couldn't help it. I burst out laughing. He was cute enough, but even if he was the wrong gender for me, he was too damn young.

"Yeah, great," he said, snatching the lead from my hand. "Tell my loser brother . . ."

I didn't listen, just turned and walked away. This gig was losing its luster.

By the time I got back, loser brother was gone, and so was my kit—two changes of clothes, my wallet, car keys, cell phone, plus the apples and a nice baguette.

Bastard.

I stormed around the enclosure for a moment, seeing if I'd moved it behind the wall, which I hadn't. Only so many places to stash a pack. The station had three wooden walls and a tarp for a roof.

I had a propane forge, a small anvil, and a handful of tools. Really all I did was heat metal and bang on it for the civilians. That and taking care of the horses on the side was paying my rent.

Now I was stuck out here with no food, no money, no car keys, and no cell. Damn it.

The woman selling weapons at the next booth over hadn't seen anything, but she spent most of her time trying to keep the kids from playing with the swords, and drunken idiots from trying to use her merchandise to start duels.

As I was on a corner, there was no one to my right, and behind me was the downward leg of the stream that kept the pickles cold.

I had my tools, that was something. The kit was a snatch

and run. Probably kids. I walked out into the market, keeping one eye on my booth, while looking around for one of the large men with quarterstaffs who purportedly were constables.

Not available. Figured. I stormed back to my smithy and rammed around a bit, considering how I was going to get home, when the girl walked by again. Okay, this was a crossroads, but how many times would she just "walk by"? On top of this, hunka burnin' knight was missing.

This time she looked at me and smiled. That got my attention.

But man, I was pissed. Conflicting emotions are a bugger. I didn't smile back, didn't wave, just stood there, impotent and frustrated over my kit. But the universe looks out for those in need.

She didn't stop, but continued across the footbridge that spanned the creek just east of me. On the other side, in the open field between the market square and the jousting field, stood the huge beer garden.

Large numbers of civilians, actors, performers, SCAdians, and other assorted camp mongrels sat under tiny umbrellas or in the open sun, drinking large tankards of beer and carousing.

Most of them were cool, singing and capering about. Them I liked.

The predators, though. Them I did not like.

Our Sir Wenceslas stood just inside the garden watching the young woman walking his way. I was about to witness his infamous technique in action.

He said something and she walked by without as much as a look.

Several of the rowdies in the beer garden started laughing and giving him grief. Not cool.

They'd spent the hotter part of the day swilling down cheap beer and growing louder and louder. They were fairly buff, decked out in chain and large floppy hats. These were the guys who hit on the beer wenches and generally made asses out of themselves.

And now they'd seen the knight humiliated.

No one was coming around, so I stood in the lane and watched them. The knight grew heated and started swearing at the guys. This in turn set them off and they spilled out of the garden and fisticuffs ensued.

Testosterone is a poison. It takes perfectly nice guys and turns them into raving maniacs. Maybe the beer helped, but I didn't think they really needed it to get into a brawl.

Pretty boy knight stood his ground and knocked one of the disorderly men-at-arms to the ground. His buddies took exception and things looked to get out of hand when the young woman walked back, giving them a wide berth, cautiously avoiding the melee.

This is when things got out of control.

One guy lay sprawled on the ground, another screamed and spit at the knight. Wenceslas had a hand on his dagger, and was shoving a third guy back against the fence.

A wolf whistle from the guy on the ground brought all their attention to the skirt.

Beer, sun, rivalry, all of these things froze as she walked by. Then the boys, for that's what they'd become, scrambled over one another to begin following her.

They were just out of my hearing range, but one of them said something a little too crude, pushed it a little too far. She turned and watched them, coldly. They didn't notice the cudgel at her belt, but I did.

One guy got in her face and made a grab for her. The next thing he knew he was on the ground and she stood back in a defensive stance, cudgel in her fist.

I'm not sure any of them had even seen her hit him, much less draw.

I liked her more and more.

But, now they were angry at her. Four beefy men directed their attention at her, as the fifth rose, spitting blood.

They charged.

Knight boy tried to stop them, sort of.

He grabbed one of them, yelling, and was shrugged off. He ended up on his ass in the dirt, and five drunken men rushed this girl.

I'll give her credit. She held her own. I had already started sprinting down the lane before the knight was eating dust, but she danced away from the toughs, clubbing one man aside, before spinning out of the grasp of another.

The guy on the ground had had enough. When he came up, he had his own weapon out, and it was a blade.

This form of reenactment we didn't need.

He lunged at her and she moved, but not quick enough. His blade sliced through her skirt and apparently caught her on the leg, because she cried out and staggered back.

About that time I dropped the knife guy with a flying kick. Seven years of tae kwon do and a first-degree black belt were not wasted. My sa bum nim would be proud.

Knife boy crashed back against another fellow and they tumbled to the ground. Before they could rise, I kicked the knife out of the guy's hand, my Doc Martens doing very bad things to all those tiny little bones.

The rest wilted when faced with two of us, and by this time Sir Knight joined us, pulling one guy aside and flinging him against the beer garden fence.

The thugs staggered off muttering and this woman pulled a whistle from her top and blew three sharp blasts. Within a minute two others, a Mutt and Jeff team carrying quarterstaffs, appeared from the market.

"Stuart," she said. "We have a situation."

I stood gaping as she directed Stuart and Gunther, the

first time I'd met them as well, to go and give chase to the drunks.

Here was one of the constables. She wasn't flirting with Mr. Knight or me. She was watching for bad guys.

Impressive.

Later I would wonder how good a job she was doing if my gear disappeared.

After blowing off Sir Knight and getting someone to replace her on her beat, she asked me to follow her to the infirmary.

The cut wasn't too deep, but she got a nice bandage. The medic was a young intern named Melanie. The young woman who had caught my attention was Katie, of course.

The Black Briar clan were working security for the weekend. They ended up finding my pack, dumped behind one of the booths. My wallet was rifled, all the money taken, but I had my license. No cell, no keys, no baguette.

After the ren faire closed for the night, Katie gave me a ride back to the city to get spare keys. She hadn't graduated from college yet, was down from Western. I didn't know that right away. I just knew she was beautiful and could hold her own in a fight.

I was smitten beyond belief.

Seven

By the time I had the fire banked, Katie had her guitar out and was drinking mead from a tall green bottle. A guy we knew from the Society for Creative Anachronism brewed it. She had three more bottles in a cooler by the door.

I started out with a raw iron bar. I wanted to get into the rhythm of swinging the hammer on something new before tackling Gram.

Between swings of the hammer, I could hear Katie's sweet voice and the quiet strumming of her guitar.

I took my time, shaping the new sword. It would only be eighteen inches long, so I'd add some cuts and stamps on the blade and sell it as an Elvish short sword. The con crowd would love it.

Every fifteen minutes I adjusted the coal, keeping the burning coke piled high, sorted out the clinkers, and banked with good, green coal. It took me the better part of three hours to get the blade tamped out like I wanted. I would temper the edge of the blade by dousing it in water. Oil would make a better edge, but I wanted the metal softer, prevent it from keeping a good edge. We sold these things to frat boys and genre wannabes. Didn't need anyone killing themselves on one of my swords.

By the time I'd quenched the blade in the trough of water, I was soaked with sweat. My muscles vibrated in anticipation. It felt good.

After midnight, with the second blade—a dagger—resting on the finishing table for me to grind down, I stepped over to lean against Katie. She put her guitar to the side and stroked my sweaty hair. I closed my eyes for a moment as she leaned forward and kissed me on my forehead.

"You do good work, my little northwest Ilmarinen."

"Who?"

She chuckled. "You'd love him. Finnish blacksmith. Quite good with his hands." She took mine in hers and kissed each of them on the knuckles. "He's not so lucky with women, however."

"Great," I said, smelling the mead on her breath, and the soft sandalwood soap she used. "How am I doing?"

"So far, no complaints."

I smiled. "Good to know." I squeezed her hands and opened my eyes. "Ready for the show?"

"I think so," she said. "More ready to go home and take a long, hot bath."

"Want company?"

She smiled. "Fix your sword. Then we'll drink more mead." A giggle slipped past her lips. "Okay, I'll drink more mead, you can drink what's left."

I patted her on the thigh. "Play me something rousing, my skald."

Raucous chords echoed across the smithy as I opened the safe and brought out the two halves of Gram. This sword made me nervous.

I've only repaired simple tools. Nothing as complicated as a sword. Theory was the same, but I broke out in chills. "Man, hope I don't screw this up."

A deep voice came from the doorway. "You had better not."

Katie squeaked, sliding off the desk and holding her guitar in front of her.

The Swedish guy, the dwarf, stood in the doorway, his skin glowing in the dim light of the forge. "You offered for me to visit you here."

"Who are you?" I asked, laying the broken sword on the workbench.

"My name is Rolph Brokkrson." He stood just outside, not crossing the threshold. I had left the big front bay doors open to keep a cross breeze going.

"I didn't hear a car," I said, nervous. Definitely did not like him sneaking up on me like this.

"I arrived while you were working on the dagger," he said with a shrug. "My truck is right out front, if you'd care to look."

Okay, possible. I made a lot of noise when I hammered. "You could've called."

"My apologies," he said with a nod of his head. "Mr.

Tuttle mentioned you were going to work on the blade this evening, and I hoped to watch you work."

Carl sent him over? I had invited him, given him my business card. Still . . .

"Just caught me off guard."

"Again, my humblest apologies," he said. "You were quite engrossed in your work. I am impressed by your skill."

I watched him, looking for mockery. When he didn't laugh, or offer more, I shrugged.

"If you attempt to reforge that sword, you must not fail."

I watched his eyes. "Are there some consequences I should be aware of?"

"This is no normal blade, as you well know." He held my gaze. "This is a test of your skill. If you fail, you will be cursed until the end of your days."

Katie made a quick hand signal and spat on the floor. She took curses very seriously.

I didn't find her reaction quaint. Not this time. Energy filled the room beyond anything I'd experienced before. "As long as there's no pressure," I said, feeling awkward.

Katie stepped around the workbench, away from the door. "Are you a dwarf?"

He stared at me, but gave a slight bow. "I am of Durin's people."

"Holy moly," Katie whispered. "Like from *The Hobbit*?"

I barked out a laugh.

"I have read this book," he said, holding his hands palm up. "But it does not tell the true tale of my people."

"Why shouldn't I reforge this blade?" I asked. This guy was an escaped lunatic, I figured. I dearly loved Katie, but elves and dwarves were make-believe.

"If you accept this task, you will risk the wrath of Odin."

I felt my eyebrows crawling up my scalp. Real lunatic. "Odin, like the All-Father? Thor's dad?"

"One and the same." His eyes shone for a moment. "But if you insist upon the course of action I would suggest you accept my assistance."

"How do *we* know you won't kill us and take the sword?" Katie asked.

Great, give the crazy guy ideas. I stepped to the workbench by the wall and took down my three-pound hammer. More heft in case I needed to brain the guy.

"I will swear on my honor."

"Honor, right." I lowered the hammer back to the table. "And why would you do this, exactly?"

"You must use Gram to slay a dragon."

"Dragon?" Katie chirped. "Like, scales and fire and wings?"

"Yes, that is one form they may take," he said. "In this case, he is an investment banker in Portland."

Katie and I exchanged bemused glances.

"Dragons accumulate wealth," Rolph assured us. "They are ingenious in their methods."

We both started laughing.

Rolph waited patiently, and when we'd calmed down asked politely, "May I come in?"

I glanced over at Katie, who shrugged. She walked over to me, placing her head next to mine. "He's likely harmless," she said.

"He's been fine out at Carl's," I said. "But his obsession with the sword is a bit creepy."

"What do you expect?" she asked, getting excited. "He's a dwarf, and a smith. Think of it as professional curiosity."

Of course she was excited. A real dwarf, and a dragon. I half expected flying monkeys next.

I waved him in. "Welcome to my inner sanctum."

Katie smirked.

"Not like I own the place and can keep you from crossing the threshold or anything," I said.

"That's vampires," Katie offered.

"Quite," Rolph said, walking into the shop. "You have a lovely forge."

"It's not mine," I said automatically. "But the Centaur is a real beauty."

"In what do you plan to quench the blade?"

"If I can reconnect the two halves, and if I don't completely wreck the blade's integrity, I thought I'd use a light, sweet oil. Something to really put a hard edge on her."

Rolph shook his head. "That will work, but if you want the best edge, the optimum choice would be to plunge the glowing blade into the heart of your enemy."

For a moment I considered JJ and his stupid hair, but dismissed the thought, weighing it against the twenty-five to life I'd get in the Washington Corrections Center for Women in Purdy. "Well, I think the oil is going to suffice. I just don't have any enemies I'm ready to murder."

"Suit yourself." He leaned against the workbench. "I can advise you in other ways, if you want."

His knowledge of the forge eased much of my trepidation. Over the next few hours, we discussed shaping techniques, the proper color the metal should glow before aligning the pieces, and the right type of flux to use while heating. I opted for powdered borax, since that's what we had in the shop. Despite his disbelief, I had no real source for crushed unicorn horn or minotaur horn this late at night. I don't know which was more surreal, him expecting we'd have bits of fantasy creatures lying around or the fact that Katie didn't consider the request to be too unreasonable.

I cleaned the ends of the break with a wire brush and dipped the ends in the borax. Then I buried them in the heart of the burning coke.

"You are a competent smith," Rolph declared as I was drawing and upsetting the face of the break.

Of course, his constant chatter made me want to hit him with my hammer. Katie sensed my stress and offered Rolph some mead. Apparently dwarves love mead. By the time I had the two halves of the blade connected and the dressed metal back into the fire, he'd drunk two bottles. Katie had no trouble convincing him to accompany her in several rousing choruses of carousal and debauchery. He even taught her a verse to "The Dwarf from Dover" that she'd never heard.

By three in the morning, I had set the weld and was dressing the blade into shape. Katie had her head down on the desk. The fact that she slept through my hammering astounded me.

Rolph examined the blade from a distance, never coming around to my side of the worktable. I could see in his eyes he yearned to work the forge, but he respected my space.

I heated the edge of the sword until it glowed a light yellow and then plunged it into the deep well of oil. The sharp hiss it made woke Katie. Her hair had come out of its ponytail and lay scattered across the front of her face.

"You should be proud," Rolph said after I wiped the blade down with a cloth. "My old master was the last to reforge this blade successfully."

I held the blade up, turning it to catch the reflection of the red embers in the runes that ran down the blade. The rune that had been obliterated by the repair was like a blank slate. A place to mark a change to the sword's destiny.

"It was whole when I found it," I said, lowering it and looking at Rolph.

"Poorly mended is not reforged," he said with a rueful smile. "The last to touch this did a service by keeping the blade from being lost." He shrugged his huge shoulders. "But that did not make the blade whole. Not in the way you have."

I held the blade in my left hand, extended it to the full reach of my arm, twisting my wrist from side to side. It seemed, for just a moment, as if some sort of energy ran from the sword, down my arm, danced along the back of my skull, and flushed through my body like a fever. For three heartbeats an intense surge grew from my belly and exploded through me in a shudder. It took me a moment to realize Rolph had continued to speak.

". . . such as it is. But, each time it was used to slay the enemies of the light. And each time, Father Odin saw fit to shatter it once again. I am pleased to have witnessed the cycle renewed once more."

"Thank you," I said, biting my lip at the shiver that echoed through me. A minor aftershock of the previous jolt. The blade felt good in my hand. The balance and weight were better than any blade I'd used in sparring at the Society. "So, the last to attempt this, he who attached the blade—why was that not sufficient?"

Rolph shrugged. "Smithing brings together the four elements, earth, water, wind, and fire. It takes a smith of great skill and spirit to accomplish such a task." He paused, watching me across the worktables, his eyes large and brimming with pride. "The previous smith failed in the joining. He was not worthy. But," he held up a thick finger for emphasis, "once the blade is properly imbued with hammer and fire, it can only be sundered by the will of Odin himself."

That thought gave me pause. Was I really that good? Don't get me wrong, I knew I'd done my best work tonight. It was like a runner's high, the endorphins were kicking in my head. I'd done something special. And it was beautiful—but magical?

"So, now, about the dragon," Rolph said.

I set Gram on the workbench. The second my hand left the pommel, a whisper of loss slithered through me. I crossed my arms and faced Rolph. "No dragons, thanks."

Katie yawned.

"But, the glory . . . the treasure . . ."

"Look," I said. "I can use this sword in the movies and make enough money to keep smithing. Besides, I have all the treasure I need."

He followed my eyes to Katie, who drooped in the chair, almost asleep again.

"But Gram deserves glory."

I could hear the yearning in his voice—the lure of fame and fortune beyond my wildest dreams.

Instead, I raked the coals with a shovel, pushing the coke against the back of the forge to be used later. It would burn down quickly, now that I'd scattered it.

"Do you not want glory?" he asked.

I set the shovel aside with a sigh, running my fingers over the pommel. "The glory of Gram will be in movies," I said. "No more bloodshed, just hack actors chasing guys like you in rubber goblin suits."

Rolph frowned. "You could cleave this anvil in two with that blade."

I glanced at the sword. The memory of its touch was a flame in my mind. I reached out, picking it up once again, letting the heft settle into my arm.

"Sure, I believe you." Honestly I did. The sword sang to me, thrilled me in ways that scared me. I could feel the pulse of power through the leather pommel. Or was I imagining it, pushed on by suggestion and exhaustion? Sometimes good work did that, gave you a thrill. "But I'm a blacksmith. I create. I don't destroy."

I turned and opened the safe.

"But you do not understand!" He slammed his fists

down on the workbench. The two blades I'd made ear-lier hopped a bit, sending the longer blade to the floor with a clang.

I tensed. My first thought was for my hammer, instead of the sword I held in my hand. I stared at him, adrena-line slipping into my veins. Gram shuddered in my grip.

For a moment I knew the sword's need—the vibration as it sought to strike the foe. I shuddered once and slipped it into the safe. Once my hand left the grip, I shud-dered again, closing the door with my hip.

As soon as the lock clicked into place, Rolph slumped against the bench, the fires in his eyes quenched in de-spair.

"So it shall be," he whispered.

I spun the combination and stepped back to the work-bench. He hadn't moved; his long black hair fell down over his face. For a moment, it sounded as if he wept.

"I'll take it tomorrow night and let JJ swing it around a bit more. Carl will pay me enough for another ton or three of coal and a good dozen sword forms. I'll drink mead with Katie and sing raunchy songs while high schoolers and old men buy my swords in hope of be-coming Beowulf."

"He was a fop," Rolph said. The disappointment was heavy in his voice. "I have searched long for a hint of Gram. To see it reforged is glorious. Perhaps that is enough."

"It's time to call it a night," I said. "I need to be back here in six hours to work. I'll see you at Carl's tomor-row night, right?"

He nodded. "But, aren't you going to put an edge on the blade?"

"Are you kidding? And have JJ cut off his left foot? No thanks. I get paid to make everything look as au-thentic as they can afford. Getting the talent mortally wounded would end all that."

Rolph sighed. "Oh, for the days of Weyland and Migard. For the Valkyries and the cries of battle."

"Go home, Rolph. Before the sun rises."

"Of course," he said, glancing at the window. "There are not enough of my people left in this world."

I watched him leave, listened as he drove his pickup truck down the gravel drive.

So much for legend and myth.

I swept the shop, letting Katie sleep while I cleaned up.

I'd done my best work and felt mighty. I could easily see how adrenaline and fatigue would make me feel the blade react. Silly, I know. That and having Katie and Rolph acting like the rainbow factory was opening up and all the leprechauns were coming to tea didn't help. This would all be silly under the light of day, I was positive.

I packed the last bottle of mead in the cooler and put Katie's guitar in its case before waking her.

"Come on, sleeping beauty. Let's get you to bed."

She leaned against me as we walked toward the door. "Only if you stay over."

I flicked off the light and pulled the door shut behind me. Children's stories. Odd, twisted myths, I thought. But who would believe for a second that there were dwarves in pickup trucks and dragons in pinstripes? I mean, seriously.

The world was stranger than the movies.

Eight

FREDERICK SAWYER SURVEYED the crowd around him and smiled. Young men and women dressed in tuxedos wandered the crowd carrying trays of drinks and small bite-sized nibbles.

Through double doors set in the far wall, rows of auction items were laid out, each to be perused by the folks there who would overbid on frippery to show their support for the homeless, or the addicts, or whatever this group shepherded through his city.

He smiled and nodded at gray-haired men and women who beamed at his attention. Each controlled a company or a board, a neighborhood committee or a council of some ilk that found themselves indebted to or in need of Frederick's generosity in one way or another.

The gaggle of octogenarians who ruled the local garden clubs each stopped to greet him. He touched each one, a pat on the hand, a kiss on the cheek. Each of the women left his presence with a smile and a livelier step. Keep them happy was his ultimate goal. Let them see how much he cared for them, how much he deserved their love. The smile on his face was genuine. He did not fake this. These were his people, his chattel. Through them, he was mighty.

The blonde carrying the champagne scooted into his view, distracting him from the briefest of greetings from an eager volunteer with the charity du jour. He nodded at the young man, shook his hand, and turned to intercept the blond champagne girl. She looked particularly yummy.

As she paused in front of him, he smiled at her, staring into her pale blue eyes. *Such a pretty girl*, he thought to himself. *The things I could do to her.*

She smiled back at him, demurely for a moment, but as the edges of his lips curled into a bigger smile, her lips parted as she let out a quiet exhalation. He pushed her, just a little, with his eyes—let her see the flames for the briefest of moments. The sharp intake of breath pleased him.

Her eyes lost focus.

He could feel her pulse racing. Given enough effort, he could enthrall her completely. The prospect was not unpleasing. With no thought to her surroundings, this young woman unbuttoned the top button of her blouse. She did not blink as she loosed the next, and finally a third. Just as things were getting interesting, and the first hint of a pink bra came into view, he blinked. Her hand paused. He watched the blush rise across her chest, up her neck, and over her cheeks—her body reacting to the heat that he called in her.

"Excuse me, sir," Mr. Philips said, appearing at his left elbow.

Frederick growled low in his throat. "This had better be important."

"Yes, sir. Of course, sir." Mr. Philips took a glass of champagne from the tray the young woman still balanced on one hand.

The movement caught her attention and she looked away from Frederick. He sighed as the connection evaporated in a puff of steam.

She glanced at Mr. Philips for a moment, blinking. When she looked back at Frederick her lips rose into a wicked smile and she tilted her head at him. Then she turned, carrying the tray into the crowd, not bothering to button up her blouse.

"Oh, I do so love pink," Frederick said, handing an empty champagne glass to his assistant.

"Playing with your food again, Frederick?" asked a man's voice, a voice of pain and mockery.

Mr. Philips winced.

Frederick turned sharply. The beast that lay so loosely below his skin shook itself. He turned an icy stare at his rival, his enemy, his kith and kin.

"Jean-Paul," he said, the loathing dripping from his voice as bitter as the acid that coursed through his veins.

"I'm very sorry, sir," Mr. Philips said, handing his master another champagne-filled glass. "Mr. Duchamp insisted on speaking with you."

Frederick looked from his able assistant, Mr. Philips, to the garish fop who stood beside him. Jean-Paul Duchamp was a bottom-feeder of the worst sort. Frederick stuck out his hand to shake, but Jean-Paul pulled a handkerchief from his pocket and held it to his nose instead of taking the proffered hand.

"You'll pardon me," Duchamp said. "I so rarely mingle with the commoners. How *do* you stand the smell?"

Frederick was slightly amused at the jibe, for while these creatures were only human, they were the crème de la crème of Portland's wealthy, mingled with the CEOs of Fortune 500 companies and the earnest young volunteers and executives who ran the nonprofit organization they were all here to honor. But then again, Jean-Paul was not one known for being subtle.

"I find it quite fulfilling to support many causes," Frederick said with a smile. "Unlike yourself, Jean-Paul. What in the world brought you out of seclusion? Another of your pig farmers forget to cover your tracks?"

Jean-Paul stiffened for a moment, much to Frederick's delight.

"He is my guest," Qindra said, moving from behind Jean-Paul, trailing her fingers across his broad shoulders and down his arm.

Jean-Paul stiffened at her touch.

"Ah, so Nidhogg's witch has deigned to lower herself to our company."

"My mistress asked that I check on your activities," she said with a smile.

Her father's Middle Eastern heritage colored her exquisite features, but it was her mother's Icelandic ancestry that lent her the breathtaking beauty.

Frederick bowed, taking Qindra's hand in his own. "I am honored by your presence." He paused, gently kissed her knuckles, then rose to watch her face. "Tell your mistress, our greatest and most ancient progenitor, that I am humbled by her interest in my little protectorate."

Jean-Paul snorted, but Qindra bowed toward Frederick. He wasn't sure, but he thought he saw her kick Jean-Paul in the ankle as she did.

"Mr. Philips," she said when she stood to her full six feet once again, "would you be so kind as to escort me through the auction?"

Mr. Philips didn't even look at Frederick. He just held out his elbow, waiting for Qindra to place her lovely caramel hand on his arm. As her long fingers lay on his forearm, he covered her hand with his, and turned, leading her away.

Once they had taken several steps, Frederick focused his attention on Jean-Paul. "So, the ancient one sends her favorite son to—what?" He shrugged. Jean-Paul was several inches shorter than Frederick, but broad like a small hill. He glared up at Frederick, a scowl on his face.

"She bids you caution in your moves of late," he said. "The witch was supposed to relay the message. I was but a reminder of possibilities."

Frederick knew full well the possibilities that awaited him. Nidhogg had no love for him. Oh, she understood his position, but he was not of her brood. Not like the derelict and wayward Jean-Paul.

Where he looked to arts and charity to grow his power, enthrall his city, Jean-Paul used drugs and vice—fear and addiction. And yet, Nidhogg, the Corpse Gnawer, biter of the world tree and most ancient of dragonkind, loved her offspring with every darkened chamber of her icy black heart.

Frederick was neither a fool nor a coward. Therefore he transgressed lightly this close to Nidhogg and her prized progeny. Still . . .

"How is your frigid mother?" he asked, with a toothy grin.

Jean-Paul snorted, not deigning to look at Frederick. Rather he watched the crowd, as if sizing up his next meal. "You know very well how she does," he said, finally. "And she leaves *me* to my affairs."

Yes, Frederick thought—if by *affairs* one meant killing prostitutes, mostly underaged runaways, and feeding their broken bodies to pigs. Frederick loathed anyone who preyed on the sick and helpless. Not that he had any problem with the hunt, or the demands of ruling his people. No, quite the contrary. He lived for the power, but understood it came as much from his people's will as from his own mightiness.

Jean-Paul, on the other hand, was not worthy of his station. There were others of their kind who had fallen in the global rivalry for power. It was their nature, of course. Predators sometimes fell to corruption, fearing no one but their own kind. And none of them had fallen any other way in recorded time.

Case in point—the last steward of Portland had fallen to the machinations of his own kind. He of the quick temper, and steady flame—Carlos Estrella—had risen to some fame during the Spanish conquest of Mexico. How he ended up the ruler of Portland had not been shared with Frederick. Not that it mattered a whit.

He had sown his own wild oats as a young stripling, of course, burning a village here or there, devouring a few children . . . but who kept count.

Frederick had been ready for the ascension before the

broken body of Carlos Estrella had been found at the bottom of Multnomah Falls. That had been a hundred years ago, when Frederick had first come to these shores.

No room for expansion in the old world. The Americas still had cities for the taking, chattel to control. More than enough for those of his kin who roamed this continent.

"Yes, you are an evil, dangerous villain," Frederick said, waving the champagne glass toward Jean-Paul, one finger pointing. He took a long drink, keeping his eyes locked with Jean-Paul's. He coughed, covering his mouth with the glass and hand, clearing his throat. "But there is a problem, you see."

Jean-Paul quirked his eyebrows upward, allowing a bit of the flame to touch his own eyes as he glanced at Frederick. "Problem?" he asked.

"Yes," Frederick said, stepping forward, entering Jean-Paul's personal space. "Unlike my predecessor, I know you are a pathetic worm who will slip a dagger into the spine of a better."

Jean-Paul stiffened, his lip curling up over his elongating incisors.

"Oh, settle down, you pathetic lout," Frederick said, sweeping his arm out to encompass the room. "Nidhogg would look on you poorly if you showed your true form here among the rabble, don't you think?"

"Let her gnaw her corpses," Jean-Paul spat. "She is ancient, not omnipotent. She does not know all that transpires."

"And yet, you are still at her teats whenever I look," Frederick said with a grin.

Those who had not yet wandered into the auction room gave the two a wide berth. While they could not possibly know the truth about him and his kind, Frederick knew them well enough to see the hesitation, to smell the fear that encircled them like a barrier.

Several breaths passed as Jean-Paul brought his anger under control. "You are in your own domain," he said, brushing a bit of lint from his sleeve, as if to appear nonchalant. "But, if you ever cross the border into British Columbia, I will—" He paused, stabbing two fingers forward, and upward. "—gut you like a—"

"Wait," Frederick interrupted. "Don't tell me." He allowed the mirth to show thick on his lips. "Like a pig?" He burst into laughter. Jean-Paul turned and stormed away, parting the crowd as much with his anger as his swearing.

Frederick watched him with amusement. So like his doddering matron, that one—living in an ancient world of broken dreams and fearful fantasies. Despite the fairy tales and myths, there was no end time coming. Nidhogg would not rise up and smite the gods. She would die of old age, for even their kind had a limit to their span. When that happened, Frederick would sweep into Seattle, assume her base, and with any luck dear Jean-Paul Duchamp might fall backward on a pitchfork a time or three.

Frederick drained the wineglass and set it on a table as he walked toward the auction. Let the old hag have her warnings. Things were changing in the Pacific Northwest. He could feel it in his bones. He straightened his tie, then his cuffs, before walking into the auction. Time to appear magnanimous before his people. Let the sheep see how gracious he was.

Then . . . , he thought, then he'd see to the young woman with the pink bra. She would make a lovely end to this already delicious evening.

Nine

KATIE HAD GONE off to catch her bus decked out in her cute schoolteacher accoutrement. She would pick up her car at the forge after school. She always had an earlier start than I did. As long as I was at the forge by nine, Julie never even batted an eye.

I slipped down the staircase, the memory of Katie's good-bye kiss lingering on my lips. The creaks and groans of the stairs elicited a wicked smile. A song for the morning after, I thought. This old building had character, and a voice to be reckoned with. The door to the street, however, was as silent as a whisper, opening and then closing behind me with the cushioned snick of the magnetic lock. I fished the car key out of the front pocket in my jeans, hefted my pack onto my left shoulder, and skipped along the front of Elmer's Gun and Knife Emporium.

Yes, I said skipped. Give a girl a break.

The combination of me reforging the sword and all that mead made Katie a little wild last night. There were moments where I couldn't remember my name. I'm just glad the apartment next door was vacant. No one to complain about the noise. Suffice it to say, even the guilt could wait while I enjoyed the ephemeral tingle—that ghostly memory of her mouth on my skin.

I shuddered, my breath coming a little faster. It was a wonderful day to be alive. Today would be a damn fine day. I could feel it in the air.

I'd parked in the only available space last night. I'd been a little preoccupied when I slid the Civic in between the Dumpster and a beat-up Volvo. Luckily I hadn't gotten towed.

As I crossed the alley toward my car, a string of swearing drew my attention to the pair of filth-encrusted pants and broken boots sticking out of the Dumpster. Could only be one person inside those, I was fairly sure.

"Joe," I called. "You okay in there?"

Joe stopped his thrashing for a moment, and then slid backward out of the Dumpster. In his left hand he held a crushed pizza box that rattled with several pieces of what I hoped was crust. He was an old man, gray and shaggy, with a beard down the front of his chest, and a mop of hair thick and ratted down past his collar. His clothes were disgusting, and he walked with a limp. He'd lost one of his eyes at some point, and the scar tissue and empty socket gave him a totally creepy vibe.

"Find anything good?" I asked.

He sniffed when he turned my way, his head cocked to the side so he could look at me with his good eye. He rubbed his nose on his sleeve and sniffed again. "Looking for apples," he said, wrinkling his nose and sniffing like a rabbit.

"Got a cold, Joe?"

He pulled a crust of pizza from the box and stuck it in the corner of his mouth like a cigar. Made my heart break, him gnawing that stale rind.

Sweet Katie looked after the old bum, made sure he had some food and didn't freeze in the winter. He refused much else. He was a mainstay in the neighborhood, but he was known to wander. We'd found him in the heart of Seattle and as far north as Everett—even out at the industrial park where Carl shot his movies.

He pulled the crust from his mouth and waved it at me. "You stink."

I took a step back. "Mighty big words, coming fresh from the Dumpster yourself," I said with a smile. "You sure it's me you're smelling?"

He shuffle-stepped away from the Dumpster, and

deeper into the alley. For a moment I thought he was going to run, but he rocked back on his heels and let out a broken-toothed whistle, shrill and off-key. "Different, I say."

I smiled at him. Maybe he smelled Katie's sandalwood soap on me. Who knows. "You like apples?" I asked. "I could bring you a couple next time I'm over."

He was like a bird, tilting his head to the left, then the right, sniffing.

"I know you," he said, stepping toward me, keeping the pizza box between us.

"Yes, I'm a friend of Katie's."

He laughed then, a cackle that turned into a cough. "Pretty Kat. She's something."

"Gotta agree with you there," I said. It was getting to be time for me to head to work, but something about the way he looked at me kept me there.

"When the sky is black, and the wind howls, who do you cry to?"

For a moment, I felt as if someone had walked on my shadow. I looked around, expecting to see a large dog, or some bogey or other coming out of the Dumpster. The sun seemed to dim as Joe stepped closer. "You hear that?" he asked.

I listened, really straining to hear anything. All I got was his ragged breathing and the traffic out on Main. "You *could* hear," he said, nodding. "You stink like someone who's found her hearing."

The wound where he lost his eye had left a long jagged scar down the left side of his face. That scar made a lopsided cross across the socket, running up from his cheek and disappearing into the ragged hair, and then across his eyebrow and over to his left ear. The white of the scar stood out against the dark weathering of his face. My eyes kept being drawn to the empty socket, the puckered flesh and the gaping wound. It was as if something hovered inside that shallow hole, something twisted and broken.

Gooseflesh broke out across my arms and back. "You really know how to charm a girl," I said, taking a step back.

He walked past me, again with a side shuffle, carrying the pizza box against his chest like a shield. When he got to the beat-up Volvo he stopped and turned. "Can you hear the cracking?"

"What?"

He dropped the pizza box onto the ground and covered his ears with his hands. "Can't you hear the bones? The bones of the earth?"

I stepped toward my car and unlocked the door, keeping an eye on dear, psycho old Joe. "Nothing here," I said, although I doubt he heard me by that point.

"The hounds are gnawing the bones!" he shouted. "Cracking open the bones of the earth and sucking out the marrow."

A jolt ran through me, staggering me against my car. Then, the Volvo hopped sideways a few inches and the alarm in Elmer's Gun and Knife Emporium began to bray. A second jolt ran up my legs and I fell into the open door of the Civic to keep from sprawling into the alley, and to keep things from falling on my head. Down the alley, I heard something crash to the ground, a planter from an upstairs window, or a brick from the façade.

Joe curled onto the ground as the earthquake did a third stutter step and vanished like a breath. Car alarms joined Elmer's up and down Main Street. I looked around, seeing if anything was damaged, but it was a pretty small quake—was there and gone in a breath or three.

When I got out of my car, Joe was gone.

That was creepy. Gnawing the bones of the earth? Not his usual, mumbling shtick.

I walked around the Volvo and found the pizza box

open on the ground. The pizza crusts had been scattered under the car.

He wasn't near the Dumpster, so I figured he had a bolt-hole to escape to. I picked up the crusts, put them back in the box, and placed it on the stoop of Elmer's back door.

I got in my car, started it up, and slipped a Judas Priest CD into the player, then donned my sunglasses and pulled out onto Main. I paused, catching a sudden movement in the rearview mirror. A pair of shadows flew from the alley behind the Dumpster, two large birds, black as a sinner's heart.

Ten

I CALLED JULIE from the road. She didn't answer after six rings, which told me she was working the forge. Or she just didn't want to answer the phone.

When the answering machine picked up, I left a message. "On my way, boss," I said, as I pulled in front of a pink Honda Odyssey. New color made me think of stomach medicine. Nasty. "Hope the quake didn't shake things up over there too much."

I hated talking to machines.

I tried Katie's cell a few times, but kept getting the *all circuits are busy* message.

The rest of the drive took forty minutes, as everyone and their sister was on the roads. I hoped Katie was okay. I tuned the radio to NPR, listening for news. Katie was in class by this time, so I didn't want to wreck her day by calling. I was just being silly. Overreacting. *I'm sure she's fine. Really.*

I pulled over at the convenience store to get some

caffeine. I cut the engine and climbed out. The store was open; that was a good sign. I recognized the guy behind the counter, but he didn't give any indication of knowing I was alive until I set two bottles of soda on the counter.

I could see he was watching a small television and listening through an earbud.

"What's the news?" I asked.

He glanced at me and shrugged. "Few lights out. One of the buildings in Pioneer Square lost some bricks again, and they are considering closing the schools."

"Lovely," I said, handing him a fiver.

He handed me my change and turned back to the television.

Closing schools. Maybe Katie was getting out early. Now, if I could just get through to her cell, I'd feel better.

Back on the road, I could see that some of the lights were out in Renton, so getting through the 167 to 405 interchange was going to take a while. No good way to get from Kent to Redmond, frankly.

I didn't pull into the parking lot at the shop until ten fifteen. Julie's truck was parked at the diner across the street. I parked my car and Julie came out of the diner, waving her cell phone at me.

"Hey, Sarah," she called, motioning me to cross to her.

I waited for a break in the traffic and darted across. "What's up?"

"I've been trying to call the customers, see how they're doing with the quake. Not getting through too often, lines are all jammed."

"Yeah, sucks. Been trying to reach Katie, but can't get through," I said.

"Tried you a couple of times, save you a trip, but . . ." she shrugged.

"No worries. Any news on the magnitude yet?"

"Not yet, but Mary called from the Circle Q and the

horses are all panicked. She asked if we could come out tomorrow instead."

Damn, I thought. *No work, no pay.* "We have anything else lined up?"

She paused, which let me know something worried her. She talked like she walked, a freight train in constant motion.

"Actually, I got Puget Gas and Electric coming out. I think we broke a seal on the propane tank out back. Not gonna light any fires until they give me the all clear."

"Want me to come do some paperwork or anything?"

"No, not today. Consider it a vacation day."

"Bank account can't take too many of those," I said with a laugh. Gallows humor.

"Yeah, I'm sorry," she said. She was well aware of my paycheck-to-paycheck existence. "Circle Q is a new gig for us. May end up with some overtime at first, if you are up for it."

"Sure," I said with a smile. Overtime was straight time, but she paid me for the hours I worked. "I'll be back bright and early tomorrow."

She rolled her eyes. "Yeah, right. I'll see you at the crack of ten."

With that she walked back into the diner, waving at me as she went.

I stood there for a second, hands in my pockets, and contemplated.

If they closed the schools, Katie would likely head over to her brother's. I crossed traffic and pulled out my cell phone.

Katie's brother, Jimmy, was our seneschal—the leader of our little band of mercenaries, House Black Briar. We were affiliated with the Society for Creative Anachronism. If work was being canceled across the Sound, most of the group would head to Jimmy's for fun and frivolity. Like recess for grown-ups. Might be fun to get some combat practice in. The summer wars were a ways off, but it never hurt to swing some rattan.

It would take me a couple of hours to get out to Gold Bar with the crazy traffic, but I had the rest of the day to kill. I needed to call Carl at some point to see if they were shooting in light of the quake but I could do that. I didn't smell any gas, so I went into the smithy and pulled the black blade from the safe. Once it was ensconced in the lovely case I made for it, I carried the bundle out to my car. *Off to crack some heads*, I thought. Pleasant thought. Maybe Katie had her cell on already. I called her as I headed out toward Gold Bar, but it went straight to voice mail.

So I left her a quick message and turned up the music. Nothing like some hard-hitting metal to put me in the mood to hit people with sticks.

Eleven

THE TRAFFIC LIGHTS all the way through Redmond and Duvall were out, but I managed to use my special knowledge of the back streets to make it out to Gold Bar in just two hours. I drove through the little town, up past the tract housing and out Ley Road to the open country out beyond Wallace Falls State Park. Jimmy's place was deep in the edge of the mountain range, a damn sight farther away from civilization than most folks would like. I can't imagine what it cost to get electricity run that far out.

Turning into the gates of Black Briar, I could see that Gunther's Harley was parked by Stuart's Miata. I pulled around, pointing the nose of the Civic back toward the main road, and parked.

As I walked along the side of the house, I could see Katie inside with Jimmy's wife, Deidre. I rapped on the window as I passed, drawing a wave from Deidre and a thrown kiss from Katie. Jimmy must've gone and picked her up.

Gunther and Stuart were dragging out the oak tables and setting them up along the side of the barn closest to the house.

"Hey boys," I called as I crossed into the yard.

They set the heavy oak slab down and waved. Gunther had his hair back in a red bandana and Stuart had a green one.

I loved those guys. They've been best friends since elementary school and were thick as thieves. Both men were confirmed bachelors, but Jimmy assured me they were straight. Not many like 'em. Well, not where I'm from, at least. Bachelor farmers are one thing. Men who wore kilts, kept their hair long (like Gunther), and generally preferred the company of other men—they were labeled pretty quick out in God's country.

Gunther was a lanky man, all gristle and grit. He stood six foot six in his stocking feet, but he preferred Doc Martens like me. He rode a Harley, dressed like a construction worker, and ran a small jazz record store over in the U District. His weapon of choice was a greatsword and he could name every musician ever to blow a sax or a trumpet in the last thirty years. Oh, and he drank like a warhorse.

That would have gone over big in my hometown. Not with my da, of course. Total teetotaler. Drink was evil. Made men do all sorts of wicked things, like fornicate. Of course, that was only bad because it could lead to dancing.

Stuart, on the other hand, was a short man, broad across the chest, and could bench two fifty cold. He was an electrician—ran his own crew over at the University of Washington. While Gunther brewed his own beer and drank with gusto, Stuart preferred mead over beer and drank out of an ornate goblet he'd had made for him by a silversmith we knew up in Banff.

His preferred weapon was a two-handed battle-axe named Madeline. He fought like a dervish and never seemed to tire. They worked well together as a team, creating a wide kill zone during the melees.

Nothing like watching the two of them, covering each other's backs while a hundred or more men and women clashed together with padded weapons and full armor. Fun and games, until someone broke something. I'd been to many battles over the past few years with Black Briar. Stuart and Gunther were the best I'd ever seen.

The Society for Creative Anachronism was organized into kingdoms. Our little band played in the kingdom of An Tir. We weren't officially affiliated with the local baronies. We fell into the mercenary camp. Jimmy wasn't much of a joiner. Said the politics would kill you.

A sharp whistle brought my head around toward the house. Katie had come out onto the porch, a large bowl of potato salad in her hands.

"Come take this from me," she said with a laugh. "Then you can go play with your little friends."

I grinned. "The potato salad looks great."

Katie stuck the bowl in my hands, and before I knew it, darted in for a kiss. I stiffened, mortified. Being alone with Katie was one thing. Flaunting it in front of the others though . . .

I wasn't ready for that.

And if I thought about it too hard, I had to admit that I might never be ready for that.

Catcalls erupted behind me. Katie curtsied and opened

the screen door, laughing as the flush ran up my cheeks. I turned, glaring at the two men. "Got something to say, ladies?" I growled as I stomped across the yard.

"Geez, Sarah," Gunther said with a grin. "You're not usually so casual with the PDA."

"Public display of affection," Stuart chimed in before I could say anything.

I set the potato salad down on the table and glared at them.

"How about some public display of an ass-kicking?" I asked.

The two men backed away, their hands up, shaking and laughing. Any other time I'd join them, but this thing with Katie was too new, too raw. I wasn't even sure how I felt about the whole girl-girl relationship and I was in one. No, scratch that. I knew exactly what I thought of it. Too many years in Crescent Ridge, living in the shadow of Mount Rainier—too many narrow minds. My da, believing in sins of all natures and how anything that isn't in his rulebook is an abomination, seeking to punish rather than love. And even though I saved myself from that situation, on some deep level I guess a part of me still believed it, too.

The thing is, I made fun of girls like me when I was a kid, all the while knowing that I would never be what the locals would call "normal." Made signs, marched at funerals—GOD HATES FAGS. I hated the lying and tried for years to deny who I was. What I was. I ran away but the voices planted in my head followed me and I'm having an awful time getting them to shut up and go away.

And all of this is kinda hard to justify with what happened last night . . . and how it made me feel. My stomach ached. What had been joy was scattered to ashes by something as simple and pure as a kiss from my sweetie. Fuck you very much, Da. Thanks for the memories.

Deidre showed up with a plate of lunch meat and

Katie carried a tray with condiments, silverware, and napkins. Jimmy followed behind them with a large basket of fresh bread.

"Why don't you boys get a keg out of the barn," Jimmy said, winking at me. "Leave young Sarah here alone before she kneecaps one of you."

"Aye aye, Captain," the two men said in unison. They grinned and turned toward the barn at a jog.

"Don't let them rile you," he said to me, keeping his back to Deidre and Katie. "You know she's crazy about you, and the twins there think you hung the moon."

"It's not that," I said, feeling even more embarrassed to be talking about this with Jimmy. It wasn't just that he was her brother, but he was also our leader. I looked up to him. "I think Katie's the greatest, it's just . . ." I let it hang there, unable to voice my frustration.

"Well, Katie's comfortable with who she is," he said, patting me on the shoulder. "You'll come around." He turned, putting his arm across my shoulder, and watched Deidre and Katie walking back to the house. "She's a good kid. Don't break her heart, okay?"

Katie was his baby sister, just twenty-four and two years out of college. He'd raised her after their parents had been killed. He was seven years older than she was and took his responsibilities very seriously. The insurance money helped them, and they inherited the farm here, but he worked like a dog to see she had everything she could want or need.

"Careful, lout," Gunther barked behind us. We turned to see Gunther dancing around on one foot, holding the other, with Stuart bent over a keg of ale, holding his elbow.

"Cracked my elbow on the door," he said apologetically.

"Liked to break my durn foot," Gunther said, stepping

gingerly down on his wounded appendage. "Nothing broken, I reckon."

"You didn't bust the keg, did you?" Jimmy called, walking away from me. Gunther looked stricken and staggered to the keg, tilting it to the side, looking for a break.

He settled it down again with a sigh, drawing his hand across his forehead and flinging away imaginary sweat. "Close call," he said with a wink.

Jimmy picked the keg up, his plaid shirt straining across his back. Stuart and Gunther hobbled along behind him, heads down, chagrined.

"Show-off," I said as he passed me.

He set the keg on the edge of the table and twisted back and forth a couple of times, his back popping in several places. "Nothing to it," he said. "Can you at least tap it?" he asked the two men.

"A 'course we can," Gunther said, wounded now. "Nary a keg I couldn't breach with grace and style."

"And empty like the sodden drunk you are," Stuart said.

The world righted itself as they bickered among themselves. Jimmy gathered plates from the storage area in the barn and Katie and Deidre brought out more food.

Basically I watched while a feast was presented. It reminded me of revival meetings. Not every memory from childhood was bad. Those huge suppers in the field behind the church were wonderful when I was a kid. More food than a body could eat, and kids of all ages to play with. I loved revivals before I learned about how evil the world was. After that they became work, and then I learned to hate them. Except for one thing. No matter what happened with me, or between me and da, revivals were where Ma used to shine. She kept the food flowing like a conductor leading a symphony. Too bad, the rest of the time she was walking three steps behind Da, her head bowed. If I missed anyone, it was her.

"Penny for your thoughts."

I looked up to see Deidre standing in front of me, a smile on her face. Here was a strong woman.

"Expecting company?" I asked when Deidre handed me a plate.

"Wednesday night gathering as usual," she said. "But with the trembler, most of the clan is coming over early."

"Might get in some equestrian work if Maggie and Susan can get over here."

"I imagine they'll be tied up with all this traffic."

"Nay," Stuart said around a mouthful of pickled beets. "They are off traffic this month. Doing liaison work with the schools."

"And, I'm betting they keep the schools out for the next day or so," Katie said. "We've had three aftershocks so far, and they are predicting more. Susan and Maggie should be free soon."

The food was excellent, and the company good. The twins kept cracking jokes at my expense, but I promised them a drubbing after.

Only one tankard with the meal, that was Jimmy's rule. Then we could practice.

Later, after the meeting, the real drinking would begin.

By then, I'd be on my way to Everett. Needed to take the black sword for Carl to use in tonight's shoot. Before I got into the heavy stuff, I dropped my gear in the lockers Jimmy had set up in the barn—wallet, keys, cell phone. While I was thinking about it I texted Carl, letting him know I had the blade ready for tonight. He'd be pleased.

I picked up my small round shield and rattan hammer. Not as good as a real hammer, but we didn't want to actually hurt each other. A few bumps and bruises were expected, but nothing really damaging.

By the time I was outfitted, Carl had texted back. We were a go for the shoot that night. That eased the stress about missing work with Julie today. I'd be getting paid at one job at least.

I spent a good solid hour with faux hammer and shield, first impressing on Gunther a thing or two about weapon speed, then showing Stuart that strength was as important as speed. The old tae kwon do skills really helped. During the sparring Katie sat on a stack of hay bales and played the guitar, singing songs to keep us focused and "in the mood," as she said. Mainly Scottish battle songs she'd translated for guitar.

After my sessions with the twins, she brought me water and a towel to dry off. Neither man snickered. It was a good workout and they'd pushed me to the limit. I'd not be as good as them overall for a long time, if ever, but they were patient teachers and able opponents.

Deidre was in the house when I entered, thinking I'd help replenish the food for the latecomers.

"You are ripe," she said with a laugh. I caught my reflection in the microwave door and my hair was matted down with sweat.

"Yeah, pounding sense into Gunther and Stuart works up a sweat."

She rolled her eyes. "You weren't out there long enough to get through their thick skulls."

They were the favorites, after all. I'd known them as long as I'd known Katie, actually. She was still in college when I joined the Black Briars. Jimmy had been kind enough to teach an awkward blacksmith apprentice the business end of several weapons over the chuckles of the twins. They came around quickly, and even came to my defense at one battle out in Idaho. Good guys, standing at my back while I took down a jackass with more mouth than skill.

I picked up the basket of bread Deidre had just sliced,

but she whisked it away from me and shooed me with her free hand. "Hon, why don't you take a shower in the hall bath. Save you a trip out to your place."

I knew Deidre. It wasn't really a question.

"My pack's in the Civic," I said, heading toward the door.

"I'll get it," she said. "There are towels in the closet across the hall there. Just leave the wet ones on the vanity when you're done."

I handed her my keys and slunk off to the shower. Jimmy was big and imposing, and we all respected him, but Deidre was the real powerhouse in the clan. She was wise beyond words, and stubborn as a mule.

I grabbed a washcloth and a couple of towels from the closet. The bathroom was done up in seashells, pink sculpted wallpaper and white doilies you'd expect in your grandmother's house. It felt comfortable and safe.

Jimmy had a full bathroom with shower installed in the old barn, but it was utilitarian. This was homey.

I stripped out of my sweaty clothes and avoided looking at myself in the mirror. Smithing gave me big shoulders, and I kept my hair clipped pretty short. But I always felt plain and didn't need a mirror to remind me. The shower took a bit to warm up, but by the time I immersed myself under the steaming spray, I knew Deidre was an angel. The hot water worked on knots in my muscles I hadn't noticed. I let the water pour down on my head, drowning the constant chatter of doubt and recrimination I struggled with.

I heard the door open. Ah, my clothes. "Thanks, Deidre," I called.

I was a bit startled when the curtain twitched aside and Katie stepped into the shower with me, naked and gorgeous.

"Not here, your family . . . ," I started, but before I

could finish the sentence, her mouth found mine and I forgot to breathe.

After the water ran cold, we toweled off. I pulled out a pair of jeans and T-shirt I had stashed in my pack, and she put back on the same clothes she'd been wearing from earlier.

She watched me as I put on my bra. The smile on her face caused me to blush. "What will your brother say?" I asked. "Or Gunther or Stuart?"

"Screw them," she said, buckling her shoes.

I loved that she wore black Mary Janes with bobby socks. She looked great and was not afraid of what people thought. Not me, though. This kind of tryst was too public. "And Deidre?"

She laughed. "Who do you think sent me in here with the pack?"

"She wouldn't!"

"Certainly she would. She said you were too uptight and that perhaps I could loosen you up a bit."

A shiver ran up my spine at the thoughts of her caresses. "Yes, but what . . ."

"No buts," she said, wrapping me in a hug and kissing my left temple. "I love you, and I don't care who knows it."

I stiffened, and she felt me stiffen, and I felt awkward and then embarrassed all over again. Relationships suck.

The sad smile on her face nearly broke my heart. "It's okay," she said. "You don't have to say it, if it freaks you out."

"Well, I think you are amazing," I said, all lame like a high school cheerleader letting a band geek down easy. "I think . . ."

"Yes," she said, touching her fingers to my lips. "You think and you think. I'm waiting for the moment when you feel."

And she was past me, opening the door without looking back, leaving me standing in the steam with my pants in my hands and my heart in my throat.

When I was dressed, and my workout clothes were tucked in my pack, I walked out, my shoulders suddenly as tense as after a full day at the forge. They were watching me, I knew it. I opened the door and fast-walked around toward the Civic, hoping to escape before I was spotted and had to endure any more bullshit.

I had the hatchback open and had flung my pack into the backseat when a long wolf whistle stopped me in my tracks.

Son of a bitch, I thought. *I knew this was not a good idea.*

"Hot damn, Beauhall," I heard Maggie holler from the back. "I didn't think you had it in you."

I turned, the blood pounding in my ears. This I didn't need. I slammed the hatchback and realized I didn't have my keys. Damn Deidre and her meddling.

I stormed around the house, and saw Deidre in a gaggle of other Black Briar folks. Maggie stood on one of the benches, looking over Susan's head.

They looked enough alike to be confused as sisters, but they were not related. Well, not blood relations. They were both blond and tall, Amazons, Gunther called them—thin and angular with a beauty that caught most folks by surprise.

They'd been lovers when they became police officers, put up with a ton of shit from the rank and file. But they handled it. Tough broads, Jimmy once said. They'd mellowed a bit recently, having gone to California to be married. I usually liked their drive and focused attitude, but I didn't relish it turned on me.

"Deidre, can I have my keys, please?" I asked, stomping to the crowd, the flush of anger on my face.

"Sorry," Deidre said, holding out my keys. "I didn't think you'd mind if I shared it with everyone."

Fuck this. "It's none of your goddamn business," I shouted.

The crowd silenced and Jimmy looked at me with his stern leader face. I didn't care, this was more than I could take.

"She's talking about the sword," Jimmy said, his voice even and reasonable. Gunther moved aside, and I could see that the lovely case I'd built for the black sword lay on the picnic table, opened, with the sword practically glowing in the crushed velvet liner.

"Damn fine job," Stuart said, breaking the awkward silence. "We didn't touch her, but she's a thing of beauty."

"I'm sorry," Deidre said. "Katie told me you'd fixed it last night, and how beautiful it was. I just wanted to show the others."

Now, if you'd taken that sword out of that case at that moment and driven all thirty-three inches of blackened steel into my chest, I would have felt much better. As it was, all I could do was walk forward awkwardly, watch as my friends moved aside, embarrassed, and quietly close the case.

"I'm sorry," I mumbled. "I need to leave."

I carried the sword to my car, keeping my eyes on the ground in front of my feet.

No one said a word, but I felt their eyes on me.

I put the sword case back in the hatch, couldn't believe I didn't notice it was missing. Of course, the hatch was filled with old clothes, several hammers, and several books on weapons. How could I have not noticed? Could someone shoot me now, please?

Guns N'Roses blared out of the stereo when I fired the ignition. I rolled down the windows and glanced in my rearview mirror. Katie stood at the corner of the house, her hands in her pockets. The look on her face was the worst of it all. What a dumbass I could be.

I drove out of the driveway, away from the shame and the guilt. Only it followed me, buried deep inside.

Better to stop digging when you realize you have the shovel in your hand, my old man had always told me. Digging more wouldn't make the hole smaller.

Of course, what he taught me mostly was to run. Leave your troubles behind in the last town. I never understood what he was afraid of, but it followed us, from tiny village to rural town. I think he was moving from church to church more than anything—seeking salvation, he claimed. I just think he was afraid to face whatever demons haunted him.

It scared me how much I was like him. Better to cut off those around you than admit you were wrong, that you'd overreacted. Ma stuck with him, though. He had that rock to lean on. Me, I had no one. Anyone who got close freaked me out.

I'd promised myself I wasn't a quitter—anymore. Katie was the best thing that had ever happened to me, but the ridicule, the shame and derision, that trumped it all . . . again . . .

Maybe I'd have more luck tonight with *Elvis Versus the Goblins*.

Twelve

ONCE PAST LEY Road, I turned toward Gold Bar and let the wind whip through the car, the windows down, the moonroof open. I'd switched to Sheryl Crow, and sang at the top of my lungs, lamenting my love life, when a black and green Hummer roared out of a side street, nearly clipping my back end. I watched the driver fishtail the behemoth across the road before it came up behind me. I was doing forty in a thirty-five but this asshole was in more of a hurry than I was. I slowed, pulled closer to the shoulder, and waved them around, only they didn't go around. They rode right up on my rear and blared their horn. Jerks.

I began looking for a wide spot to pull over, knowing the road got really windy up ahead. Come on, asshole. Move around.

The impact surprised me. The Hummer had pushed right up against my bumper and nudged me. I kept the car under control and punched the gas. The Civic weighed about twelve pounds, but it had pickup. I watched the speedometer pass fifty, and the Hummer tapped my rear bumper again. I saw the twenty-five-mile-an-hour-zone signs as I topped fifty-five, and swore. A string of cars approached ahead of me, and the Hummer backed off, but I had to slow way down to keep from wrecking. Once the traffic faded, the Hummer accelerated once again. We did this several times by the time the quarry came into view. If I could make it that far, I could pull over and let the Hummer get past me. Beats dying.

I sped up after the last curve, punched the Civic to sixty, and prayed for a cop. Better to get a ticket, I thought, than end up as roadkill.

I passed the kennel and the taxidermist without the Hummer tapping me again. Another quarter mile and the quarry appeared around the corner. Of course, at that moment, one of the slow-ass trucks pulled out, causing me to hit the brake and swerve.

I managed to avoid the truck and hit the breakdown lane, but it was covered in loose gravel. I watched the empty guard shack go past my windshield as I did a bootlegger reverse, shouting over Sheryl Crow.

My car came to a bone-jarring halt against a pile of

sand. Luckily most of my speed had diminished enough to prevent any real damage. Sand began pouring into the passenger window and into the moonroof, over my head and into my car. I flipped the latch and pulled the moonroof closed, cutting off the skittering sand. At the same time I rolled up the passenger window as fast as my arm could spin the handle. Soon, my car would be buried. I jammed the car into first, punched the gas, and popped the clutch. The wonderful car of mine performed like a champ. It died, of course.

Come on, even Rocky would have collapsed if he'd been tapped by a Hummer and spun out into a huge mound of sand.

I tried the ignition a couple of times before the car coughed to life again. I eased the clutch out, and the car surged forward, trailing sand back toward the road. When I got there, the Hummer sat idling across the exit.

I stopped, shook sand from my hair, and waited. A large man, about the size of Rhode Island, climbed out of the Hummer from the passenger side. He walked toward me, his hands clenched into fists.

"Give me the artifact," he bellowed, pointing a meaty finger at my windshield.

"Bite me!" I yelled, gunning the engine. He looked from me back to the Hummer, and back to me. Making up his mind, he broke into a run toward me, swinging his fist at my car.

Holy crap. The world slewed sideways as he connected to my front quarter panel. The car didn't die, and I took the new direction as a sign, and stomped the gas. I swung around, slinging gravel from hell to breakfast. I hoped it did more than dent his paint.

I drove along the fence that kept the kids out of the quarry and prayed I didn't drive into a ditch, or a huge gaping hole that had once held sand or gravel or whatever else this place sold. At the far end, a second gate stood open. The sign said it was where the trucks entered the quarry. I jetted out the in door and veered back onto May Creek and headed to First Street. The Hummer sat behind me and hadn't moved. I drove out past the light industrial area and to the more congested intersection with the fast food joints.

The Hummer did not show up again, and I merged onto Highway 2 toward Everett and the movie shoot. If they'd wanted me dead, I'd have been shoved off the switchbacks up on the high portion of Ley Road. They just wanted the artifact. What artifact? They couldn't mean the sword? I glanced over my shoulder toward the case in the back. How the hell had this been about that blade?

Thirteen

WHEN I PULLED into the lot at the shoot, I was thirty minutes late. Carl stood by the stage door, chatting with Jennifer, the DP, and checking his watch. I opened the door and sand spilled out onto the parking lot. I'd be vacuuming that out for weeks, I just knew it. I climbed out, shut the door, and opened the hatchback.

"About time, Beauhall. You got my sword?" Carl called from the door.

I waved at them. "Yessir."

"Better late than never," he said before turning and stomping into the building.

Great, now Carl was pissed at me. Lovely day I was having. And it had started with such promise. I grabbed the case out of the car and crossed the parking lot. Jennifer watched me, a clipboard in one hand and a patient look on her face.

"If you are going to be late in the future," she said, falling in step with me as I passed her, "could you call?"

"Yeah, sure," I said, annoyed. "Did I mention some jerk ran me off the road?"

She stopped in her tracks, startled. "Are you okay?"

I waved my hand at her, the sword's case in my left hand. "Did some damage to the car, but I'm okay."

"Did you report it to the police?"

I thought of Maggie and Susan out at Jimmy's and felt my stomach flop over. "Not yet, but I know someone."

She patted me on my shoulder, nodding. "You just be careful, single girls like us, all alone in the world—we gotta look out for ourselves."

We walked into the studio to the sound of my grinding teeth.

Single gals, yep. That was us. Bitchy, neurotic balls of tension and fear, unable to commit. I am woman, hear me roar.

The transition from Everett industrial to goblin encampment really wasn't that big of a stretch. We had a run-down cityscape to work with, the third movie Carl had shot with that set. Recycle and reuse, he said with laughter when it was brought up. I think the faux Vegas ruins far outstripped the bombed-out London and the earthquake-decimated Los Angeles of the previous two movies.

Maybe this one would make a bit of money, even.

But not until the film was in the can. I quickened my step, crossing the soundstage like a metronome.

Of course no one was ready. I'm just the prop girl and the goblins had been putting on those costumes for weeks. Surely they could've gotten started without me. Instead half of them were talking on cell phones, while several sat around playing cards. Amateurs.

I stormed to the prop unit, stashed the sword on top

of a trunk full of elephant ears, and began grabbing big rubber hands.

"Come on, people," I barked at the milling extras. "Goblins, get your asses in here."

The usual crew came in and gathered their gear. I helped several of them with the gloves, then the rubber feet. The smart ones pulled the suits on first, then put on the feet. The rest had to take the feet off because the jumpsuit costumes wouldn't fit over them.

I was getting a headache.

Of the thirteen giant goblin heads that normally lined the costume cage, twelve had been handed out among the low-paid extras. Hell, they were practically volunteers. I knew I should be kinder to them, but I was in a foul mood.

"Who's missing?" I asked the assembled goblins.

One of them pointed over at the offices. Rolph stood next to Carl, the two of them with their heads together over something on a clipboard.

"Come on, Rolph," I called. "Got a shot to get in before dawn."

He didn't move, just glanced my way and continued his talk with Carl.

I made a big production of slamming a cabinet, but the two did not stop their secret meeting. This was asinine. Here I was fussed at for being late, and Carl was keeping one of the goblins from dressing out.

After twenty minutes, I started swearing. Hanging out with blacksmiths can really color your vocabulary. Add in cops, jazz musicians, SCAdians, and movie folk, and you come with a string of epithets that make a sailor swell with pride.

Both of them looked my way a couple of times when I pitched some choice word at the right volume, but neither made a move to break up their coffee klatch.

Goblin number three, a young man with a bad case of acne and a nasal voice, began to cry when I ripped out the C word. Goblin seven, an elderly woman who just loved to feel needed, shushed me, wagging her giant goblin hand at me.

That was it. I was not going to be shushed by granny goblin and the amazing wunderkind.

I stormed out of the prop cage, slamming the steel door shut with a loud clang. I'd just built up a righteous head of steam heading toward the two of them, when Rolph broke away and walked toward the offices.

"What the hell, Carl," I called. "Rolph needs to be dressed if we are going to make this shoot. Some of us have lives, you know."

I knew that crossed the line, but damn it, I was tired and still reeling from the earlier fiasco.

Carl turned, his face red with frustration. "Back off, Beauhall. This is my movie. I call the shots."

He was right, of course, but it still galled me. "I thought you were in an all-fired hurry?"

He pinched the bridge of his nose, pushing his glasses up onto his forehead. "I have a headache, which you are not helping, and a series of issues that goes beyond your current abilities, Sarah."

I took a step back. He never called me Sarah.

"Rolph is making a phone call," he punched his finger at me, "that is very important to the continued existence of this production." He started toward me, each step forward a moment of panic, his voice rising in volume with each word. "Can . . . you . . . just . . . back . . . the . . . fuck . . . off?"

I matched him, step for step, horrified. Carl never raised his voice. Hell, he had to use a whistle to calm the chatter at times.

I raised my hands, surrendering. "Sure, boss. What-ever you say."

"Just get the goblins in position, will you, please?" He turned away, his shoulders slumped, and walked toward the offices.

Something had kicked Carl in the breadbasket since I saw him last, and it was not a pretty sight.

I mumbled apologies to the extras, gathered the twelve of them in a neat little line, and finished their costumes one at a time. Every now and again I glanced over at the office, watched as Rolph talked into the phone and Carl paced, his ball cap in his hands, his thinning hair disheveled and askew.

Something bad was happening, I could feel it. There was a solution being applied that was worse than the problem. Carl radiated it, Rolph practically had it written on his face. If this was about money, I'd bet they were borrowing from a loan shark.

Nothing I could do. I concentrated on doing my job.

A cudgel here, a short axe there—eventually I had them all outfitted for battle, in the meager, rat-on-a-stick way goblins survived. They'd look great on the screen. Number eleven had real rats in a cage, courtesy of Jennifer. I just had to make sure they didn't escape, or eat the foam costumes.

Finally they got into their positions, number three and number seven comforting one another and settling onto their taped marks in front of the ferrocrete hill JJ, the wonder-mule, would mount later to decry their foulness and such.

Rolph hung up the phone, finally, and shook Carl's hand. In fact, Carl grabbed Rolph's with both of his own and pumped them like he was expecting oil to shoot out of Rolph's ears. Carl was suddenly very happy, and Rolph looked like he'd just sold his mother's kidneys. I didn't like it one bit.

When he finally walked across the soundstage to get dressed, Rolph let an impassive mask fall over his face.

"Hello, Rolph," I said, handing him his jumpsuit.

"Smith," he said, nodding at me. His eyes were distant and cold. Nothing like the gleam of excitement and hope I'd seen the night before when I forged the sword.

"What was all the hullabaloo about just now?" I asked. He donned his jumpsuit and said nothing.

"You mad at me?" I asked as he buckled the dirty, matted pelt across his shoulder and hefted his rubber head.

"You heard my plea last eve," he said, looking down at me as I buckled his feet.

"Yeah, well. That was a bit out there."

"You are a child," he said without anger. "You have no idea the powers arrayed in the world—no idea the ripple you have made in the little pond of our lives."

I looked at him. Little pond? "I know you have ten seconds to get your goblin ass in line with the others so we can shoot this scene again."

He nodded, his mouth a hard line of frustration and impotence. "Are we done here?" he asked, stepping back, one final buckle undone on his ankle.

I ran my hands through my sweat-soaked hair and sat back on my feet. "Rolph, I'm sorry if I can't do as you ask, but be reasonable. Dragon?"

"Your inability to see beyond the nose on your face is a weakness for a smith," he said, kneeling and fastening the ankle. He still towered over me, as I was practically sitting on the floor. I was not comfortable with the positions, so I stood.

He glanced upward as I rose, a look of determination and resignation on his face. "Things are out of my hands," he said, showing me the palms of the rubber goblin appendages. "The dice have left the cup."

"Dice cup?" I asked. "You spend some time out at the casino or something?" Did Carl have gambling debts?

"Nay." He shook his head and stood. "I pulled the runes today. Things are amiss in the world."

Runes? I knew a girl in college who had a necklace she wore with a favorite rune on it, but that's it. "What exactly does that mean?"

He stood, bowlegged, with the goblin head perched on his head like an ill-fitting crown. The calm look fell over his face again. "Perthro is in overview, Tiwaz is the challenge."

"Whoa," I said, holding my hand up. "Dude, buy a vowel."

"Algiz calls the action. Kenaz guides the change." He slipped the head over his own, and the last was muffled. "But Wunjo. That is where we are bound."

He turned and walked to the group of goblins, high-fiving the crybaby and patting several of them on their round foam heads.

Runes? What had he said? Wunjo?

One more thing to ask Katie. At least it gave me something to talk about. That pang in my chest returned. She was so damn beautiful. Why did I have to make this so hard?

I gathered up the remaining scraps and props, wrangling them back into the cage as Jennifer got the lighting techs in gear.

There were several long stretches of time where the goblins had to be positioned just so—continuation shots were the worst. Carl sat at the monitor watching the run from Monday and the grips moved the goblins to and fro. Finally Carl threw up his hands and called a break.

We'd been at it for an hour and a half and he calls break?

I sidled over near Carl and Jennifer, straining my ears to make out their conversation.

"Just shoot the whole scene over," Jennifer was saying. "Remember *Tri-Wizard's Blood*? The crap we took for the incongruities in the battle scene."

Carl scowled and thrust his hands in his pockets. "Shit,

that will cost us most of tonight. We'd have to push JJ's big scene off until tomorrow night. We're already behind schedule."

I winced. Katie and I had plans Thursday night. We were supposed to go out with Melanie and Dena. I'd already canceled on her twice. Not that I would be too upset. Melanie and Katie had been roommates in college, and sometimes lovers.

Melanie was okay, really sweet and all, but I had a problem with her. Didn't hurt she was doing a residency over at Evergreen Hospital. Emergency room doctor, hot blonde with a smile that melted butter. I wasn't jealous. Not a bit.

We reshot the goblin scene from the beginning. Frankly, it was a better scene this time around, but we didn't wrap until after midnight. JJ had gone home around ten, when it was apparent we wouldn't get back to his big climax that evening.

He did have a day job—used car salesman or something slimy, I was almost positive. Maybe a lawyer; he had the bottom-feeder vibe. That and the trailer trash that he hung out with kept my opinion of him just above live rats. I glanced over at the caged vermin we used in the shoot. Well, at least dead rats. It fluctuated from day to day.

Job one was to get the extras out of the goblin suits with no damage, and get the gear back into the cage before we left. It took me until two to get all the gear packed away. Then I had to get the paperwork settled with Jennifer. We were running low on gauze and tape. Really couldn't secure the foam without supplies, and she was sympathetic. She wrote down everything I asked for and nodded accordingly. I'd get half of what I needed, but it would get me through the next few shoots.

This was no way to run a railroad. And I decided to have a little early morning chat with the chief conductor.

Carl sat at the desk, going over the books. We hadn't

had catering the last few shoots, and the extras were grumbling. We'd come to expect those horribly dry sandwiches and muffins.

I knocked on the door frame and put on my best pixie smile. "Hey, boss."

Carl looked up. I could see the strain on his face. "It's been a long night, Beauhall. Is it important?"

The fact I was back to Beauhall was a good thing, but the way he dismissed me hurt. I thought I was his favorite. So much for my girlish charm.

"Sorry. I was just going to ask about tomorrow night."

He put down his pen, crossed his arms, and looked at me. "Please don't start. We are all pissed we have to do another night, but that's how the movie business runs."

"Is everything okay?" I asked. "Anything I can do to help?"

He thought about it for a moment. I could see the need in him to tell me something.

"This got anything to do with Rolph earlier?"

That was all it took. The moment passed and his face got hard. "Just be on time tomorrow night, will ya?" he asked, picking up the pen and staring at the papers in front of him.

I sighed. There was something important here and he didn't feel like he could trust me. Another little shard of ice slid into my chest.

"I'll be here," I told him quietly.

Somehow.

This would be the third time I bailed on dinner with Melanie and Dena. I had good reasons. Work was a good reason, right?

Katie was going to be majorly pissed.

Fourteen

ANOTHER SCREAM, LONG and frightened, broke Qindra's meditation and brought her to her feet, her thoughts lost in the between places. How many had gone before? One, two? Why would someone be screaming in this house?

The fumes of recently burned incense rushed back to her as she found herself conscious for the first time in hours.

She'd almost found the source of last night's disturbance. Whatever it was, Nidhogg had been in a state. Qindra had been following a ripple in the aether, trying to find the source. She'd been so close. A few more minutes perhaps.

Alas, more immediate needs beckoned, unfortunately.

She took the red dressing gown down from the nearest post of her bed and wrapped it around her naked form. Stepping into slippers, she strode across her suite and into the foyer, careful not to ruffle the silk shawls that hung over the mirrors on either side of the archway. She kissed her fingertips and touched them to the threshold as she passed through, nodding her head sharply twice. When she reached the door from her suite to the main house, she hesitated, placing a hand on the door to check for heat.

Living with a dragon presented all sorts of interesting options behind that scream—fire being the quickest to fall prey to if the mistress was angry, or confused again, which had happened more and more of late.

The door remained cool to her touch, so she opened it quickly and strode down the short hall to the grand entrance. Maids of various ages rushed about, several heading to the long staircase that wound upward to the conservatory, library, music room, and the suites for special guests.

At least they kept their wits about them enough not to run into her, nor to rush headlong back into the ballroom, where the scream sounded a third time before being abruptly silenced.

Qindra pulled a birch wand from the pocket of her dressing gown and drew an intricate rune in the air, where it hovered in an icy blue trail of smoke. After a moment, the rune began to dissipate, the smoke drifting toward the ballroom before it stopped and faded to nothing.

No one lived on the other side of those huge double doors . . . that is, no one but her mistress. She glanced to her left and spied the young maid Jai Li.

"Where is your twin, little flower?" Qindra asked the child.

Jai Li bowed deeply before averting her gaze, but managed to point toward the ballroom.

"I see. Why were you not with your sister? Do you not serve the mistress together?"

A look of horror crossed Jai Li's face and tears sprung onto her cheeks, but she did not cry out. Nidhogg had their tongues cut out at birth, to prevent any unnecessary chatter. It was barbaric. But Qindra knew it was not a subject broached with the mistress. Not something one would risk their life for.

"Has something happened?" Qindra asked.

The teapot sat behind the large potted plant, where Jai Li had set it when she went to hide.

"Ah. The mistress asked you to fetch her tea?"

Jai Li nodded once and bowed her head.

This would be so much easier if she could just speak. Qindra spoke Mandarin. It wasn't as if there was a language barrier among those who served the eldest of the dragons.

She's in a rage for some reason, Qindra surmised. And killed one of the twins. She will be most unhappy when she returns to her senses. They were special-bred to serve her. Trained since birth. Quite the delight of the mistress's little menagerie of misfits and cripples.

The air felt thicker for a moment, and Qindra took a few shallow breaths. Blood had been spilled, and more, she was certain.

Nothing more for it then. She strode to the ballroom and threw open the doors. Those maids who had lingered in the great hall scattered like church mice, into the cubbies and crannies that they each had as a safe place. This was not the first time the mistress had lost control.

Smoke hovered in the ballroom, but parted as Qindra waved the wand in front of her. It was almost as if a breeze emanated from the tip. In the center of the room lay several broken and partially eaten bodies. One would be Su Chi, the mistress's Eyes. She would have been the one screaming. Su Chi read to their mistress now that Nidhogg's eyesight was failing her in her old age.

Qindra strode to the left, not looking to the back of the room where the dragon huddled. Anger and confusion radiated through the room. With a quick intake of breath, Qindra began to sing a quiet song in the language of her mother. An Icelandic lullaby that pleased the mistress. She continued to walk the right perimeter, keeping her gaze from the dragon, as any eye contact would be seen as a challenge, trusting her instincts and experience to alert her if things went awry.

Two boys—she assumed two, but the mess could have been the remains of three—lay scattered near the open veranda. Somewhere on the balcony lay the remains of Nidhogg's dinner. *Something light, I suppose*, Qindra thought. *Now she's gone and eaten several of the children.* She glanced around. Or at least large parts of several children.

When she was past the door to the veranda, Qindra began to hum the same melody, but without the words. After a few steps, she could feel the rage of the dragon dissipating. There was a cough, and a retching, then the dragon fell silent.

Only then did Qindra look to see her mistress in all her decrepit glory.

Nidhogg—the Corpse Gnawer—was a mighty creature. Her scales shone white and silver in the light of the candelabras scattered about the room. Only the blood on her muzzle and the carnage strewn about the room marred her beauty.

"You will be angry with yourself on the morrow," Qindra said quietly to the dragon. "Mei Hua was a beautiful child, don't you think?"

The dragon cocked her head to the side, so like a bird that Qindra often thought they shared a common heritage in the long dark before the gods of Asgard brought man onto the earth. Migard, she reminded herself. Know the enemy, know thine self.

"Jai Li will be useless without her twin, you realize?"

Nidhogg would hear her. Would drink in the words and remember them later, but now she only understood the tone of Qindra's voice. No other mortal had stood before this great beast and uttered words of reproach—of disappointment.

"They were your favorites of the new generation, and now you've spoiled the set. Whatever shall we do with Jai Li now? You cannot send her to Jean-Paul and his brothels. She is too delicate." Qindra found where the girl had been killed; a cross-stitch lay abandoned on the floor, the pillow she sat upon was shredded and covered in blood.

What transgression was committed this time, Nidhogg? What minor fault sent your aging mind into such a rage?

"I'm sure the meal Cook prepared for you would have been much easier on your stomach than what you have consumed at this point." She stepped gently over the blood smear and righted a rocking chair. The chair where Nidhogg spent much of her time these days.

Qindra placed a hand on the outstretched wing tip, gently stroked the corded muscle and tendon.

"You should sleep now, settle your mind and return to us."

The dragon moved to the side, away from the carnage, and tucked her head beneath her right wing.

"Good," Qindra said, moving closer to the great, heaving chest. "Settle your spirit, ancient mother. Let your rage sink back into the earth."

Silver mist rose from Qindra, a fine fog flowing from the tip of her wand, to flow over the dragon. Exhaustion washed over Qindra. She had not slept in the last twenty-four hours and the magic took much from her.

At least now the air smelled of lilacs.

Even after the dragon had fallen into slumber, Qindra could feel the great heart beating through her hand pressed against the ancient beast's chest. *What has happened to frighten you so*, she thought. *I do not remember word of you changing like this in my mother's mother's time.*

Only a dramatic change, an awakening of the enemy or a disturbance in the fabric of the world, could cause such an event.

Nidhogg slept while the house staff waited, fearful. Thralls to the last, servants since birth, still they were not empty-headed fools. Their lot was harsh, but not unpleasant. They had decent lives under the circumstances, and this shook the foundation of their understanding.

Qindra would deal with them later. Her first priority

was to see that Nidhogg did not kill anyone else in a rage, that she did not burn down the great house, and most of all, that she did not hurt herself. She was a very old woman, after all. The stress was horrible for her.

Fifteen

I FELL INTO bed around three thirty. I did take a shower, just couldn't face sleeping with all that sand in my hair. I couldn't believe how much sand was in the tub when I finished. Of course, by the time I drifted off to sleep, I realized I hadn't checked my messages.

When I crawled out of bed at nine the next morning, I found I'd missed a call from Katie. She'd left me a message asking that I call to talk about what happened at Jimmy's. She sounded upset. Not that I could blame her. I hit my forehead with the phone a few raps, but I didn't feel any better for it.

I called her place, anyway. Of course I knew she was at school, but she sometimes checked her voice mail from work.

"Katie." I hated this. "Sarah. Listen, I'm sorry I freaked out yesterday. It was just, well . . . you know." Good, best material in years. "Anyway. I just wanted to say I'm sorry. Really sorry, actually. Things did not go well last night and we have to shoot again tonight. Don't be mad, 'kay?" Not good at all. "Call me, please?"

I hung up and leaned my head against the wall. This was so high school.

Just to be sure, I also sent her an e-mail. Lame, I know, but I wanted to make sure she understood I was canceling for the night.

I swung by the car wash on the way to work. Three dollars in quarters later, I'd vacuumed out half of the Sahara and left my car only slightly gritty.

I pulled into the shop just before ten and Julie was packing her truck. Big day at the Circle Q. I hoped they were cool. Hated those uppity owners who hovered over everything we did.

"How was yesterday?" Julie asked, closing the tool chest she kept in the back of her truck. "You see Katie?" I liked how she didn't look at me when she asked, just in case.

"Yeah," I said, scuffing my Doc Martens in the gravel. "Had a pretty good afternoon, but things got a little off-kilter late in the day."

She nodded and walked back to the shop. I followed, sullen, my hands in my pockets. I hate being sullen, but Julie sometimes made me feel like a schoolgirl again, being judged by the teachers.

Of course, she was teaching me. I had to remember that, too.

"Had a little tiff over some PDA out at Jimmy's." There, I'd confessed it.

Julie knew Jimmy from horse circles. "He's a good guy. You working on sparring?" And just like that, she sidetracked it all. I had a lot to learn from this woman.

"Yes, and making an ass out of myself."

She barked a short laugh. "Now, that surprises me."

I looked over at her, indignant. "Hey, I'm not that bad."

"Sarah, you are wound tighter than a mare about to foal." She chuckled all the way out of the shop.

I pulled my kit off the shelf, added my favorite hammer, and grabbed a box of shoes I'd made last week. I was good at shoes. Simple work that cleared my head. More and more farriers were using premade shoes to start with. Cheaper, too. Julie, however, didn't trust the work. Didn't want to buy from little kids in China.

I added my gear to the back of the truck and grabbed a second propane tank while Julie made sure she had her laptop. She kept meticulous records of every horse, donkey, mule, or pony we ever touched. The owners sometimes called us to figure out which animal needed what kind of care.

I called my voice mail before we left, just to make sure. Katie hadn't responded yet, but it was early.

We popped through the drive-thru at Monkey Shines and got coffee. Julie didn't press me for details and I was glad.

Throughout the morning, I caught her watching me. Mostly keeping an eye on my horse work, but there was something else.

Six horses today. That would give us enough money to make the trip worthwhile, and give the Circle Q folks something to judge us by.

I loaded the gear into the truck while Julie chatted up the hands.

Something I hadn't noticed until just now was that Julie was flirting. I'm only twenty-six, so Julie at forty-one seems more like my parents than a peer. But the guy she was talking to was flirting back. Now that I thought about it, it had gone on all day, I'd just been too absorbed in my own stuff to really notice.

The owner of the Circle Q, a lovely woman named Mary Campbell, handed Julie a check and thanked us for our conscientious work. She even shook my hand, which I admired. I noticed the calluses on her hand, which made me smile. I loved a woman who wasn't afraid of hard work. Today, she was dressed for town, but I bet she was a jeans-and-denim-shirt gal most of the rest of the week.

On the way back, Julie whistled something that made me think of two-stepping. I cringed, but liked the way her eyes looked. She was really happy. I didn't mention the two guys from the farm, but if I had to guess, I'd say she favored Jack over Steve. Jack was taller, leaner. More whipcord and leather. Steve was broad and deep. Like a bull. Both were cute as hell, but what do I know.

Julie took the laptop into the office and began to download her stuff to the server she kept off-site. Too many accidents can happen at a smithy, she'd told me that first day. Better safe than sorry.

I finished unloading the truck and was putting the tools away when Julie let me know I had a message on the business phone. I checked my cell immediately and saw that I had a message there, too. Damn, how'd I miss that? No vibrating jokes please; holding on to a squirming horse while you attempt to nail a hunk of metal to his hoof tends to keep your attention.

She handed me the phone and it was Katie. Katie was very polite, professional even. Asking that I please return her call immediately as it was a matter of some urgency.

I deleted the message and handed Julie back the phone. She looked at me with raised eyebrows. "Should I ask?"

"Ditching her tonight for Carl," I said, punching up messaging on my cell.

"Ouch," she said, shaking her head. "Work over love will get you nowhere." She turned back to her desk, filling out a few invoices and adding bits of notes to her database.

I listened to Katie's voice on my message. This one was not professional at all.

"Sarah, I don't know what the hell is going on with you, but after the stunt you pulled last night, you have the nerve . . . *the nerve* to cancel on our friends again?"

I closed my eyes and listened to her anger. This was indeed the third time I'd cut out on dinner with Melanie and Dena. But I had a good reason. Right? Even I thought I was copping out. But I made a promise to Carl.

Yes, how come Carl's promise means more than the

promise to Katie? Well, work, first of all. Carl paid me to work there. Katie had to understand my financial situation, we'd talked about it often enough. Things were tight, and she just had to understand.

Of course, I hit the occasional auction. But that's professional interest.

Sigh. Frankly, I didn't like Melanie because I couldn't compete with her. She and Katie had history I could never have. They were comfortable in their own skins, and neither of them gave a damn what the world thought of them.

I, on the other hand, felt like a fish out of water. When the nagging voices in my head started up—you know, those old teachers, or cranky relatives that live in your skull and tell you how much you suck, or what an abomination you are—those voices rose loud and clear when I thought about the public aspect of it all.

When we were alone, that was a different story. She was intoxicating. I could just lie with her forever, holding each other, sharing the most intimate of moments. It felt right. Pure. And I felt loved.

But when it became public, I was back in high school, listening to my friends make fun of anyone who was different. "Wonder what her favorite flavor of carpet is" rose loud and clear when the head monkeys began to chatter. And I would feel the shame all over again.

I needed sleep, and a drink. Not necessarily in that order. But I was getting neither again anytime soon.

Sixteen

I CLEANED UP the shop, putting away the tools, updating the inventory sheet we kept of supplies used, and sweeping. Julie made sure I swept every day. Not that the smithy needed it often, but it was an excellent habit to get into.

I waited for her on the back stoop, bottle of water held tightly in my fist, when she locked up. I had to be in Everett in a few hours, but I had a bit of time to kill.

"Something on your mind, Sarah?" Julie asked once the shop was locked up. "You look like you need to talk."

I took a long pull on the bottle and screwed the cap back on before I spoke. "It's Katie. I have to work tonight, and we were supposed to have dinner with Melanie and Dena."

"Should I know them?"

I waited as she sat on the stone wall beside me, just far enough to not crowd me, but close enough for me to feel her presence. It was comforting. "Melanie and Katie were lovers in college."

"Ah," she said, nodding sagely. "I see."

I turned the bottle over in my hand, end over end, waiting. When I realized she wasn't going to elaborate, I stumbled on. "So, anyway. The shoot . . . well, things were bad last night for some reason."

"Your fault?" she asked.

"Well, I was late," I said, feeling the frustration start to build. "But after I left Jimmy's, this huge guy in a Hummer ran me off the road, then punched my car."

"Really?" she said, shocked. "I saw the damage, was

going to ask if you'd fallen asleep at the wheel, or, you know. Something else."

I assumed "something else" meant drinking and driving, but I didn't usually drink—and never when I had to drive. "No, I was late because of the asshole in the Hummer, but things were bad before I got there. Carl has reached crazy stress overload."

"And with you being the poster child for patience, you helped the situation with your calm approach?"

"No, well . . ." Damn her. Okay, she was observant, but I didn't like how folks thought they had me pegged. "Things went long last night, and we need to work again tonight to catch back up to schedule."

"And did Carl understand you had other plans?"

"Yes."

"Well, you did make a commitment to him. And if he is putting any kind of responsibility in your hands, it will cost him money if you miss."

"Exactly, thank you." I got up and paced, waving my hands. "I don't know why Katie doesn't understand that."

Julie watched me, pushed her black Stetson back on her head, and crossed her long legs out in front of her, hooking one booted ankle over the other. "I bet Katie understands completely," she said. "But this isn't the first time you've canceled on her, right?"

I stopped pacing and hung my head. "Right."

"So, it's about you picking what's important to you. She's hurt you won't visit with those people who are important in her life."

"I see Jimmy and Deidre," I said defensively. Always defensively these days. I wanted to punch something.

"Sarah," Julie said sweetly, standing and brushing the dirt off her jeans. "You love this girl?"

"I don't know."

She nodded slowly. "Does she love you?"

There it was, the gut punch. "Yeah, she claims to."

"Interesting word, claims. Come up to the house and I'll make some tea." And she started walking, not even looking back.

I stood there for a moment, checked my cell for the time, and turned to follow. I'd wanted this conversation. She was the master, and I the apprentice. Maybe I could learn more than smithing. Fifteen years of additional life experience was a world of difference.

I didn't knock, but just walked on into her trailer. Well, double-wide manufactured house, as she reminds me frequently. No wheels on this sucker, not like back home where I grew up. Her place was palatial compared to my apartment, but it still felt like the little pig's house of sticks to me.

She held the teakettle under the running tap. Two cups were on saucers and lemon and sugar sat on the table in their little dishes. Julie was a kick-ass cowgirl who could take a punch and throw down tequila like it was nobody's business, but she was also a girlie girl when it came to domestic things.

I sat on a bar stool and leaned on the counter, slumped over like I used to do at my grandmother's counter. This place had the same vibe.

"You gotta understand something about love," she said as the water began to heat on the gas stovetop. "When she told you she loves you, did you tell her back?"

"No," I said, feeling sheepish. "But she said it yesterday for the first time."

"Were you naked?"

I blushed then, of course, damn the pale skin. "We'd just gotten out of the shower."

She nodded. "If she said it when you were both vulnerable like that, it's different than if she said it at the grocery, or over the phone. We are conditioned to say it in certain conditions, but being naked and vulnerable gives us more pause, makes us both wary and free, if you understand."

I didn't, not really. "If Katie said she loved me, she meant it, no matter where she said it, or what the circumstances."

"Fair enough," she said, adding several teaspoons of sugar to her mug and passing the dish to me. "Do you love her?"

I ladled sugar into my cup and didn't look up.

"Sex is not love, Sarah, I assume you know that already."

"True," I said. "But she's my first."

"First ever, or first girl?"

"There was one guy in college," I said, rolling my eyes. "But he was lousy, and controlling, and a shit, you know?"

She let a hint of a smile touch her lips. "Sarah, you just described my first husband."

Husband, I didn't even know she'd been married.

"So, Katie is new and fresh, and intoxicating," she said. "And you guys have great sex?"

"Amazing," I whispered, not looking up.

"But it bugs you at the same time?"

This I knew, cold. "No, not exactly. It's just the whole gay scene."

The kettle whistled and Julie watched me for a moment before getting up. She poured boiling water into our cups and dropped in tea bags. She sat back down and lifted out her tea bag, dunking it over and over.

"I think you are jealous of Melanie, and I think you're a bigot."

I jerked back like she'd punched me. "Bigot?"

"Sure," Julie said, dunking her tea bag with no concern. "And a hypocrite."

"Well, fuck you very much," I said, pushing away from the counter. "I have enough of this abuse in my head, I don't need reinforcements."

I stalked to the door, not looking back.

"Tell me I'm wrong," she said.

I paused, one hand on the door, and closed my eyes, trying to control my breathing. What could I say? I knew she was right, but it still hurt to hear it. I opened the door and walked out into the late afternoon sun. I tried to close the door gently to rise above the anger that threatened to flow over the levees but I didn't quite succeed.

I consoled myself as I stomped my way to my car that I hadn't broken the glass in the door.

Seventeen

I PUT IN a Black Sabbath CD and cranked the stereo up to sixteen—enough to allow "War Pigs" to drown out the road noise. Traffic was horrible as usual, but I made it over to Crossroads to my apartment as the first strains of "Changes" echoed within my car.

I hated that I was so transparent. Gunther and Stuart, Deidre and Jimmy, now Julie. They all knew what a two-faced liar I was.

It's not like I didn't like Katie; hell, part of me wondered if I didn't love her. But I just couldn't wipe out the eighteen-plus years of socialization I'd received. I never knew a gay person until I was in college, as far as I know. Whether or not it was true, I somehow knew in my bones that God hated gays and they were unnatural, and all the rest of the rhetoric the church pushes out, and the rednecks, and especially my family. So just where did that leave me?

I hadn't talked to my father in three years, not since I realized why I couldn't keep a relationship with a guy, why I had those thoughts in gym class. My father is sure people like me can be cured if we just take up the Bible and pray. I can't deny who I am anymore but I don't know if he isn't right. I just didn't know which way was up any longer. My head seemed muddled lately and I couldn't figure out why.

I unlocked the door to my place and dropped my pack on the couch. Dirty dishes sat on the coffee table, and the garbage hadn't been taken out in about a week. I crossed to the fish tank and fed the two goldfish that were still alive. The third took the last swim to goldfish heaven via the toilet, and I stripped for the shower.

I knew I was no beauty queen. Melanie was cute and curvy in all the right places. I was shorter and dumpy. Not fat, mind you, but built more like a fireplug than a supermodel. I had shoulders that were broad and strong arms from smithing. Katie said I was amazing. Maybe it was the opposite thing. She wore makeup, not a lot, and liked wearing dresses and nice shoes. Me, I preferred jeans and a T-shirt. Of course, I was pretty damn particular about my footwear—Doc Martens, baby. They were my first crush, and my first rebellion. No girly shoes for me. And no jokes about comfortable shoes. I just liked how they looked—well, and how they made me feel. I totally understand why Katie feels a certain way based on the shoes she's wearing. My Doc Martens made me feel strong.

I glanced at myself in the mirror and cringed at my reflection. The Doc Martens were my rebellion as a kid. I couldn't even cut my hair until I moved out. Scandalized my mother, bless her heart. Da said I looked like a guy, and gave me shit about my clothes. I don't think he's understood a thing about me since I got my first period.

I tried to see what Katie saw in me. It's not like I'm a

beast. I have all the right curves, and Katie thinks I'm sexy. I should be happy with that. Just hard to overcome a decade of hiding my body, dressing in baggy clothes and fixating on what's wrong with being a woman in my parents' world.

Maybe I just needed therapy. Not like I was going to get a new face or a new body anytime soon. If I turn on a hottie like Katie, maybe I have something worth considering. I squinted in the mirror, trying to see myself through different eyes, holding my breasts in my hands, turning from side to side.

I dropped my hands with a sigh and turned the shower on full blast, heat all the way to the fore. Let the steam fill the room and block the mirror. That's what I needed at the moment. Obscurity.

I showered quickly and dressed in jeans and a T-shirt advertising another punk band that Carl would've never heard of. I think I had a dozen left he hadn't seen. Tonight I was going to treat him to D'Hammerschmiedsgselln, a cool band I'd seen in Portland a couple of times. The name is a German folk dance about a blacksmith's apprentice. I find it ironically appealing.

Okay, if I was being honest with myself, I had a nice figure, proportional and all. But why would Katie pick me over Melanie? Melanie was willowy—tall, blond, intoxicating . . . Anyway, how could I compare?

Enough introspection. I needed to get my ducks in a row and get to the shoot on time. Couldn't afford to piss Carl off.

While I toasted a bagel I checked my mail. More bills, and some guy who wanted to sell me a house. As if I could afford a house.

There were no messages on the home phone. No missed calls. I double- and triple-checked while I poured a glass of milk that was near expiring, and buttered my bagel.

Time to bite the bullet. I picked up the phone and punched in Katie's number. It was nearly six. She'd be home from school for sure, and probably eating something out of a box. She was not one to cook unless she had company. I hoped she would get over being mad at me, and let me explain about the movie.

The phone rang four times, and I almost hung up, before she answered.

"Katie, hi."

"Hello, Sarah. You calling to apologize and meet me?"

What the hell? "Um . . . no. I'm getting ready to go to the shoot."

There was a long silence at the other end. "Fine," she said. "Good luck with that." She hung up on me. Omigod. This was out of control. I thought we were adults.

I called her back, and she answered during the first ring.

"What?"

Okay, fix this fast. "Look, I'm sorry, but you know how things are. I need the money, and I gave Carl my word. It's not just me on the line here."

"I know all about Carl's inability to schedule," she said, her voice a little wonky. Was she crying? "But you promised me you wouldn't cancel on Melanie and Dena again after the last time."

"Oh, come on, that's not fair," I said. "I need this job."

"You could move in with me, cut your expenses," she said out of the blue.

"I . . . What?"

"You heard me. I don't know what happened out at Jimmy's but I think I have a good idea what's in your craw about Melanie. The fact that you're jealous is cute and all, but you need to understand she's a very dear friend, and I will not be forced to give that friendship up."

My mind was spinning. "Move in?" I asked. "Katie, what?"

"Never mind, Beauhall. Just go to your stupid movie." She hung up again. I thought seriously about ripping the thing off the wall, but took a couple of deep breaths instead. Once more into the breach.

As I dialed, I realized how much I hated phones. If I was looking at her, could touch her, I could fix this. But all I got was static and . . . indifferent silences, damn it.

She picked up again. "This had better be good."

"Katie, look, I'm sorry. I know you hadn't planned to stay home tonight, but maybe I could come over after the shoot, we could talk then."

She barked out a laugh. "I'm not staying at home, Sarah, if that's what you think," she said. Suddenly there was anger and steel in her voice again. "Just because you are ashamed of who you are doesn't mean I have to give up my life. I'm meeting Melanie and Dena for drinks and dinner, just like we've planned three times."

"But . . . I thought . . . ," I stammered.

"You thought I'd stay home because you are being an ass?" she asked, laughing again. Laughing and crying, it was creepy. "I'm going out with my friends. You understand the concept, right, Sarah? Friends, people who you care about, who you see when you want companionship. People you love."

She hung up the phone and I stood there dripping butter off the knife onto the counter. What the hell had just happened?

I needed to work, damn it. Why couldn't she see it? Hell, I hardly knew Dena, and Melanie would be just fine without me in her life.

Katie would say I'd know Dena a hell of a lot better if I showed up to dinner, like I'd promised. Of course, she'd be right. She was usually right, but what was I supposed to do?

Relationships are a bitch. Much harder to deal with people than horses, for example. When a horse kicks you, it's because they are hurting or scared. They don't want to hurt you, but they react out of frustration and pain. The echo of Katie's hurt laughter cut me and I wished I knew what I could do to make this mess go away.

Eighteen

THE BAGEL SAT in my stomach like a rock, but I made it to the set on time, early in fact. Jennifer was in the parking lot, pulling cases of bottled water out of her car and loading them on a cart. I grabbed the sword case out of the back of the Civic and hurried over to see if she needed help.

"Hey, Jennifer," I said, jogging up.

She looked around and squared up to face me, her jaw in a firm line. "Oh, good. Sarah. Look, we need to have a little chat."

That sounded less than good. "Okay."

"Help me get this water inside for the crew first, then we can talk before the goblins start dressing."

I slipped the sword case on the bottom portion of the cart and helped her load the remaining flats of water. We wrestled the cart across the gravel and once we had it up on the sidewalk, I let her push it. I held the door and let her go through. She smiled as she passed, but it was a sad smile. I was getting worried.

Once inside, I took the case with Gram and walked over to the props cage. Two boxes of gauze and a large box of tape were stacked against the door. Someone had come through pretty well.

I unlocked the cage, slid the sword between two cases of foam elephant ears, and carried the boxes inside. The gauze and tape went on the metallic shelves in their proper order before I broke down the boxes for recycling. I tidied up the cage, moving some out-of-place goblin hands to their proper spot, and noticed that several things were misplaced. Someone had been rifling through the weapons, and the axes were mixed with the swords. Not that it was a big deal, but I spent a lot of time keeping the place inventoried so we cut down on expenses. The only people with access to the cage were Jennifer, Carl, and me. Of course, it was a padlock. I'm sure about a million people on the planet could pick the lock, but still. I'd have to check with Jennifer.

I placed the broken-down boxes outside the cage, straightened things up, and walked out, locking the cage behind me, making sure Gram was hidden. Hidden? I paused at that. It's not like I wasn't going to let JJ swing it around later. For some reason I couldn't really explain, I didn't want it out when I couldn't be around to take care of it.

I picked up the boxes and headed over to where Jennifer had unpacked all of the water. The bottles filled one of the banquet tables we kept in the back for food and drink. No food again today, I saw. The crew would be glad of the water, just the same.

I added my boxes to the top of the cart and pushed it a bit, signaling to Jennifer that I'd get the water flats out as well.

"Hang on," she said, grabbing two bottles of water. "I'll walk out with you."

We pushed the cart out past the restrooms and onto the loading dock where the city kept a Dumpster for recycling. Jennifer didn't say anything the whole walk, just kept glancing at me out of the corner of her eye.

We pushed the heavy fire door open with the cart and stepped out into the fading light of dusk. After we had everything in the recycle bin, she handed me a bottle of water, and settled down on the edge of the loading dock, her feet dangling down. I opened my water and sat beside her, taking a small drink.

"What's up?" I asked.

She toyed with her water for a moment, then turned to face me, cocking one leg up on the flat of the dock, leaving the other dangling off the side. "About last night."

Uh-oh. Was I getting fired?

"Hey, I'm sorry if I was a bitch," I started.

Jennifer blinked at me, startled. "No, no," she said, waving her empty hand at me. "We're all on edge."

I nodded, keeping my mouth shut.

"It's just that, well . . ." She hesitated. "There's no easy way to say this, so I'll just launch ahead."

I felt a pain start to form in my gut, a tightness that spoke of black days ahead.

"We're broke," she said with a hitch in her throat.

"Broke?" Not what I expected, but with no food for the crew, and the shortness of supplies, I guess I shouldn't have been surprised.

"Yes, broke. Carl has been funding this shoot out of his 401(k) since the DVD sales of *Blood Brother II* were so lackluster. Didn't help that the reviews were so horrible for *Tri-Wizard's Blood* that our distributor refused to ship it. We've limped along on Internet sales, but we are seriously in the red."

"So, what then?" I asked. "We bag this one?"

She shook her head rapidly. "Oh, God no. Carl would rather die. No, he's screwed with the market, and he's being forced to start paying back the 401(k) or pay penalties he can't afford."

She stopped to take a long pull from the bottle and carefully screwed the cap back on. "I haven't been paid in a month," she said. "And I've been purchasing supplies out of my own pocket."

"What? That's not acceptable."

"Tell me," she said, smiling. "But this is important to

me. Important to Carl." She glanced off to the fading skyline.

My God, why hadn't I seen it before. She loved him. Jesus, it was like a plague. "Jennifer, you can't float this out of your teacher's salary."

"Oh, I know," she said, turning back to face me. "The tape and gauze came out of your check this time."

"My check?"

She put her hand on my knee, a gentle touch, comforting and scary. "I'm so sorry, Sarah. You said we couldn't shoot without more supplies, and we have to get this film in the can. The distributor loves it. He thinks we may make the Seattle International Film Festival with this one. He's even talking foreign sales."

"But I need that money," I said, feeling like I was going to cry. "I need to get paid. I have bills."

Jennifer turned away again, pulled her hand from my knee and brushed her eyes. "He hasn't paid the city in two months, Sarah. None of the directors have been paid. We've cut off the food, and the extras are starting to grumble."

"But," I started, then saw it was no use. I wasn't getting paid. Damn it.

"When some thugs came by the other night, looking to collect on some debts Carl had acquired, we knew things were bleak."

Thugs? Bleak? "Jennifer, he went to loan sharks or something for this?"

She didn't answer right away, didn't nod, or even seem to breathe.

"Not his most stellar moment," she said finally. "But there is some hopeful news. Rolph has introduced Carl to a guy he knows from Portland. Investment banker who loves pet projects."

My mind blanked on that. Rolph, Portland, investment banker. Alarms were going off in my head.

"He's a philanthropist, just so you know. Well respected in Portland nonprofit circles."

I must have moaned, because her hand was back on my knee. "It's going to be okay," she said. "Carl is going to sell him part of the company." She turned away again at that.

Selling part of the company? That was like selling part of his soul. Only Carl, Jennifer, and Carl's parents owned parts of the company. Now with an outside money man, things would be really different.

And if that man was who I thought it might be . . . "Fuck me," I said finally.

Jennifer laughed at that, laughed and wiped the tears from her face. "Yes, Sarah. I thought you might see it that way. But this time next week we will either be shut down, or flush with money. Carl will pay you and you'll be fine."

The hurt in her voice was obvious. Did I always make things about me? "I'm sorry, Jennifer. I know this is hard on everyone."

"Thank you," she said, patting my hand. "Just don't argue with him today, okay? He's under an inordinate amount of stress and shame."

"Shame I totally understand," I said, standing. "So, I guess we better get the place hopping if we are going to impress this money man."

She stood as well and faced me squarely. "He really likes you, Sarah. Just so you know."

"I know," I said. "He's a sweet guy."

"Yes, well . . ." She nodded, her mouth set in a frown. "Just don't hurt him."

"Wait," I said, holding up my hands. "Jennifer, I'm in a relationship."

"You are?" The look on her face was precious. "But I've seen you flirt with him. He's mentioned how cute you are."

I laughed then, I couldn't help it. After all that had gone on in the last two days, this was too much. "Jennifer," I said, stepping closer to her and putting my hand on her shoulder. "I have no interest in Carl."

She actually looked a bit affronted. "I don't understand."

"If I flirted with Carl, it was innocent, honest."

She looked at me in a way that confirmed to me that she loved him.

"Jennifer," I said quietly, "you've been with Carl so much longer than I have. Why haven't you two hooked up?"

"Oh." She blushed. "He's a thirty-two-year-old man who lives in his parents' basement."

"Well, true," I said, seeing how that would be a turnoff. "But he has a steady job, and runs this movie company. He only lives there to put more money into the films, right?"

She pondered that a moment, like it was a fresh idea. "Yes, that's what he's always said." But I saw doubt on her face. "It's just that . . ." She waved her hand as if to clear the air. "That's neither here nor there."

I waved my hand at the door. "Back to work, then?"

She hesitated. "Are you sure?" The vulnerability was painful. To want something so bad, and to be so afraid to take it.

I was surrounded by irony. "I'm not interested in Carl, honest."

A limo pulled through the parking lot, past the loading dock, and headed to the front. She turned, taking in the car, then looked back at me, biting her lip.

VIP visitor, something big was going on. And Jennifer was so torqued about Carl that she hadn't made a move to the door.

I knew what I had to do. It was a kindness, really. I

couldn't let her wonder, let the doubt and fear fester in her. I liked her. She deserved better.

If I could've I'd have punched someone at that very moment.

I took a deep breath and plunged forward. If she laughed, I'd just get in my car and drive home. I wouldn't even pick up my gear.

"Jennifer, I'm . . ." And there it was. The one thing I had never said, the one thing I could not say for fear of losing my family, my friends, my self.

But she looked at me, confused and scared. She honestly thought she would lose Carl to me, and didn't know how to deal with it. This woman who had more nerve, more vim than anyone I'd known.

"I'm gay," I said, keeping my eyes level with her own.

"Oh," she said—then, "Oh, really?"

And just like that the light was back in her face. The hope that she kindled for Carl had returned and I was no longer a threat to her world.

I counted three breaths before I realized I hadn't spontaneously combusted. The look on Jennifer's face gave me a bit of hope. Maybe if I could tell her without dying, I could tell others.

My father's face hove into view, and my heart skipped a beat. Of course, not everyone was as sweet and open as Jennifer. Maybe I'd just keep it to myself a while longer.

How long until this little secret got around? And was I brave enough to deal with it?

Nineteen

JENNIFER STRODE ACROSS the set, barking out orders and making the crew jump with the vigor I was used to. Now maybe we'd get back on track.

I corralled the goblins and began the transformation of computer geeks and housewives into bloodthirsty humanoid killers.

Once again, Rolph was not with them, but I could see he was in the office with Carl and two well-dressed gentlemen. That was a meeting I didn't want to be anywhere near. After suiting up twelve goblins, many of whom grumbled and fussed about the lack of food, I decided to get JJ ready instead of waiting around for Rolph. Who knew how long they'd be ensconced in the office. I grabbed Gram out of her case, and picked up the mighty Elvis shield from the back of the prop cage. Time to find the *talent*.

I had no problem tracking down JJ. All I had to do was follow the smell of whores. Well, that was not totally fair to the whores. Did I mention I hated the man?

In the back of the studio, through the fire exit, in the smoking area just outside, JJ stood with his arms around two women while a third stood to the side. All four of them were smoking. Of the two hanging on JJ, one was a fortysomething bleached blond ex-stripper named Cherie, like Cherry. The second was a young woman, maybe nineteen, who hailed from the same side of the tracks as Cherie, only she'd been ridden less. Her name was Barbara, but insisted everyone call her Babs. The third groupie, Juanita, was a slightly dumpy Hispanic woman who had told me she wanted to marry JJ so she could get her green card. She said he was a lousy lover, but he doted on her. Things like that I needed to know like I needed an acid-washed brain. She stood to the side, watching the three of them laugh.

I stepped into the doorway, the sword in one hand, the gaudy shield in the other. "Come on, Elvis. Time to gird your loins for battle."

He loved it when I said loins. A sly smile crept over his face and he shook his head. "We got time," he said, kissing Cherie on the left ear.

"Costume time, lover boy," I said, gritting my teeth.

"Fuck off, Beauhall," he said, turning a rather nasty face my way. "Carl said we could take it easy since he's in a meeting. We have plenty of time."

"You might want to reconsider," I said, stepping out the door and facing him with the sword and shield. "Jennifer thinks we need to impress the suits."

"Fuck her," JJ said. The three women laughed. All I could think of were hyenas.

"Look, pretty boy," I said, losing my cool. "You can snuggle with your groupies after the shoot."

"Hey," Babs said. "I gotta work at eleven."

"Isn't that past your curfew?" Juanita asked, stubbing out a cigarette.

Cherie wolf whistled and JJ grabbed Babs by the ass, leaning down to kiss her neck.

I stood there, fuming, as JJ looked up at me and licked the side of Babs's neck. He winked at me and nibbled Babs's ear.

"You're a pig," I said, turning back to the studio. Babs laughed and Cherie made kissy-face noises.

"Better be careful," JJ said with a laugh. "You might give her the wrong idea. Our mistress of props is a dyke."

I stopped just inside the door, clutching the black sword as the anger flooded over me. The sword vibrated, humming like a tuning fork in my brain. The women's laughter rose shrill and torturous. The urge to turn and kill them all, run them through with the sword, began to fill me, anger and violence filling my legs and arms, rushing up my torso, approaching my heart like a rocket.

Then, for a moment, I saw Katie in the shower, smiling at me through the steam, and the conflagration of anger simmered down to a manageable crackle. I stormed across the studio, around the set, and toward Carl's office. I didn't have to take this kind of shit.

Just past the set, Rolph came striding across the stage toward me. He took one look at me and, obviously hearing the laughter that trailed me, grabbed me by the sword arm in an attempt to prevent murder.

"This is not your fate," he said, his eyes large in the shadowy stage. "They are buffoons, chattel. Your calling is greater than this."

I shrugged off his hand, but the moment of murder had passed. "Fate? Fated for what? Killing your dragon? Are you still after that fantasy?"

He paused, bowed his head a moment, and looked up at me, his face a mask of conflict and pain. "I owe you an apology," he said, finally. "I pushed you with something you are not ready to accept. It was brash and uncaring on my part. I did you a harm, and I wish to make amends."

"Harm?" I asked, confused. "What harm have you caused?"

"I mentioned your relationship with the young skald to Mr. Montgomery yesterday evening before he left."

For a moment, I think I blacked out. It was one of those moments where you hear something, and all the words are in your native tongue, yet it's like listening to the adults speak in *Peanuts*. All white noise.

"I'm sorry, what did you say? Who is Mr. Montgomery?"

I am uncertain of the emotion I displayed on my face at that moment, but Rolph took a step back, holding his hands in front of him.

"JJ, James Joseph Montgomery. The star of this film." He ran on, before I could speak. "It was a grievous mistake, in hindsight, but I thought I was protecting your honor."

"My honor?"

"Mr. Montgomery had said something about your inadequacies in certain areas, and I explained that perhaps the reason you had not fallen under his spell was that you were involved with another."

That explained that, as it were. I took several deep breaths, attempting to clear the fumes of anger that swam around my head. "Rolph, I understand your concern. Thank you for your efforts, but in the future, please let me fight my own battles."

He looked at me and shrugged. "As you wish. I had just assumed you avoided battles of any kind."

"Nice. Look, I'm not going off to Portland to kill some investment banker for you." Then I paused. "You don't mean that fellow in the office with Carl . . . Is that your dragon?"

"One and the same," he said, spreading his hands in front of him, palms up. "If you would not go to him, I thought it best to bring him to you."

"By having him buy into the movie?"

Now it was Rolph's turn to sigh deeply. "You are naïve. I have seen more of this world than you can imagine. You are a child of privilege. You know nothing of suffering, or of want. This creature you so easily dismiss has spread wrack and ruin in his lifetime. He may not be eating virgins these days, although one cannot be too sure."

"I get your point," I said, glancing at the office. "But you can't honestly believe he's a dragon. He's wearing Armani."

"He is adaptable, a shape-shifter," he said. "If you doubt me, go ask Carl when we are to resume shooting. I will get dressed. See for yourself."

"Oh, fine," I said. "If this will put an end to all this, I'll go meet your dragon."

"Would you like me to take your items?" he offered.

For a moment I saw a glint in his eye as he looked at the sword. Instead I handed him the shield. "See that JJ gets this, will you?"

I moved the sword to my right hand, away from him, and he shuddered.

"As you wish." He took the shield and walked past me out to the smoking area. Dragon indeed. There was more than one who coveted pretty things.

Twenty

THE SECOND I agreed to go to the office, to confront this stranger, the sword felt different. I know it was adrenaline and nerves, but for a moment, I got a rush.

I walked over toward the office. Carl was talking to the banker, and another man. Jennifer stood beside the desk, a clipboard in her hand, taking notes.

Maybe by facing this man, Rolph would be appeased. He really was a sweet guy, if a bit odd. I'd just as soon he gave up on the mad scheme on his own. It would make things easier. I strode toward the office and the four of them walked out. The entire facility is about the length of a football field, with several soundstages and a ton of middle ground for forklifts, props, stages, and so on. I guess I was fifty feet from them when they emerged from the office. The banker passed by one of the stage lights and his shadow was cast high on the wall.

If I hadn't been holding Gram, I would have totally peed myself—as it was, I thought I might lose bladder control. The shadow that rose across the floor and up the closed loading dock doors was not that of a man.

Gram shuddered in my hand, a blood haze fell over my vision, and the world slowed. Between one breath and the next, everything stopped except for the dragon. Banker or no, I had no further doubts. I stumbled forward, pulled along by the sword, it seemed, because the fear that flooded my body told me to run while I could, run and hide before he turned his eyes on me.

When he turned to me, I knew fear—real holy-shit-the-world-is-going-to-end fear. All I could see was fire. His eyes found mine and I fell screaming into a charnel pit. Bones and refuse littered the studio, blood coated the walls, and every single person I'd ever loved lay eviscerated before me.

I must have cried out, because the next thing I knew, Carl was at my side, pushing my sword arm down and turning me away from the dragon, one arm across my shoulders, speaking rapidly in my ear. I craned my neck around, keeping the dragon in my sights, until he turned, his vision honing in on JJ and his harlots as they came laughing into the studio.

"Jesus Christ on a crutch, Beauhall. Are you out of your mind?" Carl's voice penetrated the fog of blood. "Sarah." He shook me slightly. "Jennifer," he called. "A little help here?"

Jennifer appeared at Carl's side and took my arm. "Come on, Sarah. Let's get you some water, what do you say?"

"I'll take the sword," Carl said, but I growled at him, pulling the sword out of his reach.

"No," I barked. "Mine."

He stopped, making eyes of panic at Jennifer, who just grabbed me by both hands and led me away. Away from the fire and the death and the fear.

Once we were safely back with the goblins, back on the far side of the prop cage, near the office Jennifer kept, that I'd never once visited, the fear began to recede. I shook then, as the adrenaline that had flooded my body took hold of my muscles. I almost fell, but she held me up, helped me to a chair by her desk, where I collapsed.

"Let's get you something to change into, shall we?" she said, sympathy and embarrassment warring on her face.

I guess my fear had won. I had wet myself.

And the dragon had just glanced at me, had not given me the attention one gave a bug.

I lay the sword on the desk beside me and felt the warm wetness of my jeans. I lowered my head into my hands as the tremors racked my body.

Holy Mother of God.

Twenty-one

FREDERICK FELT THE sword before he turned his head. This was it. He'd felt the disturbance the night before. Knew something powerful had come into being, but he could not name it. There were rumors of rumors, of course, but his kind had acquired all the relics long ago. How had this sword suddenly appeared from nowhere? It was a power he had never felt before. Something about it raised the hackles on his neck. Items of power were dangerous, especially in the hands of humans. Legends told of foolish deeds perpetrated by the humans, fanciful rantings that urged the one who controlled the artifact to attempt to kill his kind. He motioned to Mr. Philips with a jerk of his head, and his faithful servant approached, leaning in to exchange quiet words.

"Our foolish dwarf was as good as his word," Frederick said.

"Yes, Mr. Sawyer."

He always appreciated Mr. Philips's efficiency and no-nonsense attitude. "See that he is rewarded adequately. We may have need of his services again in the future."

Mr. Philips nodded and turned to walk toward the back of the studio.

Immediately, Frederick turned his attention to the next bit of business here. "Who was that excitable young woman just now?" he asked Carl, who had just returned.

"That was Sarah Beauhall," Carl said. "She's our prop manager." He clenched his hands a few times, nervously, Frederick noticed. "She's been having a bit of trouble the last few nights."

"Yes, I can imagine the stress of budget woes, and an erratic schedule, must be playing havoc on your fine crew."

Carl blinked at him, confused.

Silly humans. "Of course, this remains your studio as we agreed," Frederick said calmly. "I wouldn't dream of telling you how to run your business."

"Right," Carl said, his attention focused on the back of the studio, following Jennifer and Sarah's passage long past the time they'd moved out of sight.

"I think we can clear up your immediate cash flow problems," he said, pulling a thick envelope of money out of his jacket pocket and handing it to Carl.

Carl took the envelope, glanced inside, and looked up, shocked. "Yes, this will get us back on track."

Nothing like an envelope stuffed full of hundreds to make them putty in your hands. They are so much easier to manipulate than conquer, he thought. *Money truly is power.*

"Of course," Frederick continued. "A twenty-five percent stake in Flight Test, Limited and any current or future project will be a lovely addition to my portfolio."

Carl shuddered. "This will get us through the next few weeks," he said, almost apologetic. "But it won't clear all the debts and make us liquid."

"Oh, of course not," Frederick said, waving his manicured hand. "This is just a good-faith gesture. Mr. Philips already has a list of your creditors. I will be settling up with them in the next few days."

Carl gawked at him. "All of them?"

"Well," Frederick said with a predatory smile. "We won't be paying off your parents' mortgage, but any debt acquired or owned by this studio will be free and clear by close of business Friday." He paused. "I include your obligations to the less-than-savory influences."

"That's a lot of money," Carl said, breathless. "I don't think you understand just how much."

"Tsk, tsk, Mr. Tuttle. Don't insult my business acumen."

"I meant no insult," Carl began.

Frederick waved him off. "No insult taken, Mr. Tuttle. But my job is money. I make quite a lot of it, and I know a good investment when I see one. Your prior work alone would be a good enough résumé for me to invest."

"You know my work?"

Flattery was next to money when it came to power. He chuckled, despite his best effort. "Carl, my new friend," he said, placing his arm around Carl's shoulder and turning him to face the working stage.

"This is your canvas. You are an artist I can appreciate. You work your magic here, I will handle certain monetary transactions and see to a few glitches in the distribution channels you have found in the British Columbia area. I have connections." He grinned, and Carl seemed to relax.

"It would be great to see *Blood Brother II* released in Canada."

"Not to worry." Frederick steered Carl toward the set, walking briskly. "Later I would love to meet your prop girl." He smiled. *Meet, eat, whichever worked out for the best.* "But for now, I must meet this leading man of yours. I have heard many interesting things about him."

Yes, Frederick thought. *There was a man both vain and shallow.* He could mold JJ Montgomery, guide him to stardom, and sweep the power from his shadow.

An excellent pawn in the long game.

Twenty-two

JENNIFER WAS A doll. She hustled me back to the locker room and basically stripped me down and shoved me into the shower. I stood under the spray, letting the hot water run over me while my brain processed what had just happened. Either I had suffered a blow to the head when I was sparring with the twins yesterday, or I had lost my mind.

The thought that the dragon could be real, no matter my body's reaction, just couldn't fit inside my brain. I was under a ton of stress. People under stress see and hear strange things. That had to be it. Besides, Rolph had set me up. First he mentions the dragon at the smithy when I'm exhausted, both physically and mentally, then he messes with me here at the set. No wonder I hallucinated a dragon. I was dealing in the land of make-believe every day here on the set. Just my imagination running amok.

In the meantime, I'd have to be careful around Rolph. I didn't like the games he was playing.

I scrubbed myself with the bar of soap Jennifer had in her shower caddy, and let the stress and anxiety flow down the drain with the suds.

When I got out, she had two large towels waiting next to some clothes. I dried off, packed the shower caddy, and examined the clothes. These were sorority sweats. I'd be spending the rest of the evening with Greek letters across my big pink ass. That wasn't humiliating. At least it didn't read SPANK ME.

I draped the towels over the shower rack and bundled my dirty clothes into a very tight ball. I dropped them into the washer in the costume area and walked back into Jennifer's office. The sword lay right where I'd left it. I was surprised at the sense of relief I felt seeing that black blade.

I picked it up, comforting myself with the weight of it, and walked back to the crew.

I had to go through three doors to get to the set. No outside noise, and all that. I walked to the prop cage, slipped Gram into her case, and settled to the left of the stage where I normally watched the shooting.

Jennifer was there, watching rapt as Frederick regaled the cast and crew with his love of film, and his entrepreneurial spirit.

"He's a shark," Jennifer said as I stepped up to her.

"Or some other predator with large teeth," I said.

She looked at me and smiled. "You can be very pretty, when you don't dress down so much."

Dress down? Hell, I was in sweats. My jeans and T-shirts were cool. And the boots I normally wore were totally kick-ass. Of course, now I was two inches shorter and padding around in my bare feet. I guess to Jennifer blond hair, bare feet, and pink sweats were hot.

"You trust him?" I asked.

She turned back to the crowd and shrugged. "You know what they say about things that seem too good to be true."

"Yeah. You gonna read those contracts before everything is finalized?"

"Too late," she said. I could tell she was angry about that. The clenched jaw and tight shoulders were a good clue.

"Carl is a big boy, knows his business and all that."

"True," she said, letting out a long-held breath. "But I have a stake in this, too.

"He's already complimented JJ on his fine acting ability, and even winked at one of the young grips."

"Eww," I said. "Not Kimmie."

Jennifer nodded. "So, shark and lecher. She's only sixteen."

"We'll keep her out of his way," I said, patting Jennifer on the shoulder. "The JJ thing, we can't help. He's a dumbass, no matter how big his head gets."

This brought a laugh from Jennifer that was good to hear. Frederick stumbled a bit in his soliloquy, looking over at us with a bemused smile. Real bastard, that one, no matter my stress levels. I may have hallucinated the dragon thing, but my instincts told me he was bad news all around.

It took another twenty minutes to get things back in order and start the shoot, but things went amazingly well after that.

The goblins were all in rare form, and JJ belted out his lines like a pro. I was fairly impressed, until he swung the sword up to smite the goblins, just like Monday night. Only this time, he let go on the upswing and the sword sailed through the air, slicing through an aluminum support light and sending it shattering to the ground.

While the techs replaced the light and the grips cleaned up, I assured Carl and JJ that the sword was not sharp, and that he just didn't know his own strength. This seemed to mollify the little pisher.

The second take went even smoother. We were up to JJ's big line when things went wrong.

"I declare this land free from oppression," he called out. His white sequined armor glowed, and the lighting was immaculate. He held the sword above his head and his voice rang clear and sonorous.

"I claim this, my birthright. This sword—"

Rolph, I know it was him, started forward, his goblin hand outstretched, with a mewling cry loud enough to interfere.

"—made from the shattered horn of Memphisto . . ."

JJ wound down, not sure how to proceed, so Carl called cut, and we started all over again.

By the third take, things went perfectly. So well, in fact, we wrapped the night with that scene. Carl called cut on the final take and everyone cheered. Finally, we'd beaten the fickle fates and sunk another scene.

JJ stood on the stage, holding the sword, more amazed than the rest of us. He was really good, I hated to admit. Frederick walked onto the stage and began congratulating the cast and crew, a handshake here, a high five there. I walked from the opposite direction, making a line to JJ. I needed to get the sword back in its case before too long.

"James, my good man," Frederick bellowed, holding his arms out as if to hug the fop. "That was astounding."

JJ lowered the sword and grinned like a little kid. It was almost cute.

"Thank you, sir," he said.

Sir? Holy . . .

"Fine blade you have there," Frederick said, walking up to the ferrocrete rocks and craning his neck up to JJ. "Fine indeed."

"Thanks," JJ said, glancing over at me. I started walking his way as fast as I could without running, or losing the sweats that didn't quite fit.

"I'm a collector," Frederick said, working his way over the cables, through the milling goblins, and to the ramp up the rocks. "I'd love to see it up close."

"Um." JJ looked between Frederick and me, unsure of whose wrath to risk. He knew what kind of bitch I could be, but Frederick Sawyer was money. "Sure, I guess," he said, turning.

"JJ, you've done enough damage tonight," I bellowed, storming up the right side of the stage. "Give me my damn sword, before you hurt the suit, you ham-fisted hack."

Not my best work, but I was under pressure.

The word "hack" was the final bit. JJ swung around and snarled. "It's just a piece of trash. Not unlike certain people around here." He dropped the sword on the stage with a clang and stormed off, past the blinking Frederick Sawyer and straight to the smokers' exit.

"Nice," I yelled, bending to pick up the sword several steps ahead of Frederick. He stopped as soon as I touched the hilt, a smile slowly spreading over his face. For a moment I shuddered at that toothy grin, but I turned and stormed back down to the prop area, clutching the sword like it was the last line out of the water.

"Smooth," Jennifer said to me as I stomped past her, my bare feet slapping on the concrete floor. "You have his attention now, that's no mistake."

I just kept walking, straight to the prop cage and through the door. Once Gram was nestled in its case again, I carried it with me to the back to switch my clothes into the dryer.

I locked it in the prop cage again, and began disassembling goblins. Once all the assorted pieces were stowed, and I had the stage hands putting away the extra bits, I began to calm down. He was going to touch my freaking sword. For the briefest of moments it was as if I'd stood before him naked or something, vulnerable and weak. Bastard.

Finally, we finished breaking down the set, now that we were finished with this god-awful scene, and wrapped at two in the morning. Late night, but we'd finally be on to the next scene. That was enough to put a spring in my step.

Jennifer let me know my clothes were dry, and I slipped to the back to change. I folded her sweats on top of the sword case, not daring to let it out of my sight for even a moment with him in the building.

Jennifer smiled when I tried to return the clothes. "Keep them," she said, holding up her hands. "After a long night commando, they belong to you now." She smiled when she said it, so I smiled back.

I liked her. Classy and hard-working. Not sure what I'd do with a pink outfit, but maybe Katie would approve. If she ever spoke to me again.

I said good-bye to the crew and gathered my stuff to head home. As I walked past the office, I saw that JJ stood in the doorway, ranting at Carl.

"Yes, I'm familiar with your differences with Ms. Beauhall," Carl said diplomatically. "But I'm sure she's just tired like the rest of us."

"Jesus," JJ barked. "Before I found out she was a dyke, I thought she must be giving it up for you, but dude. She's a menace, and you aren't even getting any nookie."

At the word "dyke," Carl turned to me, a look of shock on his face. Another Kodak moment.

I just shrugged and walked past them. I was not going to argue with the idiot, and Carl was a big boy. I'm sure Jennifer would explain it all to him. I just wanted to go home.

Of course, before I made it through the door Sawyer's lackey stepped in front of me.

"Pardon me, miss. My name is Mr. Philips," he said, his accent nonexistent, his manners faultless. "Mr. Sawyer would like to have a word with you about the sword you used in tonight's theatrics."

"Theatrics, or histrionics?" I asked with a smirk.

"I'm sure I don't know," Mr. Philips said, nonplussed. "My employer is a man of considerable power as well as compassion. I'm sure a few moments of your time could not be so hard to share."

"Tell your boss," I began, but a shadow fell across my heart then. A touch on my arm sent a chill running down the back of my neck, down my spine, and into the soles of my feet.

"It's quite all right," Frederick said at my left ear. "I appreciate Mr. Philips's civility and candor, but I'm capable of speaking to a pretty young woman without his assistance."

Mr. Philips bowed, literally bowed at the waist, and stepped away from us before turning on his heel and walking around the office and out of sight.

For a moment, I saw myself following him, running after him, no less. Anything to avoid that hand on my arm.

"My dear," he said, his voice warm and moist on my ear. "I so rarely want something as badly as I want . . ." He paused, sliding his hand up my arm to my bicep. "My, but you are a strong one," he said, squeezing my arm.

I spun around then, fed up with his games. "Don't you ever fucking touch me again," I said, pushing him by the shoulder. He stumbled back a step and anger flashed on his face. "You're scum of the worst sort," I shouted.

Carl pushed past JJ and stumbled out of the office, sputtering. "Now, hang on a minute," he said.

"See," JJ said, hot on his heels. "She's a psycho."

I didn't even glance at them, they were so inconsequential at that moment. All I could see was that feral look on Sawyer's face.

"You are a bottom-feeder," I said, feeling my courage surge upward. "You prey on the weak and the fearful. And I for one do not believe your pandering, simpering act for a moment."

"Sarah," Carl bellowed. "That will be quite enough."

"No one touches me without my permission, Carl. I don't care how much money he throws at you."

Carl stopped next to Frederick, his mouth hanging open, like he'd never seen me before.

"And," I said to Sawyer, "if you lay a hand on me again, I'll give it back to you in a box."

Before Carl could react, before JJ could add his stupid retort, and before Frederick could twist that feral grin onto his face again, I pushed past them and stormed out of the studio.

All hell broke loose behind me, but I kept on walking, the clip-clop of my boots echoing down the corridor. I slammed the fire door open and stood aside as it ricocheted back to close with a bang.

The night was clear. Stars winked down from the heavens. I leaned back against the brick building and let my breath settle for a moment. But only a moment.

I wanted to be well away from the studio before any of them thought to come after me—away from the yelling and threatening. Just to be gone before I learned who the real monsters were.

Twenty-three

I TOSSED AND turned the rest of the night. At first I had a nightmare about a giant man-eating pink bunny.

This triggered a trip to the bathroom, a glass of water, and a quick pace of my apartment. It was a short trip. I only had the one bedroom and a living room/kitchen combo.

Once I'd slipped back to sleepland, I spent some quality time running from my family and friends as they took turns being horrified about who I'd become, or laughed at me for being such a prat.

When the weak sunlight began to slip between the blinds I knew I was done, but I fought it. The garbage truck backing up to get our Dumpster was the clincher. The incessant beeping, followed by a floor-rattling crash as the idiot operator slammed the now empty metal box down onto the parking lot, ensured I wouldn't sleep again, maybe for days.

I arrived at the smithy early, wearing my sunglasses and drinking a triple espresso mocha latte. Nothing like caffeine and sugar to kick-start your day.

I slipped Gram in the safe with my other swords, just to keep her secure for the time being.

I spent the morning making shoes to replace the ones we used over at the Circle Q. Julie quizzed me on the different techniques I was using to temper the steel, and I left out the blood of my enemy. I didn't figure she'd find that an acceptable business model.

After I finished the shoes, she had me work on making a chain. Chains are delicate work and force you to use much more control than I used on a shoe, or one of the swords. Not that I was wild with the hammer or anything, but one of the key things she always told me was to learn to feel the metal, understand the weaknesses and strengths in every piece, every blow. She was very Zen about the whole endeavor.

She let me place the order for another ton of coal, and check if we needed more propane out in the big tank by her house. By buying gas for her place and the smithy at the same time, she got a better deal, and they split the bill for tax purposes.

I filled out several forms, made three phone calls, and was balancing a pencil on my upper lip while leaning back as far as I could go in her ergo-enriched office chair. I would have had the new record, too, if she hadn't dropped an envelope on my head.

Some teachers . . .

"What's this?" I asked, sliding out of the chair, grabbing up the pencil, and sliding over to the door so she could sit down.

"How am I supposed to know?" she said, picking up my order forms. "Most people would either look at the address, or open it."

But of course. I looked at the envelope, and there was no address, no stamps or other postal marks. Just my name, Ms. Sarah Beauhall, in thick black script.

"No address."

"Noticed that," Julie said with a smile. "Delivered by courier."

I tapped the envelope against my forehead and looked at her. "Pretty odd, don't you think?"

She initialed my order forms and set them in the to-be-filed pile on the corner of her desk.

"Oh, fine," I said, sliding my little finger under the envelope flap and ripping it upward.

She didn't even turn. Just tapped on the keyboard of her laptop and began entering records into her accounting program.

I peeked inside, then tilted the envelope on top of her desk.

Julie glanced over as three pieces of paper slid out: a bill of sale made out between Frederick Sawyer and Sarah Beauhall, a smaller envelope, and a check for fifty thousand dollars.

Heat flushed across my chest, a brushfire of anger. "That son of a bitch."

"Jesus, Sarah. This is a lot of money," Julie said, holding up the check.

I picked up the bill of sale. "He wants the sword."

"Is that all?" she said, looking at me over her shoulder. "One sword. That's a lot of scratch for a hunk of metal."

"Not just any hunk of metal," I said. This was beyond slimy.

"What's in the other envelope?"

I opened it and pulled out a letter.

Dear Ms. Beauhall,

In the off chance the cashier's check isn't enough incentive, I can sweeten the pot with a recent acquisition.

Give me the sword, of your own volition, and I will add in my stake in Flight Test, Ltd.

In case you are wondering, I have already acquired several hundred thousand dollars of debt incurred by Mr. Tuttle. These would, of course, be a further stake you could have in this little movie venture.

Please consider these options. Mr. Philips would assist in having the documents notarized and filed with the proper authorities. I assure you, this letter is contractually binding.

Yours,
Frederick Sawyer

I handed the letter to Julie and walked out into the shop. I fired up the propane and began heating a longsword form I kept on hand. I let the metal get white-hot before I started hitting it for all I was worth. Fire, strike, turn. Repeat.

The reverberation of the hammer on the steel felt good. Each jolt pushing aside the anger and the fear. Nothing was as it seemed with this man. Any offer this good had to be a lie. What was so important about this sword?

Of course, hadn't Rolph already explained it all? But if I believed that Rolph was a dwarf, and Sawyer a dragon . . . If this sword was Gram, really a magic sword . . . what I needed was not a big fat payday. I needed a rubber room.

Julie came out of her office with the papers in her hands and watched me. I hammered and hammered, fired and turned.

Finally, I stuck the metal into the rain barrel we kept to cool shoes, and the roughly hewn blade split with a loud, echoing pop and a cloud of steam.

"Nice," she said. "Ruined it."

I turned, dropped the broken hunk of metal into the waste bucket we kept by the anvil, and placed the tongs and hammer on the table. Then I took off my gloves and laid them on top of the tools.

"I can't take it," I said, leaning against the table. "It's too good to be true."

"Sarah," Julie said, stepping to the back of the workbench. "This is a cashier's check. You can cash it with no contractual obligation."

I laughed. "Of course, but you and I both know I won't. Sawyer could, I would bet my life on it, but I can't."

"Dishonest?" she asked.

"Dishonorable."

She pulled the papers through two fingers until she hit the corner, then she turned them and began sliding them through her fingers again. She repeated this at each corner, watching me, her face a mask.

"It's just a sword," she said. "You could buy a house, or start your own smithy."

There were many things I could do. Hell, just not having to worry about money every single week would be a blessing. But at what cost to my soul? Never bargain with the devil, my da would say. No matter how good the terms.

"I'm not ready for my own smithy," I said, pointing at the waste bucket.

"True," she said with a smile. "But it would make a lovely nest egg for when that day comes."

Tempting . . . very, very tempting. But wasn't that the point?

"He's a predator, Julie. Flatter and take, obfuscate and pander."

She shrugged. "He's a businessman, a little less ethical than you prefer, but the offer sounds like everything you've dreamed of." She walked around the side of the workbench and stopped at my side. "Sarah, this is a lot of money."

"Yes, you've said that."

She nodded. "So, what is the problem, exactly?"

How did I explain this to her? She couldn't feel the fear, or sense the danger just by me telling her. This was at the animal level, the crocodile brain. This man would kill me if I stood in his way, or likely do some other dark and purely undesirable things to me beforehand.

"I have to trust my gut, ya know?"

She watched me, waiting.

"He's a scumbag. In my heart of hearts I think he tortures puppies and worse."

She raised her eyebrows. "Puppies?"

I shrugged. "That's all I got."

The silence stretched between us, neither moved, until we heard tires crunching into the gravel drive. She placed the papers on the bench beside me and patted them. "Sleep on it," she said. "Don't do anything rash."

I scooped up the papers and jogged them into alignment. "Okay."

She walked out to greet the customer, and I put everything back into the envelope and tucked it into my messenger bag. I'd think about it overnight, sure, but I highly doubted my opinions of the man would change in that time. I started to sweep the shop when Julie came in with one of the hands from Circle Q. It was Jack Marlowe.

"One of their horses has a limp," Julie said, coming into the shop. "Jack here was out picking up some supplies for the ranch, and asked if I could come out and take a look."

"One of the ones we worked on yesterday?" I asked.

"No, ma'am," Jack said. His voice was more tenor than bass, but it had a sweet drawl, more Okie than Texan.

"Good," I said, relieved to have the distraction. "I'll get our gear into the truck."

"No need," Julie said, giving me the strangest look. I think she actually crossed her eyes at one point, trying to get me to get with the program.

"Oh . . . okay," I said, catching on, finally. "I'll woman the fort, as it were."

"Don't mean to impose," Jack said. "It's just, well . . ." He pushed his hat back and rubbed his forehead. "Mrs. Campbell is a mite upset about this one. Blue Thunder is one of her prized high-steppers."

"I'll just get a few things and follow you in my truck," Julie said to Jack.

"All right," he drawled. "Anything I can fetch for ya?"

Julie almost giggled. I could see it in her face. She knew it too, and turned it into a cough. "No," she said, patting her chest and coughing again. "I'll only be a minute. Why don't you head over to the grange and get what you need. I can meet you and follow from there."

"Sounds good," he said, tipping his hat in my direction. "Afternoon, miss." Then he turned to Julie and smiled a whole faceful of teeth. "I'll see you over there."

Julie didn't move. Hell, I'm not sure she breathed until we heard the pop-pop of his tires on the gravel. When she let out her breath she giggled a little twitter and turned away from me.

"You okay there, boss?" I asked, not bothering to hide my own smile.

"Yeah, I'm fine," she said, grabbing her hoof doctoring kit. "Oh, don't forget to order the coal and the propane," she said, and was out the door with a bang. I stepped over to the screen door and watched her scamper to her truck. Scamper, I say. For a moment I thought I'd giggle myself. He was a cutie, but Jiminy Christmas.

I returned to the shop and began putting things in order, deliberately not thinking about the envelope in my pack. What would Katie say about that much money? It was more than she made in a year teaching, and almost twice what I made at both jobs combined.

A house would be nice. A place to call my own. And a smithy someday. I could feel the place around me, the power it contained. These walls absorbed it, squirreled it away. Every job, every moment we worked here, fire and forge, hammer and anvil, fed the smithy. It was Julie's, but I was allowed to play here, to soak in the overwhelming sense of creation and strength.

If I had my own smithy, I could call the shots. I could make armor, even. No time with the horses, but imagine learning to forge plate. I dreamed of the delicate work needed to shape a helm. Someday.

Katie would love it.

I couldn't believe I hadn't heard from her. I checked my cell, then logged on to Julie's machine and checked my e-mail. No messages. No mail, no angry voice mails, nothing.

I'd close the shop at four, like we advertised, and head home alone. Katie likely needed a few days to come around. I'd give her some space.

Yep, that's what I'd do.

I checked the voice mail a few more times, just to be sure.

Twenty minutes later I called her cell.

No answer.

I left her a message, and then called her apartment where, guess what. She didn't answer. I knew she had to be at school.

But I did leave another message. Don't get your knickers in a twist. It was nothing sappy. I debated on the merits of groveling and begging, but went for nonchalant. Smooth.

"Katie, hi. It's me, Sarah. Just want to talk. Been a weird few days. You wouldn't believe what's been happening. Call me, 'kay?"

Same message on both phones. I couldn't be more lame if I'd written it down and read it from a script. At least I didn't whine.

Then I wondered if I should have apologized. Damn. I could call the school and leave her a message. Or I could call out to Black Briar. Deidre would know where she was.

Instead I scurried around, trying to stay busy, trying not to call and leave another message.

E-mails. I hadn't sent an e-mail yet. Within five minutes I'd solved that problem. Three e-mails later, each one more desperate than the last, I shut down Julie's computer and sat pounding my head against her desk.

I gave up and spent the last hour filing invoices that Julie never got around to. Then I straightened her office, more nervous cleaning than protracted need for order. Quite the contrary. I craved chaos in most things. Well, music, mainly. I'd really like it if my love life were more orderly, but that didn't look like it was going to get there any time soon. And knowing that it was mostly my fault didn't help matters at all. I just kept puttering around the office in a mad attempt to keep my mind off the check, and the fact that Katie wasn't returning my calls. Yeah, that sure helped the afternoon crawl by.

Twenty-four

BEFORE I LEFT the smithy, I pulled Gram's case out from beneath the workbench and opened the safe. I pulled her from the safe and held on to the pommel, letting the comfort of it roll over me. Something about how it fit my hand gave me a sense of completeness. Must be artist's pride, I thought as I lay her in her case.

As I snapped the lid closed, I decided what I really needed was another coffee, and maybe a cruller. Looks like I'd be doing some research at Monkey Shines before heading home.

Of course, on a Friday night, they were out of crullers, so I had to settle for an orange-banana muffin. The coffee was up to their regular standards, and I grabbed a fat comfy chair near the back with a little table for my laptop.

I was anxious to see what secrets the Interwebz could give up on our Mr. Frederick Sawyer of Portland, Oregon. I had the fuel, I just needed some quality online time.

I slipped on my headphones, cranked a little Dream Theater, and fired up my browser. Rich people got lots of press, I found. Philanthropist, entrepreneur, socialite.

It seems Mr. Sawyer was last known to be in the company of a buxom blond grad student named Trixi Smythe. He was photographed dancing with her at a fund-raiser just this week.

She was dressed like one of the staff, instead of a date, but you could just never tell with college students. I figured she was twenty years younger than him if she was a day.

Of course, he looked just a bit older than Julie. Younger woman, older man. Nothing going on here, move along.

The muffin just wasn't doing it, orange and banana, what was I thinking? Better to get one of their killer peanut butter brownies.

I paused the music, took out my earbuds, and locked my computer screen. I could see it from the counter, and we were all adults here. I'd be between the laptop and the door. Anyone touching it would enjoy a knuckle sandwich. Part of me hoped someone would try.

The place had filled up, so I asked the accountant on the couch to watch my stuff while I went to the powder room.

When I came out, the line was no shorter, but I really wanted a brownie. I fought my way forward through a pack of college kids and worked my way around to the end of the line.

Then I heard the laugh. Now, when you've been in a relationship with someone, when you've tickled them until they couldn't take it anymore, when you've listened to them talk because you loved the sound of their voice, you knew instantly when you heard it.

Katie was in the crowd. I turned around looking, and spied her standing near the pickup station. Must have missed her when I swam upstream of the college kids. Man, I was glad to see her, and to hear her laughing.

Then I saw Melanie.

Katie had her hand on Melanie's arm and they were laughing together. And in that moment I lost it.

"What the hell are you doing here with her?" I asked a little louder than publicly acceptable.

Katie stopped laughing and Melanie looked around, confused at the shift.

"Sarah?" Katie asked. Her whole demeanor slammed closed and caution flags sprouted all over the place.

"I've tried to get ahold of you all day," I said. "You can't bother to return my calls, but you can go out for coffee with . . ." I waved my arm at them, crazed, I knew, out of my gourd with jealousy, but it was one of those moments when I couldn't stop myself. ". . . Her?"

I knew I was being an ass. Part of my mind sat back and evaluated the entire scene. Hysterical young woman verbally accosts her friend and lover because she was laughing with her old lover, whom I knew to be a much better fit for said girlfriend.

Seriously . . . therapy could be in order.

But that didn't stop me from putting the second foot in my mouth and ranting like a complete fool.

"Does Dena know you two are out together?" I asked, stepping past the stunned coffeemongers. "Or are you two sneaking around behind her back, too?"

"Don't be an ass," Katie hissed.

Melanie grabbed the coffees that had just come up, and mumbled apologetically, "I'll find us a table."

Then she skulked off to the back of the shop, leaving Katie to suffer my wrath.

"Have you lost your mind?" Katie asked, squaring herself up in front of me and crossing her arms over her chest.

Okay, she had her book bag, which meant she likely had just come from school. Melanie could've just met her here. But I wasn't buying it.

"Color me stupid," I said, feeling the engine picking up steam. "What do you expect me to think? You here, with your old lover. Not bothering to even tell me."

"Oh, Sarah," Katie said, her voice softer and full of pain. "This is so far over the top."

"Over the top?" I asked. "I'm not the one sneaking around."

"Oh, for God's sake. It's a coffee shop. It's not like this is a no-tell motel."

"Was that your next stop?"

Katie's face flushed red. For a split second I thought I'd hit it correctly, then I realized I'd finally crossed the line. She wasn't chagrined, she was pissed.

"You need"—she took a step toward me—"to back"—and another—"the fuck"—she punched me in the shoulder—"off!"

I stumbled back, more surprised than anything.

"Fine," I said, feeling the tears pushing against the back of my eyes. "I see how it is."

I pushed past her, the coffee shop blurring as tears welled into my eyes. What was wrong with me? Maybe I had lost my mind.

I grabbed my laptop, slamming it shut, and shoved it into my messenger bag. I left the orange-banana muffin and the half-empty mug o' coffee on the table and turned, dashing tears from my face and slinging the bag over my neck and shoulder.

"Sarah, wait," Katie said, one hand held out.

"I don't need this," I said with a hiccough.

The cool air of the early evening began to dry the tears on my face as I made my way across the lot to my trusty hatchback. I fumbled the door open, slung my gear inside, and jumped in.

As I roared out onto Redmond Way, I saw Katie in my rearview mirror, standing in the middle of the parking lot, her hands shoved into her pockets.

Twenty-five

MELANIE SAT AT the table Sarah had so abruptly abandoned. She had their coffee on the table, and sat back with a worried look on her face and a manila envelope and several loose papers on her lap.

Katie collapsed into the overstuffed chair and let her head drop into her hands. Sarah had totally flipped out for no reason.

"You okay?" Melanie asked quietly.

Katie looked up, brushed a tear from her face, and picked up her coffee. "She's under a ton of pressure."

"Uh-huh," Melanie said, picking up her own coffee. "I'm guessing she melted down after the shower, then?"

Katie thought back with a smile. "She was quite surprised, and Deidre, the evil wench, set the whole thing up. She knew Sarah was overloaded and needed a bit of unwinding."

"I remember her not-so-subtle hints," Melanie said, sipping her coffee.

"Sarah's just not comfortable with this whole thing," Katie said. "She's only been out for a little while."

"Little while?" Melanie asked.

"Well . . . the first time I kissed her, I thought she was going to punch me in the face."

"Interesting reaction."

"Yeah," Katie said, nodding. "I just stood there, watching her face. I could tell she was having an argument with herself."

"How'd that go?"

Katie shrugged. "When she didn't react, or leave, I reached out and touched her face. She flinched but didn't pull back. So I leaned in and kissed her forehead, whispering how beautiful she was."

Melanie leaned back and sipped her coffee.

"I could feel her melt in my hands. Then it was like a switch was thrown. She became the aggressor, practically ripped my clothes off."

"She wasn't rough? Angry?"

"God, no," Katie said, waving her hand. "She was very tender. Urgent, and fumbling, but caught on pretty quickly." She smiled, thinking back.

Melanie leaned forward and put her hand on Katie's knee. "So, you were her first?"

Katie nodded.

"She hasn't had time to adjust. You and I, we knew early."

"High school," Katie said, nodding.

"Right. And you and I were comfortable together in college. Sarah hasn't even come out to her family, has she?"

Katie barked a laugh. "No chance. She said her father barely speaks to her now with the blacksmithing thing."

"Not the most open-minded group of folks?"

Katie just shook her head once and sat back, holding her coffee with both hands. "There's got to be something else," she said. "She totally flipped."

"Well, she lost this," Melanie said, passing the stack of papers. "This could have something to do with it."

Katie flipped through the papers, saw the check, and whistled a descending tone. "Holy mother."

"Yeah," Melanie said. "What kind of trouble is she into?"

"I'm not sure," she said, scanning through the letter. "But I know the sword this guy is trying to buy. I bet this is part of it."

"Well, we'd planned to talk about Sarah tonight. I just didn't realize we'd have a floor show."

Katie glanced at her sideways and quirked a smile. "Bitch."

"Guilty as charged," Melanie said. "But I have to be back at the hospital in an hour, so spill the rest of it. What's special about this sword that makes it worth so much?"

"You remember the summer my parents died? Remember the bunker?" Katie began.

"How could I forget," Melanie said, setting her coffee cup down. "Jimmy caught us fooling around down there, before he showed you the letter."

"Well, I think all that crazy stuff my parents were on about . . . I believe them," Katie said, steeling herself for an argument. "I think Sarah may have reforged *the* Gram."

"Jesus," Melanie said. "This is huge."

Twenty-six

KATIE CALLED SARAH at home several times the next day and decided to just swing by the forge. Sarah usually worked on pet projects on Saturdays, with Julie's blessings.

She grabbed two coffees and a dozen crullers on the way.

When she pulled into the smithy parking lot, Julie came out of her trailer and walked toward the shop.

"Morning, Katie," Julie called.

Katie balanced the bag and the coffees, while closing the door to her car with one hip. "You seen Sarah?"

"Nope. Not since about two o'clock yesterday afternoon."

"Damn," Katie said, her shoulders sagging a bit.

"You two have a fight or something?" she asked.

"Something."

"That coffee?"

Katie shrugged and handed the one she had for Sarah to Julie. "Not sure you'll call it coffee, but it's got enough sugar and caffeine to stop a mule."

Julie took a sip of the triple espresso mocha latte and grimaced. "Definitely something Sarah would drink."

Katie smiled. "Might as well go for the whole diabetic rush," she said, holding out the bag of crullers.

"If this is how you visit her," Julie said, fishing out a sugar-laden donut, "we're gonna need to talk about her weight."

"I only break out this level of sugar when there's real trouble," Katie said. The tears were near enough to feel the sting. "We had a bit of a row at Monkey Shines yesterday."

"What for?"

"She accused me of sneaking around with my friend Melanie," Katie said. "Melanie was between shifts over at the Evergreen Hospital and she agreed to meet me for coffee."

Julie took a second cruller and sat on the tailgate of her truck, kicking her feet. "And Sarah took exception?"

"Lost her freaking mind," Katie said, pacing back and forth behind the truck. "Sarah left this at Monkey Shines." She held out the envelope. "This mean anything to you?"

Julie glanced at the envelope, but made no motion to take it. "Came yesterday by courier."

"Some guy wanting to buy her sword," Katie said.

"I told her to take the money and run," Julie said, reaching over and taking the bag of crullers from Katie.

"What did Sarah say?" Katie asked, facing Julie.

"Said it would be dishonorable."

A warm smile blossomed on Katie's face. "That's my Sarah."

"She says you told her you love her," Julie said, changing the subject.

"Yeah, Wednesday." She stopped, her jaw hanging open. "You think that's what caused all this?"

Julie shrugged, munching on her cruller. "Sarah's full of conflicting emotions, Katie. What the two of you have been doing so far has been play. Now you went and made it all serious."

"But I do love her."

Julie set the bag of remaining donuts on the gate of her truck and stood, sucking the sugar off one thumb. "Give her some time. She'll come around at her own pace."

"You think so?"

"She's stubborn and convinced of her direction, 'cept when she's not," Julie said, brushing the dust off the back of her pants. "Let her come around to it. Better in the long run if she sees it herself."

Katie let her head droop a little. "Does it have to be so hard?"

"Nothing worth having ever comes easy," Julie said, clapping Katie on the shoulder. "Why don't you go on home and let Sarah work this through. When she's tired of beating her head against the brick wall, she'll come around asking for help. I've been watching her for over a year. She's a damn fine apprentice, but is bound and determined to do things the hard way."

Katie stared at the envelope a moment and shrugged. "Well, if she comes in, will you have her call me?" she said, walking toward her car.

"Sure thing."

When had things started to go crazy? Katie thought back. It was fine until the earthquake. Cats and horses got a little nuts when earthquakes happened, maybe it was the same with Sarah. Of course . . . She glanced over at the envelope. The sword had been reforged the night before.

She started the car and pulled out of the lot. Jimmy was being so damn cautious. What if this was Gram they were dealing with? Mom and Dad had urged caution, keeping a low profile, but sometimes things just got out of hand.

She rolled down her window and cranked up her stereo. Pink's "So What" blasted over her. Somehow this was screwing with her relationship with Sarah and it was starting to piss her off.

Twenty-seven

I WOKE AT the butt crack of dawn. I don't remember crying as much as I had last night, but I sure remember sleeping more. Another night of short sleep rations and psychotic dreams. Thunderstorms and giants battling for the high ground. Each time I dodged a bolt of lightning, or hurled boulder, another obstacle rose before me, bigger and meaner than the last.

At least I recognized they were nightmares. That was an improvement. What I needed to do was really push myself. Hammer my body into oblivion, then I could sleep.

That trail out between Issaquah and Marymoor Park was just the thing I needed to clear my head. Eleven miles. I'd run it last summer when I was getting ready for that marathon down in Bend. I could run as much as I could and walk the rest. Piece of cake.

Of course, I rarely ran more than four or five miles in a given day, so this would kick my behind.

I drank a large glass of orange juice after my shower, then dressed in my running clothes. With the MP3 player strapped to my bicep, and a healthy dose of sunscreen on my neck, face, arms, and legs, I was as ready as I was going to get today. I packed in several bottles of sports drink for the run along with a couple packs of power gel in case I could fill the water bottles at the public fountains along the way. Not looking to win any races here, just to finish and be able to walk.

I deliberately left the cell phone on the counter. I needed time to think. Didn't want any interruptions.

The drive to Gilman Village was rather short, given that it was Saturday traffic. I parked across from White Horse Toys, cranked up a long playlist of random metal, and began to stretch.

Once I was really aligning to the tunes, and had stretched enough to allow a light jog to get the rest of the way, I packed my fanny pack with wallet and keys and headed down the trail.

Eleven miles. That's a long damn way.

I started at a light jog, but as I cleared the strollers and the talkers, I stepped it up. The first few miles were smooth, finding my rhythm, hitting my cruising speed. After mile five, I walked a bit, then jogged, and walked, alternating for endurance. It was that first moment where my heart thudded in my chest, and my breath stuttered in and out with a near sob. This was when my mind felt clear, when the voices and critics were shut down, pushed aside by fatigue. I figured it was time to take stock.

Carl had a thing for me, but now knew I was gay.

Jennifer loved Carl, and felt a kindred spirit to me now that she realized I wasn't the competition.

JJ was a dumbass, surrounded himself with strippers, and Sawyer was telling him what a great actor he was. Amazing. Of course, if I was honest about it, he was pretty damn good. He was just a jerk. At least I knew where he stood in the grand scheme of things.

Rolph, on the other hand. He was a puzzle. Had he sold me out to the damn banker? Why was he twisted up in this? Why would he call in Sawyer, other than to put him in my face? He seemed so damn earnest about both the sword and the dragon.

A shudder slipped across my shoulders but I ran through it. There was something scary about Sawyer. On the surface he seemed fine, real humanitarian, but with Rolph's story and the sword, things didn't synch.

It all came back to the sword. Maybe I was just too damn tied up with it emotionally, making me imagine things. There was something about Sawyer that set my teeth on edge—a sour taste below the surface that told me he was a very dangerous man. But what evidence did I really have?

And my gut had worked so well on many levels in the last few days. Just look at the mess I'd made with Katie. She'd told me she loved me, and I managed to piss that away pretty quick.

But, dear sweet Katie. I thought of the wicked smile on her face when she stepped into the shower. How she looked in the morning just waking up. How she liked her coffee and how, when she was really tired, she'd sleep curled up on top of the blankets, instead of burrowing under them like I would.

But Katie was in another league—one I wasn't sure I wanted to play in. I could see a relationship totally working with her, but when you added in Melanie, and Dena, and the whole Gay Pride agenda, I balked. I didn't want the lifestyle. No marches, no banners, no rainbow T-shirts and spangled pink pyramids emblazoned on my car.

Whom I chose to share my sex life with was my own damn business. If straight people didn't have to declare who they were sleeping with, then why the hell did I have to? Why did I have to make some proclamation to the world on the subject? Anyone who needed to know, already knew. Hell, some folks I wish didn't know already knew, and the world hadn't come to an end . . . yet.

Maybe Katie and I could just come to a quiet understanding. She could handle all the rallies and sit-ins, and I'd read her notes or something.

One movement is as bad as the next, frankly. First Da has us running all over God's creation looking for the perfect church, and we'd sit in on meeting after meeting, joining the team with the TRUTH. Only, each version of the truth differed, depending on who you talked to.

This whole Gay Pride thing was no better. Individuals preaching to the converted masses, telling them things they already knew, making the world a little more sparkly in the name of equity . . . as long as you believed what they believed.

Sigh. What I needed to do was to clear my head, air out the cobwebs a bit and maybe make some room for new thoughts, an alternate perspective.

So I ran on, head down, concentrating on my breath.

Back when I took tae kwon do as a kid, my sa bum nim told me that my mind was too busy. She said I needed to learn to concentrate, to focus my actions and my thoughts on a single target, a single goal.

I don't think I really understood what she meant until I started smithing. That's where I found my ability to give myself to the task at hand. Become so engrossed with the art, the work, that everything else fell to the side.

Running didn't fix that, but it got close. Of all the things in my head, only Katie's face interceded for the next few miles. I kept catching glimpses of Katie—the way she held her mouth when she orgasmed—the way she drew in her breath in quick gasps.

There was power in that moment. Not unlike the power I felt when I created something with steel and fire. Taking her to that edge and riding with her as she crossed into bliss—that was when I was at my best. Focused . . . dedicated . . . invincible.

I wish I could keep that feeling after, when I was out in the world. To be able to hold that fire, keep the overwhelming confidence and surety of that precise moment. That would be bottling the lightning, that's for sure.

At the hour mark, realizing that I was *not* going to solve the whole sexual orientation conundrum, I switched my thoughts to the other huge thing in my life at the moment.

Like what to do about that damned sword.

Swords and dwarves, dragons, bankers, movies, prima donna actors, and desperate, well-meaning directors.

If I used the sword to kill Frederick Sawyer, what would that cost? Oh, the prison time notwithstanding. I understood all that, but where did I stand morally?

That moment at Carl's, I knew fear like I'd never known before. Something there triggered a primal instinct in me. I could've killed him, if I had been within reach, but instead I let the fear wash over me, shutting down my defenses, closing off my mind.

The next several steps jarred through me as my pulse thundered in my ears. In that moment, the world narrowed, folded in to nothing but the trail and the sound of my feet.

The Fear rose in me then, caused me to stumble. For a moment the world was consumed with the black shadow that had engulfed my heart. While the certainty of the monster others could not see had faded with sleep, the overwhelming feeling of powerlessness had not diminished. If anything, it was growing stronger.

I stutter stepped as pain thrashed across my left calf—cramp of an alarming category. For a moment, I nearly lost my balance as the trail seemed to slide around. Then I realized it was another quake. This one about like the last, several hard jolts and a semilong rolling shrug as the Pacific shelf slid north toward Canada.

I walked after that a long bit, wishing I'd brought my cell phone. At least I had the sports drink. Should've drunk one earlier.

I managed to work the cramp out of my calf, but the knot I felt forming below the skin would not dissipate altogether. I did the best I could to get it eased back enough to walk, but I foresaw a foul-smelling muscle ointment in my future.

I limped the last two miles, hoping I could borrow a phone long enough to get a cab back to Issaquah. No way I was making that jog back.

As it was, I could see collapsing into a hot bath and then going back to bed.

When I arrived among people again, I made my way over to a women's softball game, purchased two bottles of water, and sat in the stands to watch. Eighteen- to twenty-four-year-old women of all colors and creeds dotted the field. The pitcher was excellent, and the outfield superb. They played ball well, too.

Definitely a little surge of joy watching them. Watching the way they moved, the way they looked in their uniforms—all the curves in all the right places.

The guys on the rock climbing wall to the left did nothing for me, however. Oh, I could appreciate the way they were toned and all, but they didn't light my Bunsen burner.

I watched the doubleheader, eating hot dogs and drinking several bottles of water over the next few hours. Several times I had to pace around the bleachers as my legs threatened to cramp up, but I knew the drill. Work the knots, stretch the muscles to prevent further damage, and drink enough to get my electrolytes back into balance and to hydrate.

Around one, I found that there was a bus that ran to Issaquah so I made sure I was on it. Getting from the bus stop to my car proved a bit challenging, but nothing compared to trying to drive a clutch.

When I got home, I would medicate, steam, and sleep. In that order.

Twenty-eight

THE ANTI-INFLAMMATORY DIDN'T kick in until after I'd soaked in the tub for an hour or so. But when the knots began to finally loosen, I limped to the bedroom and crawled deep into the nest of blankets, not even bothering to dry my hair.

I woke around midnight. I'd slept for almost nine hours, and had no recollection of dreams. My left leg burned where the knot had been, but overall it felt pretty good.

I slipped on the pink sweat suit—hey, it was comfy. I grabbed my satchel and sat on the couch to check my e-mail.

Maybe I'd won the lottery or something.

As my laptop booted, I remembered Sawyer's offer. That was one big-ass check. I opened my messenger bag and rifled through the notebooks and assorted papers. The envelope was not there.

I panicked. Had I lost it? No, wait. Did I even put it in my kit? Was it sitting on Julie's desk at this very moment?

That was the likely scenario. I put on a pair of white socks, and my tennies, grabbed my fanny pack, and headed to the car. If that envelope was at Julie's I wanted to get my hands on it immediately. It was imperative that no one else got ahold of that check.

I drove over to the smithy, making the best time and

within the speed limit. Julie's truck was in the driveway, but the lights were out in her trailer. Of course, it was nearly one in the morning by this point.

The crunch of the gravel seemed louder than normal, but I pulled over to my normal space and parked. This would only take a moment.

I had the keys in my hand, and had already thrown the light switch in my head, when I stopped short. The door was ajar.

Had Julie left the door to the smithy open? I couldn't imagine it.

I crept forward, keeping my hands free and my profile low as I approached the door. Through the crack, I could hear someone swearing in thickly muted whispers, and the sound of a shuffling body. At least one, couldn't tell if there were more.

Robbers in my domain? This was the fight I'd been itching for. I slowly pushed the door open with my foot and listened intently. Whoever was rummaging around inside had not heard the door. I scuttled around the edge of the door frame, keeping my profile as small as I could. When I reached the tool bench, I quietly picked up a two-pound hammer and stood, flipping on the lights.

Not exactly what I'd expected.

Rolph lay on the floor in front of the safe, bloody and beaten, his hands and arms covering his head, as if to ward off another blow.

I fell to my knees beside him. "Craptastic," I muttered, touching him on the arm. "Hang on there, big guy."

"Apprentice?" he mumbled through a smashed mouth. "Is it you?"

"Yeah, I'm here," I said, a cold wave of nausea and fear warring with the horror and anger that threatened to overwhelm me. "What happened?"

"The dragon," he said, his breath coming in sharp

stabs. "He sent some giants to take the sword. He thought I had acquired it for him and was holding out." He lowered his left forearm over his eyes to block the light, but his right hand fell to his side.

"First, I have the sword, so you don't need to worry."

He peered at me under his arm, his eyes intense, searching.

"It's fine," I said. "Now, don't move. Let me get the med kit."

"You are an angel," he said, barking out a laugh.

I stood, set the hammer on the table beside the anvil, and walked to the emergency kit Julie kept in the smithy. We could handle damn near anything short of an IV or blood draw.

I sat on the floor beside him and checked him for immediate trauma. No bones appeared to be broken, and his blood loss was limited to the wounds on his face and head.

"We should get you to a hospital, get some X-rays," I said, opening a bottle of antiseptic and a bag of cotton balls.

"No," he said, as I knew he would. "Cannot risk being out after the sun rises."

"Right, gargoyle time," I said, covering the lip of the bottle with a cotton ball and tipping the liquid out. Hell, what did I know anymore? If he believed it, best to humor him. "This is going to sting a little."

I placed the cotton against a shallow cut on his forehead and he drew in a sharp hiss. "Little," he mewled.

"Probably needs stitches," I said. "But I'm not a sewer. Different trade."

"You are humorous," he said, his lips swollen like two pink slugs.

Tires popped on the gravel parking lot and I stood, snatching up the hammer and killing the lights. "Hang on, Rolph," I said, squatting next to him and patting his arm. "If the bastards show again, I'll be ready for them."

"They were never here," he whispered. "They did this at my home."

"Then why are you here?" I asked as voices approached the smithy. Julie and a male voice. I listened a moment and knew. Jack Marlowe.

"Friendlies," I said, and stood. I flipped the lights back on and stood in the doorway, waiting for them to come inside.

"What the hell is going on?" Julie asked, standing square in front of me. I stepped away from the door and swung my arm out to take in Rolph.

"Someone has used one of the movie extras as a punching bag," I said, being cool. "And he decided this is the safest place to land."

"Cute outfit," Jack said to me with a wink.

Julie and I both looked at him. Neither of us had a pleasant expression on our face, and he took a step back. "Just saying," he mumbled.

"Never figured you for pink," Julie said, craning her neck over me to see Rolph. "He gonna live?"

"Likely," I said, stepping aside and setting the hammer down. "I thought I'd do a bit of doctoring and see how he cleans up."

"No hospital?"

"I can do stitches," Jack offered.

"I'll go up to the house and get some things," Julie said, shaking her head. "Jack, you come with me."

She grabbed his hand and walked out the door. I peeked and caught her grabbing his ass just as they reached her front door. Interesting night, indeed.

I knelt back with Rolph and began cleaning the smaller cuts and abrasions. He mewled and moaned but his blood was as red as mine.

"So, giants, huh?"

"Yes," he said through gritted teeth.

"How many?"

"Only two."

"Two?"

"They are giants, after all," he said. "Tall, arms like twisted steel, hands the size of . . . well, rubber goblin hands."

I laughed at that and he tried to smile despite the pain.

I sat back on my heels, a bloody cotton ball in one hand, and considered. "Did you see their vehicle?"

"Hummer," he said. "Black and, I think, dark green."

"Bastards," I said, letting the anger bubble near the surface.

Rolph stared at me a moment. "You know of them?"

"Maybe," I said, getting a clean cotton ball and dipping it in the antiseptic. "Couple of goons ran me off the road Wednesday, fit your description. One of them punched my car."

"Could be them," he said. "I would advise caution."

"Gee, ya think?"

I finished working on him and sat back to contemplate the situation. Julie and Jack didn't come back. After thirty minutes, I heard a truck leaving and Julie came into the smithy. Her hair was mussed up, and she had on a different . . . "Is that Jack's shirt?"

She waved at me, batting away my comment, and knelt by Rolph.

"He can't go home," I said. "They know where he lives."

"Who are they?" she asked, pulling a hooked needle from her kit along with some fine thread.

"They want the sword," he said, eyeing her suspiciously. "You have done this before?"

"Oh, sure. Dozens of times," she said, squatting over

him. She handed him a pint of whiskey and examined the cut over his eye. "I've sewn up horses and such. Skin is skin."

"Comforting," he said.

We helped wrestle him up to a seated position against the anvil and he took several large swallows of the whiskey.

"Ready?" she asked, kneeling in front of him.

"Aye," he said, closing his eyes.

He winced a bit, but didn't really make too much of a fuss. The stitches went swiftly; she really had a delicate touch. Seven little black Xs dotted his forehead, and he would heal good as new. Mostly.

"He could bed down here for the rest of the night, if he needs," she said, packing her kit.

"No sunlight," he whispered, exhausted.

Julie raised her eyebrows at me.

"Right. Julie, just roll with this, okay?"

"What am I rolling with, exactly?"

Okay, here was the next test. Rolph believed this, and Katie did the last time I'd had a rational conversation with her. But how could I tell Julie with a straight face? Hell, I couldn't exactly say I wasn't having my doubts about my sanity. There were moments where I was afraid all this could be true, but those moments were fleeting.

"I am of Durin's folk," he said.

I shrugged at her. "He says he's a dwarf."

Julie held up her hands. "Wait a minute. Dwarf?"

"At your service," Rolph said.

"If you say hobbits or wizards, I'm tossing both your asses out onto the street."

She was smiling when she said it, but I could tell she was a little discombobulated.

We waited for a few breaths. She brushed the hair out of her face and nodded. "Okay, goons want the sword, you're a dwarf, and can't be out in the sunlight." A look of comprehension crossed her face. "Tell me you have Gram," she finished, facing me.

If you'd have hit me with a feather I'd have collapsed into a heap of pink cotton. "Not you, too?" I asked. "Am I the only sane one here?"

Julie laughed. "He's a smith, I can tell by his hands and arms. Besides, I just get the vibe from him. And you've been freaking out about the sword, and, face it—I'm a blacksmith. How many blacksmiths do you know?"

"Um, besides you and me . . . two," I said, confused.

"Yes, two. But I know dozens, and we all follow the legends, the culture, the mythology. I have seen Wagner's *Ring Cycle*. Seattle Opera does it every few years."

"I've never seen it," Rolph interjected.

I shrugged. "I'd rather gargle drain cleaner than listen to opera."

"It's a good story," Julie said, leaning against the door frame. "I think Warner Brothers did it best with Bugs and Elmer Fudd."

"Oh, I saw that," I said, nodding. "Valkyries, battles, Viking warriors with winged helms and magic swords . . ."

"And lightning bolts," Rolph said.

We looked at him and he shrugged.

"I like Bugs Bunny."

"Anyway," Julie said. "Sigurd or Sigmund, I can never remember . . ." She waved the air. "One of them slays the dragon Fafnir with the sword. Blah, blah, fat lady sings."

I winced. "Sigurd, actually."

"My father claimed to have met him," Rolph said.

I rolled my eyes. "So, Julie, do you believe my sword is Gram?"

"It doesn't matter what I think," Julie said, sitting on the edge of the workbench. "There are people out there who believe it. Enough to hurt your friend here."

Touché.

"So, he can sleep in the storeroom. No windows in there. I'll run up to the house and get him some gear."

And back she went, out the door at a skip. Skipping and whistling, actually. I bet this would be a perfect moment to ask for a raise.

We got Rolph bedded down and Julie headed up to the house with a promise to check on him the next day.

"I miscalculated," he said as I was pulling the door closed.

"Sorry?"

"I thought as soon as you saw what he was that you would kill him on the spot."

He was a dim shadow in a room of shadows, so I couldn't see his face, but I let that little puzzle piece rattle in my head a moment.

"You set me up?"

"I knew you would see his true form, recognize him for the beast he is. Was I wrong?"

I shook my head, remembering the fear. The doorknob slipped from my suddenly sweating hands and I leaned against the door frame. "Terrifying."

He didn't say anything for a long time. When I was convinced he had gone to sleep I straightened up and pulled the door closed.

Twenty-nine

OKAY, TIME TO take this up a notch. I had the sword in my car, and there were at least two thugs looking for it.

What I didn't understand was why Sawyer would offer to buy it from me, then send guys to rough up Rolph. Something didn't add up.

I sat in my car a moment, resting my head against the cool vinyl of the steering wheel and thinking. This was just too much. I needed to talk to Katie. Hell, I just flat needed Katie. I couldn't breathe. So I drove instead.

I parked in the same spot I'd lucked out on a few nights earlier and walked down the alley with the sword in its case in one hand and my favorite hammer in the other. No plan to take a beating.

I passed the Dumpster and thought of Joe. His odor usually preceded him. I'd almost passed the alley when he stumbled out, reeking of sour sweat and cheap wine.

"It is beneath you, smith."

I turned, nearly jumping out of my skin, the sword and case on the ground at my feet, my hammer pulled back for a blow. I rolled onto the balls of my feet and let out a breath.

"Jesus, Joe. Why the hell do you have to scare me like that?"

He stopped by the Dumpster, his features shadowed and twisted by the glow of the streetlight on the corner. "You truck with dwarves, smith."

"Dwarves?" I asked. "Does everybody know about this?"

"He will bring you ruin," Joe said, stepping toward me. He leaned on a rough-hewn tree branch and hobbled toward me a step. "You bear the runes, you bear the sword."

My left leg cramped then, sending me to one knee. I'd really overdone it with that run. I breathed through clenched teeth and stretched my calf, trying to get ahead of the knot.

"You fight the truth, that is plain to see," he said, turning his one good eye toward me. "And your spirit is cloven, sundered by your own fear."

"What the hell do you know?" I whispered, massaging my leg with both hands, the hammer at my feet.

"Know?" he asked with a cackle. "I know you have wounds upon wounds, smith. When will you mend the break within yourself?"

I lifted the hammer and stood, favoring my left leg. "Listen, you creepy old man . . ."

But he was not there. I looked around the Dumpster and as far back into the alley as I dared. No one. I edged back, picked up the sword case, and hobbled out of the alley. Overhead a pair of crows cawed into the blackness before the dawn.

Thirty

I LIMPED TO the doorway up to Katie's place and realized I'd left her keys at my apartment. Better to ring up, anyway. Only polite. No real way of telling if she'd even see me. Of course, she'd want to know about Rolph, and the things that had been going on . . . right?

The buzzer stuttered a bit as I held in the button and waited. After a minute, I buzzed again, waiting. On the third try, Katie's sleepy voice called down on the intercom. "I will kill you," she said.

"Katie?" I asked.

"Sarah?" Her voice was suddenly more awake.

"Yeah, can I come up?"

She didn't answer right away and I leaned against the brick.

"Are you drunk?" she asked, finally.

Fair question, but . . . "No," I said. Still hurt.

"It's really late."

"I just want to talk. Rolph's been attacked. There's news about the sword."

"Oh," she said, hesitant. "How do you know I'm not having a Sapphic orgy up here as we speak?"

That was absurd. "What are you talking about?" I asked.

"Never mind. You can come up for a minute."

Okay, that was something. The lock buzzed and I pulled the door open, finagled my gear through, and began the painful climb up to the second floor. My calf burned like nothing I'd ever experienced.

Katie met me at the door dressed in her summer pajamas and a robe. Usually she slept naked, so the tone was set. She watched me with a cautious expression as I pulled the sword case through the door, and tried not to drop the hammer as I pushed around the couch and collapsed on the loveseat. "Could I get something to drink?" I asked. "Please?"

She stood there a moment, contemplating, and then nodded. Schoolteacher till the end.

"And some ibuprofen?"

I took the two pills and the glass with a smile. The water wasn't the only thing that was cold.

Katie sat at her kitchen table, toying with her own glass of water and yawning. "What's going on?" she asked, looking up.

I could see the redness in her lovely brown eyes. Likely crying as much as sleep loss. Katie never cried. I hated that I did that to her, but . . .

"I'm sorry about last night."

She didn't nod, or say anything. Just took a small sip of water and held the glass on her lap with both hands.

"Right. Well. Things aren't going so good right now. Rolph was beat up, and . . ."

"New girlfriend?" she asked.

"What?"

"Little old to be banging college kids, but I guess I'm not much older, huh?"

The room spun for a moment. "Me? What are you talking about?"

"You didn't have to wear her clothes over here," she said, the bitterness thick in her throat. "Melanie and I are just friends. We were just meeting to talk." She hiccoughed a catch, trying not to cry. "I wanted to talk about us," she held her hand at me, open palmed, and drew it back to tap on her own chest. "You and me. About Jimmy's and . . ." She turned her head and sniffled a bit, taking a napkin from the table and dabbing her eyes. "All we did was talk."

"O-okay," I said, lost. "I believe you."

"Fine, then can you go, please?"

She rose and stepped toward the door. "If you needed to sleep with someone else because you were scared, or uncertain, or just didn't understand your sexuality yet, that's one thing." She was angry now, not sad. I sat there, holding the empty water glass to my chest and trying to breathe.

"Katie, what are you talking about?"

"You didn't have to fuck her, and then wear her clothes here. That's just low . . . beneath you."

I looked down and realized I was still wearing the pink sorority sweats. I laughed. Wrong move, and it sent her blood pressure up about fifty points, but I couldn't help it. This was surreal.

"Jesus, Katie," I said, standing. I walked to the kitchen and set the glass into the sink. "I didn't sleep with anyone, and how I got these is part of the story."

I walked back into the living room and she stood at the door, holding it open with her hand pointing toward the hall.

"I swear to God. I'm wearing these because I pissed myself at the movie shoot."

A moment of doubt crossed her face, and she softened a pinch.

"Don't lie to me," she whispered. "Just tell me you needed to get it out of your system or something, but don't lie."

I walked up to her and fell to my knees at her feet. "Katie, I swear to you. I would never do that to you, and I would never flaunt it like this, never hurt you like this."

She looked down at me for the longest time. I didn't move, just sat at her feet, looking up and praying. Then the cramp exploded in my calf again and I spasmed sideways, knocking the end table askew. I growled a wounded cry and clutched my calf, all dignity gone, all pretense vanished in the white-hot pain that seared my calf.

"Sarah, my God," Katie said, letting the door close with a bang, and kneeling beside me. "Charley horse?"

"Yes," I managed to hiss.

She worked my calf, pushing my hands out of the way for a moment. Then she slid the sweats up over my calf and stopped, rocking back on her heels. "What the hell is this?"

I rolled up on my shoulder and looked at my calf. There was a marking of some sort there, like a T with the arms drooping down at a forty-five-degree angle. "No idea," I whispered.

She got up, ran to the kitchen, and returned with an icepack. The coldness took the bite out of the pain, and the muscles began to unclench.

Soon I was lying on her couch, on my stomach, with my legs in her lap and my sweats pulled up to my knees.

She examined both calves, looking for further markings, but the marks on my left calf were the only ones.

"Looks like a brand," she said, gingerly touching the tissue. "But it could be a tattoo of some sort."

"I didn't have anything done," I said, feeling fairly vulnerable at that moment. "I swear."

"These are too healed, sort of," she said, scribbling on a piece of paper. "It looks as if they are coming through the skin, pushing outward, as it were. Here," she handed me a notebook with five symbols.

"Symbols like on the sword," I said, rolling over and slipping my feet to the floor. "This is too damn creepy."

I pushed the pant leg back down over my calf and limped to the case, which now sat on her kitchen table. I opened it and pulled the sword out. Once my hand firmly grasped the pommel the light in the room dimmed and then brightened. Colors seemed to shift into a brighter shade and I felt invigorated, pain free.

"You okay?" Katie asked, standing.

I did feel a little woozy, drunk almost. "Light-headed."

I held the blade under the light and turned it a bit to allow the runes to appear all along the blade. Sure enough, several looked like the ones on the paper, like the ones on my calf.

"You left this at the coffee shop," she said, dropping the envelope on the table beside the case. "Melanie found it at Monkey Shines after you stormed out."

I looked down at the envelope. Considered the contents and what they meant. "Thank you." What else could I say? I'd been an ass.

"You know," she said, sliding into a chair at the table, looking up at the blade as I turned it in the light. "There are three schools of magic in Norse mythology. Bardic singing. That's my realm." A shadow of a smile touched her lips.

I watched her face, looking for hints of mockery, but none came. She was being serious. "You think you're magical?"

"You thought so at one time." She shrugged. "It's a matter of perspective. Do you feel motivated—charged up—when I sing during your practices with Stuart and Gunther?"

I thought about it, really considering it. I did feel invigorated, heady almost. "Yeah. I think it helps."

She shrugged again. "Magic is a matter of perspective. If you believe, then you believe."

Hard to argue with that.

"Anyway," she continued, "the other two are illusion, which seems to include astral projection or out-of-body experiences, and runes."

"Seriously?" I asked. "That's pretty random."

She shrugged. "Or so says the infinite Internet."

I sat down beside her and placed the sword back in the case. When I turned to her, reached for her hands, she slipped them from the table and into her lap.

"Runes play a major component in Norse magic," she said. "Something has marked you."

"Definitely odd," I said with a shrug.

"Odd?" she asked. "Sarah, does none of this faze you?"

I was too damn tired. Tired of being angry, and tired of trying to figure all this out. If there were runes magically appearing on my calf, and dwarves and giants . . . Maybe it was time to roll over, accept the madness, and move on to something I could affect.

"If you'd asked me about this just five days ago, I'd have laughed, thinking you were off on one of your fantasy trips."

She stared at me, not smiling.

Pretty damn uncomfortable here, thank you very much. "Anyway . . . Things have started getting squirrelly ever since I reforged the sword."

"So, is it coincidence, magic, or just . . ." She yawned. "I don't know what you think anymore, if I ever did."

I'd royally fucked things up, that was obvious. I'd tried to touch her three times, and she'd avoided it since I got here. How was I supposed to fix this?

"I think we should look them up, see what their meaning is." That's the ticket. Change the subject. I ripped the page from the notebook, dropped it and the envelope inside the sword case, closed the lid and latched it. Time to roll the dice. "I'll look them up after we've slept. I'm beat."

Katie looked away. "Have you decided then?"

"About the dragon and the sword?"

She sighed. "I'm talking about you, Sarah. You need to accept who you are, how the world works." She got up and paced across the room, her arms crossed and her hands grasping either arm. "Accept things for what they are."

"Oh, I'm not selling the sword to Sawyer, if that's what you mean," I said. "He's horrible. This dragon thing doesn't jive with my headspace, but the runes sprouting on my leg are hard to argue with."

"No," she said, shaking her head. "Sarah. Right now, I don't care about dragons or dwarves, swords or runes. I want to know if you have made a decision about us. About what we mean to one another." She paused. "I think until you come out, until you accept who you really are, and learn to forget what other people think about your sexuality, we can't move forward. Until you can face yourself, this just can't work."

"But the runes . . . What about Rolph and the giants?"

"Sarah," she said sadly, and I saw it in her face, heard it in her voice.

This was it. I started hearing the closing sequence of the *Get Smart* television show—all those walls and doors closing.

"I don't think we can see each other anymore."

And that was that. I could see it in her face. At that moment, a glacier stood between my heart and hers.

I don't remember the alley, or getting to my car. I know I didn't see Joe again, but the next clear moment I was driving up 167 and the oncoming headlights sparkled like diamonds through my tears.

Thirty-one

I DIDN'T GET out of bed Sunday until well after three. I don't recall any dreams, but when I crawled to the shower, I felt like I'd been worked over with a sack of hammers.

I showered and paid special attention to the runes on my calf. They didn't wash off, of course. They didn't hurt anymore, either.

Dressed in a pair of white boxers and a wife-beater T-shirt, I sat at the kitchen table and fired up the laptop.

Sawyer's offer sat underneath a pitcher of wilting daisies on one side of the table. I purposely ignored them, really.

The Inter webz proved to be pretty useful. I found several conflicting Web sites on runes, but when I cross-referenced it with Gram, I came up with tons on Norse mythology. There were several good pages on runes.

The ones on my leg were:

Thurisaz: Reactionary force. The focused energy of destruction and defense. Conflict and change. Oh, good—weapon, destruction, anger. Very obvious given the last few days.

Dagaz: Dawning awareness, clarity of morning as opposed to the confusion of night. Signals a personally driven change in direction.

This one was harder. I know I struggled against change. It's something I work through all the time.

Kenaz: Fire of transformation. Fire of life. Power to create a new reality. Sexual love, passion.

Blacksmith . . . girlfriend . . .'nuff said.

Gebo: Gifts balanced. Sacrifice and generosity. All matters of relationships, business, personal, and partnerships.

I could put a twist on each of these, I'm sure, but again, pretty obvious given my current series of problems. Just hoped it meant I was going to work through the relationships in a positive fashion. Sacrifice is a scary thought.

Tiwaz: Honor and justice, leadership, analysis and rationality. Knowing where one's true strength lies. Willingness to self-sacrifice.

Goes with Gebo, but how does one gauge their own true strength? Did it deal with smithing? Or perhaps it's the power to stand up to Frederick and his games. Pretty sure the relationship aspect didn't play here—not with my track record.

And of course, each of them have an opposite, depending on which way the rune is presented during the reading. So, while my runes read positive when you started behind my knee and read down, when I looked at them in the mirror, they were reversed.

Interesting, regardless. I looked at the blade in its case, one flat side shining under my kitchen light. Runes ran down the entire fuller, except, of course, where the blade had been repaired. As it was, I could make out most of them. The sword hummed with power when I grasped it. I seriously considered what might change if I added new runes over the repairs.

I pushed my couch and coffee table into the kitchen area and moved the lamps into the bedroom along with the television. Once the room was empty, I took the sword from the case and began to run through several warm-up exercises with it. It felt good in my hand although the weight was all wrong. It didn't feel natural like the hammers I preferred, but this sword knew me. I can't explain it any other way. My arm suddenly felt thirty-three inches longer when I worked with that sword, an inorganic extension to the organic. It both thrilled and horrified me.

With breath heaving and sweat dripping, I danced

around the room, cutting and slashing, letting the demons in my head suit as targets. After an hour I collapsed onto one of the kitchen chairs with an oiled cloth in one hand and a liter of water on the table in front of me. Rubbing the sword, concentrating on the places where I'd touched the blade, was cathartic. The sword glowed by the time I'd drunk all the water, and I put it back into the case with care.

This sword sang to me. Filled my head with the songs of victory, the glory of battle. But it could not hide the blood. Always the blood.

I closed the case, comforted in the snap of the latches, and turned out the kitchen lights. I didn't even move the furniture back, just climbed over the couch, took a shower, and collapsed into bed, exhausted.

Thirty-two

QINDRA KNELT ON the mat across the table from Frederick Sawyer; watched as he quietly poured two cups of tea and mused.

"It's not a difficult question," she prodded. "You are encroaching on Nidhogg's interests, and she wants to know why."

Frederick carefully set one of the cups in front of her, then placed a second in front of himself, ignoring the question. The Japanese waitress stood far enough back to not eavesdrop, but close enough to be of assistance if they asked. The teahouse had been his idea. A way to allow him to feel relaxed in what was essentially enemy territory.

He raised the china cup to his lips and sipped. Steam

rose thick from the liquid, hot enough to scorch her own lips, yet Sawyer just smiled and nodded once to the server, who bowed deeply and turned away.

Patience was long Qindra's best gift, learned at her mother's knee as she served the dragons before her coming of age. There were many who tested her, and so far, they had all failed. Yet, this creature vexed her.

"It would seem," she went on, "that you have knowledge of recent events . . ." She paused, worried about how much to reveal. "My mistress is uncomfortable at the moment."

"She's old," Sawyer said quietly. "Perhaps she is tired, out of sorts."

He watched her, looking for signs, worried glances, fidgeting . . . but she would not play into his game. "You know as well as I, Nidhogg remains the greatest of your kind."

Sawyer barked out a laugh.

Qindra couldn't help but react. Her head rocked back as if she'd been smacked.

"Greatest in this immature country, perhaps." He leaned forward, resting his forearms on the table, inches from her folded hands. "There are those back in the homelands who would disagree."

Old argument. She waved a hand between them, clearing the air of tension. "There are none who would dare challenge Nidhogg." She paused, raising one eyebrow into her hairline, seeing if he would protest. "Unless you have taken leave of your senses. Maybe she feels you losing control, succumbing to the beast."

This time, Sawyer reacted. He darted his head forward a breath, snapping his jaws with a clack, flame rising in his eyes.

" 'Ware your tongue, witch."

Qindra nodded once but did not break eye contact

with him. Keep them off balance, and never show them fear. "Nidhogg requests what knowledge you have of recent events."

The moment passed and Sawyer settled back, the fire smoldering in his eyes, a hint of the rage that could consume him. "I'm sure I know not of which you speak."

Perhaps he was telling the truth. There was no sign of anything special, no hint of direct malice toward Nidhogg. Jean-Paul, now—that was a different subject. Sawyer hated Jean-Paul almost as much as Jean-Paul hated everyone.

"I am dabbling in a bit of a hobby, here." He shrugged, dismissing any relevance. "If Nidhogg is desperate for the artistic talents or monetary options of my little movie adventure, I'm sure they would welcome other investors."

Another probe, a foray to see her weaknesses. But they were halfhearted attempts, more social parrying than actual digging.

"Her holdings are more than adequate," Qindra said, lifting her own cup. "It behooves a wise ruler to keep track of her allies." She nodded in his direction. "And those forces that may be squabbling among the dogs for scraps."

"If she looks for villains," he offered, "she needs look no farther than her own offspring."

Qindra let a smile touch her lips. "Jean-Paul is a nasty creature, full of hatred and the need for darkness."

"You mean torturing prostitutes and drug addicts, I assume."

Qindra sipped her tea. The liquid did not scald her, as she'd feared, but the bitterness of the tea was surprising.

She must have made a face of some sort, because Frederick slid a bowl of rice sweets to her. "This will cut the bitterness. It is an acquired taste."

The sweet melted on Qindra's tongue, a light sugary

flavor that flattened the harshness of the tea, making the taste almost pleasant.

"There is something afoot," she said. "I have felt something recently, some ripple in the fabric of things. I am not afraid to share with you my concern, as you have proven yourself honorable in past dealings."

Frederick considered. She could see it in his face. Here was one with whom respect and deference went a long way. Quite unlike Jean-Paul and his distasteful need for power and pain.

"There is a sword," he mused, twisting his teacup from side to side. "But it is as likely I felt the woman who held it as anything."

She let him gather his thoughts, gave him room to explore the situation.

"She was quite thrilling," he said finally. "There is power there—"

Qindra sat up straighter, alarmed at the implications suddenly.

Sawyer shook his head. "Individuals may exude power, untapped and never realized. I'm sure you have seen it yourself."

"But the covenant," Qindra said as a shudder ran through her. "If she is one of the fallen, one of those destined to return, you know what must be done."

Sawyer laughed again, only this time it was pleasant, almost jovial. "You would fear a fairy tale? You, the shining star of your kind?"

Ah, flattery. He was most adept. Qindra nodded thanks, allowing him to continue.

"I have tasted the blood of the last of them, witch— long before your mother's mother's mother slid, mewling, into this world. You and your mistress need not fear."

There had been rumors. Her mistress had never spoken plainly of it. Had one of the ancient ones been reborn within memory, one of the Æsir—those ancient gods who once ruled the seven worlds? Did he speak the truth? Had he actually discovered one and slain him or her?

"Who?" she asked. "Which of the Æsir have you slain? Do not brag, it is beneath you."

He tilted his head to the side, his nostrils flaring a bit as he remembered. "She was nearly insignificant, small near to nothingness."

"A child then?" she asked, her stomach twisting. "You slew a child?"

The shrug reminded her how little his kind thought of her and hers. They had ruled her kind since before the rumors of civilization. Their complacency would be their downfall.

"She was a beautiful baby," he carried on, lost in the memory. "Hair of the finest gold. Some say she would have rivaled the sun if she had grown to maturity."

Sif, then, Qindra thought. *Thor's bride.* How many others had been reborn in the centuries since the dragons had hunted them down, slain their thralls, broken their fabled rainbow bridge between Migard and the ancient lands of Asgard? Had any slipped through the dragons' nets? And could this new threat be another of the ancient blood? "So which is it? Sword or woman?"

Sawyer shrugged. "This young woman is full of life—angry and passionate. I could feel the fire in her, see it coursing through her veins like molten steel. But she is daughter of man, not Æsir."

"And this woman, with the fire of life? You think she is nothing to fear?"

"Fear? What an odd thought. Do we have any to fear among your people?" he asked. "You are the most powerful of your ilk, and I do not fear you."

She knew it was true. He had no fear in him, only bravado and something else, a hint of compassion she did not think his kind capable of.

"The sword then, an artifact of power?"

He sipped his tea in silence, breathing slowly.

She began to relax, took another sweet and sipped her own tea. Perhaps it was Nidhogg's age after all. She'd never known one of their kind as old.

"I think," he said finally, "if this were some relic from the ancient past, we would have felt it before. The sword was whole and then broken. She reforged it to be used in a movie. If it were a weapon for my kind to fear, I'm sure we would have known about it before this."

That seemed logical. How many ancient weapons had they discovered over the millennia—seven? Eight? Did any exist beyond the dragons' hoards?

"So it remains a mystery."

He shrugged a final time, setting his empty teacup down on the saucer, upside down. "Perhaps your mistress ate someone who disagreed with her."

Not even a little bit funny. Did he have a spy within her house?

"Besides," he continued, "if there is something amiss on Nidhogg's doorstep, I'd suggest she look north to the last of her wayward brood."

Qindra pressed her palms together and bowed slightly toward Frederick Sawyer, the last dragon to enter America from the Continent. Perhaps she'd have tea with Jean-Paul as well. She needed to get to the bottom of this. Her household had seen enough turmoil.

Thirty-three

MONDAY WAS A good day at the forge. Julie had spent Sunday with Rolph, apparently, deep in shop talk, and she was in a fine mood. He'd parked his truck at the Crankshaft Tavern across the street, so after sundown on Sunday, he'd beat feet for safer climes. She thought he was going to stay with one of the other goblins from the movie shoot.

Suited me just fine. One less thing to worry about. I had three orders for worked andirons and fireplace tools requested by the owner of the Circle Q. She wanted to replace those in her house, and loved, loved Julie, hence more work for me.

When I'm overloaded with stress I crave the forge—to swing the hammer, strike the steel, feel the heat. I let the conscious mind fade back to the training, the rote. Firing the steel to the correct color, striking the correct points, each took finesse and knowledge that came from doing, from working and reworking until you were exhausted. Like martial skills, blacksmithing could be taught only so far with books and lectures. Until you held the hammer and tongs, felt the hair on your arms curl and whither as you got too close to the heat, felt the agony of failing at a task. Then you could improve, work upward to better skill, better patience.

That's what it was all about. If you rushed it, if you looked for shortcuts, you failed. If not this hammer stroke, or this finish grinding, then when the tool was put into use, when the item was displayed, or utilized in its intended fashion, your mistakes would show, your flaws would appear to mar or ruin the piece.

So I worked—firing each piece, hammering at the right moment, learning to understand when things did not go my way, knowing I had a second chance, another opportunity.

It was hope and it was breath.

And when I opened myself to the possibilities, it was joy. I had missed joy of late.

Julie called lunch long before I was ready. The earth could have frozen in the heavens for all I knew. The work consumed everything, became the center of the world. Became a place of peace.

Lunch? How could it compare?

Of course, I reminded myself. Every tool needs to be tended, and that included myself.

I agreed to pick up teriyaki today, so Julie could arrange for a second inspection with Puget Gas and Electric. She wanted a new set of fittings on the propane tank. The old ones were cracking from weather and wear.

On a whim, I stopped at the florist and had a small vase of daisies sent over to Katie at school. Daisies were our favorites, one of many similarities. The card just said *Thinking of you*.

The spicy beef warred with the garlic pork to fill my car with an amazing hodgepodge of odors. Meat and rice were good fuel for the body. I also picked up diet soda for Julie, and orange juice for me.

There was a stretch Hummer in the lot when I got back. I parked in my spot and set the food on the roof of my car while I fished the drinks from the backseat. No cup holders in my car.

When I straightened, I noticed that Mr. Philips stood beside the Hummer. I flinched, but Mr. Philips didn't react.

He walked toward me, pulling the black leather gloves off his hands and holding one hand out for me to shake.

"Ms. Beauhall," he said in his crisp, polite voice. "How does this day serve you?"

I crossed my arms and leaned back against my car, scanning his face for any smirk or quirk. "You have some nerve coming here," I said. "You got Sawyer in that beast?" I pointed toward the Hummer with my chin.

"I'm afraid Mr. Sawyer is tied up in a business meeting most of the day. He asked me to stop by, proffer his apologies for the other night, and see if you'd made any decision on the very generous offer he had couriered to you on Friday."

"Busy. I see." I didn't trust Sawyer as far as I could spit, but my gut told me Mr. Philips was a straight arrow. He'd do Sawyer's bidding with every ounce of his quiet fortitude, but he was not a spiteful man. "I have not made up my mind," I said.

He didn't react at all.

"Mr. Sawyer felt you may not be quite ready to come to an agreement," he said without as much as a smile. "If you would like to make a counteroffer, I assure you he is open to negotiation."

"Yes, I'm familiar with his oratory skills, and his ability to bring pressure to bear. I just had no idea the lengths, and depths, to which your employer would stoop. If he is so interested in negotiating, why did he send those goons to run me off the road? Huh?" I stood up straight, leaning a bit into his personal space.

This brought a small flicker of doubt. "I assure you Mr. Sawyer would not stoop to such tactics," he said.

"Yeah. Well, he sure stooped pretty low when he sent the same goons out to beat on poor Rolph the other night."

He actually blinked, twice. "Mr. Brokkrson has been injured?"

"Nothing permanent," I assured him. "But enough to send a clear message of intimidation."

"Mr. Sawyer can be ruthless in business, I assure you," he said, regaining his calm exterior. "But he is neither a ruffian nor a fool."

"I know what he is," I said. This was my place of power, I realized. The smithy held power that I tapped just by being open to the possibility. "You can tell your boss, for me, that I'd rather see the sword shattered again than let him touch it."

"I see," Mr. Philips said, taking a small notepad from

his jacket pocket and jotting something down. "Are there any other options besides shattering? Melting down? Dropping into a live volcano, sinking at the bottom of the sea? Burying with a great hero, perhaps?"

I think I could like this guy; too bad he worked for the wrong team. "Cute," I said, turning to gather up our food. "I'm going back to work, Mr. Philips. Tell your boss that I may have considered the deal if he hadn't gotten impatient and roughed up Rolph."

Mr. Philips let his mouth harden before speaking. "I give you my word of honor that neither Mr. Sawyer, nor any of his associates, had anything to do with this."

I began to walk around the car, but paused and turned. "For the record, Mr. Philips, I honestly believe you believe that. But I have a friend who needed stitches and who is afraid to return to his home because of all this. Whether or not you believe Sawyer capable of this, tell me. Who else would be so desperate to get their hands on that sword?"

Mr. Philips nodded. "Who indeed?"

"I need to get back to work," I said, walking toward the smithy. "Have a good day, Mr. Philips."

Mr. Philips tilted his head, made an additional note, and turned on his heel. By the time I had the food sitting on Julie's desk, the Hummer had pulled out of the lot.

Thirty-four

I ARRIVED AT the set early. After last week's debacle, it would be good to be prompt. I pulled into the lot and noticed right away there were a few new cars, and a large panel van with EMERALD CITY CATERING emblazoned on the side. Dinner tonight at least.

I didn't see a Hummer, or any luxury vehicles to speak of, so I figured Sawyer was absent this evening. Good thing. I was in no mood for more *Let's Make a Deal*.

I dropped my shades on the dash and stepped out onto the gravel. Something was different. More money, better catering. And, was that a rent-a-cop? Carl was going all out.

I grabbed my case out of my car and strolled across the lot. My encounter with Mr. Philips earlier in the day had me feeling a little like I was under control of something. A little, anyways.

The guard was a young guy, pretty buff with a flattop haircut and an attitude that was a mixture of boredom and eagerness. If you've seen security guards, you know the type. He sat at a small table covered in clipboards. Each was color coded and held several pages. I smiled, tipped two fingers at him, and cut by him, to get to the door.

Only, I didn't quite make it.

"Excuse me, miss," he said, standing. I didn't slow down, and he darted in front of me, clipboard in hand. "Sorry, ma'am. Closed set."

"Closed?" I chuckled. "I've worked here for a year. Closest we've come to closed was when Carl left his keys at home."

He nodded at me and squared up, planting his feet shoulder width and holding the clipboard in front of him like a shield. "Regardless," he said, looking at my stern expression. "I'll need your name, and you have to sign in."

I rolled my eyes. "I'm the props manager. This is a waste of my time."

"Please, ma'am. Your name and an ID?"

"This is something Sawyer has cooked up, isn't it?"

"I wouldn't know, ma'am."

I fished for my wallet and dug my driver's license out for him to see.

"Beauhall, Sarah J.?"

"Yes," I said. "At least that's what my dear old da calls me."

He didn't so much as acknowledge the comment. "I'm afraid you're not on the list."

"What?"

"Hang on a second," he said, holding up one hand. "Don't move. I have two other lists."

Probably on the management and production staff list, I figured, so I stood there and counted to ten—backward—really, really slowly.

"Nothing on the vendor list," he said, setting down a clipboard. He didn't look too happy. He picked up the last clipboard and there was a bit of red yarn tied around the clip. Red was never good.

"Ah, yes," he said, placing his hand on the nightstick looped at his belt and stepping back toward the door. "I'm afraid you are on the banned list, Ms. Beauhall."

"Banned?" I asked. This was not happening. Christ, I'd worked here longer than most of the folks on Carl's roster. Maybe Jennifer and a couple of the camera guys, but I was in the top ten, easily.

"There's some mistake," I said. "You have the clipboards mixed up. I'm the props manager."

He glanced down at the first clipboard and watched me out of the corner of his eye. "Says here that Eastside Novelty and Props is handling that job. They have not assigned a manager for this position yet."

Now I was getting pissed. "Of course they haven't, you little pisher. I'm the props manager." My left calf began to throb and I felt the rising urge to smack something. I stepped back, trying to control my breathing, but it just didn't work. One second he was pulling out a walkie-talkie and babbling about calling the local police, and the next I'd kicked over his table, shoved him against the wall, and was screaming obscenities. People came around the building from the loading dock and the smoking area.

I saw JJ with his whores, laughing, and Jennifer darted back around the corner in a panic.

As I was considering wind velocity and trajectory as to Mr. Uniform and his likely landing point if I threw him from the doorway, Carl came through the door yelling.

"Jesus Christ on a crutch, Beauhall. Have you lost your ever-loving mind?"

I spun toward him, anger flaring.

He stepped back, flinging his hands in front of his face. "Back off, damn it."

The effort to keep control was enormous. I wanted to fight, wanted to push him through the wall. This little shuddering man was keeping me from . . .

Carl?

Holy mother.

I took two more stumbling steps backward, feeling the adrenaline crashing through my system. My hands hurt from clenching them into fists. I turned, looking for the sword, and saw the case lying in a shrub several feet from the door. It had not come open, but I could tell it had bounced a time or two.

"Hey, Carl. Sorry, man." I held up both hands, palms outward. I knew that was weak by the fear in his eyes, and the way yon guard had pulled out his nightstick and was chattering into the walkie-talkie.

"Sarah!" Jennifer screamed, running through the door. She stopped, assayed the scene, and grabbed Carl by the arms. "Are you okay?" she asked him.

"I'm fine," he said, the fear leaving his eyes. "Sarah has lost her mind, but no one has been hurt."

"Local police are en route," Guard Boy said.

I slumped down to the ground, sitting flat on my backside. "You banned me?"

Jennifer looked from Carl to me, then came over and

squatted down beside me. "We're really sorry," she said. I could tell she was sincere.

"Sawyer hired an outfit to come in and evaluate our setup, see about upgrading our gear." Carl looked at me, his chin out, but doubt in his eyes. "Seemed like a good idea."

"And banning me?" I asked. "That a good idea, too?"

No one said anything.

Jennifer patted me on the shoulder and stood. She held a hand out to me, waiting. "I'm sorry," she said.

I took her hand and stood.

Carl picked up the sword case and handed it to me. "Me too," he said. "But you have been a bit out of control lately."

He and Jennifer exchanged a look. Her eyes softened and she shrugged.

Carl smiled a bit and turned. "Why don't we call it a vacation," he said. "Take a couple weeks, get some rest."

"Yeah," Jennifer said, stepping up to Carl and placing her hand on his arm.

Things were moving fast. I smiled at her and she only blinked.

"I can't afford a vacation," I said. "You already took the supplies out of my last check."

"Yeah, we'll fix that," Jennifer said. "Right, Carl?"

"Sure, sure," Carl said, nodding. "We'll send over a check."

I hugged the sword case to my chest, trying to breathe. I needed that money to cover my rent. Things were tight enough as it is.

"This is about Sawyer, isn't it?"

No one spoke.

"You know he tried to buy the sword?" I asked. "Offered me his stake in Flight Test plus a bonus?"

Carl looked at Jennifer, questioningly. "Really?"

"News to me," she said, looking my way. "For the sword?"

"Yes."

"Are you going to sell?" Jennifer asked.

"No. Not a chance."

Carl's jaw dropped. "Why not? Hell, I'd much rather deal with your mood swings than . . ." He turned away from the guard and lowered his voice. "Sawyer creeps me out."

"He's an odd man, that's for sure," Jennifer added.

"And he loves JJ," Carl added. "He's been pumping him up all weekend, telling him he can do better, telling him he should go off to Hollywood."

"Good riddance to bad rubbish," I said. "JJ's a prima donna who needs an ass kicking as much as anything."

Jennifer laughed a bit at that. I liked her laugh.

By the way Carl looked at her, he liked her laugh, too. Nice to see them maybe getting together. They made a good couple. Hell, the way they ran the movie set they were just like everyone's parents.

"Two weeks?" I asked, battling back tears. "You sure, Carl?"

He hung his head then. "I'm sorry."

"I'll talk to Sawyer," Jennifer said. "But you'd better go before the police arrive. Wouldn't want this getting totally out of hand."

"And if I leave, you all save face, right?" I asked. This was pissing me off again. "I thought we were friends."

A police cruiser pulled into the lot, parked by the walkway up to the entrance, and a young officer stepped out. She was cute, and totally hot in her uniform, but I think bored best described her. Something about the way she looked snagged in my mind, something about passion and control.

I shook my head and glanced away. What the hell was

wrong with me? It was like I was losing control of my emotions.

Jennifer walked out to talk to her, hurrying to get ahead of the security guard.

"Hey, Sarah," Carl asked, stepping to my side. "You seen Rolph?"

My alarms began to vibrate. "No, why?" I asked.

"Oh, nothing big. He's not here yet, and he's always early," he said, rather lamely. "And we tried to find him this weekend to no avail."

How far had Carl slid here? I gotta tell you I was beginning to have my doubts. Money can be a great enticer, and blind even the most honorable man to acts of desperation and deception.

"Sorry, Carl. Haven't seen him."

"Okay, just asking." He stuck his hands in his pockets and glanced over at the police officer. She was listening to Jennifer and the security guard tell their tales and her boredom was not getting any better.

"About the sword," Carl said so nonchalantly as to be painful. "Any chance we can borrow it for the rest of the shoot?"

I laughed then, out loud, more bark than mirth. "You fire me, give me over for a handful of shekels, and then you ask to use my sword?"

"Just for this flick," he said, "if we have to reshoot any scenes." He shrugged. "You know the drill."

I took a step away from him, assessing the way he stood, and the look on his face. "Sawyer tell you to ask?" I didn't wait for an answer, just turned and began walking to my car.

"Beauhall, wait," he called to my retreating back. "We could rent it. I know you need the money."

That was the last blow. I showed Carl the better half of a peace sign and climbed into my car.

As I backed out, I saw Homeless Joe over by the Dumpster holding a catering tray with lunch meat and cheese. He watched me, training his one good eye on my progress, munching something as I passed. He mouthed a word, crushed cheese falling from his lips.

The word was "dragon."

Thirty-five

I THINK I was numb. When I saw the signs for this cowboy bar where Julie went dancing, I pulled in and parked. The sound of the engine cooling, the pinging of metal, sang a song to me—a song of sadness.

It was early, about seven forty-five, so the lot was half full. When I bellied up to the bar and began a tab of tequila shooters, the bartender didn't ask, just dropped a bowl of limes and a shaker of salt beside me. The first three went down rough, like swallowing fire. After that, things began to blur a little.

The fifth shot finally broke through the barrier. I got up from the bar and moved to the dance floor. No one was dancing, but I needed to move. There was something inside me, something that needed to spin and twirl, thrust and jab. I needed a battle, something to vent my anger, some outlet for my rage.

Only there were no battles, so I danced, let the redneck, boot-stomping twang roll over me, ride along my nerves and direct my body into a frenzy of motion. I wanted to be out of control.

I never liked how I danced, but at that moment I was grooving. Then, when the sweat ran down my back, and the fire ran through my belly, I blinked and shifted. It may have been the alcohol, but one minute I was gyrating on the dance floor to the wolf whistles of a couple of cowboys, and the next I was sitting at the bar, one hand on the bottle, the other on my calf. Only I was still on the dance floor. If not for the stereo vision, I'd have chalked it up to being so drunk, but I was as lucid as I'd ever been. Something was happening here that I didn't understand. I didn't have long to think about it, though. Events got out of control too quickly.

One of the cowboys got up to dance with me and I swung into it with abandon. Soon a second was on the floor, and things got crazy. If I could've figured how I was sitting at the bar, watching myself being pawed by those two cowboys, I would've stopped it.

As it was, I recognized them. They were the hands from the Circle Q. The dancing got dirtier, and their hands were touching me in ways that both excited and mortified me. Apparently I was enjoying myself with them enough that when the bartender came out and asked us to leave, I went with them willingly.

This out-of-body experience was a bit too trippy for me, and since I was leaving with the guys, I thought I'd better try and follow.

When you don't have a body, or are no longer connected with it, you forget how important gravity, and physics in general, are in helping with movement. I sort of hovered there a bit, in a way that made me think of astronauts, and I panicked. Luckily, when I lost sight of myself, it triggered a survival instinct that propelled me out of the bar, through the wall, and across the parking lot.

What I saw there was worse than on the dance floor.

If I could have died of shame at that moment, I would have. I think my spirit form, or astral projection, or whatever the hell I was at this moment, was significantly more sober than my physical self. As I watched, horrified, I shimmied out of my jeans, wadded them up, and tossed them into the back of the pickup truck we all stood behind. Then I was back at it, making out with first one guy, then the next. Dancing in my Skivvies and my T-shirt.

"She's a real firecracker," Steve Wilding said.

Jack Marlowe didn't say anything, just pulled my shirt over my head, undid my bra, and whooped like he was at a rodeo.

Why I didn't stop them, I just can't figure. I was mad at Katie, and Carl, and damn near the whole world. I was also very, very drunk.

But I didn't want to have sex with these men. It had nothing to do with sex, or love. It was about power, and powerlessness.

So, I let them feel me up. Felt their hands and mouths on my body in ways that hadn't happened with anyone but Katie. I watched, horrified at the expression on my face, and if I could have cried, I would have.

"We gonna take her back to our place to party for real," Steve said, raising his head from my left breast.

Marlowe laughed from the foot of the truck. "You know who this is, don'tcha, Wilding?"

Steve looked closer, but didn't recognize me in my mostly naked and drunken state.

"It's that dyke that works for Julie."

Steve shook his head.

"The blacksmith," Jack said, standing beside Steve and trailing his hand where Steve's mouth had just been. "We could take her back and do her a few times, see if we can break her from munching carpet."

Stop it! I screamed in my head. *Don't do this, make this end*.

"She's pretty drunk," Steve said. He leaned me against the truck and looked into my face.

"Her eyes don't look so good, Jack. Maybe we should . . ."

He didn't finish that statement because two things happened. I snapped back into my body, felt the world crash into pain and humiliation.

And I hit him.

He was off balance and not expecting it, but when my fist connected to the side of his head, I stepped into him, punching him over and over, face, chest, arms, anything I could reach. The final cross took his feet out from under him and he landed with a thud.

Jack hollered something I didn't make out and lunged at me. I felt the bile rise in my throat as I realized everything that had occurred had been condoned by me on some cellular level, and I lost it. Felt the anger and the hatred swell up in me, burning the alcohol, filling me with a rage I'd been nursing and walling off for days now.

I stepped forward, blocking Jack's first feeble punch. Those years of martial arts I'd studied as a kid came to me and I followed his awkward stutter step and hit him with a haymaker that rattled my teeth. He got one arm up and absorbed part of the blow, but I dazed him.

I caught him in the breadbasket with my left, and he went down to his knees.

My roundhouse kick caught him in the chest and all the air rushed out of his lungs.

He flopped back, gasping for air. I was just about to stomp my heel into his throat when Steve tackled me from behind.

We both went down on the gravel, but I was on the bottom. Rocks, beer caps, and assorted broken bottles broke my fall. He rolled off me, climbed to his feet, and staggered over to help Jack up.

I rolled over, ready to defend myself, but the cowards ran.

They climbed into Jack's pickup and tore out of the parking lot, showering me with gravel. The fire that burned inside drove me to try and stand, but the flame guttered and thankfully I blacked out.

Thirty-six

THE NEXT VOICES I heard were deep, very deep, and sounded like rocks grinding against one another. I cracked open one eye, and saw a huge man with hands like catcher mitts, leaning over me. I moved my arm to cover my breasts, but found that he'd already covered me with a jacket.

"Hang on there, little miss," he said. His voice was not unkind.

"Eh, Ernie. She alive?"

"Aye, Bert," he called over his shoulder. "She's awake."

"Good," Bert called back. "See if you can bring her this way. The boss would like a word with her."

"Can you stand?" the first man asked.

"We'll see," I said, attempting to sit up. I could feel blood encrusted over several parts of me, and I hurt all over.

He stood back while I stood, but put a steadying hand on my shoulder when I swayed. "I found this shirt," he said, holding out my top. "And these boots, but I can't find any pants."

I pulled the shirt over my head, no bra for me. Then I stepped into the boots. "Mind if I keep this?" I asked, gesturing to the jacket.

"Be my guest," he said.

I wrapped the jacket around my waist and followed him across the lot.

As we neared the limousine I thought the world might just tilt right off its axis, so I staggered over to my car and leaned against the hood. "Sorry guys. This is as far as I can go."

Bert leaned down to the window of the limo and spoke with whomever was inside.

Ernie stood beside me and made sure I didn't fall down again.

"The boss wants to know where the sword is."

I didn't flinch, even though I knew it was inside my car. Hell, I could see the case through the hatchback, if I looked. "Go to hell," I said, my voice weak in my own ears.

"Be polite," Ernie said, sternly.

Bert cocked his head at the limo and nodded.

"He says you have twenty-four hours to come up with the sword, or things will get ugly."

"Yes, bad," I said with a nod. "You have no idea how ugly my life is right now."

"I guarantee it can be worse," Ernie said.

"Yeah?" I asked.

"You got guts," Ernie said, stepping away from me. "But the boss don't play. You've got twenty-four hours."

I pushed myself to standing. "Tell your boss, the coward, that if he can't drag his sorry ass out of the car to ask me himself, he can take his offer and shove it where the sun don't shine . . . then rotate."

Ernie looked over at Bert, who just shrugged.

"I'll tell him myself," I said, stepping toward the limo. "Sawyer, you coward. Sending thugs to do your dirty work?"

Ernie looked at Bert again, confused.

"Tell you what, Frederick. You can just kiss my lily-white ass."

Bert chuckled and shrugged. Ernie stepped around me and opened the front door of the limo. "Even Frederick Sawyer may be disinclined to take that invitation," he said. "Twenty-four hours. We'll be in touch."

I tried to push past him, to get to the rear door of the

limo, but he blocked me. "Come out of there, you coward," I yelled, struggling to get past the huge man.

"Step back," Ernie said, pushing me.

I stumbled then tried to go around him again. He backhanded me. As I spun away from him, falling awkwardly, I was glad he hadn't closed his fist. The world spun and I felt the crunch of gravel against my back again.

My body gave out then, succumbed to the abuse, and faded.

Then the sirens came from the distance, and folks were streaming out of the bar. Better late than never.

Thirty-seven

MELANIE RUSHED TO the next room, anxious and dreading the new patient. All she knew was they had a female drunk who fought the EMTs and, given the lack of pants, had most likely been raped. Another wild one to round out her perfect shift.

Only, when she pushed through the curtain to help the two nurses, who were obviously struggling, she saw it was Sarah.

"Jesus, Sarah," she said, stepping up to grab a flailing leg.

"She's out of control," Nurse Alana said.

"If we can hold her legs, I can get this strap over her," Nurse Carol said.

Melanie did the only thing she could do. She lay over Sarah's legs, pinning them to the bed and allowing Carol an opportunity to get the strap over her left arm. Then it became a battle of attrition, one limb at a time.

Once Sarah was tied down, Melanie got an IV in her and got her sedated.

"Her blood pressure is out of control," Alana said. "Heart rate is one ninety and not slowing."

"Get a blood draw. Let's see what she's on."

"My vote's PCP," Carol said, walking past the curtain. The nurses did their job with efficiency. Melanie examined her. While there was no evidence of intercourse, there were bites and bruises on her that told her Sarah had been in a very bad situation.

Elevated alcohol numbers and an exceedingly high testosterone level surprised her. This was not like Sarah.

Sarah's heart rate was not slowing, but at least they got her sedated enough to prevent injury. Melanie had never seen anything like it. Her breathing was deep and quick, like a marathon runner. Totally weird for someone asleep. Melanie stepped out to call Katie.

It was three in the morning by this point, and Katie answered just as Melanie was about to hang up.

"It's Sarah," she said. "We have her in the ER. She's been assaulted. Lots of cuts and bruises, but nothing too damaging."

"I'll be right there," Katie said. The shock was obvious in her voice.

Melanie tended to the other patients that came in, but checked in on Sarah often. When Katie arrived, she let her in as family.

"Nothing permanent," Melanie assured her, but she wasn't sure Katie heard her. "We just can't account for the elevated heart rate and the breathing."

"Sounds like she's fighting," Katie said, watching her tied to the bed. "She's breathing like she does when she's sparring."

Katie sat by Sarah's bed and held her hand while Melanie finished her shift. Sarah didn't wake up, but after another hour, her body began to slow.

Thirty-eight

I CAUGHT THE sounds of a heart monitor and the smell suddenly made perfect sense. I opened my eyes, saw the industrial beige of the walls around me, and turned my head slowly. No giants. No cowboys, no battles, and definitely no dragons.

An IV stand hove into view, then I noticed Katie nodding asleep in a black plastic chair. Damn.

The events of the night came crashing back. The out-of-body experience didn't allow for a nice hazy memory. Everything was crystal clear. I turned away from Katie and vomited.

Which woke her up, caused her to scream for the nurses and make a general fuss. The nurse on duty came in and made sure I wasn't going to drown in my own sick. An orderly sauntered in and added the special odor of stale mop to an already odiferous situation.

"Oh God, Sarah," Katie said, holding on to my hand and pressing her forehead to my shoulder. "Jesus."

"You left out the Holy Spirit," I offered.

She raised her head and stared at me. Her eyes were puffy from lack of sleep. "Not funny, Beauhall," she said.

"Yeah, I guess not."

We just sat there and absorbed each other's company. Actually, I lay there, and she stood, but you get the meaning. Neither of us said anything else, and when the orderly left with his magic mop, I let my shoulders relax. I was on edge, ready to fight or fly. Katie could feel it, I guess, because she held on to me with both hands.

After a few minutes, Melanie came in with a police officer.

"Sarah," she said, glancing at Katie, who stepped back to the wall. "This is Officer Simpson. I explained that you were sexually assaulted, but that you fought back. She's here to take a statement."

Katie squeezed my hand tighter. I couldn't look at her, so instead I looked at Melanie. Melanie who I measured myself against, who had never said a cross word to me, and who loved Katie unconditionally.

I don't think I could have hated her any more if I tried. I'd be damned if I'd let her see me helpless and weak. "I wasn't assaulted."

"What?" Katie and Melanie said at the same time.

"I saw the trauma," Melanie said. "The cuts and bruises are obviously from a struggle."

I stuck the arm without the IV behind my head and looked at the officer. "I was very drunk."

She began jotting down notes.

"I was dancing and being all wild when these two guys came onto the dance floor . . ."

And so it went. I gave them every detail. From the dirty dancing to the parking-lot teenage groping. I explained how it got rough, and how it had ended.

But I didn't mention the sword, or Frederick. And I definitely did not mention the astral projection. Drunk is one thing, certifiably crazy is another.

Katie, bless her, stayed through the whole thing. She listened to every word that I said, and then left. She didn't look at me, didn't say anything to Melanie, just picked up her sweater and walked through the curtain.

The officer turned to Melanie and closed her notebook. "Sorry, Doctor. Doesn't sound like assault to me." Her face was pinched. "Just sounds like a night of drunken stupidity coupled with a need to hurt someone who cared for her."

Melanie stood with her mouth open, uncomprehending.

Officer Simpson exhaled loudly. "What a waste. I'm out of here." She turned to leave and stopped, turning back. "Oh, and I'd get some counseling," she said. She looked at me for a moment, anger and disgust on her face, before turning and pushing through the emergency room curtain.

"Sarah," Melanie said, barely at a whisper. "Why?"

I realized the nurses had heard, as had anyone else within hearing.

I didn't hate Melanie, I realized. I hated myself.

"Can I get out of here?" I asked.

Melanie looked at me, checked my charts, the monitors, and my blood pressure. "Yes," she said. Her voice was very neutral but I could see the strain on her face. "Why don't you let me get you a pair of scrubs."

"Thanks."

When she left, I sat up and swung my feet over the side of the bed. I was in a hospital gown and had several wires taped to my body. I could remove those, but I was not comfortable pulling the IV.

Of course, Melanie had thought of that. A nurse, Stephanie, came in, tsked at me until I lay back down, then removed the IV, turned off the monitors, and removed all the stickies.

By that point, Melanie had returned. She handed me a set of scrubs, tops and bottoms, and a plastic bag with my shirt and the oversized jacket I'd been wrapped in when they found me. Oh, and my boots. I loved those boots, damn it.

She stepped out of the curtain and let me get dressed.

When I opened the curtain, she was standing there with a clipboard. I signed several pages and she handed it to the discharge nurse. "Come on," she said, turning and walking toward the exit sign.

"What?" I asked, hobbling after her. "Where are we going?"

"I assume to get your car, and possibly your pants," she said, not looking back.

"You can just leave?" I got my feet planted firmly in the boots and rushed to catch up to her.

"I was off shift three hours ago," she said. "I just stayed because I thought Katie meant something to you."

That didn't hurt, nope. Not one bit. I followed her in silence. I was one huge walking lump of pain, and the scrubs rubbed against several cuts in a bad way, but I was not going to make a peep.

Thirty-nine

SHE TOOK ME to the bar. My car was there, but I didn't have a spare set of keys. I'd have to get the other set from my locker at the smithy. I could see the sword case was where I left it and felt a bit of relief.

The lot looked very different with the rising of the sun. No mystery shadows, just gravel and refuse. Pretty place for a girl to give it up.

We walked through the field beside the lot looking for my pants, and then around the bar itself just to be sure. They wouldn't be open again until much later, so I couldn't check inside.

"I can take you somewhere," Melanie said, standing next to the car.

"Thanks," I said, staring at my feet. "I guess you can take me to the smithy. I need to get my spare keys and such."

She nodded and climbed into her car. I crossed the lot toward her, scuffing my boots and feeling thoroughly miserable.

As we pulled out, my stomach rumbled and Melanie

glanced over at me. "Geez, Sarah. When did you eat last?"

I had to think. Dinner? No . . . "Lunch yesterday."

She drove on in silence for a moment. "I've been on all night, I'd kill for some coffee."

This was new.

"Want to grab some breakfast? Maybe talk about what's going on?"

Most any other time I'd have laughed it off, told her no, and resented her asking. But at that moment, when Katie had heard me at my ugliest, and the world had stopped making any kind of sense, I decided to throw caution to the wind.

As the man said: *I've tried nothing, and I'm all out of ideas.*

"Sure," I said, letting my head fall back against the headrest. "That sounds nice."

We pulled into this little dive Melanie knew about. "Lots of doctors and such come here," she said. "They keep the coffee full, and don't hassle you if you stick around a while."

"Sounds good," I said, sliding into a booth and grabbing a menu from behind the catsup.

"They make good omelettes."

Then I remembered—no money. "Damn, Melanie. I don't have my wallet or anything."

She just shook her head and rolled her eyes. "I know. I'll buy. Then, you'll feel obligated to talk."

I laughed at that and smiled up at the waitress, who set two glasses of water in front of us.

"I'll have a coffee IV," Melanie said.

"Orange juice," I said.

The waitress turned to get the drinks, and Melanie called out, "Oh, and a pitcher of water, please."

She just waved at us over her head and walked on.

"She know you?" I asked.

"Janie?" she said, shrugging. "She knows I work over at the hospital and have fairly rough nights from time to time. She can usually tell if they are too bad."

I drank my glass of water and crunched the ice as I set the glass down.

The juice arrived and I drank half of it in one long swallow. We ordered eggs and hash browns. She added bacon and I chose ham.

I hoped the food would give me some strength back.

"So, tell me," she said, adding sugar to her coffee. "Anything you'd like to get off your chest?"

I shrugged. "Lot been going on," I told her. I toyed with my juice glass, turning it from side to side and sliding it between each hand on the film of moisture that had built up under it. "Lost my job last night."

"The smithy?"

"No, Julie's cool. This was the movie thing."

"Ah," she said, picking up her cup. "Katie's told me about that."

"It's not just playing, if that's what you think," I said.

She blew on her coffee and watched me. I felt a frown slide over my face and my shoulders began to ache.

"Sarah," she said, taking a sip and closing her eyes for a moment, "I have no idea why you'd get yourself into the position you did last night—"

"No kidding."

"—but I do know that it's self-destructive."

I only nodded. That was a no-brainer.

"And if you want to fuck up your life," she said, putting her coffee down ever so carefully, "I can't stop you. But if you continue to hurt Katie, I may just have to kick your ass."

The anger in her voice appeared out of nowhere. I felt

an answering call rise in my chest and she reached out and took my hand.

"She loves you, you idiot. And I can see why . . ." She paused. "Most times."

The anger that had begun to uncoil in my chest evaporated like a mist.

"I'm not a threat to you, Sarah. No matter what Katie and I had in the past, we are just friends."

"I know," I lied.

"Uh-huh." She took her hand off mine and picked up her coffee again. "So, care to explain what is causing all the turmoil?"

So I did. If she loved Katie, which I was sure she did, in that way you love old friends, then she knew of Katie's crazy notions, her fantasies of elves and dwarves, her musical jaunts and her ren faire excursions.

So I told her about the sword, and the dwarf, the movie, and the dragon.

Funny thing was, as I told her the tightness in my chest began to ease. She was a good listener. Didn't judge, just nodded and asked leading questions when I lost my way. I could see why Katie thought so highly of her.

When our food arrived, I ate like a wolf, while she told me about the first time she'd ever heard Katie sing.

Then I talked some more while she ate. Told her about meeting Katie at the ren faire. About the last time we'd made love, the shower, and the fracas afterward.

"You realize," she said, spreading apple butter on a last piece of toast, "you are horrified that folks will think you're a freak."

I didn't need to answer that, she could see the truth on my face.

"Sarah," she said. "Who you love is up to you. Straight or gay, it's no one's business. I just wish you could accept it."

"I know what I am," I said, and stopped as she looked at me with horror.

"What you are? What kind of talk is that?"

The blush rose over my face like a tide. "You know what I mean."

"Yes, I do. I know exactly what you mean. It's what your father says, what your preacher says. Katie's told me about your folks, about their attitudes toward women. And anyone else who doesn't fit into their version of reality."

I was too damn tired to be mad anymore. I wanted to crawl into a ball and block it all out. It was just so hard.

Her hand covered mine again.

"Do you think Katie is evil? Do you think her a fool?"

"Of course not," I said. "She's sweet and caring."

"Yes, she is. So, if she can be wonderful and light, and if you can love her . . ."

I didn't protest that. I couldn't.

"If you can understand her and her lifestyle, if you can accept it in her, why can't you accept it in yourself?"

And that, ladies and gentlemen, is how you win an argument.

Of course I couldn't accept one without the other.

"I can see the need in you, Sarah. I know the pain and the confusion. We've all been through it in one form or another. You want something so badly it overshadows everything in your life, and yet you think it's horribly wrong. And sometimes it feels so wrong that you are willing to totally destroy yourself because of it."

What could I say? Funny thing was, on some level I felt that this wasn't just about sexual orientation. Everyone had their demons they wrestled with. I just let my battles get public. Loss of control, inability to trust myself—and by extension anyone else. Old story, million of them just like it out there.

So I switched the subject. She knew it and let it go.

We talked about Frederick and the sword, about his erratic behavior and the thugs and the check.

"Doesn't make much sense to offer all that, and then send goons after you and your friends," she said. "Is Katie in any danger?"

"Surely not," I said. "It's a sword, not a nuke."

We finished and Melanie took me by the shop to get my keys. I grabbed the spare to the shop from where Julie kept it inside a hanging flower pot on her porch. I was careful to be quiet, not to knock things around and wake her.

I left a note about a hospital visit and apologized for missing work. I tucked the note and her keys under her keyboard. She'd find them there for sure.

Melanie took me back over to the bar to pick up my car.

Seeing my trusty hatchback, with my sword in the back, I felt relieved and horrified by the last few days.

But I'd made some headway with Melanie. Mended a bridge or two on that front.

We'd talked a long damn time, and I felt fairly good about it.

As I walked across the lot, Melanie pulled around and stopped. "Give her some time," she said through her open window. "She's pretty freaked out by all this."

"Yeah, I guess."

"Give her a chance here, okay?" she asked.

I waved. "I'll give her a day or so."

She yawned then, and waved at me. I watched her pull away, thinking I really should just go home and sleep.

Forty

JULIE WAS PISSED. It wasn't like Sarah to just no-show. They had a big job out at the Smithfield Farm, and it would take her most of the day to handle it alone. But, she'd swing by and see Jack on the way home. That would be nice.

The horses were ornery, and the owner was annoyed at the time it took, but Julie finished all the shoeing and some hoof doctoring with her usual skill. Old man Smithfield grumbled a bit, but in the end was happy with the work.

But Sarah would get a talking to, that was a fact.

Julie washed up and packed her supplies back in the truck while Smithfield wrote out the check for her services. *And no apprentice to pay today*, she thought. *Maybe I'll just take Mr. Marlowe out for a nice dinner. Make it up to him for the other night when Rolph showed up unexpectedly.*

Not that he was a bother, either. Julie liked the strange man. He loved smithing and knew a ton about things that Julie had only read about.

They'd shared a few meals and exchanged some ideas for improving certain techniques. Julie found it refreshing to be learning from someone again. She missed her own apprentice days sometimes.

When she arrived at the Circle Q, she spotted Jack's pickup right away. She checked her watch, nearly six. He'd get off soon.

He straightened up from a tractor and smiled at her as she got out of her truck, wiping his hands on a rag and placing a wrench in his back pocket.

"Tractor acting up on you?" she asked, seeing what he'd been working on.

"Nah, nothing serious. Just changing out the spark plugs."

She sauntered up to him, pushed his hat back, and kissed him.

He flinched back a bit, which surprised her, and she saw he had a split lip.

"Oh, baby. What happened to you?" she asked, stroking the side of his face, noticing the long bruise running along his jawline.

He grimaced and took her hand. "Had a tussle last night. Things got out of hand over at the Triple Nickel."

She laughed then, backing up and looking at him from head to toe. "You and your sidekick get in a fight?"

He shrugged. "Nothing we couldn't handle."

There were several marks on him, she noticed. A bruise on his forearm, and maybe on the scruff of his neck. His hands had several small cuts and his left hand was swollen, knuckles bruised. She thought maybe she'd take him back to her place and see about playing a little nurse. The thought sent a shiver through her. Definitely a good idea.

He kissed her on the ear, and let his hand glide down her back in that way he had. Such big hands.

And his cell phone rang. The tinny strains of "Super Freak," the version with the banjo, echoed from his back pocket. He pulled out the phone, saw who called, and shrugged. "Boss calling," he said, and flipped open the phone. "I'll only be a few minutes."

She patted him on the ass as he turned and walked back to the tractor, talking about hay and mowing. He glanced back at her, winked, and limped around the side of the tractor.

Helluva fight, she thought. *Hope they didn't hurt someone.*

While he talked, she walked past his truck, trailing her hands along the side, and then hopped up on the tailgate to sit and wait for him. The call took a while, and she was just wondering how a man could have so much crap piled in his truck when she saw something that caught her breath. A bra poked out from beneath an old feed bag. She climbed into the truck and pulled the bags away. There was not only a bra—with a bigger cup than she had, she noticed, wounded—but there was also a pair of pants.

Son of a bitch, she thought, picking up the jeans. The design that was sewn down the left leg looked very familiar. She held her breath and felt for the pockets. In the back right pocket, she pulled out a wallet.

Now her heart was thumping in her chest. This was not happening. Not now, not this guy.

She opened the wallet and dropped it with a cry of anguish. There on the bed of his truck lay a picture of Sarah Jane Beauhall's smiling face. It was her driver's license.

Julie slowly put the wallet back into the pants and rolled them up, wrapping the bra inside the roll. Then she climbed out of the truck and stomped over to the tractor, and the lying sack of shit.

"How could you?" she said, hitting him with the rolled-up jeans. "Is that where you got those marks?" she asked, her voice rising to a shout.

Jack turned around, startled, and quickly hung up the phone, while holding an arm up to protect his head.

"Is that a hickey on your neck, you lying bastard?"

"Calm down, Julie. Let me explain."

That's all it took. If he could explain, then she was done.

"What, am I too old for you? Huh?" She was full-on crying now and hated herself for it. "You fuck her in your truck and can't even return her pants. Where is she?" The moment turned black and she took a step back from the rather tall man, seeing him as a threat for the first time. "What did you do to her?"

"Her," he said, his own voice rising. "The little whore about killed me and Steve!"

Julie turned. "If you've hurt her," she choked back a sob, "I'll kill you. Where is she?"

"We left her at the bar," he said, pulling his shoulder back. "She wasn't fighting it until the end, just so you know."

"Stop it," Julie said, her vision sparkling with tears.

"You want to get into it, then fine," he said, stomping past her. "She wanted it. Wanted it bad. But all of a sudden she went psycho—" He spun around, waving his hands in the air. "—began punching and kicking. We didn't sign up for that craziness so we left her. You happy?"

Julie shook her head, crushed the jeans to her chest with both hands, and ran for her truck.

He didn't move, just stood and watched her as she drove away.

Forty-one

I WAS SWEEPING the floor of the smithy when I heard Julie coming across the lot from her place. I'd gotten in pretty early for me, hoping to make up some time for missing the day before.

I was in a whole world of hurt and probably needed to stretch to loosen up, but for now the pain was a steady reminder of my stupidity.

I'd had a hard time sleeping, as you might expect, and made sure I got the sword back in the safe this morning.

Watching it disappear as I closed the door, hearing the locks synch home, gave me a bit of peace.

We had several orders to get out, and a day of shoeing ahead of us. Would be nice to do some work, feel useful again.

Julie opened the door, and stopped. I didn't turn immediately, as I was digging some dust out from under a worktable. When she didn't say anything, and didn't move, I turned. "Hey, Julie," I said. "Sorry about yesterday, I would've called, but . . ."

She threw a roll of cloth at me. "Here's your pants," she growled, her voice tight with anger.

I didn't even try to catch them. They bounced off my chest and landed at my feet. "Julie, where'd you find . . ." And I realized where.

"Left your pants in his truck," she said, seeing my face. "No idea how you got home without them, but by the look of you, it was a rough night."

"You have no idea," I said, sagging against the broom. "Look, I'm sorry."

She held her hands in front of her, palms out, and opened and closed them into fists. "You have a lot of problems, Sarah. I've tried to be there for you, but you've crossed a line."

I looked up at her, tears filling my eyes.

"What I can't figure is your angle. I know you were struggling with Katie and all," she said, walking into the shop. There were tears in her eyes, and more anger than I'd seen outside my own mirror in a while. "You lament your fate and all that horseshit, then you go out and try and bang the one guy I'd found to like? The one guy who didn't assume I was a dyke because I'm a blacksmith, or work with horses. You have to ruin that for me? For what, Sarah?" She'd crossed into yelling. I'd never seen her so angry before. "Is this a game to you? You move on from Katie to a couple of guys you pick up at a bar? What's that do for your reputation, huh?"

I couldn't breathe. She just kept yelling and pacing. She was a strong woman with many more years swinging a hammer than I. And she looked like she'd like nothing more than to punch me right in the face.

I didn't screw them, but did it matter? Was that line really important at this point? "I don't know," I said, honestly.

"Word of this gets around the horse community, I'll be out of business, you think of that?"

Of course, I hadn't been thinking at all. "I'm sorry."

She looked at me, disgust and pain battling across her features. "Damn it, Sarah. I liked you."

And the fat lady began singing. I felt that I might just slip out of my body again, like I'd done at the bar. The pain and anguish were so sharp, so visceral, that I felt I could float out of my body and leave the hurt for just a moment.

Instead I bowed my head and sobbed. "I'm so . . . so . . . sorry." And as I said it, I knew it didn't matter.

"Get out," she said, her voice frigid.

I couldn't look at her, I just laid the broom on the workbench, knelt to pick up my pants, and shuffled around the anvil, touching it with the side of my hand as I passed. "Sorry . . . sorry . . . sorry . . ." I kept repeating, thinking that this was not happening. This was the one safe place, the one true place.

As I reached the door, my hand on the knob, she called out to me.

"Sarah, wait . . ."

And I turned, hope blooming in my chest for a moment.

But when I saw her, the hope fell to embers.

She pointed at the safe. "Get your shit out of my shop."

I just wish she'd hit me. Hell, I deserved it. But that last was worse.

I opened the safe, took out two short swords and a dagger. I laid them on the table and turned to get the case for Gram, but she'd moved to stand in front of the workbench. She leaned forward, placing both hands on the surface with her head sagging down. She was crying. I could hear her sobs, feel each racking breath like a spear in my heart.

I couldn't get Gram's case without asking her to move, so I unrolled my pants on top of the safe, and rolled Gram, the swords, and the dagger all together, tucked them under my arm, and walked out.

I dumped the lot in the back of my car and opened the driver's door. I hesitated, looking back at the shop, wishing that she'd come out. But she didn't, so I got in and drove away. I'd done a lot of leaving lately. Caused a lot of pain. The universe, or karma, or whatever the hell you think keeps the balance, well, as far as I'm concerned, they could all take a flying leap.

I was sick of crying.

Forty-two

I DROVE AROUND a while, not really caring where I ended up. Drove over to Seattle and wandered around Gas Works Park for a few hours, then drove out toward Black Briar before I realized Katie could be out there. And I couldn't really face that lot yet, not with everything that had happened.

So, I drove out to Tiger Mountain, parked the car, and hiked up onto the plateau. Getting lost in the green felt right.

At first, there were a ton of people, but the farther I walked, the less crowded it got.

Eventually I was alone with the trees. I found a nice secluded spot with a trickle of water, far off-trail, and sat against a tree. I cried a while, but felt I was running out of tears. I dug my hands down into the humus, stirring up the dry smell of decay, and the rich moist smell of growth. Death and life intermingled to provide fertile ground for the next generation of trees and plants.

I drew strength from that earth, from the roots of the trees and the living energy that surrounded me. I sat there for hours, just letting my mind empty of everything except the cool wind and the deep richness of the soil under my fingers.

The temperature dropped by a good ten degrees when the sun set, and I felt the transition of the day into the mystery of twilight. The woods felt different suddenly, quieter, like a moment before the world wakens.

I was only slightly surprised when my cell phone rang. This was the Pacific Northwest. Somewhere on one of those ridges nearby, one of the trees was really a cell tower in disguise.

I looked at the number, and almost didn't answer since I didn't recognize it. But something compelled me. I answered on the third ring.

"Blessings and victory," Rolph's voice said into the phone. "Where are you?"

"Out," I said, annoyed. "Why are you calling me?"

"You must come to the smithy," he said. I caught a hint of panic in his voice.

"I seem to not work there any longer," I said, but the bitterness I half expected did not arise. Somehow I'd let it drain from me, let it fade into the earth, and be replaced by a more peaceful energy. "And since I don't work on the movie any longer, Rolph, I'd say we don't have anything in common."

"Don't be a fool," he hissed. "Someone has broken into the smithy. The safe is empty. They have the sword."

His anguish flowed through the phone, in the inflection of his voice, the quality of his tone.

"It was not in the safe," I said. "And why would you be looking for the sword in any case?"

He stammered a moment, making excuses of concern. I tuned it out, frankly. The exhaustion of the last few days had not been purged by my time in the green. Just pushed back around the borders.

"And besides," I said, cutting into his ranting, "the sword is in my car."

"Father of crows," he breathed. "Where anyone can see it? Are you mad?"

"As a hatter," I assured him. "I'm done in, Rolph. I have nothing else to lose. I've lost my love and my livelihood. All I have is this stupid sword, which, frankly, I'm beginning to think is cursed."

"Cursed? Why would you think such?"

"Yeah," I said, sitting up from the tree. "Didn't you say if the sword was forged incorrectly, the smith would be cursed?"

"Yes, true," he said, hesitant. "But I witnessed its remaking. It was done with grace and skill."

I must have finally hit rock bottom in the last few hours, because that small compliment buoyed me. Gave me a modicum of hope. "Thank you, Rolph. That means a lot to me."

"You are quite welcome."

I stood up and brushed the pine needles and dirt from my jeans. "Is there anything else?" I asked. "I'm going to hike out now, and I don't know how good this signal will be."

"If you are sure the sword is safe," he said, the worry thick in his voice. "I am afraid."

"What's got you spooked, Rolph?"

"The dragon has begun to move into the open. He will not be long dissuaded from his prize, unless you act."

"I'm not gutting an investment banker, no matter how creepy he is," I said. "Dragon or no, I don't relish spending the next forty years in prison for a bad feeling."

"Then you are a fool," he said, and hung up the phone.

I hiked out; the cell lost signal as soon as Rolph hung up, funny that.

Rolph's call had spooked me, though. I'd been here a long time. What if someone had broken into the car? What the hell was wrong with me, leaving it out where anyone walking by could see it?

I chafed at the pace to get out of the woods, but it was getting harder to see as the light faded. When I got back to my car, it was full-on dark. I stood and looked back toward the city, toward Bellevue and Seattle, enjoying the lights.

To my relief, no one had broken into the car. Time to take the damned sword home, hide it under my bed or something.

Somewhere to the west, fireworks exploded into the sky. Too early for the Fourth of July, I thought.

Then this wave of anger and fear washed over me like the blowback from a nuclear explosion. Fireworks over the city? Was that more east?

I got in the car and drove down the access road as fast as I could. No one was left on the mountain. When I hit 90 West, my phone rang.

"It's too late," Rolph cried into the phone, not even waiting for me to say hello.

I could hear explosions in the background, and sirens.

"Rolph, what's going on?"

"The dragon has awakened," he said. "You must act, or face the consequences. No one is safe."

Then the line went dead. A mushroom cloud appeared

over what I assumed was Redmond. The explosion sent fire high into the sky.

Damn, was Katie in trouble, too? I flipped the little car across the median at a NO U-TURN sign favored by the cops, and headed east to 18. That was a more direct route to Kent.

I punched Katie's number into the cell and called.

The phone rang, and rang, and rang.

Forty-three

EIGHTEEN IS NOT the safest road to do a hundred miles per hour on, but I was pushing it. I tried calling Katie over and over, but she did not answer.

I called Evergreen Hospital, but Melanie wasn't on shift, and they wouldn't give me her number.

I had no one else to call.

Julie wasn't speaking to me, but if the smithy was in trouble . . . I punched her number and a recorded message informed me that all circuits were busy.

I stared into the night, watching the white lines flash under my car, and prayed to whomever was listening that Katie was okay.

No one stopped me when I careened through downtown. I parked in front of a fire hydrant and jumped out, heading for Katie's door.

" 'Ware, smith," Homeless Joe yelled at me as he hobbled around the corner. "Flee, child, before it is too late."

I spun around. Joe was nearly running with a large staff in his hand, limping along with a bad knee or hip, I never knew which. I took a step toward him, curious about his sudden outburst, when two very large bodies came out from the alley and hit Joe. The first man, whom I recognized as Ernie from the other night, clipped Joe on the back of the head, sending the old man sprawling onto the sidewalk.

The second thug, Bert, kicked the staff away and stomped down on Joe's elbow. I heard the pop from the street. Joe let out a guttural cry, and Ernie kicked him in the chest.

"Leave him alone," I shouted, balling my fists at my sides.

Ernie kicked Joe again, and Bert turned to me with a feral grin. "You again," he said. "I'll squeeze your head until it pops."

He took a step toward me, and Joe lunged forward, grabbing him by the ankle and causing him to trip.

I turned to the car, fumbled the keys a moment, and then got the hatch opened. My hammers were in the back, along with the rest of my personal smithing gear.

I found the first hammer, and at the same time, found the roll of pants and swords. My left hand fell on Gram's pommel and the world shifted slightly. The grunting and yelling of the two brutes took on a more rough and grinding quality, like the sound of a landslide.

I spun around as Bert ran up to me, and I stepped aside, swinging the hammer back to clip him in the elbow. I didn't stop, but ran forward and launched myself at Ernie, hammer in my right fist, Gram in my left.

That was when I got a good look at them. With Gram in my hand, the glamour that hid their true appearance fell away, and I saw them for who and what they truly were.

Giants. That's what Rolph had said. These guys were twelve feet tall and as wide as a bus. How they managed to fit in even a Hummer astounded me. I leapt at Ernie, landing to his left side, and brought the hammer around. He dodged at the last moment, and instead of me catching him in the head, he absorbed the blow on his shoulder.

If felt like striking a granite wall.

However, he felt something, because he stumbled away from Joe and grunted with the blow.

Bert rushed me from the rear, sounding like a freight train. I spun, letting him come to me, and feinted with the hammer, only to bring Gram around in a short thrust, and then a quick flip of the wrist.

The blade bypassed his outstretched arm, and flicked against the side of his neck, sending a spray of blood into the cooling night.

He grabbed his throat and fell to his knees, his eyes as big as lamps.

Ernie had not been idle, however. The whistling sound of a large object being swung was the only thing that saved my life. I jumped backward as a full-on street post came crashing into the spot I'd just vacated.

Unfortunately, I did not avoid the blow altogether. It clipped my right arm, and the hammer fell to the ground. That arm went numb.

I rolled across the ground and back to my feet in time to parry a clumsy swing of the pole. Ernie did not slow, just swung that pole at me, over and over, pushing me back toward the alley.

Bert lurched up, his hands and jacket covered in blood, but he was not down. He punched me in the side, knocking me to my knees. He would have brained me, but Ernie swung the light pole again, only this time he ripped down the power lines overhead and electricity arced down the pole, which hit Bert as I ducked. Both giants fell back, stunned.

I struggled to my feet, pain shooting up my right arm from the elbow, and staggered over to Joe, who sat against the front of Elmer's Gun Emporium. Bert began to rise from where he'd fallen. Ernie struggled to his knees, reaching for the post that he'd flung away.

I knelt down, looking at Joe. "Can you stand?" I asked. I held the sword to my left, glancing back over my shoulder to the two giants.

"I will survive, child," Joe said.

I turned to look into his weathered face. His beard was encrusted with filth, and his eye did not focus. He grinned and I could see several broken teeth. "Sorry, Joe," I said. Bert was on his feet, but staggered. He'd taken the brunt of the electricity, and he wasn't looking too good.

This was ugly. They were much slower, but had enormous strength. I would lose in a game of attrition.

" 'Ware the Jotuns," he said, brushing the hair from my eyes.

Energy flowed from his touch, drawing a line of fire along my scalp.

I looked up, shocked by an intense moment of clarity and peace. A blackness had been burned from my mind.

In the reflection of the storefront, I saw Ernie swinging the lamp, and I spun around, raising the sword with both hands.

My right arm no longer hurt.

I deflected the energy of the blow, redirecting it upward. Unfortunately, it crashed into Elmer's window. Alarms shrieked into the night.

"See if you can get away," I said, rising and spinning on my left heel. "I'll hold them as long as I can."

"You are a brave one," Joe said in his slurred, drunken voice. He placed a hand on my left calf and said, "Wodiz."

The night glowed like the day as power and strength surged into me. My calf throbbed with pain and a euphoria flooded through me. I could feel each rune like a fiery brand. My numb arm felt as right as rain. Every inch of me vibrated with power—seeking release.

I glanced down at Joe and he glowed as well, the color of bruises.

Ernie lunged in at me with the pole, like a lance. I batted it aside with Gram and lurched forward, smashing the blade along the post, only stopping as I cut through flesh and bone. Several fingers on Ernie's right hand fell to the ground, wiggling like maggots.

He dropped the pole, bellowing in pain, and held his hand to his chest. I took that moment to lunge forward and pick up my hammer.

When Bert rushed me, I cried out, screaming something in a language I didn't recognize. Ernie spun around, shock on his face, and Bert stumbled. I swung the hammer, catching Bert on the side, just above the floating rib, and he grunted from the impact.

I brought Gram around at the same time and felt it bite into his left arm, the blade slicing deep before sliding free.

Ernie turned and ran, leaving his fingers to flop around on the sidewalk. Bert fell to the ground, bleeding from several wounds, his breath rushing in and out like a bellows.

"Finish him," Joe said, sitting up. Blood ran down his face, and he held his left arm at an odd angle. "Send him forth to Hel."

I did not hesitate, but leapt forward, slipping Gram into Bert's chest, just over the left breast. He cried out as the first six inches of the blade sank into him, and he fell back, nearly wrenching Gram from my hand.

I spun, looking for Ernie, but he had already fled around the corner of the building.

Only then did I walk over and step on the flailing fingers. They popped like overstuffed sausages, but they stopped moving.

I wiped Gram on Bert's shirt and watched as his movements slowed, and then stopped.

"Police soon," I said in Joe's direction. I walked to the hatchback, dropped the hammer inside, and carefully wrapped Gram inside the jeans once again. Then I walked back and helped Joe up, helped him into the narrow backseat of my car, where he collapsed, perhaps losing consciousness.

I desperately needed to find Katie. Power surged through me as I pushed Katie's door open and bounded up the stairs. At the top of the stairs I didn't stop, but smashed through her door.

"Katie," I called out, running through her place.

She wasn't there.

Okay. No Katie. She was likely out at Jimmy's or something. I ran back to my car, taking the stairs three at a time. Soon I was speeding up 167 toward Renton. "Next stop, the smithy," I called back to Joe, who may or may not have heard me.

About Exit 5, on northbound 405, the adrenaline crash arrived, and I started shaking.

Forty-four

I'D JUST KILLED a man. Well, a giant, but the emotion was the same. My hands rattled on the steering wheel and I found I was breathing in short gasps.

I pulled over to the breakdown lane and put on my flashers. "Hyper . . . ventilating," I said aloud, looking over to Joe. He had not moved since I'd put him in my car. How badly was he hurt?

"Here," he grunted, handing me an empty fast-food bag. I held it over my mouth and breathed, feeling the panic slow. Luckily I had the window open, because the stench of old french fries and Joe's special odor combined with the thought of those fingers, and Bert kicking on the sidewalk as I pierced his heart.

I leaned out my window and vomited.

This was not a good habit to get into. I rested my head against the window frame and tried to keep my breathing even and slow. "I killed him," I said.

"Aye."

I sucked in exhaust and grit as the southbound traffic whizzed by on the other side of the divider, but I couldn't move. It was like something popped in my head . . . this *shit* was really happening. The sword, and giants. Holy Mother of God. Was I losing my mind?

"I need something to drink," I said, turning off the flashers and checking the traffic. "Let's stop at this tavern over by the smithy," I said. "I want to check in on my friend."

"I could use a drink," Joe said.

I pulled into traffic and adjusted my mirror. Joe stared at me with his one good eye. Pain etched his face, and he cradled his arm against his chest.

Traffic was relatively light for the Eastside, but I still chafed at the pace. Weaving in and out of the slower moving vehicles bought me some time, but I had to be careful. With all the hot-rodders out there, adding nitrous and such to cars exactly like mine, I was more prone to police scrutiny. Tonight, I didn't need the delay.

I cut through Bellevue and over to Redmond, noticing that the lights were out and smoke hung heavy in the sky.

God, I hoped that wasn't coming from the smithy.

Joe raised his head and sniffed. "Fire," he said, and passed out.

"Hang on, Joe. We'll skip the drink and head to the hospital. Just don't die."

I barreled down Bel Red and over toward Kirkland. If I took Seventy-second, I could pass the smithy on my way to Evergreen Hospital.

The flutter in my gut became a full-on ache. Flames like I'd never seen before roared upward into the night sky.

I turned past the car wash and the full brunt of the tragedy came into view. The smithy was a total loss. Several fire trucks and police cruisers had the area cordoned off. Traffic had come to a standstill due to the crowd milling around the Crankshaft Tavern across the street. I nosed the hatchback through the crowd and cut into the tavern lot. I parked near the back, glanced back at Joe to see if he was breathing, and got out, letting the sound of chaos wash over me.

"I'll just be one minute," I said to Joe, who let out a low moan. "Let's see how bad it is," I said, walking toward the road.

Jesus, that fire was hot. Must've been the propane exploding I'd seen earlier in the night. I was surprised there weren't more buildings burning.

I cut across the street to get a better angle, and sure enough, Julie's trailer home was a smudge of ash.

A police officer approached me, holding his hands out to his sides to block me from approaching the fire.

"Sorry, miss," he said in a strained but kind voice. "You need to stay back."

I wanted to jump up and down and scream. Instead, I took the calm approach. No use antagonizing the nice officer. "Sorry. It's just that I work here," I said. Mostly not a lie.

His face was stone-cold sober. Serious. "It's not safe, miss."

"Yes, of course," I said, taking a step back.

He seemed to relax. If I was nice, he'd play nice.

"Has anyone seen Julie?" I asked, holding down the panic. "The owner. Did she get out?"

A fireman with a clipboard approached. "You worked here?"

"Yeah," I said. "Black smithy."

"If you could answer a few questions, then," he said. "We can't get into the shop, the fire is too intense."

"Is there a truck in the lot?" I asked.

"No truck, but there is a car over to the side," he said, pointing.

It had been burned out as well.

"Whatever started this seemed to spread across several target areas," he said. "We heavily suspect arson, but until we can know more . . ." He shrugged.

"I guess that mushroom cloud was the propane tanks going," I said.

He nodded. "Happened before we were on the scene."

"We got coal out back, about a ton and a half," I said, walking along the fire line.

He relayed the information over a walkie-talkie and let me walk with him around to the side of the shop. As I got closer, I had a very bad feeling about the car. It had been totally burned out, but the shape was familiar. Could be Katie's, I thought. But how many of those are on the road today? And the fire had done a good job burning it down to the rims.

We walked a bit farther, so I could see the front of the smithy, farthest from the road, between the shop and Julie's place. He pointed out several heavily burning sections, and I confirmed one was the coal pile. The second seemed to be a collapsed shed.

"We stored supplies back there. Borax, welding gear, that sort of thing."

"More propane?" he asked, making notes.

"No propane, but several tanks of oxygen."

"They blew early," he said. "Oxygen doesn't like fire." I nodded. "Yes, I know."

He stopped and spoke with one of the young men holding a hose and directing water into the fire.

Between the car and the smithy, I saw the firelight glint

off something lying on the ground. The fireman didn't see it, and while he was distracted, I darted over and picked it up.

My heart leapt into my throat. It was Katie's phone.

Blessed mother, what was Katie doing here?

I spun around, overwhelmed by the noise, and the smell, the heat, and the flashing lights. I had to get out of here. And I needed to get Joe to the hospital.

I began walking around the fire line. Too many questions danced in my head. Hadn't Rolph been here? Did he start the fire? Where was Julie? Her truck was not here. Had Katie and she met to talk?

I ran across the street, pushing through the crowd toward my car, when I remembered that Rolph had called me from near the smithy. I turned, looking for the pay phones, and sure enough, there he was, talking.

I pushed past several goth kids who were trying to gawk and act bored at the same time.

"Rolph," I yelled over the noise.

He turned, panicked, and hung up the phone.

"Sarah, thank the Norns."

I grabbed him, even though he had a head on me. I pushed him back against the wall and growled, "Katie was here. Where is she?"

"They took her," he said. "They came and ransacked the smithy. Someone was hurt." He cringed when I raised my fist.

"Who was hurt?"

"A woman, I could not tell." The anguish in his voice was real. "If they had seen me, I would be dead right now."

"Unless you started this," I said. "Unless you lured Katie here and killed her and burned down the shop when you couldn't find the sword."

He pulled back, shock on his face. "I would not," he said, his voice strained. "The bard, your lover? I could never harm her. And Julie? She showed me kindness. Do you think this is how I would repay them?"

I eased back a bit. Julie had nursed him.

"Then why'd you bring Frederick into this to begin with?" I asked.

"To force your hand," he said, letting his head drop. "You would not see reason. I thought if you met him, you would see the horror of him."

"He wasn't bothering you, nor me," I said. "You invited him here, into our lives."

"He killed my kith and kin," he said, the anger returning to his voice. "He burned their village, slew the men, ate the children."

A shiver of nausea slithered up my chest, causing my shoulders to shake briefly. I lowered my hands, releasing Rolph. "I had no idea."

"And now, will you confront him?"

I closed my eyes; it was all too much. Katie and Julie hurt, kidnapped, dead, or dying? The smithy burning.

"They will not put out that fire," Rolph said, turning to look across to the smithy. "That is dragon fire. It will burn itself out when the fuel is consumed, or when the light of day approaches."

"Are you serious?" I asked, stepping around him to look at the firemen. "They are putting on a serious amount of water."

He just glanced down at me.

I thought for a moment, trying to make sense of all the chaos.

"Okay, so I need to find Frederick. He wants the sword, so I have a bargaining chip."

Rolph reached out, grabbing my shoulder so hard it hurt. "Never even say that aloud," he said. "I would rather see all you hold dear burned to ash than see the sword given freely to one of his kind."

I shrugged his massive hand off, and thought. What did I really know about this man—I mean, dwarf.

"Oh, Joe." I turned and started walking to my car. "Rolph, do you have your truck?"

"Yes, why?"

"I have a friend who needs to get to the hospital. We were attacked earlier by a pair of giants."

Rolph grabbed me by the arm again. "Giants?"

"Yeah, Ernie and Bert."

He looked at me blankly.

"Same goons that threatened me the other night, and ran me off the road a few days before."

"Perhaps the same two who beat me," he said, his voice full of venom.

"Well, one of them won't be bothering anyone else," I said, moving toward the car. "I killed him."

Rolph nodded, his face grim. "Not a small feat. And the other?"

"He's missing a few fingers," I said. "Maggoty things that kept on moving after he fled."

"Yes, foul creatures, giants."

I made a face. "I smashed them, but he got away."

Two kids on bikes sat beside my car, so I shooed them away, and opened the back door.

There was no one there. I looked back at Rolph, who had fallen to his knees.

Two ravens flew out of the car, their caws piercing through the general hubbub. Several people turned to see, and the world slowed for a moment. Rolph held his hands over his ears. "Mercy, Woden," he cried.

I squatted down beside him. "What the hell is wrong with you?"

"The one-eyed beggar," he whispered.

"Joe? Yeah, the giants hurt him, but I rescued him."

He reached up with his left hand and brushed the hair

out of my face. "He has marked you, I see," he said, letting his hand fall.

I spun around and looked into the side mirror.

Just inside the hairline above my left temple, there was a series of small runes. "Son of a bitch," I whispered, letting my hair drop. "He branded me."

"He has marked you as one of his own," Rolph said. "Can you deny your call to arms now?"

I stood, looked over at the smithy and the flames that still roared into the night sky. "Not anymore," I said. "I'm going after Frederick."

"He's at the movie shoot," Rolph said, his voice flush with emotion. "I was talking with Juanita, she says he is there."

"Juanita?" I asked. "One of JJ's girls?"

Rolph flushed. "She is kind to me."

I shrugged. "Never underestimate kindness," I said. "Let's roll."

I got in my car and began pulling through the crowd. Getting to Everett would be a bitch.

Forty-five

I WAS ALMOST to the Woodinville cutoff when I had a quick change of plans. Rolph was following me fairly close, so I put on my blinkers and waved out the window, pointing toward the exit. He followed without a hitch.

If I was going to confront a dragon, I wanted some better gear. And I wanted to let someone else know, just in case.

We pulled into Black Briar around eleven. The house was dark; Jimmy and Deidre were likely already asleep.

We parked and walked up to the barn.

Gunther and Stuart were sitting on bales of hay, drinking and working. Stuart was mending a leather rigging of some sort, and Gunther was sharpening a dagger.

"Hey, guys," I said, striding up with Rolph.

"Hey, Beauhall," Stuart said. "Was wondering when we'd see you out here again."

"Yeah," Gunther said, putting down the sharpening stone and polishing the blade with a cloth. "After that little scene last time, we figured you'd be too mortified to come back."

They watched me, expectantly. No bullshit this time, Sarah. "They took Katie," I said. "I need some gear."

"Who took Katie? Melanie?" Stuart asked.

"No, not Melanie." I paused a moment. I'd known these guys for years. "It's a long story," I said finally. "*Armageddon Rag*, gentlemen. The real deal."

I'd thought about this on the way over. How could I convince them without looking like a total freaking idiot? But then, I'd been worried about how others perceived me for a long damn time, and that's served me so well.

I thought back to those long nights of wishful thinking, of planning for the end of the world, or dreaming of a life where one lived by wits and skills alone. A time when a single man, or woman, with a sword could right the wrongs. They'd be skeptical, but deep down, they needed to believe.

"Remember all those nights we talked," I paced in front of them, waving my hand, "the game we played about what if? Like if the world was different. If we had to live by our wits and our swords?"

Stuart laughed. "You been drinking?"

I punched him in the leg, eliciting a hurt cry. "Not joking, you ass. One of you go wake up Jimmy. I'm going in to get my chain."

Gunther and Stuart looked at one another and laughed.

That was it, I wasn't getting through to them. I shoved the bales of hay, and the two men tumbled to the ground. "Either help, or get the hell out of the way," I shouted, storming past them and into the barn.

I stood in the center of the barn, considering how best to proceed, when Stuart and Gunther came stumbling in. Gunther stormed right up to me, pissed off, and grabbed my arm. "What the hell was that about?"

I spun around, shoving him. "I told you. They took Katie. And likely Julie. Or . . ." I choked. "Or she's dead."

Stuart came up with Rolph behind him. "I think she's serious."

"Quite," Rolph said. Both men turned to look at him. "There is a dragon who has taken the form of a man to hide his true self."

"He wants Gram," I said. "I need to go rescue Katie. Are you going to help, or laugh more?"

Stuart started to smile, but looked at me, cocked his head to the side, and a look of dawning comprehension crossed his face. "Gram . . . ," he said. "You called the sword Gram."

"Yes."

"Fafnir's Bane," Gunther said, looking back at Rolph for the first time.

"Rolph," I said, "these two geniuses are my friends Gunther and Stuart."

All three nodded, in that territorial way men have, and I turned to the lockers.

"Rolph's a dwarf, boys. I know you're familiar with the stories."

"Jesus and Mary," Stuart said, crossing himself. "You ain't fooling?"

I didn't even answer. I opened my locker and pulled out my chain mail. The stitched cotton underarmor smelled musty as I pulled it over my head, but it would keep the chain from cutting into me, I hoped.

The chain was a bit trickier, but as I was laying it out on the bench, to try and get it over my head just right, Gunther stepped up and helped.

"You'll need a scabbard for that pigsticker," he said. "I think Stuart has something you can use."

"Yeah," Stuart said from across the barn. "Look in locker six. I'll run up to the house and wake Jimmy."

"Thanks," I said, looking back at Rolph. "Helps when you have friends," I said.

He looked back, his face impassive.

Once the chain was in place, and the cinches were tightened correctly, I could move with only a small amount of restriction. "Decent armor," I said, brushing my hands down the chain. The links were done with skill. "One day, I should try making some armor." I thought how lovely that would be if only we all lived through this nightmare. And Katie. Dear God, I had to not think about what she might be going through at the moment or I would fall apart.

Gunther grunted and began fishing through locker six. He came out with two belts and a scabbard.

"Not sure which of these fits better," he said. "You want the sword over your shoulder, or at the waist?"

"I think I'd like a belt to hold the hammers," I said. "And a shoulder mount for the sword."

"Can do," Gunther said, digging into the locker again. "We can make this work."

I had the scabbard in place and the hammers on my belt by the time Jimmy came jogging into the barn.

"What's going on, Sarah?" he grumbled. He had on a pair of workout pants with half-moons helter-skelter across the legs, and a T-shirt that read: ONCE A KING ALWAYS A KING, BUT ONCE A KNIGHT IS ENOUGH.

Scruffy and torqued as he was, he still gave me the warm fuzzy I always got around him. Jimmy's was a safe place. I hated to disappoint him. "They took Katie."

I fished her cell phone out of my back pocket and handed it to him.

He took the phone, opened it, and looked through the files. "It's Katie's," he said, motioning to a table. "Sit down and tell me what the hell is going on."

I wanted to leave, to get to Frederick, but I needed Jimmy on this. That had come clear to me during the fight with the giants. Kith and kin, that's what made this worth anything.

So I told him. Granted, it was the quick version, but I tried to include as many details as I could remember. He poked and prodded with questions, but didn't tell me I was a liar, or a fool.

Even though I glossed over it, I could tell he knew about my drunken night. That explained the strained look on his face.

"This homeless guy," he said. "Joe?"

"Yes," I said.

"Woden," Rolph added for the first time.

Gunther and Stuart exchanged a look, but did not interrupt.

"Woden, right," Jimmy said. "So, you fought a pair of giants, which don't look like giants unless you are holding the sword, right?"

"Yes," I said. His level of reasonableness was a bit maddening.

"So, these giants were beating on a guy who your friend here thinks is Woden."

"Who is Woden?" I asked, looking around.

"Do you never read?" Stuart asked. "Woden . . . Odin . . . the All-Father. King of the gods."

"Not king," Rolph said. "He is their jarl."

"Works out the same," Stuart said, disgruntled.

"More chieftain," Rolph said. "King would be Konungr."

Jimmy and I looked at them for a moment, and they stopped talking, chagrined. "Continue," Jimmy said.

So I described arriving at the burning smithy, how I saw Katie's car, and where I found the cell. I especially impressed on him the point that the fire was pretty fierce.

"Dragon fire," Jimmy said, nodding. He turned to look at the others. "Stuart, your buddy still work over with the Redmond Fire Department?"

He nodded. "Yeah, EMT."

"Okay, get on the horn and see what he knows. If this story holds water," he looked back at me, "and I assume it will, give him a clue that there could be some nontraditional flammables there, and that they may want to back off and just work on containment."

Rolph nodded and Stuart hightailed it out of the barn.

"Show him the runes," Rolph added from the back.

Jimmy looked at me, raising one hand toward me, giving me the stage.

"During the battle with the giants, one of them pulled a streetlight out of the pavement and began swinging it around. I was holding my own, but could see a short end coming, when Ernie—that's the nice one—clipped the power lines above the street, and managed to catch both himself and Bert with a substantial shock."

"Lucky break," Gunther said.

"Nay," Rolph said. " 'Twas Woden, calling the lightning."

Jimmy looked over his shoulder. "Wasn't Thor the one to call lightning?"

Rolph shrugged. "Woden is the most powerful, his powers are legion."

They argued among themselves for a bit, Odin versus Zeus, and the traditional roles of gods and beggars. It ran on for a few minutes before I could get a word in edgewise. Luckily, they had to breathe sometime.

"Anyway," I said.

They all turned back toward me.

"I went to check if Joe was going to be okay, and he

brushed the hair out of my eyes." I pulled my hair back, exposing the line of runes just inside my hairline.

Jimmy leaned forward, pushing my hand out of the way, and moving the hair to see each rune separately. "Did it hurt?"

I didn't hesitate. "Like fire. But more a cleansing fire than a destructive one, you know?"

All of them nodded. It was cute, like bobbleheads.

Stuart came running back in. "They are all set," he said, a little winded. "Deidre's making coffee, started the calling chain."

"What?" I asked. "Calling chain?"

"If someone has Katie, we are going to mobilize the troops," Jimmy said. "Standard procedure. We'd do it with any one of us."

I sat back and looked at him. He didn't seem to be fazed by any of this.

He smiled and patted me on the leg. "Go on, Sarah. Finish your story."

He had the strangest look in his eyes. Creeped me out. He should've called me a liar, or crazy, or something. But he just looked at me, with patience and . . . understanding, perhaps.

"When the fire flashed through my mind, much of the fog lifted." I paused a moment, considering. "I've been a mess lately, if you haven't noticed."

"Since mending Gram," Rolph added. "You were fighting the geas of the blade, ignoring the purpose for which it was originally forged."

"I just can't kill an investment banker from Portland, or anywhere," I said, raising my voice. "Even with everything that's happened, with the things I've seen. That is just murder."

No one spoke for a moment, and Gunther was the first.

"Sarah, if the president of the United States can invade

another country based on a suspicion, I think you can move out on probable cause here."

"He's right," Rolph said, barely able to contain his glee. "You have no idea of the depredation this beast has caused."

"Before we send her out killing folks, I want to hear about the rest of the fight, and the significance of these runes," Jimmy said, turning back toward me and focusing things.

I explained about the runes on my calf, and how Joe had infused me with some power. "He cried out 'Wodiz,' or something." I stood and pulled up the legs of my jeans. Couldn't get them high enough to show all the runes, but I wasn't dropping trou with this crowd.

"Ah," Rolph said. "Woden of the one eye has many gifts: first among them is the gift of prowess in battle. Those who are favored by the All-Father are unmatched in combat. They become an army of one, feared by friend and foe alike."

"Berserker," Stuart said, the awe apparent in his voice. "Great, Beauhall. I'll never take you in sparring again."

I laughed at that, and the mood lightened a bit.

"Okay, final bit," Jimmy said. "I'd like to see the sword."

I looked over at Rolph, who watched intently.

"It's in the car," I said, rising.

"I can get it," Gunther said.

"NO!" Rolph bellowed.

Everyone stopped and stared at him. Gunther looked ready to fight, and Jimmy had on his I'm-the-boss face.

"It is hers to bear," Rolph continued. "Hers to wield."

"I'll just go get it," I said, jogging past everyone. "I'll be okay."

I left them in the barn. As soon as I was through the door, I could hear them talking excitedly.

I pulled the sword from the hatchback and slid it into the sheath over my shoulder. It fit perfectly. I had a feeling that no matter what container I put it in, it would be an excellent fit.

Deidre opened the door, carrying a tray with a large thermos of coffee and several mugs. I helped, grabbing a tray with sugar and milk, and walked with her back to the barn in silence. When we got in, the men stood around one of the workbenches, and Jimmy was pulling topo maps out of the cupboard.

"Planning a battle?" I said, walking in and setting the tray on top of a map of the Mount Si area.

"Call's gone out," Deidre said, pouring a mug of coffee and handing it to Jimmy. "First team should arrive in half an hour."

I shook my head. "And what will they be doing, exactly?" I asked. "You can't all follow me to confront this guy, and I can't wait any longer."

Jimmy stepped beside me and placed his hand on my shoulder. "We will prepare," he said. "If we need to do search and rescue, or donate blood, or just offer support in a time of crisis. We'll be here."

I watched him, perplexed.

"May I see the sword?" he asked. I was slightly puzzled, as they had already gotten a look at the sword, but realized that Jimmy needed to see it now in a different way.

I pulled it out of the scabbard and lay it on the table beside the coffee. He leaned over, running his finger down the fuller without touching the blade. He moved his lips as he read the runes, nodding at each one.

"Turn the blade, please."

I grabbed the pommel and turned it over. While I held it, the room shifted a bit, became clearer. Everyone looked the same, just a brighter, shinier version of themselves.

Jimmy read the back side of the blade, hesitating at the point where the reforging had obliterated the rune on each side.

Jimmy straightened, a serious and thoughtful look on his face. "Put it away, please."

I returned the blade to its scabbard and turned to see Deidre holding a helm.

"Take this," she said. It was typical skullcap with a nose guard. A white tree was painted on the front.

I smiled and took it from her.

"This was to be a birthday gift," she said, smiling. "But if you must go to battle, better to protect your head."

"Ah, Yggdrasil—the tree of worlds," Rolph said, approvingly.

"Well," I said with a chuckle. "Actually it's the white tree of Minis Tirith."

He looked confused.

"*Lord of the Rings*, again, I'm afraid," I said.

He rolled his eyes and turned away, asking Gunther something about ale.

"If you get into trouble, call," Jimmy said. "If any of this is real, you will need backup."

"She likely needs therapy," Deidre said, pouring a cup of coffee.

"I'll be careful," I said. "But if he has help, or . . ."

"Thralls," Stuart offered.

"Yes, thralls, or thugs, or three-toed sloths," I said. "I have no idea, but I know he's at the movie shoot in Everett and he's not expecting to see my smiling face."

Deidre's cell phone rang. She spoke into it, then asked Jimmy a few questions. While they talked, I put on a pair of leather bracers and greaves we used for sparring, and considered myself as armored as I was going to get.

"Maggie and Susan are already on the phone with the police in Kent," Deidre said, closing the phone and turning to us. "They found Elmer's broken into, and a really big guy stabbed to death out front."

Everyone looked at me. I shrugged. "Told you."

"Why don't we let the police get this banker?" she asked.

"Not possible," Rolph spoke up. "He is too powerful. The smith must confront him herself."

"I don't like it," she said. "Not one bit."

"Like it or not, we'll be ready," Jimmy said.

I shook hands with everyone and when I got back to Jimmy, he held my hand a while, looking into my eyes. "When you get back, ask me why I believe you."

I nodded. "I figured you thought I was nuts."

"Nuts," he said, laughing, "but not insane." He closed his eyes briefly and then opened them and I saw a world of hurt and worry there. "Find my sister, Sarah. Find her and bring her here safe. And when you do, you can ask Katie to explain why she is so steeped in lore. Why we started all this."

Deidre patted Jimmy on the arm, and walked over to Rolph, Stuart, and Gunther. "Come on, boys. Let's get a bonfire going out back, what do you say?"

Gunther and Stuart groaned, but Rolph looked happy.

"Just means more toting for us," Gunther said, pulling Rolph along with him. "You can help stack the posts."

"About Rolph," I said.

"Your friend will be safe here," Jimmy said, picking up his coffee cup. "He's not the first of Durin's folk we've had sleep in our barn as dawn approached."

I shook my head. Maybe I wasn't crazy. Maybe the whole world was crazy. There were just too damned many mysteries. I'd be pressing him for answers when this all settled down, you can bet your bottom dollar.

But it would have to wait. I needed to get out to Carl's.

Forty-six

THIS TIME, WHEN I got out of the car, I was dressed like something from a medieval shoot. I pulled the hammers out of the back and set them in their holsters. I slipped the shoulder mount over my head and slid Gram into the sheath, then shut the hatchback with a solid thump.

When I walked to the door, the rent-a-cop glanced at me and did a double take.

"You can't go in there," he said, lunging forward to grab me. I swung around and clipped him on the back of the head with my forearm. He staggered past me into the shrubbery.

I slammed the door open and jogged down the short hall to the interior doors. Once there, I pulled Gram from the sheath and kicked the bar, sending the door flying backward with a bang.

They were in the middle of a shoot. Now, I'd read the script, even gave Carl some suggestions on combat sequences, but I did not remember, at any point, JJ leaning over a gorgeous blonde, pouring wine over her bare breasts.

"What the hell?" I said to no one. I scanned the room. Despite my explosive entrance, much of the crew remained fixated on JJ and the blonde.

I strode across toward camera two, where I'd spotted Carl and Frederick.

"Hey, you," I growled as I approached them. "I want a word with you."

Carl and Frederick turned at the same time. Carl's face slid from concentrated amusement to open shock. He glanced from my face to the sword and stepped between me and Frederick.

"Nice try, Carl," I said, shoving him aside.

Clyde, who ran camera two, jumped off his seat and scampered across the stage toward JJ. The crew turned toward me as I stepped within striking distance of Frederick.

"Ms. Beauhall," he said, his voice silky smooth. "Going to a costume ball?"

The urge to smash the pommel of the sword into his pretty, smiling face rose in me like a carpet of red ants. I lunged forward, and turned the blade at the last moment. Instead of hitting him in the face, I locked my right forearm against his throat, with the tip of Gram just under his left ear.

His hands were in his jacket pocket and he made no move to defend himself.

I stared into his eyes, fury filling up the hollow spots inside me. "Where is she?" I hissed through gritted teeth.

He smiled, amused. "Breath mint, dear?" he asked, pulling a half roll of mints from his jacket. The paper trailed off the end, white and silver.

"Sarah," Carl shouted behind me. "What the hell are you doing?"

"He burned down the smithy," I said, my voice shaking with rage. "He took Katie and Julie."

"Crazy's back," JJ yelled from the stage. "Where's security?"

Jennifer approached from Frederick's left, her hands in the air. "Sarah, he's been here all night."

"She speaks the truth," Frederick said.

The calmer he was, the angrier I got. This time, I recognized the feeling, understood the source. The berserker frothed beneath my skin. I loosened my grip on the sword a micron, letting my hand relax instead of throbbing.

"You're lying," I said. "Only dragon fire burns that way."

Of course, I had no idea what the hell I was talking

about. How good was Rolph's word? I'd known Jennifer and Carl much, much longer.

Still . . .

"Why would you offer to buy the sword?" I asked. "Give me your share in Flight Test, and then send goons after me? Why'd you burn down the smithy?" I drew a breath, giving him a chance he did not take. "Were you angry that you couldn't have what you wanted?" I continued. "Found the swords weren't in the safe, so you torched the place?"

I leaned in, breathing into his face. "You are a coward, Frederick Sawyer. Afraid to fight your own battles."

He snapped his teeth at me, fire flashing in his eyes. "Careful, little smith. I might lose my patience with you and your silly games."

"Excuse me, sir," Mr. Philips said from behind me. "I hate to interrupt."

Frederick tilted his head a little to the left, looking past my shoulder. "I'm a bit tied up at the moment, Mr. Philips."

"Yes, sir. I'm very sorry, sir," he said.

God, the man had control.

"It's just . . . well . . ." He stepped around to my left, well out of reach, and held up a cell phone. "I'm afraid this call is for Ms. Beauhall."

"Nice try," I said, letting the tip of the sword press into Sawyer's skin, drawing the tiniest bead of blood.

"Put it on speaker," Frederick growled.

One of the grips ran up, dragging a cord across the floor. He handed it to Mr. Philips, who inserted it into the cell phone and said, "Go ahead."

No sound came through the phone.

"No more games," I said. I could feel my pulse throbbing in my temples. I was close to losing it. "Just give her back to me, and I'll let you live."

"Oh, my," a man's voice sighed all silky and sweet out of the speakers.

I jerked my head toward the phone. What the hell?

"Frederick, dear cousin. I guess the events of this little drama are approaching the climax."

"Jean-Paul?" Frederick asked, his face losing some of the humor and control.

Laughter rang from the speakers. All around the movie shoot, people cowered, stepping into shadow or behind sets.

"While you dabbled in the movies, and philanthropy, I got to the heart of the matter," Jean-Paul said. There was a moment of shuffling, and the sound of crying, and a sharp smack, followed by a yelp of pain. "Talk to your lover, insect," Jean-Paul's voice said in the distance.

"Sarah? Oh my God, Sarah, are you there?" Katie's voice echoed throughout the stage.

Sawyer stared into my eyes, and I knew he told the truth.

I stepped away, lowered the sword, and watched his face. The blood from the cut in his neck had trickled down to stain the collar of his shirt. He bowed his head and I turned, facing Mr. Philips.

"Katie, are you okay?" I asked, reaching for the phone.

"Julie's hurt," she said. "This bastard said he was going to kill her. Sarah, he wants the sword."

I sank to the floor, placing Gram on the ground in front of my knees. "Is he a dragon?" I asked. "Did he burn the smithy?"

"Yes," she said, her voice angry, but frightened. "He hurt us, Sarah." Her voice dropped, filled with shame. "He's . . . he's beyond evil."

He hit her; the meaty smack sounded clearly over the speakers. She moaned as Jean-Paul took over the conversation.

"I'll kill you," I said. "Mark my words."

"Yes, the little girl playing at smithing and movies. You are more pathetic than Frederick, and I had no idea that was possible."

Mr. Philips pulled the cord from the phone and the laughter died. Several of the crew were crying around the edges of the sets, and Frederick took the phone.

I watched him, afraid to stand. If I moved, I would lose control. Already the berserker in me clawed at the inside of my brain, calling me to kill, maim, destroy.

I took a long, shuddering breath, searching for calm. I could not succumb to that instinct.

"So, Jean-Paul," Frederick said in his sweet voice. "Tired of feeding hookers to pigs, time to move up and snatch schoolteachers?" Of course he knew all about Katie. He knew all about me.

So the goons were from this Jean-Paul guy. The fire, and the threats. And Sawyer, dragon himself, had only invested in a place I worked.

And suddenly the world got a whole lot weirder—if that was possible—as I realized not only that dragons existed but also that Frederick wasn't the only one in the world. How many more of the damned things were there?

I'd been played for a chump. Only question was how far was Rolph into this? Did he know, or was he a patsy as well?

Frederick closed the cell phone and walked over to me. He held a hand out to me, and I stared at it for a few moments. I stood on my own, stepping back from him and holding Gram between us. There might be another wolf in the chicken coop, but this one still had all his teeth.

Frederick nodded and lowered his hand to his side. "Jean-Paul is—" He paused, considering. "—unsavory."

"Why did he call?" I asked, looking over at Carl and

Jennifer, who were in each other's arms. Jennifer had her head on Carl's shoulder, and I could hear her crying.

"We have both been played the fool," Frederick said. "As has your dwarf friend, Rolph Brokkrson."

I realized that he wasn't snowing me. Gram allowed me to not only see through the glamour of the giants, but allowed me to know that Frederick was telling the truth. "Rolph set me up?" I asked.

Frederick chuckled. "I recognized him the moment I smelled him," he said with a feral grin. "Let's just say I've had a chance to interact with his family in the past."

"You killed and ate them, you mean."

He shrugged. Ballsy.

"So, now what? Did he say anything? This Jean-Paul?"

His cell phone rang. "This would be Qindra," he said, holding up the phone. "May I?"

Just who the hell was Qindra—another dragon? I nodded wearily. Sure. Lovely. Regular day at the office. I stepped back from him, looked over at Carl and shrugged. I really couldn't live with them being afraid of me, hating me. "Sorry about this."

He looked at me, assessing me. "He took Katie," he said, holding Jennifer tighter. "You do what you need to do."

Relief from one corner, at least. Jennifer straightened and looked at me, horror and fear on her face.

Was it fear of the situation or fear of me?

She nodded once and a hint of a smile touched her lips. Not me, then. I'd won a bit with that.

Frederick spoke into the phone in a language I did not recognize. He waved and Mr. Philips came over to him with a briefcase. Frederick opened it, took out pen and paper, and wrote on several pages. Then he put everything but one page back into the case, and Mr. Philips closed it with a snap.

"Very good, sir," Mr. Philips said, turning on his heel and moving toward the exit door. He passed the security guard, who stood in the doorway, confused. They spoke a moment, and the guard left with Mr. Philips.

Frederick closed the phone and walked over to the three of us.

"My apologies," he said to Carl. "But we need to shut down the shoot for a week or so."

"Wait a minute," Jennifer said. "We're already behind schedule."

Frederick waved his hand. "Just a week, and see that everyone is paid," he said.

That was generous.

"In the meantime . . ." He turned to me, holding out a piece of paper. "I'm returning to Portland for the next week or so. It has been suggested I've overstayed my welcome."

I took the paper. On it was a single phone number. Seattle prefix.

"Qindra will arrange a meeting," he said. "Exchange the women for the sword."

"Who is Qindra?"

Frederick looked at me, considering. "She is the face of Nidhogg. She has no love for Jean-Paul, nor myself."

"Pity," I said, wishing I had been paying more attention when Rolph and Jimmy were going on and on about Norse mythology. I had a feeling that I would be needing this stuff real soon.

"Yes, well. Enemy of my enemy, and all that," he said with a shrug. "She is trustworthy and indifferent. She serves her mistress and her interests. Neither mine nor Jean-Paul's are of any real concern to her."

"So why is she setting up this meet?"

He considered it, unhappy at the thought, I could see by his face.

"I have trespassed," he said, finally. "And I will make

amends, but Jean-Paul has violated certain precepts and this must be handled delicately."

For a conniving, baby-eating fire-breather, I could see how Mr. Sawyer became a pillar of his community.

"So, I call this number, set up an exchange, and we all go away happy and healthy?"

He laughed. "My dear Sarah. Jean-Paul has undoubtedly done some harm to your friends, and will likely kill them before he is done. He will take the sword and make you watch while he hurts them . . . a very lot."

I shuddered. His tone was like he was ordering dinner. "And I should do this why?"

"Because I see the fire inside you, Sarah Beauhall. You wield that which my kind fear. My kind who has ruled you for generations beyond counting. Most of you are chattel who go through their lives unknowing of the power that controls your fates. But you? You have the will and the . . ." He paused, assessing. "Something about you is beyond my remembrance. It reminds me of a cautionary tale told to me by my nursemaid."

I clutched the paper in my fist, nodding.

"There was a time, before my mother's mother," he said, stepping closer and lowering his voice, "at the dawn of time, when others held power. There are rumors of rumors of one such as yourself. One who wielded the great sword, who made the world anew. Are you this great one?" he asked.

Then he turned, laughing. "Childish fears," he said, waving his hands. "No matter. I would go, if I were you, because it is your one chance to strike at him, to exact your vengeance while he thinks you are weak with fear and grief."

Vengeance I understood. It burned in my veins, swelled in my brain like the cry of carrion birds.

Forty-seven

I WALKED OUT of the studio, slipping Gram back into the scabbard.

"Good luck," someone shouted from behind me. I think it was one of JJ's bimbos. Maybe Babs.

The security guard watched me from behind his little card table but did not get up.

The poor guy really was out of his league here. I stopped at the bottom of the stairs and turned back, walking toward the desk. To his credit, he didn't move.

"I'm sorry," I said, taking the helmet off and running my hand through my hair. "You are just doing your job. I have done you a dishonor."

He blinked at me. "Mr. Philips told me they grabbed your girlfriend," he said. "I can't blame you."

"Doesn't excuse my behavior," I said, bowing my head. "I'll make it up to you."

"Just get the girl," he said.

I turned and walked briskly to my car. More debt to repay.

I unhooked my weapons and placed them inside the hatchback, stacking the helmet on top of the pile.

I leaned against my car and called Jimmy. Time to make this happen.

"Jimmy," he said. He always answered the phone the same way.

"It's Sarah."

"How's Katie?"

Right to the heart of the matter. That's our Jimmy. "Wrong dragon," I said, feeling ridiculous. "She was snatched by a guy out of Vancouver. I need to set up an exchange. Sword for the women."

"I see," he said. "Why aren't we calling the Feds, again?"

I tapped my forehead with the knuckles of my left hand. "Dragon, Jimmy. Remember. Giants and crazy shit. You think the Feds are going to believe this?"

"Right," he said. "I'm not sure all of us aren't certifiable. What do you need me to do?"

"Drive your truck out to the big field behind the barn and get me the GPS coordinates for that spot. I'll make a call and they'll show up."

"So, you think they are going to fly in? Drive?"

"No idea yet. Haven't called the facilitator."

He laughed, a strained and tight laugh. "Facilitator. These dragons of yours are pretty organized."

"Likely more than we ever imagined," I said.

"Hang on," he said.

I heard him close the truck door, and the *bing-bing* of his seat belt warning. "Okay," he said after a minute. "You ready?"

"Shoot."

I wrote down the coordinates on the back of the page with the contact number. "Might clear everyone out, just in case."

"You don't worry about us," he said. "You just set up the meeting and get out here. We gotta bring Katie and Julie home."

Great, I thought. *Only Julie has no home . . . and the blame for that can be put squarely on my shoulders.*

I got in the car, put on my headset, and dialed the number. While it was ringing I pulled out of the lot and began making my way to Black Briar.

The phone rang six times, then an old woman answered. "Yes, may I help you?"

"Uh, this is Sarah Beauhall. I'm calling to arrange . . ."

"Yes, yes," the woman said. "I know why you are calling, Ms. Beauhall. I just wanted to make sure it wasn't that nice man who insists on selling me the local paper again."

Funny woman. "I have the coordinates."

"Yes, I understand you are having a bit of trouble from two of the boys."

Boys? I bet this was not Qindra. "Who is this?"

"Oh, dear. Names are not important."

Yeah, right. "Is this Nidhogg?"

The woman laughed. "Now that is a name rarely spoken. There is really far too much drama in the world to be dredging up such a volatile nom de plume, don't you think?"

Yeah, whatever. "Sorry," I said. "I meant no insult. I just want my friends back."

"Of course, dear. I'm sure Jean-Paul will make the exchange in good faith. The deal is both women for the sword, do I have that correct?"

"Hell yes!"

"Noble," she said. "I will be sending an emissary of my own to make sure things are aboveboard."

"Thank you," I said.

"No thanks needed," she said. "And as one of my many thralls, I will insist that you also bargain in good faith, and hold up your end of the deal."

Thrall? I was no one's slave. "I don't know who you are, lady," I said, letting the anger creep back into my voice, "but no one owns me. If your pet Jean-Paul shows up and gives me the women unharmed, I'll give him the sword. If he's hurt them, I will cut him down."

The woman laughed, a creaky titter that sounded like the rending of desiccated flesh. "What a delight you are, my dear. So full of vim and vigor."

"Yeah, whatever," I said. "Are we setting this meet up, or what?"

"Oh, the impatience of youth. Yes, dear, I am ready

for your silly numbers. Jean-Paul will arrive within the hour."

I gave her the coordinates and hung up the phone. One hour. I could be at Jimmy's in twenty minutes. I stepped on the gas and sped through the nearly empty streets.

When I hit 5 South, I pulled Katie's cell phone out of the console and pulled up Melanie's number. She'd want to know. Want to be there. Hell, she might not even know something was going down.

As the phone rang, I thought of a way to explain this to her. I'd promised her that Katie was safe, not involved.

Truth was likely the best answer. No beating around the bush.

"Hello," Melanie said wearily.

Obviously I'd woken her.

"Melanie, it's me, Sarah. Katie's in trouble."

Forty-eight

I PULLED OFF the main road and onto the gravel thirty minutes later. Construction south of Everett kept things tied up. Nothing like Seattle traffic to get a girl's panties in a bunch.

Things were totally out of hand, I'd decided on the drive down. Learning about dragons and dwarves, magic swords and Norse gods was worrisome. I had spoken to three dragons, one in each of the major cities in our region—this concerned me.

How many of them were there? Did they control all the major cities? What kind of world did we really live in? What if they controlled everything? Government . . . military. This was beyond the bomb, beyond Armageddon.

If I hadn't completely lost my mind, it seemed that we lit-tle humans didn't know squat and our world was domi-nated and run by a nonhuman force. Like *War of the Worlds*, only everyone slept through the war. How could we have missed this?

But, then again, not everyone had missed it, had they? Rolph had warned me, Katie told her tales, Jimmy and the Black Briar had a deep, dark secret.

It was overwhelming.

I pulled up to the house, trying to keep my hands from shaking. Instead of being deserted, as I'd expected, the driveway and surrounding field was packed with vehicles. There were a dozen or more pickup trucks, three sedans, and a pair of motorcycles. Too many peo-ple here.

Looks like Jimmy hasn't cleared the place.

I parked and got my gear out of the back, strapped on my weapons, but did not put the helm on. Not yet.

The house was all lit up. As I walked around to the back, I could see into the kitchen. Melanie stood at the counter, rolling bandages, if you can believe it.

Deidre was washing dishes and directing several oth-ers; Carolyn, Tim, and his partner, Jason, were bustling around, prepping for catastrophe.

I wanted to speak to Melanie first, before going out to the barn. I had to fix this before I got myself killed.

The screen door squeaked on opening, and everyone turned to watch me come in. No one said anything, but they kept their hands busy, watching me. I stepped across the kitchen and placed my helm on the counter beside the stack of bandages Melanie was rolling.

"Thanks for coming," I said.

Melanie shrugged. "Anything for Katie," she said.

Deidre came over to me and cupped the side of my face in her hand. "You are a stubborn woman," she said.

"Hard to read, but easy to love." She kissed my cheek and walked into the living room, shooing the rest of the house before her like a mother hen with her chicks.

"I'm sorry," I said, looking back to Melanie.

"Just get her home safe," she said, her voice strained and quiet.

"If something happens," I began, but she turned and put two fingers on my lips. I stopped speaking and just stared into her lovely blue eyes.

"Sarah," she said, "Katie loves you. Learn to live with it."

What else could I do? "You have everything you need?"

She shrugged. "Never know. Got an EMT crew out at the Denny's on Eighty-first, taking their sweet time returning the wagon after their shift."

I smiled. "Anyone I know?"

"Well," she said, turning and picking up a strip of white muslin, "there is this dreamy redhead on that crew that I kinda prefer to sleep with."

"Dena?" I asked.

Melanie nodded.

"God, what she must think of me." I rolled my eyes and bent my head forward into my left hand.

"She thinks you are a raving bitch, if you must know," Melanie said with a wicked grin. "Said if you are stupid enough to lose Katie, you didn't deserve her sympathy."

"Nice," I said. Dena moved up a couple notches in my world.

I reached over and hugged her from the side. "I'll bring her home."

Melanie patted my arm and leaned her head down on top of mine. "I know. Just be careful."

I let her go and picked up my helm.

"Prepare for blackout," Deidre said into a bullhorn from the back deck.

I looked over at Melanie with raised eyebrows.

"Deidre insists that too much light provides targets of opportunity."

I laughed. "Leave it to Deidre to go into blitz mode." I pushed open the back door and jogged across the gravel turnaround. When I was halfway to the barn there was a loud pop and the farm plunged into darkness.

Forty-nine

HURRICANE LANTERNS BURNED on either side of the barn's main door. Out in the practice field the boys had built a bonfire that looked like it would burn until dawn.

I fished my cell phone out of my jeans and checked the time. One forty-five. Go time in fifteen.

Jimmy had the rest of Black Briar's crew in the barn, of course. Each man and woman was dressed in some form of mail, from chain to scale to full plate on Susan and Maggie.

Weapons lined one wall. Crossbows and falchions, swords and shields. The real items, not our rattan practice toys. The metal of the double-bladed axe that stood by the lockers gleamed gold in the flickering light of several more lanterns.

The twins, Gunther and Stuart, sat against the wall with real weapons at their sides. Gunther had a huge claymore and Stuart a tall, double-bladed axe. They were impressive. Everyone else stood in a circle around Jimmy. Three score fighters. Even Rolph stood with them, a smaller axe held loosely in one hand and a shield in the other.

". . . last chance," Jimmy was saying. "When we hear

the signal, we beat feet out into a skirmish line, just like we practiced."

I walked over to the twins, tipped two fingers at them, and stood at the back of the crowd, listening to Jimmy's pep talk.

He saw me and nodded, but kept on with his speech. "We'll have medics on duty," he said, looking from one individual to the next. "Deidre will be working with any wounded, along with Melanie Danvers, a real emergency room physician."

"We aren't playing here," Gunther said from the sideline.

"Aye," Stuart added, standing. "No heroes needed."

"Good point," Jimmy said. "If you are ready to fight, then stay. If you are afraid, or just don't want to risk this, no harm, no foul. Head into the house and Deidre will put you to work doing something equally useful."

To their credit, not a one of them moved. If anything, they were more excited than ever.

"This is a clean swap," I said from the back. Everyone turned to look at me. I quelled the urge to run and squared my shoulders. "We have one badass for sure, likely shock troops to boot." I looked across the line, putting each face in my memory—accountant, two cops, at least one hairdresser, Chloe. Students and truck drivers, construction workers and one retired librarian. This was my clan, the family I chose.

"Listen up, people," Jimmy said, clapping his hands. "They come in, Sarah makes the swap." He looked over at me for confirmation.

I nodded.

"Excellent. Sarah makes the swap and we get the women up to the house. Once the bad guys have left the property and the women are safe, we can stand down."

"Should be no need for all this," I said, waving my

hands around the room. "But it's nice to know you are there if I need you."

Bob, the accountant, lifted his fist in the air and grunted, "Hoo-rah."

Everyone else broke out into giggles and began pounding their neighbor's fist.

Lord protect us.

Jimmy signaled to the twins, who got up and began lowering the lamps. Soon, the only real light on the farm was the blazing bonfire.

I put the helm on my head, cinched the chin strap, and made sure the hammers had just the right amount of play in their holsters.

I took a deep breath and walked out of the barn.

Three steps from the door, Rolph jogged up to me. "Smith."

I turned. "Yes, dwarf?"

He patted the flat of the axe on his thigh and looked around. "I await your signal."

"I'm really going to trade this for the women," I said, watching his face in the shadows.

If he flinched, I couldn't see it.

"Do what you must," he said, bowing. "Love before honor."

I tilted my head to the side, trying to read him. "You are an odd dwarf."

He chuckled. "You have no idea," he said, moving to stand behind me, to the right.

Together we crossed the ring of light from the bonfire and out into the blackness of the field. Fire to our back seemed a decent position to be in. I knew they were coming from the north. I could feel it.

"Luck, Beauhall," Gunther bellowed from back by the barn.

"Can it," Jimmy said, and the sounds fell away to where only the crackling of the bonfire reached me.

Fifty

THE HEAVY THRUM of choppers pounded in my chest moments before three of them crested the trees and flew toward the bonfire. One broke left, one right, and the third hung back a little, forming an inverted point. Each of them scanned the field with searchlights, starting at the bonfire and working outward.

Once they found me and Rolph, the other lights settled on us, covering us in the bright halogen glow.

"Something is wrong," Rolph said, taking a step away from me.

"You didn't see choppers in our future?" I asked.

"Yes, helicopters. But there should only be two."

I jerked my head around, and Rolph shied back another step, panic on his face.

I grabbed his arm, pulling him to a halt. He spun around, his eyes wild.

"Two? You expected two?" I shouted over the noise. "Whose side are you on?" I asked.

He clutched the shield against his chest, with the axe tight against the shield. His breathing was coming fast. "I honor the sword," he mewled.

"Meaning what?" I asked, punching him in the arm.

He looked at me, glanced at the sword over my shoulder, and nodded. "So mote it be," he said, kneeling down and bowing his head, with his arms out to his sides. His axe and shield dropped to the ground.

I stared at him, contemplating his liability, when a new set of lights bounced at us from the south.

"Limo," Stuart shouted, and I half turned, shielding my eyes to see a stretch limousine coming down the drive toward the bonfire.

To my left, the choppers began to land. To my right, the limo pulled around sideways between us and the barn. In front of me Rolph Brokkrson, dwarf and smith, knelt at my mercy.

Okay, this was unfair.

"Get up, dwarf," I barked, and he lifted his head. "We'll sort this out after Katie is safe."

"Are you sure?" he asked.

"Give me your word of honor you will help me."

He stood, eager. "You have my word."

"Excellent," I said, turning northward. "Get your gear."

As he recovered the axe and shield the spotlights winked out.

The choppers were landing. Two of them were the big twin-rotor types—troop carriers. The third was a sleek attack chopper. The wicked chain gun on the front could turn this whole field into hamburger in a matter of seconds.

Real military-grade equipment here. Not comforting in the least.

The one on the right landed, disgorging its cargo. Thirty bulky men I assumed to be giants. The second chopper, on the left, didn't wait to land before dozens of lanky men leapt out. Once the chopper's wheels touched down, two large, square figures stepped out, not even ducking under the turning blades.

"Trolls," Rolph breathed, pointing to the many. "Another thirty or more. And ogres," he said, pointing his axe at the two hulking brutes. Even with the glamour I knew to be on them, they barely looked human.

The trolls were only smaller in comparison to the thugs on the right. The ogres had a head on me, and were as lithe as boulders.

Once the third chopper was on the ground, the enemy fanned out, forming a half circle between me and the chopper. All they had to do was rush forward, and they could close me in a circle of large, brutish bodies.

Oh yeah, this was looking better by the minute.

A person I could only assume was Jean-Paul emerged from the middle chopper. He was much shorter than I expected, but bulky, like a football player. The light from the choppers and the bonfire gave me a good view. Jean-Paul was a fop, a dandy.

I'd say pimp, but he dressed more like a jester than a power broker. He straightened his jacket and reached back into the chopper, yanking someone through the door and out onto the ground.

It was Katie. She fell at his feet, her clothes shredded and in tatters. But she was alive and that's all that mattered to me.

He kicked her. "Get up, pig."

Rage erupted in me. I had both hammers in my hands and was running across the field toward the bastard. *Twenty yards*, my mind read. *Eighteen more then I can smash his brains in. Fifteen, twelve.*

I screamed. The words were an ancient Swedish dialect, my mind said, the part of my mind that sat off to the side, like the astral projection. The rational superego that kept score, watched for transgressions, filing grievances.

The id blossomed into a mantra of smash, maim, kill.

"Stop," a woman behind me called, and to my utter astonishment, I did.

Not because of any desire on my part, mind you. I nearly frothed in fury, grunting guttural epithets in obscure languages.

When I realized I could not approach the dragon, I turned to see who compelled me to stop.

She strode from the limousine, tall and beautiful. I sensed more than saw her beauty. The ground around her shone with a pale blue glow. She seemed to float toward me.

A knee-length cloak swirled around her in varying shades of blue, giving her the illusion of moving in murky shadows. She pushed back a fur-lined hood to reveal an exotic beauty: pale hair and dark, dusky complexion. Around her neck hung a necklace of feathers and leaves.

She chanted as she approached; the words were quiet, just beyond hearing, but as the sound washed over the field, a bluish mist fell from her lips and pushed along the ground. The fog swirled around my feet, creeping up past my ankles, only to fall away again, like it wanted to take shape, to form an appendage of some sort and grab my legs.

Fear began to creep into the fury, tingeing the world in a mixture of red and blue.

This beauty paused, puckered her lips, and blew. The fog that swirled up to my knees collapsed back into a fog and rushed forward toward the choppers.

"*Seið-kona*," Rolph muttered off to my side.

"You interfere, witch," Jean-Paul called, closer than I'd remembered.

I turned slowly, letting my gaze fall on him. Four yards, twelve feet. I could cover that distance in a sneeze.

Katie lay at his feet. Through the tears in her clothes I could see the lash marks on her back, and dried blood on her face as she looked up toward me.

As the fog rolled forward, the glamour that surrounded the men fell away, revealing the true forms of giants, trolls, and two rocky ogres.

"You bargain in ill faith, Jean-Paul," the witch said, gliding forward. "Nidhogg gave her word that you would meet your original bargain."

Jean-Paul bristled at the name Nidhogg. Frederick had called it right.

The witch stepped up to me and pulled a furred glove from her left hand. She kissed the tips of the first two fingers, and placed them on my left cheek.

The rage vanished. Muscles I had been clenching relaxed, aches vanished, and my mind was clear of the anger and fear.

"Be at peace, warrior."

"Who are you?" I asked, relieved to be in control of my actions once again.

"I am Qindra," she said. "I am the mouth of Nidhogg."

"Bitch," Jean-Paul spat. "Lapdog." He put his boot on Katie's back and stepped over her, forcing her to sprawl forward onto her stomach. "Whore."

Qindra laughed, stepping around me and wagging a finger at Jean-Paul. "Silly boy," she said in a lovely condescending voice. "You are spoiled and petulant. Perhaps it is time for you to be punished." She raised her hands in front of her face, as if to clap them together, and looked at him sideways between her palms.

Blue energy crackled up her palms and danced in the air above her fingertips. In their light, I could see that the nail of each finger was painted with a single rune.

"Is there no chattel to bed for your mistress?" he asked. "No overwrought sheep that needs your special attention?"

She smiled at him and touched the smallest finger of each hand together. Thunder rolled in the distance, and lightning played across the horizon.

He threw his head back and laughed.

Cruelty played in that noise, evil and vain. He would not sleep without vengeance. Would not let pass the slightest transgression. Those who offended him paid a heavy price. That is what that laughter said to me.

He raised one hand and swung it forward, arcing toward us.

From the darkness a boulder soared. Qindra flicked her wrist, and a rock the size of a pony spun aside, smashing into the ground.

"That is but a taste," he said, the ego rising in him.

She smiled and touched two fingers together.

The smaller chopper exploded. The concussion rolled across the field like a wave, knocking everyone to the ground, Rolph, Jean-Paul, the giants, and the trolls.

Only Qindra remained on her feet as a mushroom cloud of flame rose into the night.

"Peace," Jean Paul said, climbing to his knees. Katie rose to her feet first, before any of us, and kicked Jean-Paul in the face. His head snapped around as blood flew from his mouth.

Jean-Paul lashed out, spinning on his hands, his booted foot clipping her leg, and she stumbled to the ground. He quickly rose, stepping on her hair. He touched his mouth, brought his hand away, saw the blood, and spat on her.

Some barrier prevented me from lunging forward. A wall of energy stood between us. I struggled to my feet and glanced around at Qindra, who shrugged.

"Bargain in good faith," she said.

Jean-Paul stepped to the side, squatted, and pulled Katie's head up by her hair to stare into her face. "Still have some fire in you after all we've shared," he said, jerking her hair tight and twisting her neck back farther. "Shall I tell your lover about our adventures?"

"Stop this," Qindra said, the quiet sibilance of her voice cutting through the night.

He stood, wiping the blood from his mouth with a handkerchief he pulled from his shirt pocket. "Quite right," he said. "We have business to attend to."

He waved his left hand and two of the trolls broke ranks, jogging to the chopper, and returned carrying a stretcher. They placed it on the ground to my right.

They smelled of carrion, the overwhelming sickly

sweet stench of decay. Their bodies were covered in sores—pustules that wept a foul ooze. One of them lifted the corner of the sheet and whipped it away, before running back to the line on the left.

Julie lay on the stretcher, battered and bloody. The right leg of her jeans had been shredded, and her broken femur stuck out of the thigh muscle. The whole leg was swollen, and looked shorter, twisted. I couldn't imagine how much pain she had to be in.

At this moment, she wasn't even moving, and in that instant I feared she was dead. She drew a shuddering breath and I did the same.

"Here is the first," he said, flipping his hand at me as if to dismiss my very existence.

"Medic," I shouted.

Jean-Paul rolled his eyes and turned to stare down at Katie.

Gunther and Stuart ran up, looked at me, and I nodded. They glanced over at Katie, but I tipped my head at Julie and they grabbed the stretcher.

"Melanie will see to her," Stuart said, and they carried her back toward the house.

Katie looked up at me, past Jean-Paul's legs, and our eyes met.

"Let her go," I said, my voice thick.

"Get up, bitch," Jean-Paul said.

I growled and leaned forward, straining the barrier that contained me, but Qindra held up one hand and I fell back. *Get her out alive*, I told myself. *Get her to safety. This guy can pay another time. Do whatever it takes.*

"Really rather vulgar, even for you," Qindra said, looking at the back of her hand.

Jean-Paul snapped his head around and I could see the dragon struggling to come out. "I thought you were a neutral witness," he hissed.

"I thought you were a whore killer and pedophile," Qindra said sweetly.

Jean-Paul lurched forward, his fingers curled inward, like claws. "I will kill you, witch. Kill you and make flutes from your bones."

My fear painted the dragon in his stead—a shadowy form that spread above and beyond him, a black echo of what he could truly become.

The part of my brain that was still a little girl cringed. I wanted nothing more than to abandon all this and hide behind someone larger than me, someone stronger and more powerful.

Qindra laughed.

And with the high tinkling gaiety of that sound, the fear fell to the ground, shattering into a thousand shards of old dreams.

"I could take your eyes for daring to look upon me," she said, the power and venom in her voice making her every bit as threatening as Jean-Paul, or Frederick in his own right. "Nidhogg would hurt you in ways beyond even your cruel fantasies," she said.

Jean-Paul stiffened, holding his head high. It took him a moment, but he managed to contain his wrath. With a shuddering breath, he let his shoulders sag, nodding once toward Qindra. "My apologies," he said, his voice as poisonous as a viper.

Qindra smiled and bowed to me. "I believe you have a transaction to complete."

Jean-Paul motioned to Katie, who stood beside him. For a moment I thought she would fall, but she looked at me, her face determined, and she steadied herself, holding her head high.

Why hadn't she said anything, I wondered.

I settled the hammers back into their holsters at my waist, slipped my right arm through the leather strap that kept the sword sheath secure on my back, and slid the whole rig around and over my shoulder. I eased the scabbard from the harness and held Gram, ensconced in leather, in front of me.

"Bring it to me," he said, his voice full of contempt. I knew this was wrong. I could feel it emanating from the sword, through the leather. Gram did not want to be turned over to this beast, this murderer. I could feel the need to draw the sword, lunge forward, and let it drink from his black, black heart.

"Set it before me," he said, his voice commanding and bitter.

Qindra scratched her thumbnail across the rune on her left middle fingernail. The wall that held me ceased to exist. I stumbled forward onto my knees, slapping the sword against the ground at his feet. If I looked at him, if I glanced up and saw his face once more, I would balk, renege on the deal, and Katie would be lost to me.

Fifty-one

"No!" ROLPH SHOUTED before my hands left the sword. His footsteps echoed through the earth like the staccato of pebbles falling on a drumhead.

Gram throbbed, power pulsing through the leather. In my mind's eye, I saw Rolph leap forward and I rolled to the side.

Too late. His axe careened off my helm and ricocheted off my shoulder with a painful crunch, although the chain kept the blade from biting into flesh.

I pulled the sword in against my chest, and continued rolling onto my back.

Rolph was on me in an instant, his hand reaching for the sword.

"You cannot," he bellowed. His eyes were full of sorrow and madness.

Rolph dropped onto me, his weight crushing the wind from me. I brought a knee up into his thigh, and he shifted his weight, allowing me to get my left arm under his.

"Get off . . . ," I grunted.

He grabbed for the sword, and I punched him in the throat. Any normal man would have fallen to the side, gasping for breath. Instead, he head-butted me in the chest.

Breasts may be lovely cushiony things, but they do not like to be punched. Pain exploded in my chest.

I cried out and thrashed to the side, throwing him off balance. I twisted, getting my legs free, then wrapped them around his waist and rolled.

He slipped to the side and just like that, I was on top of him. I smashed my gloved fist into his face, breaking his nose. Blood sprayed across the ground, and his grip loosened on my bad arm. The sword lay on the ground between us and Jean-Paul.

As long as I kept Rolph at bay, Jean-Paul would get the sword and this would all be over. Only, when he looked at me, grinned that carnivore's grin of teeth and hell, part of me balked.

When Jean-Paul moved toward the sword, the overwhelming urge to keep it from him flooded me. If he ended up with the sword, everything I loved would fall to ruin.

I launched myself off of Rolph and reached the sword half a beat ahead, pulled it against my chest, and rolled.

Jean-Paul stomped the ground where my head had been and twirled to face me. He crouched in a fighter's stance, ready for anything I could throw at him.

Only, I didn't want to fight him. I wanted him to take the damn sword and get out of our lives, hopefully forever. The conflicting emotions warred in my head, one asking to end this, the other screaming to keep the sword from him, no matter the sacrifice.

I tried to rise by pushing off with my right hand, and nearly fell on my face. Jean-Paul smiled and offered me his hand.

"Bite me," I said, smacking his hand and standing without his help. My right arm hung at my side, twitching. In my left I held the sword, letting the power wash over me like a rising tide.

"As it shall be," Jean-Paul said, stepping back, the flames returned to his eyes. "Perhaps I'll take the sword and keep this plaything." He stepped toward Katie.

Katie called out, a guttural choke, her hand reaching for me, but the warning was too late to prevent Rolph's full-body tackle. The world dimmed for a moment as I hit the ground with him on top of me again. As much time as I'd spent under him, I should demand dinner. At the moment, I'd settle for a breath.

"I claim the sword," Rolph bellowed as he swung his right fist into my side.

Pain blossomed along my ribs and I drew a ragged breath.

"You forfeit . . ." He flailed at me. ". . . any claim . . ." His voice broke and I could tell he wept. "Unworthy . . . ," he moaned.

"Oh, hang them," Jean-Paul shouted. "Kill them all."

Fifty-two

I BROUGHT MY knee upward and this time, I caught Rolph in the groin. He fell to the side and I pushed away from him. Once I was out of his reach I scrambled to my feet, breathing in gulps.

Jean-Paul smiled at me, holding Gram in its sheath. Bastard. I ran forward, only to be knocked to the side by a fifteen-foot-tall wall of ugly.

I landed on my ass, and the giant stumbled with two crossbow bolts in his chest.

"Leave her," I shouted.

My only answer was laughter. Jean-Paul faded back toward the chopper. He had Katie on her feet and was pulling her along by her arm.

"Katie," I choked out. She whipped her head around, and they were swallowed in a wall of bodies.

A wave of huge bodies, each fifteen feet of muscles and bone, ran at me.

I turned, looking for Qindra.

"What a mess," she said, holding her two index fingers together and pointing them like a gun. Lightning leapt forth, swallowing a giant that had swerved toward us.

"The covenant is broken," she said, pulling a feather from the charm at her neck and flicking it at me. She vanished in a puff of smoke.

I tasted stale tequila, if you can believe it, in that moment.

And the rage in me was freed once again.

I strode into the battle, a haze of red coloring every image.

Behind me I heard the distinct sound of crossbows, and several of the giants stumbled in their lumbering gait. Of course, they did not fall.

"Black Briar!" someone shouted behind me.

I drew a hammer in each hand and swung the left at a giant that lumbered past me, shattering his elbow. He swung his left fist at me, and I rolled to the side, smashing his ankle with the second hammer.

He fell, tangling up two others, and I leapt over him, bringing both hammers down in a spray of blood and brains.

The rest of the giants surged past me only to smash into the Black Briar skirmish line.

No matter the hours we trained, nor the coolness of our gear, we were just not equipped to handle this type of fight.

The skirmish line looked good, shields locked, their spears bristling out like a porcupine.

Several giants fell back when they impacted the wall, but the momentum and weight carried them forward in several places. Once they were through, they decimated the line.

There were sixty people in that shield wall. Good, strong people I thought of as family. More than my own mother and father.

Chloe, the hairdresser, died in that next instant, crushed by a maul-like fist. She had done everything right, held her place, shield up. A giantess writhed on the ground in front of the line, Chloe's spear piercing her huge throat.

But Bob the accountant hadn't held. He'd buckled and was crushed beneath the stomping feet of two giants.

The hole that opened split the Black Briar line and Chloe never even saw what killed her.

Spears were dropped and swords drawn. The SCAdians broke into groups of twos or threes, guarding each other's backs while fending off the giants.

I paused at a downed giant, kicked the spear that pierced his chest. He threw his head back, bellowing in pain.

I crushed his throat.

Whirling around, I saw that two of our people were hard-pressed by a giant with a telephone-pole-sized club. On his backswing, I darted in and drove a hammer's spiked head into his spine.

As he fell to the ground, my people scrambled forward, hacking and cutting. He would not rise again.

Gunther leapt over one fallen warrior, Trisha, I think,

and swung his great sword, severing a giant arm. He stood over his fallen comrade and screamed like a banshee.

The giant did not fade, but swung a club around, catching Gunther in the leg, collapsing his knee, driving him to the ground.

I sprinted forward, racing the swing of the giant's club. I threw myself at the back of the giant's legs.

He fell, startled, blood showering the area with arterial flow from his flailing stump. Gunther rose up on one knee and drove his sword into the giant chest, and I rolled to my feet, hammers at the ready.

From the haze, Stuart darted forward, grabbing Trisha and Gunther, dragging them both back toward the barn.

I ran after them apace, ensuring they were not followed.

Then the ogres hit us.

One sword shattered against the body of an ogre, and crossbow bolts fell to the ground, splintered and bent.

I fell upon the closest, striking it in the back, blow after blow, as it staggered forward, trying to turn to face me. It swung its arms around, pinwheeling, but I danced in, hammering. On the fourth blow, a seam appeared. On the sixth blow, the whole shoulder shattered and the ogre fell to the ground, a heap of broken stone.

We could not stand against their strength, their numbers.

"Fall back," I shouted. "Form on me."

Two warriors stumbled to my side, shields up. To my left, another group fought toward me.

"Left flank," I said, moving to meet the second group. Between us, we slew two trolls and then we were five.

We battled forward to a giant who was pounding his club down on a fallen SCAdian. I didn't even recognize them any longer, but those with me pulled the giant down, stabbing it over and over—our cries of anguish and horror rising into the night.

Several giants rushed the far right flank, nearest the barn.

One of them snatched up a smallish warrior, maybe Robert, one of the young computer programmers. Whoever it was, he was flung high into the air. The body hit the barn and rolled down to fall on the ground, broken.

"Right," I shouted, sprinting toward the giants. Several people stood shoulder to shoulder, spears in hand, but they weren't warriors, they were the support crew.

One of ours took a blow just below his shield with a short spear. He went down, keeping his shield up enough to divert the next blow. We rushed forward, swords and glaives catching the troll unaware.

"Thank the Maker," Kyle George said, leveraging himself up onto his feet. The leather breeches he wore had absorbed some of the blow, but blood soaked his leg.

"Get him behind the line," I bellowed.

"I'll take him," Samantha said, wiping her sword on the rough hide armor of the troll. She sheathed the blade and lifted Kyle's arm over her shoulder. While we watched, they lumbered back toward the safety of the barn.

Or, I thought it was safe. The sound of a shotgun blast erupted from that direction.

"Who has that?" I yelled.

Brett, an insurance salesman and damn fine fighter, pointed back at the barn. "Deidre," he shouted. "She's in trouble."

I turned, torn. The barn was behind our skirmish zone—a safe place for our wounded.

A second blast erupted and I saw a giant fall to the ground, where the support crew turned it into a pincushion.

Deidre stood on top of the picnic table, chambering another shell into her shotgun. *Helluva woman*, I thought.

"Let's move, people," I bellowed. "Troll at two o'clock."

My crew surged forward, taking the troll down. Brett took a hard blow to the head, but the others pulled him back, away from the battle. Then we were four.

Just past the troll that had got a lucky shot in on Brett, we heard chanting.

Once the troll was dispatched, we moved in that direction. I could hear Stuart's voice rising above the rest.

"Black Briar," he called.

"Black Briar!" his squad returned.

"Cut 'em down."

"Cut 'em down!"

A troll fell back, turning and stumbling, blood covering his torso, his armor in shreds.

Imagine his surprise when we stood between him and freedom.

I hit him with both hammers—Redondo—each circular blow striking with practiced precision. One hammer caught his left arm, the second hit the same arm, shattering it, forcing him to drop his spear. I stepped forward, letting the third blow strike the head. He fell with a finality that let my squad ignore him and rush the giant that harassed Stuart's squad.

Between us, the giant had no chance. Once he fell, our two units met and merged. We paused to breathe, twelve stoic Black Briar clan members, winded but alive.

"Too many down," Stuart said, once he'd had a chance to catch his breath. "Too many of them standing."

"Aye," I said, looking across the field. One of the giants had fallen into the bonfire, scattering the logs out into the field, and fires had begun in the surrounding grass.

"Rally to the barn," I suggested, clapping Stuart on the shoulder.

"What about Katie?" he asked.

I turned and looked across the field. Through the haze and smoke, I could see Katie struggling against Jean-Paul as he dragged her back to one of the choppers. *Good girl*, I thought, *keep fighting the bastard.*

I'd been so swept up in rescuing folks, taking down the next target, that I'd lost the ball. Time to rescue Katie, before it was too late.

"Save the wounded, protect the barn," I said to Stuart, and sprinted away from them.

"Come on, ladies," Stuart shouted. "Let's show Gunther what real warriors can do."

I glanced back, saw them sprinting back into battle, moving toward another knot of us holding our own against the onslaught.

"Black Briar's gonna rock your world," they sang, cadence and call.

They would be okay. They had to be.

Fifty-three

I'D LOST COUNT of the fallen, but we were not the only ones thinking on the field. Four giants and several trolls had followed our lead and were rallying together. Only this group followed the chaotic path of the remaining ogre. As I sprinted past, I saw them mow through four warriors who had taken a stand.

"Swords don't work against him," I growled. "Come on, people. Use your heads."

Of course they couldn't hear me. Hell, they were likely dead.

Stuart and his crew had taken down another troll and were dragging some of the wounded back toward the barn when I climbed atop a fallen giant to get my bearings. It was like walking on top of a mattress, but I needed the vantage point.

Katie was on the ground again, and Jean-Paul kicked her, shouting and waving Gram at her, holding the sheath halfway down the blade.

Why hadn't he drawn it?

As I got closer, I started seeing burning debris from the attack helicopter scattered across the field. Several bodies lay among the wreckage. I guessed one had been the pilot, based on the helmet he wore.

Jean-Paul looked around, like a hound catching a scent, and turned toward the copter that had delivered the giants. The pilot there had the blades spinning already. That one was earning his pay.

A sound rose in the distance, a clear high call. I glanced around. There it was again. Horns. Two horns blew, signaling . . . I stopped and looked back. Jimmy, Susan, Maggie, and Brendon thundered across the field, warhorses in full bardic armor, lances lowered and shields locked onto knees.

The knot of giants and trolls that were following the remaining ogre scattered as the lances ripped through them.

The four of them split two and two, banking around the crowd. They turned in unison, dropping their shattered lances. Susan and Maggie drew swords, Brendon and Jimmy horsemen's maces.

They came around for a second pass, the two men attacking the ogre as they rode by. Susan and Maggie ran down fleeing trolls.

Stuart's crew caught up with them and rushed in, cutting down one of the remaining giants. The battle had turned again.

Smoke covered the field, and the smell of petrol and burning flesh choked me as I ran for the first chopper.

A troll stepped in front of me, through the smoke. I nearly ran into the long bill-guisarme he'd managed to swing around in my direction. He was as surprised to see me as I him.

I smashed his weapon to the side, and the hooked bill snagged in the sleeve of my chain, ripping a gash into my arm and pulling me off balance. Instead of stepping back to catch my balance, I lunged forward, spinning to the outside. I brought a hammer up under the shaft, flipping it upward and out of his hands. The momentum brought me around for a solid strike, allowing me a chance to smash his right shoulder with my hammer.

He lumbered to the side, tripping over the pole arm, and sprawled facedown in the trampled grass of the field.

I leapt forward, smashing his right hip with my left hammer, and dropping onto his back with my knee, bringing the second hammer onto the back of his head.

Trolls have very thick heads, it seems, and spines that don't actually follow expected rules of physics.

I hurt him, there was no doubt by the way he shrieked, but he rolled aside, flipping me onto the ground, and was nearly upon me before I pulled my knees up and launched both feet into his chest.

Heavy mother, I thought, as I lifted him off the ground and deposited him to the left side, away from my right hammer. The left one lay on the ground five feet beyond our skirmish.

We were both on our feet at the same time, but he had taken more wounds. He dove forward biting at me, much to my surprise. I brought the hammer up, smashing the side of his face, and he fell.

I didn't have time to bother checking him. I limped over to my other hammer, picked it up, and hobbled after Jean-Paul, holding my side as breathing became more of an exercise in pain.

The breeze carried a thick waft of smoke away and I saw Jean-Paul punch Katie. She fell like a sack of flour.

"Katie!" I yelled, lurching forward.

Jean-Paul bent over and grabbed her in a fireman's carry. He glanced back at me and lumbered to the chopper. She didn't move.

Don't let her be dead, I prayed as I ran.

The chopper hovered just off the ground. The pilot had the blades spinning at full torque. Jean-Paul leaned against the frame, dropping Katie unceremoniously into the open bay. He slid the sword across the chopper floor, planted both hands on the edge of the door, and jumped in after her, shouting for them to go.

I wasn't going to make it.

He slid the door shut, watching me as I ran toward them.

They were barely off the ground when I caught up to them, but the chopper hovered fifteen feet in the air. I couldn't reach them.

I looked around, thinking I could climb on something and jump, when the sound of the chopper faded. It's not like sound stopped, it just faded back, the battle cries and the heavy beat of the dual blades. Instead, cutting through it all I heard the quiet chanting of Qindra once again. I could not see her in the smoke and chaos, but her voice sang in my head. "*You know what to do, sister. Follow your heart.*"

The runes along my left calf flared to life, burning into me with the intensity of an acetylene torch. I buckled with the pain, dropping to my hands and knees for a moment.

A shard of metal lay on the ground near my hand. I snatched it, ignoring the blistering heat, and twisted around. I used the shard to split my left pant leg open, revealing the glowing runes. Here was my answer.

Using the metal shard, I was able to cut my hand, drawing a line of fire across my palm from thumb to pinkie. Not too deep, but blood welled up quick and dark. I bent, dragging the bloody hand down the length of my calf, feeding the runes with my lifeblood. Power surged into me. I rose, taking three loping strides, and launched the hammer into the air.

The chopper had swung around and was picking up speed when the hammer smashed against the rear rotor housing.

Smoke billowed from the rear motors, and the chopper twisted in the air, seeking stability.

I raised my bloody hand and wiped it across my brow. The painful clarity of all my mistakes, my near misses and could-have-beens, flashed through me. I did not need strength, I surmised. I needed accuracy.

I let fly the second hammer. This one arced high into the sky, only to fall back and strike the rising chopper near the front. I watched with held breath as the hammer smashed into the cockpit, shattering the window with a thunderclap. The echoing explosion blasted outward, knocking me to the ground, and flashing across the battlefield, leveling anyone lucky enough to be on their feet. Lightning exploded from the cockpit. I had to pray that somehow the chopper wouldn't completely fall apart. That I could somehow get to Katie in time.

I rose to my feet and stumbled after the smoking chopper. It didn't fall from the sky, but slid sideways across the tree line, the body spinning counter to the blade rotation.

I stopped at one of the dead pilots, ripped off a long swath of cloth from his flight suit, and wrapped my hand three times, clenching the ends in my fist. Blood soaked the cloth, but I felt no pain. Not yet, anyhow. I slipped the .45 out of the holster under his arm and awkwardly chambered a round.

I stumbled along, watching for the enemy, keeping the chopper in my peripheral vision. The wounded started getting to their feet, and the battles began anew.

Fifty-four

THE CHOPPER SLICED across the sky. Whether guided by a dying pilot, or carried by the winds of fate, the huge machine veered back toward the battlefield and crashed with the horrid shriek of rending metal.

The front rotors smashed into the ground like cannon fire. Brendon Lord had been pushing Titan hard to get out of the way, but the chopper came in too quickly. Titan was smashed to the side by one of the blades and Brendon's mailed body flew toward the barn.

Several giants and trolls were either crushed by the body of the craft, or cut to pudding by the blades as they beat themselves into the ground.

Katie, dear God.

The wreckage was catastrophic. Could anyone survive that?

I ran forward, determined to pull that damn machine apart with my bare hands if I had to.

The chopper lurched upward, almost a bounce. Then lurched again.

On the third time, the doors on the top side exploded into the air.

The dragon erupted from the metal cocoon, large black wings unfurled, eighty feet from tip to tip. With a large sweep, they pulled hard against the night sky, launching the sleek, scaled body upward.

I raised the .45 and pulled the trigger. The first shot belched from the gun with an odd snapping sound. If I hit the dragon, I couldn't tell. He didn't slow. I pulled the trigger four more times, but the gun never fired again. I pulled the clip, and there were rounds there.

I'd lost the dragon, in any case. I tossed the pistol

aside and rushed forward. "Katie!" I shouted, reaching the copter. I could see the dead pilots inside the shattered cockpit as I scrambled up over the wreckage.

I jumped, catching one of the front wheel wells, and leveraged myself upward. Climbing up the bottom of the chopper proved easier than one may think. From the damage, and the protruding bits, I managed to reach the peak and look over into the twisted ruin.

Katie lay crumpled in the bottom, against the far door. I grasped the lip of the opening and lowered myself as far as I could. I swung a little before loosening my grip, so as to not land on Katie.

The chopper shook when I landed. I was at her side in an instant.

"I'm here, Katie," I whispered.

She didn't move, so I sat on a smashed cabinet and stroked her face, crying. "You're okay, baby," I said. "I'm here."

Outside, the screams of the dragon echoed across the countryside, but they sounded tinny inside this shell.

"I'll kill the bastard," I whispered, feeling her for breaks and searching for life-threatening wounds.

She stiffened and I froze. "Katie?" I asked.

She lived, thanks be.

"Hey," she said, relaxing a bit and turning her head toward me. "You feeling me up?" She winced when she moved.

I laughed through the tears, a moment of pure joy.

"Anytime you'll let me," I promised.

"Liar," she said with a smile.

Things in my life had been murky. Shadows and hidden meanings. In that chopper, with the smoke and battle swirling around us, I finally understood the only thing that mattered. I leaned forward and kissed her forehead.

"I'm sorry," I said. "Sorry for everything—the fear, and the shame . . ." I trailed off, overwhelmed.

She watched me, not saying anything. After a moment she reached up and stroked the side of my face. "You're bleeding."

"It's nothing," I said, capturing her hand in my own. "I love you, Katie."

She smiled. "I know, you freak."

Of course she did.

"You are just stubborn, and pigheaded and afraid," she said.

"Is that all?"

"No," she said. "There is one more thing."

I waited, knowing that I had much to atone for in my fear and anxiety. "Only one?" I asked.

"Kiss me," she said.

I leaned forward and pressed my lips against hers. Her skin was ashen and her lips were split, but I touched mine against hers, gently.

"That's better," she said. "Can we go home now?"

I helped her sit up. She was covered in welts and bruises. He'd hit her, a lot, the bastard. I'd pull his wings off him, if I had the chance.

"Not sure how we are getting out," I said. "We could . . ."

Something large smashed against the top of the chopper. I looked up to see the dragon perched on top of us, his long neck craned down to press his narrow head into the doorway. He smiled, darted his head forward.

I dove over Katie, covering her with my body. She gasped as my weight pushed on her chest. Gnashing, foot-long teeth snapped together in the space I had just been in.

"Sorry," I said, pushing myself upward, and launched a full booted kick to the side of the dragon's head.

He whipped his head to the side, bouncing against a dislocated luggage rack, and bellowed in pain.

"Come on, you pussy," I growled, scrambling off Katie and darting forward again. Talk about target of opportunity. Before me was his gorgeous eye, about the size of a dinner plate. The iris was black with a mixture of gold.

I punched it for all I was worth. It felt like punching a bag of pudding. My arm sank forward, past the wrist, and a thick, milky liquid splashed over my arm and down the front of me.

His shriek reverberated inside the chopper, and I fell, covering my ears. His right eye gaped as he blinked bloody tears. Noxious vapors rose from his nostrils and a smoking liquid dripped from between his teeth, splashing on the shattered seats. The thick canvas material began to smolder.

He swung his head around, faster than I imagined possible, and smashed me to the side, the scales along his cheek grating along my chain. The links parted with a ringing snap.

I fell onto my side, the impact of his face knocking the wind out of me. I couldn't draw enough breath.

Breathe.

Why didn't he breathe inside the chopper? Turn us both into charcoal.

Then I saw it. The sword was wedged under one of the shattered seats. If he toasted us, he toasted the sword.

The first breath I could suck in hurt like a bitch, but it was better than the alternative.

He pulled his head back out near the top of the hole and looked around with his good left eye.

"Come on . . . you . . . coward," I gasped, trying to stand. "Fight . . . like a . . . man."

He swung his good eye around to me and snorted. Smoke and ash spewed over me, blinding me for a moment, causing me to cough.

My chest burned. I needed fresh air.

I fell, blacking out for a bit.

Katie's mouth was pressed against my own. She

breathed into me, pushing air into my battered lungs. I rolled over, coughing.

"Where's . . . ?" I choked.

"He's gone," she said, cradling my head. "He's gone." Then we were moving.

"He's lifting us," Katie said. She had crawled onto one of the cushioned bench seats that had remained bolted to the floor, huddling with her knees up to her chest.

I looked forward to the busted cockpit windows as we swung around.

"Hang on," I shouted, and we flopped through the air.

I dove for Katie's seat, covering her with my body, protecting her from more harm.

We bounced when we smashed to the ground.

"That chain is a bit rough," Katie said when I rolled off of her.

"Sorry," I said, grinning sheepishly. Somewhere high above us, the dragon roared. "We gotta get out of here."

She sat up, looking around. We were right side up this time, but tilted forward. We'd landed on something or some things and the tail of the chopper rose into the air at a good thirty-degree angle.

There were openings on either side of the chopper. To my left, a pair of giant legs appeared, and something large and heavy smashed against the rear of the chopper. To my right, there was an opening between several broken bodies.

"Come on," I said, crawling forward.

We made it to the door as the first giant reached in, ripping out the seat we'd just been in. Katie scrambled past me to the churned-up grass and I rolled out of the chopper as the seat was flung after us.

A face like a smashed penny poked in, followed by a pair of large hands, ripping the opening wider.

The chopper rocked forward, the rear going higher into the air.

We ran a few steps, Katie hobbling along across the broken ground, and I stopped. She'd make it from here.

"Run for the barn," I said. "I have to go back."

"For what?" she asked, turning.

"The sword," I said. "They can't have it."

She looked past me, concerned. "Be careful," she said, scrambling back to kiss me on the nose. "Don't get killed."

"No chance," I said, running back into the gaping wreckage. I'd seen the sword near the back, wedged in behind one of the benches that ran along the last half of the cargo area.

Fifty-five

I HAD TO climb upward at a pretty stiff angle while one of the giants scrambled the insides of the mangled chopper, searching for the same thing, no doubt.

He was wedged inside the wreckage. How so many of them had fit inside here was beyond me. Powerful magic, that. I slipped past a fallen set of cabinets, and he reached round, clipping my hip.

"Get off," I said, pushing his hand away. I slid down to catch my feet on a broken cargo support strut, and the calloused hand raked along my body, bouncing my head against the metal floor, sending stars racing behind my eyes.

I grabbed a twisted punched metal strap and hauled myself upward toward the sword. The giant poked his head around the cabinets, getting his bearings.

There was no loose debris near me, having all rolled down toward the cockpit. I felt naked without a weapon. I could've punched him, but he outweighed me by a few hundred pounds. Instead, I continued climbing.

We saw the sword at the same time. I leapt from a bench support, assisting my momentum by grabbing the bench and pulling upward.

The giant scrambled after me, forcing the balance to tip toward the back, and I fell ass over teakettle toward the rear of the chopper, past the sword and against the rear wall.

I covered my head as loose debris, metal plating, and shattered Plexiglas rained down on me.

The giant caught himself on a broken bench. He pulled one of the cabinets loose and dropped it on top of me. I twisted, taking the brunt of the force on my back and shoulder. I didn't feel anything get past the chain, but it was worse than getting kicked by a horse.

The sword hung by the leather harnessing, trapped on one of the many twisted bolts that stood out. I pushed the cabinet to the side as the giant pulled himself upward to the front of the chopper, tipping his balance too far forward. He grabbed the sword by the scabbard, tangling the harness in his fingers.

"Not today," I said, pushing off the floor—wall—whatever, and jumping. I was just able to wrap my hands in the harness, pulling the giant more off balance. He slid backward, catching some part of his clothing on a piece of the wreckage. I swung in a slow circle, my boots a good four feet from the pile of debris and sharp, pointy metal bits.

We remained in that position for several seconds, each debating our next move.

I pulled myself upward. All those hours hammering metal had some benefit. The giant pushed with his feet against the remaining bench, leveraging himself toward the front. If he could tilt the balance back, I'd fall into his lap.

Someone else must have caught on. For one moment

he had a panicked look on his face as I pulled myself closer to the sword, and the next he was grinning, as the chopper tilted back toward the front.

Once we rose far enough, a second giant scrambled into the chopper and I knew I was dead.

I swung my legs toward the wall, pushed off the roof, and pulled myself upward, bending at the waist and wrapping my legs around his arm.

He swung his free hand, pounding me on the back as I pulled the blade free of the scabbard. We flew forward as a third giant climbed in and we flipped back to the fore. He lost his hold and I fell after him, yanking on the sword for dear life. Once the blade was free of the scabbard, I twisted, slashing it out in a wide arc, catching the giant in the face, slicing through temple, eye, nose, mouth. The sword did not stop, just parted his skull like paper.

He fell onto the next giant, who had just found his footing, and I landed on top of them both. The third giant fell onto his knees, nearly falling out of the opening.

I landed on top of the first giant, who thrashed against the cockpit, his brain not recognizing that he was already dead. I rolled out of the chopper, landing on my knees, looking around for bad guys. The two remaining giants scrambled out after me.

The first went down as I whirled and brought the sword through his knee. He bellowed as he fell, nearly drowning out the sound of battle in the distance.

From above, the dragon screamed again, and we all looked up.

The black shadow filled the sky like a bruise for a moment, then dropped toward us like a plague. I steeled myself against the fear that threatened to swallow me. At the last minute, I dove. The dragon strafed us, claws out. The standing giant shrieked as the claws ripped through him, slamming him against the chopper, bits and pieces spraying the ground around me.

I scrambled to my feet and ran around the end of the battered machine. A battle line had been drawn at the barn, and the remaining SCAdians fought against a wall of trolls and several wounded but lethal giants.

The sword sang in my head. The runes along the blade glowed with energy, fueled by the blood of the enemy.

Here was power, here was strength. With this blade, I could bring down that dragon. If I lived long enough.

I wove in and out of fallen bodies, approaching the barn from the west. The SCAdians had built a berm around the barn with two horse trailers, several barrels, the rough-hewn feast tables, and the overturned limousine that had brought Qindra to this little soiree.

One of the giants lifted a dead horse with obvious effort and flung it over the wall. It was Titan, Brendan Lord's trusty Belgian warhorse. He had been a steady and loving animal, bastards.

Cries rose from the defenders as the horse fell among the stretchers, scattering the wounded like pick up sticks.

I ran along the left flank and darted in among the enemy. They didn't expect an attack from that quarter, focused as they were on the small wall. I managed to hamstring the first giant when the dragon roared over us belching a stream of fire.

Napalm blasted across the roof of the barn and rained down on friend and foe alike. More smoke billowed over the battle, and SCAdians began an orderly retreat toward the house. Many of the wounded struggled back under their own power, but too many had to be carried or dragged on their litters.

I slashed at the enemy as they fought to escape the flames as well. I don't have a clue how many I touched, but more than one troll left the field with fewer appendages.

They were not stupid, just panicked. One troll slammed me aside with a shield I recognized from our crew. They'd scavenged from the fallen.

I ran to the line, calling out to the survivors.

Fifty-six

STUART MET ME at one of the breaches, a bandage around one arm, and the double-bladed axe in his hands. I noticed several notches. I'd be needing to make him a new axe.

"Katie ran past us," he said, watching the enemy fall back. "Melanie has saved several who would've died otherwise."

He didn't look at me at all, I realized. His eyes were haunted.

"You okay, Stuart?" I asked, clapping him on the shoulder.

"Too many hurt," he said, his voice thick with exhaustion. "This is madness. We're children, playing at games."

A group of the support staff returned from the house, carrying stretchers out away from the burning barn.

"Guns next time," I said with a smile. "Automatic weapons?"

He barked a laugh. "Not much use." He rocked his head back toward the barn. "Deidre did well with that scatter gun of hers for the first few shots. Then it jammed."

"Happened to me, too," I said. "Picked up a .45 from one of the pilots. Only got off a single shot."

"Too much magic," he said, stepping forward a couple of paces as the smoke shifted. "Tom tried one of the rifles Jimmy keeps for hunting, and it never fired a single cartridge. Susan and Maggie both tried their service revolvers with the same results."

I watched the smoke with him, looking for the enemy to return. "Sword and shield, then," I said.

"Aye." He thumped the flat of his axe against the huge boot of a fallen giant.

The dragon soared above us, watching. The few giants and trolls that remained alive were probably running for the last chopper.

"How's Gunther?" I risked.

Stuart grunted. "Surly and mouthy," he said with a smirk. "And pissed off to be rescued by a little girl."

I laughed. "Sorry to interrupt his imminent murder."

"You did well," he said, glancing my way for a moment. "This has been one huge clusterfuck, but I think we may just beat the bastards."

"Gonna lose the barn," I said, glancing back. "That fire will burn until dawn."

He shrugged. "Dawn ain't that far off," he said, yawning.

"You got this under control?" I asked, stretching my arms above my head.

He just looked at me.

"Yeah, right," I said. "Oh, and I'll be needing a new rigging for this pigsticker."

"Always treating your gear like crap," he said with a shake of his head.

I patted him on the shoulder and turned to the house. "I'm gonna go check on Katie. That dragon ain't done with us, and I want to make sure she's safe."

I'd made it three steps, before turning back. "Stuart? Did you see what happened to Rolph?"

He shook his head. "Last time I saw him, you were tussling with him over the sword, then all hell broke loose."

I'd look for him after. There were more questions than answers.

I jogged toward the house, pondering. Why the dragon hadn't attacked again confused me, but I wasn't arguing about having a breather. I slowed as I passed several other warriors, each bloodied and grim.

"Good work, folks," I said. "Shocked the hell out of 'em."

One of them wept openly somewhere down the line. I turned aside, not wanting to intrude on their grief.

I crossed the yard toward the barn and was startled when Jimmy came riding out with Deidre draped across his saddle. Susan and Maggie came riding behind him, their armor covered in gore, but they appeared unwounded.

"They'll think twice before carting off anyone else," Susan said, scanning around.

Jimmy didn't say anything—just walked the horse forward. Smoke had already begun to collect inside the barn, but obviously they needed to clear it out first.

"Wounded are up at the house," Maggie said.

"Let me get Dee over to Melanie," Jimmy said, his voice thin.

I stood at the barn entrance, and he passed me without a word or even a glance.

Maggie nodded at me and cantered her horse back toward the battle line. Susan stopped in the practice yard, her horse skittish and dancing.

"Where's that damn dragon?" she asked, scanning the sky.

Without thinking I closed my eyes and held the sword out, turning slowly, letting the pull of the sword guide me. When I could feel the dragon the strongest, I stopped, and opened my eyes. The blade pointed straight up.

Fifty-seven

ON THE ROOF of the burning barn perched the dragon.

"Scatter!" Susan yelled, pulling her gelding, Nightingale, around. I dove to the side as the huge lizard dropped on us like a hawk. He spread his wings as he neared the ground, and swooped across the yard, snatching Susan and Nightingale in his massive claws before climbing into the sky.

I rushed forward, swinging the sword, and nicked the long tail, scoring several scales off and cutting into the meat.

The dragon roared and faltered in his rise, veering around the burning barn with Susan pounding madly on the claw that gripped her. Nightingale screamed like only a horse can scream, the horrifying sound that warriors had learned to hate for centuries. One claw had pierced its side, and blood rained down as the dragon gained enough altitude to clear the skirmish line and head toward the rallying giants and trolls.

The snap of crossbows echoed down the line, and bolts soared after the beastie.

"He's got Susan!" I screamed, running back toward the battlefield.

Maggie twisted on her saddle, caught sight of the dragon, and roared in fury. She turned her mare, Dusk, spurred it back into the burning barn, and emerged again on the other side, a lance in one hand and the long plume on her helmet burnt to a nub.

The dragon landed in the no-man's-land between the defender's line and the rallying trolls, smashing the horse to the ground with the audible crunch of mail and bones.

I faltered, my heart breaking at the sight of Nightingale's life being snuffed out. I'd worked with these animals for several years and loved them as if they were my own.

Susan bounced once as the dragon landed, escaping his claws for the briefest of moments. Those on the line yelled and screamed, more crossbow bolts flying across the field to bounce off the dragon's armor. She scrambled away from him, but he lunged forward with a wing, clipping Susan in the back, sending her sprawling onto the ground.

The giants and trolls roared with laughter, shaking their weapons in the air. Several of our folks scrambled over the wall only to be called back by Stuart.

"Keep your heads," he bellowed. "No suicide runs."

Susan was back on her feet and scrambling as best she could in the armor. Jean-Paul swung around, herding her with his other wing. She fell hard, clattering to the ground, and rolled over, panting.

I gripped Gram in my left fist and sprinted to the line, clambered over a few strategically placed steps, and jumped to the ground on the opposite side. My knees would be angry for a long time coming, I reckoned.

I was getting damn sick of chasing after this guy.

Susan screamed when he snatched her up in his claw again. This time, she had her dirk out, and stabbed his claw, the blade skittering off the thick hide. He cackled a deep-throated rasp that raised the hackles on the back of my neck.

Faster, damn it. There was no way I was reaching him in time.

He fell back onto his tail, flipping her into the air. She arced upward, screaming and flailing.

With hideous clarity, I watched him lunge forward with his long neck and smash his iron jaws together. Only her armor kept him from cutting her in two.

The dragon shook her in his teeth, like a dog who'd captured a rat.

The emotion of it should have overwhelmed me, should have taken me to my knees, but the rage kept all else at bay.

From the right, the sound of thundering hooves caught everyone's attention. Maggie rode at the dragon, shrieking. She leaned forward over her lance, driving her horse with reckless abandon.

When Dusk saw the dragon, she shied, rearing and whinnying in fear. Maggie pulled the reins around, leaning into her long neck, calling to her. In a moment, she had her back on all fours. Dusk tossed her head and surged forward again, reassured by her master.

The line of Black Briar survivors began to cheer; hell, they were doing the wave, rising up to match her progress.

I had a very bad feeling about this.

The dragon spun, flinging Susan's broken body to skid past me, her armor punctured and twisted. I glanced away as it tumbled into a mangled pile.

I think that was the moment I realized I could not kill him enough.

Black Briar screamed their anger behind me, and the dragon darted his head to the side, trying to keep the enemy in sight. He was favoring his left side, being unable to see from the right. The right side was vulnerable.

I sprinted forward, hoping to stop what I knew was about to happen. "No, Maggie!" I shouted as I ran, but she only kicked harder, Dusk running with heads-down concentration.

I assumed the dragon determined Maggie to be the greater threat, so he ignored the rest of us. He crouched down on his belly, supine, stretching his long neck out toward Maggie.

"Watch out," I yelled as I neared him.

Maggie was within fifty paces when he flamed, engulfing her in liquid inferno.

But she did not falter. Like a comet, Maggie and her trusty steed hurtled onward, lance first.

I reached him, then. Striking forward with Gram.

The blade cut through the scales like parting silk. The three-foot-long gash in his side was not deep, but it did catch his attention.

Jean-Paul twisted, trying to swat at me with one large wing. I dove as the wing clipped me, rolling with the momentum. It hurt, but it was a glancing blow.

Too bad for him. With a horrendous crunch, Maggie slammed into him, her lance piercing his side just above the rear left leg, biting deep.

He swung his tail around, smashing into Maggie and her horse. They bounced, rolling across the yard in a fiery tumble.

Cries of horror rose from the SCAdians. How much was too much? Maggie and Susan had been leaders in our community for as long as Black Briar had existed.

I rose, spinning on my heel, Gram in front of me. The dragon stumbled backward and fell onto its left side.

I risked a look over at Maggie, who managed to crawl two paces toward Susan before she collapsed, burning. I turned away. The vision of her reaching for Susan, her hand burned to the bone, would live in my memory forever. If I survived.

There was the power of love. That was what sacrifice was worth.

Jean-Paul raised his head into the air and roared. Think lion, only about two hundred times more scary.

Trolls and giants fell to the ground cowering. If I had not been holding Gram, I would have lost all control of my bodily functions, I'm sure.

I could not imagine how the Black Briar folks took that cry.

He snapped at his leg, biting at the lance, but only succeeded in ripping off more scales.

One of the giants, brave soul that he was, ran forward, dodging and weaving. The dragon snapped at him, but his heart was not in it. The giant slid under the long neck and scrambled forward, only standing when he could grab the lance.

"Hang on, boss," he bellowed. "I'll get it."

The first tug caused the dragon to scream in pain. His right leg collapsed, and he fell onto his chest.

The giant dove aside, avoiding being crushed by inches.

But he did not give up. This time he grabbed the lance and yanked it with all his strength, showering the ground in black blood. I'd be willing to bet that nothing would ever grow there again.

The dragon roared, lashed his tail around, and knocked the giant off his feet.

The giant scrambled across the ground on all fours until he was out of the dragon's shadow then lurched to his full eighteen-foot height. He was the largest of his kind I'd seen so far. Here was a being of power who was likely used to getting his way.

"It's okay, boss," he shouted, holding up his hands and backing away. "That thing is out now, you'll be okay." He did not stop backing up, just moved slowly and carefully.

The dragon thrashed his head back and forth, howling a high-pitched cry of pain.

"Get the girl with the sword," the giant said, pointing in my direction.

Giant, yes. Stupid, no. He had no intention of fighting his boss.

He circled to the right, and Jean-Paul weaved back

and forth. The giant, apparently not the brightest of the bunch after all, turned and fled too soon.

The dragon, in the pain and confusion, attacked.

"No quick movements," I muttered.

Before I could blink, he pounced on the giant like a cat, pinning him to the ground with his front claws and raking him with his right rear claw, gouging out great bloody chunks. The giant flailed, punching the dragon in the left side of his head. But that was his final effort. His arms fell to the ground and his legs spasmed.

A final bite severed the giant's spine and he stopped moving altogether.

I learned two things from this.

At least my boss didn't kill me when she fired me.

And . . .

Jean-Paul's rage knew no friends.

I recognized his state. He'd lost control, succumbed to the fury and pain. No one was safe within reach of him. Not even his own people.

As I watched him lash out, I was horribly reminded of my own actions since forging the sword.

Trolls and giants fled his rampage. He attacked anything that moved.

I stalked forward, but stayed low. No use drawing his attention.

The final chopper started to rise, dropping trolls who had not found their way safely inside, but perhaps they were the lucky ones.

Jean-Paul whirled on them, dragging his left leg, and breathed a spear of liquid fire.

The chopper rocked on impact, flipping on its side, and fell thirty feet to the ground, where it exploded.

The dragon raised its head high into the air and roared, shooting fire into the night.

I took the chance and rose into a crouch, running along

the ground as low as I could. My legs screamed in pain, but I had to get to him, had to put this to an end.

Only he and the fates thought otherwise. I have no idea if he even knew I was there, but intention didn't really matter. He swung around, his tail moving counter to keep him balanced. That's the point of a tail. I knew this, saw it coming at me. Hindsight and all that rubbish.

Regardless, he clocked me, clipping my head and shoulder. I flipped through the air, a full-body flip, and landed on my back, hard enough to see stars.

He leapt upward, his wings beating a broken cadence as he limped into the air.

I wanted to rise again, to go after him, bring him down, but I couldn't. I just didn't have it in me. The enormity of it all washed over me and I closed my eyes.

Fifty-eight

WHISPERED VOICES SLIPPED into my mind. Sweet voices of young women. I thought of Katie right away, but the voices were wrong.

I opened one eye and saw a tall, lithesome blonde in scale mail and winged helm leaning over me. She had a short stabbing sword on her hip and wore a skirt of overlapping scales. For a moment I thought I recognized her. Not sure from where.

"What of this one, Róta?" she asked, glancing over her shoulder.

Another woman, taller than the first and older, glanced over from where she stood, her head turned, with a golden torque nestled at the base of her exquisite throat. Stunning. "Nay, Skuld, not that one," she said. "It is not her time." She rocked her head past me. "See to the next."

Skuld looked down at me, her face angelic. She bent lower, touching one long finger to my forehead, pushing back the hair above my left temple. "He has marked her, so he has," she said, turning. "Placed his claim on her."

Róta walked over, glancing down at my face, and shrugged. "Comely enough, but he has never been one to quibble over looks."

"Aye," Skuld said with a smirk. "He's never kept you from his bed."

A sharp smack brought Skuld upright, her hands thrust behind her.

"I am not alone in that matter," Róta said, laughing. "Leave this one. There are plenty of others."

They both scanned the field, evaluating, it seemed, the better part of carnage.

"So many valiant fallen," Róta said. "It has been many a long year since we had the like to choose from."

"Warriors there have been aplenty," Skuld said with a sad shake of her head. "They die by the thousands every year, but so few are worthy of his table."

"And fewer still, his bed," Róta added with a quiet sigh. "What I wouldn't give for another night with old one-eye."

"The greater or the lesser," Skuld said with a giggle.

Róta gasped, covering her mouth with that beautiful hand. "You are scandalous," she said, straightening. "He's been gone so long, I'm not even sure he remembers us."

They strode away, each taking a different direction, but neither moved toward the fallen giants or trolls.

Valkyries, I realized. How bad did I have to be injured to be considered by the Valkyries?

And who knew Valkyries were so randy? Katie was

not going to believe this. I prayed to whatever gods there might be in the world that I would get to tell her.

I sat up, my arms and legs stiff and aching. I still clutched Gram in my left hand, though. Some small favor there.

It took me a few minutes to rise, first to my knees, then to my feet.

The farm was a blasted wasteland. Somewhere in the east, the sun was rising, I could feel it in the air, but the light had not reached us yet. Soon.

I looked around, seeking friend or foe.

Skuld or Róta, I couldn't tell them apart at this distance, stood over Susan's broken body.

"Rise," Skuld commanded. Her voice was sweeter, less husky than Róta's. Susan's spirit rose like mist. Her spirit was dressed in armor as she had been in death.

"Let's have a look at him," Róta said, waving her hand.

The visored helmet spun away in a swirl of fog.

"By the Tree," Skuld said, taking a step back. "It's a woman."

"There are plenty of women warriors," Róta said. She twirled her hand and Susan's spirit twirled slowly before her.

"But when was the last one that fell battling one of the wyrms?" Skuld asked, turning to Róta.

"Few indeed. It will be a shock to those in the great hall, I'm sure."

"What of this one?" Skuld said, crossing to Maggie. She drew her spirit up, correcting any unfortunate kinks or contortions with a wave of her hand. "They were lovers."

Róta nodded. "Aye, and worthy as any I have seen."

Skuld drew forth the spirits of their horses and directed the women onward to the great hall.

"They will put a twist in Eric's tail, don't you think?" Róta asked.

Skuld nodded with a smile. "Should rile the lot."

I turned away, leaving the Valkyries to their task, not wanting to see who died a glorious death, and who just died the final death. Either way, they were lost to the rest of us.

The barn burned feverishly, pouring black smoke into the sky.

No one moved out from the final battle line. The giants and trolls had either fallen or scattered.

The SCAdians tended to the living, as best they could.

I yearned to go to them, to see who yet lived. For a brief moment, I even considered falling into a warm bed with Katie and sleeping until winter.

But, alas—something remained undone.

As I walked, the stiffness eased and Gram's urgency began to rise. She had tasted Jean-Paul's blood, and craved more. It was not a sentient craving, more of a base need. I didn't argue with it. The sooner Jean-Paul died, the happier the world could be.

And the sword could find him. It pulled at me already, urging me to follow the long slope downhill to the stream, then onward to the river and eventually to the lake. That's where I would find him.

To the north and east . . . into the mountains. There, perched along the shores of a lake he lay, nursing his wounds and his pride.

But how to get there?

Fifty-nine

MIST BEGAN TO rise from the earth, the chill moisture that had always reminded me of ghosts. This dawn would not dispel that fantasy.

Out farther than any other, a lone figure walked, kneeling, working. I strode in that direction.

Stuart moved among the bodies, one at a time, friend and foe alike. I watched him, shy about breaking his solitude, but pacing him. When he found a SCAdian, he checked them, desperate to find them alive.

It was painted on his face, the momentary hope then the black acceptance. He would close their eyes, cross himself, then rise, planting a spear in the ground to mark their fall.

He carried a thin bundle of short spears, each trailing a small white flag.

I don't know how many he started with, but he would run out all too soon. I glanced back along his path. The flags were thick across the field.

The enemy he bypassed without a pause, until he found one alive. The troll had been wounded. Who knows if it would have recovered.

Stuart did not hesitate. He stepped forward, knelt on the troll's chest, and drove the spear into its throat.

He saw me then, looked into my eyes, and dared me to question him.

I just nodded and turned aside. Who was I to judge him?

I paused at the wreckage of the first chopper and recovered the sling and scabbard from the giant's dead hand.

Once I had the sword in the rig correctly over my

right shoulder, I walked on to the tree line, massaging my left arm. Carrying that sword for so long was tiring.

Past the tended fields, deeper into the woods that ran wild along the back of Jimmy's border, I found what I was looking for.

There in a clearing, I discovered another legend, another fantasy come true. Three winged horses were picketed there, munching on fresh green grass. They were outfitted in fine white leather harnesses and saddles of ermine. Add in a kitty cat with huge brown eyes, and I would have melted on the spot.

Of course, I was not alone. I had seen two Valkyries, but there were three horses, so there had to be another around.

She could wait, as far as I was concerned. I wanted to meet these beautiful horses. One let me approach, even nuzzled my hand when I raised it to her nose.

"You are stunning," I said, running my hand down her neck to where the wings joined her back, just below the withers.

She let me lift her front leg to inspect the hoof.

Sue me. Professional curiosity.

"Does she meet with your approval?" a woman asked, stepping from the deeper shadows beneath the trees.

I lowered the hoof gently, patting the horse on the shoulder. "Shoes are in good shape, the hoof is trimmed nicely."

"High praise from a smith such as yourself," she said, reaching out and placing her left hand on the horse closest to her. "We love them as the children we will never see again," she said, almost in a whisper.

"They are remarkable," I said, meaning it. I had never seen finer horses. And let's not get started on the whole wing thing. My inner eleven-year-old was about to wet herself.

The Valkyrie bowed, placing her right hand on her chest. "Gunnr, at your service."

Service, eh? I nodded at her. "There is a service I am in need of," I said.

"You seek the wyrm," she said, eyeing me.

I nodded.

"And you think I should let you take one of our children, one of our light into this folly?"

What could I really say to that?

She watched me, assessing. "What thinks you, mortal? What madness afflicts you to pursue this course?"

I stepped away from the horses and drew Gram, laying the blade across my right arm.

She craned her head forward, staring at the sword. I waited.

"That bears his mark," she said.

"That is not all," I said, flipping the sword up and slipping it back into its scabbard. "There is this." I took a step toward her pushing my bangs up off my forehead.

She stepped closer, tracing the runes on my scalp with one long, thin finger.

"And this," I said, turning, holding my calf up, pushing the cut jeans to either side.

"These are different," she said, kneeling. She cupped my shin in one hand and ran her hand down my calf.

Her touch sent shock waves rippling through my body. The delicate way her fingers traced the runes on my calf caused my heart to skip a beat.

"Kenaz is emboldened," she said, tracing the rune, trailing her fingers along its path.

"Hum . . . hmmm . . . ," I said, clearing my throat and pulling my leg away from her. "Mad enough for you?"

She stood, staring into my face.

Her eyes were the blue of a jay's egg, crisp like a winter's morn. If I reached out and touched her, I think she would not mind.

"You are comely," she whispered, reaching out and tracing a finger down my left cheek from the runes to my chin. "Not unpleasing in the least."

"Yeah, well . . . ," I stammered, blinking.

Nothing like getting hit on by a Valkyrie.

Her lips were the color of winterberries, red and plump. I could imagine the way they would taste. I imagined the way the muscles along her neck would feel under my lips.

"Is it hot in here?" I asked, stepping back and rubbing my hand across my cheek.

Gunnr shook her head, as if giving up a dream. "You may ask of me," she said, stepping forward.

I stepped back again, just out of her reach.

"Anything," she said, her voice husky with need.

Holy cats. What had I gotten myself into?

"This is a little over my head," I said, stepping back again, pacing her movement. "You are way out of my league."

"But you are receptive, I can feel it."

My pulse was definitely quickening. "I'm sorry," I said, stepping around the rear end of one of the horses, putting the elegant beast between us. "I'm spoken for."

Gunnr's expression melted, a pained look sweeping aside the teasing and the joy. The sadness that painted her face was like a punch in the heart.

"You reject me?" she asked, dropping her arms and bowing her head. "I have become anathema."

Oh, the drama. "No, no," I said hurriedly, sidestepping along the horse, trailing my hand over her shoulder and along her face. "You are beautiful beyond words."

She did not turn to me, but kept her head bowed. After a moment, I realized she was crying.

You really have a way with women, Sarah.

I continued my circuit around the horse, and stood behind her now, feeling like the fool.

"Honest," I said, crossing my arms across my breasts,

tucking my fingers under my arms. "You're definitely hot."

She sniffled and turned her head halfway, glancing back at me.

If not for Katie, that look, that vulnerable beauty would have won the day. As it was, I began thinking of different types of coal to keep out otherwise overwhelming thoughts.

"You do not jest with me?" she asked, turning farther toward me. "Having a play at my expense?"

"Oh, lord no," I said. This much attention from anyone else but Katie was very uncomfortable. Nice, but scary. "I can think of worse ways to spend an evening."

This brought a smile to her face.

I closed my eyes, thinking of Katie. This creature was a rare beauty. Powerful and intoxicating.

I felt her aura and opened my eyes. She'd stepped forward, invading my personal space. She smelled of leather and cloves.

"A kiss, then," she said, the words tripping off her lips in a soft buzz.

I gulped, trying to keep it together. "Pardon?"

"That is the price," she said, touching her tongue to her lips, wetting them slowly. "One kiss, and you may take Meyja to pursue your folly."

One kiss, she says. I drew a breath, intoxicated by her scent. Would one kiss betray Katie? Would she care?

"Best decide soon," Gunnr whispered. "He flees with his remaining strength."

I'd never find him later, and if he returned to his home base, it would be like rooting out a badger with a spork.

"One kiss," I said, knowing I was doomed. "That's all . . ."

And she melted into me, her lips like honey, her skin smooth as silk.

I forgot myself for a moment, lost in the sheer pleasure of that one kiss.

Later, I would remember it as a dream. But in the moment, it was victory and release, ecstasy and fulfillment.

An eternity later, I drew back, gasping for breath.

"Katie," I whispered.

Gunnr's smile turned to a frown, and she stepped back, her hand sliding from around my hip. How she'd got it under the chain shirt and against my bare skin, I had no memory, but the second her hand left the small of my back, an ache shuddered through me.

"You love her, truly," she said with a sigh. "It is unfortunate."

I stood there, mouth agape, trying to remember my own name. She walked over, untied a long lead from the tree nearest the horses, and brought it over, placing it in my hands. For the briefest of moments, she held my hands between her own and stared into my eyes.

"You have but to call, smith. Whisper my name in the night and I will ride to you."

Of that I had no doubt.

I stepped into the stirrup while Gunnr steadied Meyja. I took up the reins and turned her away from the farm. Just down the hill, the valley opened up, and I could take wing.

Holy crap, I was gonna fly!

Gunnr placed her hand on my knee, squeezing softly. "He rages," she said, looking up at me. "Do not take Meyja into battle. Ride low and set down a distance away. Sneak up on him as he thrashes about."

"Aye," I said, gently patting her hand, and pushing it off my knee as subtly as I could. "I will not bring this beautiful creature to harm."

"She is my heart," Gunnr said. "Bring her back to me."

I reached down and brushed her cheek.

She leaned into my palm, capturing my hand with her own, holding it against her face. "I will count the moments until your return," she said, taking my hand away from her face and kissing the palm.

"Right . . . hum, hmmmm . . . yes," I said, clearing my throat. "I have to go kill a dragon now."

She stepped back, her face serious again. "Yes, of course. The foul wyrm must pay for his centuries of depredation."

"At least," I said, and turned Meyja with my knee.

We walked only a few steps, when Gunnr called out to us. "Warrior, wait."

She ran up, holding out a shield. "Take this," she said, holding it so I could loop my arm through the leather strap.

It was tall, really a tower shield, which would cover the greater part of my right side. If I didn't have a second weapon, a shield was a good addition.

"Thank you, Gunnr."

She bowed, touching two fingers to her forehead. "Be safe, warrior."

Warrior it was now. Before, I was smith. I don't know if I'd been promoted or demoted.

I nudged Meyja into a gallop, figuring speed was required to fly. At the edge of the hill, she loped into the air, her great wings rising and falling.

The ride was amazing. Magical. My only regret was I couldn't share it with Katie.

Yes, I remembered Katie.

I held the reins in my shield hand and reached back, pulling Gram free from her sheath.

"Okay," I said, closing my eyes. "Let's find us a dragon."

Sixty

WE FLEW NORTH by northeast for twenty minutes before I felt a good solid tug on the sword. We were on the trail. And I could feel water. He was definitely near water.

The tilled farms scrolled below us, getting smaller and smaller as we gained altitude. I'm not sure how high we went, but I never had trouble breathing. A time or two we flew through clouds, which were not fluffy in the predawn sky. They were dark and wet, soaking through my jeans and quilted cuirass.

If the dragon didn't kill me, I'd likely end up with pneumonia.

The sky to the east had begun to lighten, the first rays of the sun scoring the cloud cover in hues the Easter bunny would be proud of—blues, purples, pinks, and all shades in between.

Frankly, I was surprised I didn't see a news chopper or airplane anywhere around me. Definitely over the more rural parts of the county. Once we crossed Woods Creek I thought I had him, so I sheathed Gram and gave my arm a rest.

Lake Chaplain was good sized, only about a quarter the size of Lake Sammamish, but big enough.

"Come on, Meyja. Let's take 'er down a bit and see what we can see."

She whickered and tossed her head, but angled down. We passed through a thick layer of clouds and the predawn darkness rose around us once again. When you fly high enough, the day starts sooner. I liked that.

I could see the lake coming up in the distance, and my stomach began to tighten. Already most of my body hurt from the fighting, and that whole getting hit thing.

Add in the flying horse, and now my thighs were screaming at me.

I'd be hobbling for a while after this, that's for sure. Like any of it would matter soon enough. I was taking a sword to a dragon fight. My odds of survival were pretty damn low. The sword sang to me, though—filling me with bravado and hope. Gram was made to kill dragons. I knew this now with all my heart. That's why Frederick wanted it, even if he couldn't articulate what drew him to the power. Nidhogg likely wanted it, if she was aware of its existence. Jean-Paul just wanted it so no one else could have it. That much had been made clear.

The fact he never touched it was the final clue. I could kill him with it, if I could survive long enough. So many had died already because of that bastard. I wasn't going to let him walk or fly away and spread his terror elsewhere. He was going down.

I didn't notice the smoke until we were almost to Lake Chaplain. I'm not sure what caused me to look back, but a quick glance showed me the thin black smudge above Lost Lake. We flew right over him in all that cloud cover. He wasn't at Lake Chaplain at all. The sneaky bastard.

I turned Meyja and we banked south, toward the smoke. I drew Gram again, and immediately a teeth-grating thrum ran up my arm.

We settled in a clearing about a mile from Lost Lake. Meyja touched down with a soft, graceful landing that I hardly felt. "She takes you into battle?" I asked, patting her neck. "A beauty like you?"

Meyja threw her head back and nickered. I slid from her back and surveyed the field to the north.

"Seems safe enough," I said, grabbing for the lead. Meyja had other ideas. She tossed her head and ran across the field like a shot. I stumbled forward about three paces, and my thighs and ass just couldn't take it. I stopped, cramping up, and slipped Gram back into her sheath.

Stretching was in order. I spent a few minutes keeping an eye on Meyja and stretching out my thighs and calves. A bit of yoga can do wonders.

When I could move without crying, I picked up the shield and walked out into the field.

"Come on, Meyja. Don't be a bitch."

She danced across the field for a moment, head high, tail in the air. Sassy. I covered my mouth to hide the smile. She was amazing to just watch. After a minute, she turned back to me, settling under a pine on the edge of the open field.

"He's just over at Lost Lake," I told her, running my fingers through her mane. "If I'm not back in a while, you head on back to—" I paused. Didn't really want to say her name. I had enough unwanted attention.

Seriously.

"—that woman," I whispered. "You understand?"

She bowed her head and let me rub her ears. Then she bumped me with her nose, pushing me away.

"Okay, okay," I said, holding up one hand. "I can take a hint."

I turned, picked up the shield, and drew Gram.

"Wabbit time," I muttered. "Come out and play, Jean-Paul. I have many debts to settle with you."

I crept through the underbrush for a bit, but came upon a hiking trail soon enough.

Hope there wasn't anyone at the lake this morning.

Gram kept me on a steady course, running down to the lake. At a quarter mile I could hear the dragon—Jean-Paul—thrashing about. Sometimes I heard water, and others I heard his shrieking rage, and the crash of trees.

The trail ended at a park. Benches and tables were strewn along the beach, many of them smashed.

Several cabins around the bend of the lake were burning. If they held anyone, they were beyond my reach.

I skirted along the forest line, not wanting to cross open ground just yet.

Out in the lake I could see several small boats sunken in the shallows. Out a little farther floated a scattering of busted wooden decking. Likely the end of the broken pier and boathouse smashed to bits by his nibs.

I watched him from hiding. He stormed up and down the beach, hobbled and wounded.

It was pissing him off. He'd limp along a few strides, practically dragging his left hindquarter, and he'd stop, throw his head into the air and roar. Let him tire himself out, my internal logic said. Give him a bit longer.

On his next pass down the beach, he held his head high into the air and sniffed, scanning the tree line.

I fell, dropping into a ditch beside the trail. He snorted, growled, and turned to walk into the water.

When the water was up to his front shoulder, he bent and drank.

Drank, and it had been hours since I'd touched water. An ache flooded through me. It's like my cells had suddenly shrunk, dehydrated. My tongue felt like an old sock, and my eyes hurt from lack of sleep and too much smoke. One little drink could fix that right up.

Down the beach, near the burning cabins, there was a concrete building that remained standing. I could see he'd smashed in one side, but concrete didn't burn, and wasn't worth his time, apparently.

On the side of that building stood a public water fountain.

Looked like heaven to me.

I watched him for another moment and then crept farther along the trees toward the building. He was drinking so noisily, I could tell where he was without seeing him. I dashed across the soft lawn and pressed my body against the back wall.

Peering around, I saw that he had not moved. I bent,

twisted the knob, and drank a deep swallow of public water-fountain water.

It was tepid and tasted too metallic, but my body craved it. I ignored the gum stuck in the drain and drank for three breaths. Any more and I'd throw up. I sidled up to the edge of the wall and looked around. He was just climbing out of the water, heading south around the lake.

In the distance I saw several more cabins—maybe a mile away. Smoke rose from one of the chimneys.

Civilians, I thought. Time to cut this scene short.

I lifted the shield, adjusted my grip on Gram, and stepped around the side of the building.

"Hey, Jean-Paul," I shouted, feeling very brave in that instant. "You . . . dirtbag."

He froze, like a cartoon bad guy with one foot in the air, and slowly turned his head on that long, skinny neck of his.

Smoke rose from his nostrils and he grinned. Teeth as long as my arm shone in the early morning light.

"That's a boy," I said, stepping away from the building. "Time to pay the piper."

He rose up, stretching his neck out toward me, and roared.

Sixty-one

ROARING WAS NOT flaming. Make all the noise you want, big boy. I sprinted across the beach to get between him and the water. If he was gonna play with fire, I wanted to be near the antidote.

Especially since the sun was up. No magic fire with the sun up. Of course, I only had Rolph to trust for that knowledge.

And that'd been a mixed bag.

My legs felt like they'd been soaked in brine for a few days, bloated and squishy. I ran through the pain, sprinted as best I could.

He swung his head around, turning his body, and moved to meet me.

I'd seen this move before. I felt his wing sweeping in as much as saw it. Angling the shield above my head, I diverted the wing tip, letting the energy pass over my head, glancing off.

When the claw lashed out, I flung myself to the right, tucking into a shoulder roll and coming up on one foot and one knee, the shield between me and teeth, the sword flashing out to nick the left leg.

It was a glancing blow, barely a scratch, but it was a game of tag at this point. Who gets in first, who gets in last.

Speed was the game. He had me on size and strength.

I was cuter, but that goes without saying.

He was big—forty feet from nose to tail, with a wing-span twice as wide. I was under six feet tall. As long as he didn't sit on me, I was damn hard to hit at this range.

Twice I slipped in past his claw, delivering little cuts. Each stroke sliced through his scales like parting a cabbage. Not too hard with a really sharp instrument.

And it pissed him off. Hell, if I was him, and I had those awesome scales, I'd be pissed.

Snick, off went a few scales and dragon blood dripped onto the sand.

He was tired and pissy, I was beat to hell and exhausted. We danced like two old people. Of course, he'd been doing this a long damn time. This was my first dragon.

Totally forgot the tail. Rookie mistake. I caught a head butt on the shield, keeping the ridges along his skull from smashing my ribs in. But I never saw the roundhouse.

Armor is your friend. One second I was thinking I'd take his ear off, or maybe go for his good eye, and the next I was spitting sand out of my mouth and wondering which bus had landed on me.

I didn't lose anything, fingers and toes, that sort of thing, but the shield went one way and the sword went the other.

"Crap," I spat.

The shadow clued me and I rolled to the left, vacating the kill zone. He stomped with his good front claw so hard, me, my gear, the sand, all hopped up in the air a good three inches.

Did I mention he was heavy?

Shield was closer, so I went for the sword.

Yes. Logical, but I could not win a defensive battle. I feinted to the shield and when he drove his head down to intercept me, I dove to the left, did a shoulder roll—grabbing the sword and sprinting around to his blind side.

His head swung around faster than I liked, trailing sand down from his teeth. I could still feel the grit in my own mouth, so I smiled as I ran. He wasn't doing anything fancy on this side.

He brought his wing down and I slashed upward, parting the thin membrane between two long bones without as much as a pause. It wasn't a big rent, but it allowed me to pass without getting smacked to the ground again.

I slashed the sword down his right side, opening a wide gash, showering the beach in his blood. It sizzled and smoked, burning. Everything about him sucked.

I ran past him, reaching for the shield as I moved. He flipped his tail around. I dove to the side and he swatted the shield, sending it arcing toward the burned-out cabins. So much for defense.

He roared and reared up on his back legs, beating his wings for balance. Now he towered so far above me I couldn't see his head.

Damn! I turned and ran.

The first blast of fire soared over my head by a good three feet. It was like running under an open broiler. I smelled the distinct odor of burning hair.

Fire, fire, run for the water.

I ran along the remains of the dock, slipping Gram into the sheath over my shoulder. Then I dove off the end of the pier, driving deep. When I found the bottom, I struck out for deeper water, out toward the wrecked boats and dock. Out where he couldn't get me.

I hoped.

I swam until my lungs began to burn, then I kicked upward, struggling against the weight of my armor. I reached an overturned boat, and pulled myself into fresh air, coming up under the gunwale. The bottom had been smashed in, and I could see sky, but I couldn't see Jean-Paul.

God, could he swim, too? I looked down between my feet, but didn't see anything.

This sword, jeans, cuirass . . . I'd be drowning soon when I ran out of strength to kick and keep my head above water.

Maybe not the best choice.

I pulled myself under the boat until I reached the edge and ducked under, coming back up on the outside, and looked around for him.

He was on the shore, water up to his shoulders. I flinched when he belched a long stream of fire out across the water. A boat to my far left rocked back when the napalm struck it, and it sank under the waves.

Nice shootin', Tex.

Okay, new plan.

I swam under the water as far north as I could, paralleling the beach, and running to shallower waters among the water lilies. I was able to walk at that point, getting my head above the waterline to breathe. Several fires were burning on the water as he picked off the larger debris. I was running out of places to hide.

Time to head back to dry land. I was almost to the burned-out cabins when I cut in to the shore. He was a good fifty yards south, scanning the water for me to pop up.

Thanks Mom, for all those swimming lessons.

But swimming had sapped even more of my strength. I was running on fumes.

I dragged myself onto shore, stumbled to a bit of cover behind one of the cabins, and caught my breath, dripping.

There, tangled in a rhododendron, was my shield.

I needed that shield, and I needed him closer, close enough to attack.

When he faced south on his sweep of the water, I stood and launched a piece of wood out as far as I could into the lake. It plopped into the water with a rather weak splash, but it caught his attention.

I ran to the next cabin, snatched the shield from the bush, and flattened myself against the wall.

Sucker was fast, faster than I would have believed. He sped north along the beach, roaring. He covered the distance to the cabins in seconds, but he remained focused out in the water.

How was I going to finish this guy?

Hoping I could outmaneuver him, I crept around the cabin to the east, thinking I'd come at him from behind.

Did I mention that dragons hear really, really well?

I'd gone about halfway when flames struck the cabin. Fire splattered all around, splashing off the timbers to rain around me in tiny smoldering drops. I instinctively held the shield over my head and hunkered down.

That shield was large. I found if I curled up tight, I could keep everything covered.

When the sizzling drops stopped falling, I moved eastward toward the trees. I dodged across the open ground to the next cabin and realized I was nearing the concrete building where I'd gotten a drink.

Okay, full circle.

Concrete would shield me from his flames, at least until he worked his way around to get close and personal.

Speaking of which, I felt something, a quick jolt in my core. Badness was about to ensue.

I stopped and spun around, dropping to one knee just as he flamed again.

The shield covered me from head to toe; as long as I crouched down behind it I'd be safe. That's what I'd learned so far. That's all that mattered for the next twenty-eight seconds as napalm struck the shield and parted around me like the Red Sea.

I held on to that shield long after it was too damn hot. Long after I could smell burning flesh. When he paused to draw in breath, I dropped the shield, ignored the large circle of black on my right forearm where the point on the shield had transferred some of the heat through to me.

His neck was extended, his ears back, and his good left eye turned a bit toward me. I screamed as I leapt forward, over the line of fire, and brought the sword down.

I'd intended to sever his godforsaken neck, but his survival instincts were greater. He jerked his head up, pulling his neck out of reach. Fortunately for me, it exposed his chest. I sprinted in, closing the distance to his bulk. He twisted, having little else to do, and took the blow on the right shoulder, just below the wing. It was a meaty blow. Thick corded muscles parted and the blade rebounded off the shoulder blade, jarring my arm like striking a stone wall.

I held on to the sword, but again could not protect myself from his tail. At least this time I saw it coming.

Fools me once, and all that. Okay, twice . . . I'm a slow learner.

He caught me across the midsection while I was extended, the blade in his shoulder. I'm not sure, after all this, how I kept hold of the sword, but lost my . . . well . . . gravity.

I flew through the air, sixty feet into the trees. Several branches were kind enough to break my fall as I dropped through the trees and landed on my back.

Cuts and scrapes covered my face and hands, but I did not lose that sword.

Breathing hurt. Each inhalation made me actually move my chest, and the muscles along my ribs hurt so bad, I thought I would cry.

I slowly sat up and climbed to my feet as Jean-Paul limped to the trees, blasting fire out in a wide swath. The local fire crews were not going to be happy about this, not one bit.

"Come on, you bastard," I croaked when he stopped to breathe. "You are losing to a girl."

Okay, losing was a matter of conjecture, but I just needed to keep him pissed, keep him off balance. I had done some serious damage so far and, thankfully, had nothing permanent to deal with on my own part.

At least, if things were bad I didn't know it yet.

If he weren't so damn despicable, I'd almost feel sorry for him. He was in rough shape. He'd not fly again soon, with that right shoulder cut up, and he was bleeding from half a dozen cuts.

Part of me wanted to sit and watch him. He was so majestic—a powerful killing machine. I could appreciate his strengths. Here was a beast nature intended to treat us as prey.

We really had no predators. Well, none that I'd ever known.

How many like him were out there?

I staggered forward, leaning on each tree as I worked my way back to the beach. He hadn't followed me into the trees, which was sound on his part due to the bulk thing.

But I now had some serious ground to cover to get back inside his optimal danger zone. Too far out and he'd rule the battle, claw and wing, bite and tail. I needed to be in close to deny him those advantages.

My right arm had begun to hurt, but I couldn't think about it. Couldn't imagine the burn and the damage there.

I walked out of the trees, dragging Gram behind me, too exhausted to lift it again. It whimpered in my mind, this close to its enemy. That's what I understood. This sword was made to kill dragons, just like Rolph had said.

Jean-Paul staggered, weaving from side to side. He was exhausted as well, from battles and loss of blood.

How many calories did a beast his size burn up? Hell, how many calories did he lose raining fire down so frequently?

He obviously had limits.

So I approached him, planning to end this one way or another. If I died, he'd be so damn hurt that the National Guard would finish him off. Or the local sheriff. Someone. I just needed to drag him down, keep whittling away at him.

"Aren't you done yet?" I grumbled when he flipped his left wing at me. I just ducked. Didn't even raise the sword. I saw him with a clarity that spoke of near total collapse. Exhaustion was diverting more and more energy into certain activities so that for the moment, I had a sense of time slowing, of each tiny motion highlighted and telegraphed.

When he lashed out with a taloned claw, I countered, bringing Gram around in both hands, cutting deep into his foot, severing one whole claw.

His guttural moan was worse than the roaring. Pain was a stranger to this man—dragon. At least pain inflicted on him by others.

Once more, as the world honed in to a pinpoint, I heard Qindra's voice in my head. "*Finish him*," she said.

The runes along my left calf flared with an explosion of energy, flooding my exhausted muscles with adrenaline and something I've never experienced. Magic, perhaps?

I launched myself at the beast one final time. Claws raked down my side, shredding the chain and my flesh. Blood flooded down, but I had to end this. I lunged forward, diving under a sweep of his bleeding claw.

The blade bites deep into his chest, only stopping when the crossguard smashes into shattered scales. Then I'm flung away once again and the world is reduced to the roar of the dragon, the smell of burning flesh, and pain.

Sixty-two

OKAY, I HOPED I was dreaming, because the afterlife could not suck this much. I zoomed into the scene, like any good dream, flying one minute and jolted into the action the next.

I rolled down the street carrying a tray of tall fluted glasses, each filled with champagne. The golden liquid rose to just inside the lip of each glass and I knew if I spilled a single drop I would die.

I was dressed in a tight skirt, and high-heel roller skates, which I would not wear on a bet. In my right hand I carried a branding iron. The tip rotated, like a slot machine, the head glowing red, the image shifting from one rune to another.

Along one side of the street were my friends: Julie

stood with Carl and Jennifer, while the extras and movie crew lined up farther down. Past them, the Black Briar clan stood in single file, each facing the street, as if watching a parade.

On the left side of the street were various clusters of individuals; some I recognized, some I did not.

In one group stood Frederick with Mr. Philips and the tall blonde I thought I knew, but could not be sure.

Next, half a block away, stood Qindra in a severe suit, clutching an attaché case. She stood half in shadow, and I could see the light glowing in her eyes, blue and bright.

Behind her, deep in the shadow, stood another. I could barely make out the form of her, an old woman leaning on a cane, but her eyes were not blue, rather flashing red, like flickering flame. This I assumed to be Nidhogg, Qindra's mistress.

I bent to remove the roller skates, and the second I touched the laces a roar echoed down the street toward me. I glanced back. A dragon the size of a 747, with scales various shades of green from a forest green so dark as to be nearly black, all the way to bright jade. His head was shaped like a shovel, only the size of a Buick.

I stood, and he stopped. I rolled slightly to the side with my friends, and he roared again, lumbering down the canyon of buildings that ran back to the horizon.

I stopped and rolled back toward Frederick, and the dragon lay down, twining its long neck around to meet its curling tail. Within a moment, it looked to be asleep.

You never could trust dragons, though. They could sleep with their eyes open, and see through their eyelids.

"Oh, Sarah," Frederick said from my left. "Be a doll and give us a glass of that nice wine."

"Champagne, silly," the blonde said, giggling, and I recognized her then. It was the breasts. The last time I'd seen her, she'd been lying on a chaise, letting JJ pour wine over her chest while the cameras rolled.

"Champagne is wine, my dear," Mr. Philips said, stepping to the curb and holding out a hand. "If you don't mind, Ms. Beauhall."

I rolled up and let him take two glasses from the tray. Instead of taking one from each side, he took two closest to one side, making the tray tip. I twisted my wrist to keep the tray balanced.

"Don't spill any," Frederick said with a wicked smile. "Your friend back there would be most displeased." He motioned behind me and I glanced back at the large green dragon.

"This tickles my nose," the blonde said, sipping her champagne. "I like it."

"I'm sure"—Frederick slurred, leaning over, leering at the young woman—"that we could find many things to tickle you with."

I rolled back a step as his long tongue flicked out and licked her from earlobe to collarbone, undoing the tie that held up one side of her top with a twist of the forked tip.

"Here, let me help you," Mr. Philips said, reaching forward to undo the other tie.

I turned away as her top fell around her waist.

"Thank you, Mr. Philips," Frederick said. "She looks good enough to eat."

I rolled across the street to Julie and offered her a glass of champagne, but she acted as if I wasn't there.

Jennifer glanced past me to the dragon and whispered, "She's not quite with us today." She clasped Carl's arm in her hands.

"But we're ready," Carl said, pulling away from Jennifer. "I'll go first." He turned, took his shirt over the top of his head, and pulled his shoulders back. "I want mine here on my left breast." He glanced at Jennifer. "Near my heart."

Jennifer smiled and began unbuttoning her shirt. "He's so brave. I'll get mine in the same place, please."

I stood there, shocked, as she opened her shirt and pulled her bra strap down over one shoulder, exposing her left breast.

"I was much happier when you told us it doesn't hurt," she said, smiling weakly.

Across the street, Frederick catcalled and Carl stiffened.

"It's okay," Jennifer said. "We'll not make any waves."

The brand in my right hand clicked into place, and the tip stopped on a symbol I had not seen before. I could not make it out, but it reminded me somehow of money.

I leaned forward against my will and pressed the brand against Jennifer's breast, half an inch above her nipple. She shrieked and tried to pull away, but Carl stood behind her, holding her arms back. He leaned his head beside hers and made cooing sounds. "It's okay," he said. "It only hurts for a moment."

The smell of burning flesh filled my nostrils and I wanted to vomit.

When I pulled away, her breast was burned and swollen, the brand a series of blackened scars on her flesh.

"Tha . . . thank you," she choked between sobs.

"We'll be good citizens," Carl said, stroking Jennifer's hair. "We will be as you have made us."

I branded them, the movie folk, one after another, the stench of burned flesh staining my spirit. I wept as I did it, wept as they each bared their chest openly and took the mark over their heart.

When I finished with them, Qindra beckoned me. I rolled to her side of the street, holding out the tray of champagne.

She took two glasses, being careful to take one from each side. It did not balance the tray, but it did not upset it more.

She turned, handing the second glass to the shadow. An old hand, gnarled and spotted, reached into the light and took the glass. For a moment, I could see the cane she carried, for it was indeed Nidhogg—the Corpse Gnawer. The silver head of the cane was of a dragon wrapped around a tree. The work was skilled, and looked very old.

I could not make out what Nidhogg said, but Qindra nodded and turned back to me, draining her glass in one long pull.

"Nidhogg thanks you for your service to her kind. She looks forward to you serving her for many years to come."

If she had slapped me I'd have felt less stunned.

"She has one demand, beyond all that you have done," she said, motioning toward the Black Briar line. "You are to breed within the year, as is Katie. The two children will be given to my mistress for her whims. Then you will be considered to have repaid the debt you owe her."

"What debt?" I asked, horrified by the thought not just of bearing a child, but of giving it over to that ancient beast.

"You have deprived her of one of her own," she said, directing my attention to the next spot down the line of buildings. A jacket lay on the pavement, rent with sword strokes and covered in blood.

"You will begin to make up for what you have taken from her," Qindra said, her voice full of pain. "Or she will destroy the lot."

I followed her gaze to the Black Briar clan. Jimmy stood with Deidre, Gunther and Stuart held Katie between the two of them, naked and scarred.

"They are worthy warriors," Qindra said. "Nidhogg gave you and Katie to them in exchange for their service. Pick as you will, but bear her a child."

She turned, dropping the glass to the sidewalk where it shattered with a loud crash. "And this . . ." She motioned for the brand. "I will mark your clan. You have not the privilege."

I handed her the brand and she flipped the end to a worm writhing around the base of a tall tree.

"She would brand you here," she said, touching me on the inner thigh. "To remind you of your obligation."

I glanced back to Katie. She already bore another mark, one I knew to be his mark, the black one. Yet she was to be doubly marked.

"And what happens if we fight you?" I asked, rolling back a few paces, out of Qindra's reach.

She nodded. "You will all die."

"Not the children," a dry and raspy voice whispered. "Just as you were raised in my service, so will we raise others."

Qindra stared at me; no emotion touched her face. "You and the clan will be destroyed, and others will be put in your place."

"We do not accept your mark," I said. "We will fight you."

"So mote it be," Qindra said, turning away from me and stepping into the shadow.

I dropped the tray, waited for the glasses of champagne to shatter on the ground. Instead the world was consumed by the roar of the green dragon.

Sixty-three

"WASN'T SHE DEAD once already?" Skuld's voice slipped into my dreams.

"Not dead, but close," Róta said. "Gunnr is quite smitten with this one."

I opened my eyes and the two Valkyries stood over me, their lean faces and long blond hair drawn back in the most severest of buns.

"Is Gunnr here?" I asked.

"See," Róta said, straightening up. "Not dead."

"Too right," Skuld confirmed, turning away. "But this one, I'm fairly sure he's never getting up again."

I pushed myself up on my elbows and looked over. Jean-Paul lay on the beach with Gram sticking up from his chest. Deep slashes and cuts covered his body. His clothing was shredded and soaked in blood.

Skuld bent down and examined him, tsking as she did.

"Don't bother with that one," Róta said. "Another will come for him."

"It's been a long time since we saw one such as he," Skuld said.

Róta held a hand out to me, and I took it, standing with neither grace nor style. "Here is a find even more rare," she said.

Skuld snorted. "Now you sound like Gunnr."

I leaned against her for a moment, allowing my body to get used to being upright.

"I've never seen anyone take such a beating and live," Róta said.

I chose to ignore the comment and went to Jean-Paul instead.

He was thoroughly dead. I pulled Gram from his chest and wiped it on his pants leg. "I need to get back," I said.

"Gunnr is expecting your return," Skuld said, watching me from a distance. "Of course, it could be she worries for Meyja, but somehow I think it may be more than that."

I didn't have time for Valkyrie crushes. I needed to get back to see who lived. I needed to talk to Jimmy and Katie, to see if Qindra was still at the farm.

I needed to collapse and sleep for a week.

Róta waved over my shoulder and I glanced around. Meyja came trotting along the beach. "Here is her beauty now."

"She's a beauty all right," I said, slipping Gram into the sheath over my right shoulder.

The world was a dull haze of pain. For some reason, I couldn't lift my right arm and didn't really care at the moment.

Skuld helped me onto Meyja's back, where I twined my left hand in the reins.

"Find Gunnr," I whispered, and she flicked her ears back and neighed.

We circled the lake once. Seven cabins had burned. God, I hope they were empty. There was enough death. I had no idea how this was all going to be explained, but for the moment I wanted to get back and see that Katie was safe.

As we flew south, Skuld and Róta flanked me. It was comforting to have them on either side. Not that I thought Meyja would let me fall—still . . . After a moment, they began to sing some ballad I couldn't understand. The words rolled over me, their singsong voices nursing me, keeping me safe.

I must have dozed.

"Look upon what you have wrought, warrior," Róta's voice said to my left.

From this vantage point, I could see the whole of the farm. It was a disaster. A thick haze of smoke hung over the entire area. The three choppers looked like toys destroyed by naughty boys. Boys who played with magnifying glasses and firecrackers.

The fields north of the barn were scorched, a patchwork of fresh brown earth, charred grass, and intermittent green where the battle had spared the growing things.

Blackened timbers stood in the fresh morning light, marking where the barn had once stood. The barn had been the heart of the farm, where we worked hard, and played harder. The sides stood in jagged ruin, while the roof had burned away to ash. From the sky, it looked as if someone had reached into the farm from above and ripped out the heart.

The house stood, undamaged, which was a blessing. I could see people moving around down there, so some still lived.

"Take us down," I said to Meyja. "Your mistress needs you and I need my friends."

Skuld rode above us as we landed, keeping watch, it seemed. Róta landed first, lighting through the trees. We followed second, coming in from the valley side. The transition from flight to trotting was subtle and sweet. I could get used to this.

Gunnr stood in the clearing, her arms crossed over her chest, and her helm on her head. I couldn't see her face for the shadows.

Meyja walked to her, lowered her head, and pushed Gunnr. "You are come home to me?" she said. "I had thought you found a new love."

She stroked Meyja's nose, but looked up at me as she spoke.

Obsess much?

I slid from Meyja's back and patted her neck. "Thank you, mighty steed. For your service and your joy."

Gunnr watched me, her eyes lost to me in shadow. Skuld and Róta walked over, leading their own mounts, and each placed a hand on Gunnr's shoulder, one to a side.

"Come, sister," Róta said. "We have *einherjar* with which to attend."

I handed the reins to Gunnr and bowed my head. "Thank you for your kindness." I looked up. "I am in your debt."

She accepted the reins with a nod. "And you, warrior. Do not forget me."

The memory of that kiss burst bright, sending a shudder through me. "Not likely," I murmured.

The smile that flared on her face rivaled the sun.

They turned, the three of them, walked to the edge of the clearing, and mounted. I watched them as they danced into the sky, followed by two others, Susan and Maggie riding their proud beasts, galloping westward.

Why westward? Wasn't Valhalla in Norway or something? Something else to find out.

The peace and quiet of the clearing began to fade and I breathed in one final hint of cloves.

Funny she didn't ask about her shield.

Now to the living.

Sixty-four

LEAVING THE TRANQUILITY of the clearing brought back the aches and pains of the long terrible night. My right arm began to throb and the weight of holding it up became nearly too much to bear. I hugged it to my chest, cradling it with my left. Something was amiss there. My scalp began to tingle as well. There was not a point on my body that did not pulse with pain.

I skirted the smashed and burned choppers. Too much carnage there to contemplate. Instead I cut west, then angled back toward the barn, avoiding the majority of the battlefield, at least for a bit.

Without really thinking about it, I walked to a small trampled area, the thigh-high hay smashed and burned to reveal a lone white marker that hung limply, soaked with the morning fog. I paused, glancing down at the fallen warrior, considering why she had not been worthy of the Valkyries.

Perhaps her death had not been valiant enough. The young woman who lay before me clutched a bloodied sword. Her armor was punctured and rent from a dozen or more strokes. However she had died, Stuart had rolled her to lay on her back and placed her sword on her chest, and her shield and helm at her feet. I struggled to remember her name. I'd known her for a year, since she'd started coming to the meetings, learning to fight. Karen, I think, or Sharon. I couldn't think clearly.

I turned, walking on. Better to not stop at each and every one of the fallen, I decided. I wouldn't be on my feet that long.

The fog seemed thicker than it had from above. It hugged the ground, lending an eerie, haunted look to the churned-up earth. Too many surprises awaited the unwary.

A thick band of pain tightened around my scalp, making my eyes ache. Every breath was an exercise in subtle muscle control. Too deep, and I wanted to fall to the ground. Too shallow, and I grew light-headed.

Things began to all meld together. Bodies of trolls I passed looked like all the others, twisted limbs and congealed blood. Death was never beautiful, but the aftermath of carnage such as this was nearly overwhelming.

Halfway to the house I ran into a wall of limbs. I raised my head slightly and saw it was two giants lain haphazardly atop one another. A great pool of blood lay around them, thick with flies. The stench hit me like a hammer, and I staggered back, away from them. I turned away only to find other limbs, broken trolls—a field of cadavers.

My head began to swim and for a moment I thought I would fall into that congealing lake of blood, either to drown or be consumed by the carrion eaters.

"No more," I mumbled, turning, looking for a way out of the maze of dead. Somehow I had to reach the house, move past this ugly harvest and find the living.

No Valkyries picked among these dead. Soon, someone would need to clean all this up. Make the world clean. Would anything grow here again?

The world began to lose focus.

"I saw her, damn it," a male voice said somewhere in the fog that covered my eyes.

"Where?" a woman's voice asked. Her voice was so familiar, so sweet and comforting.

"Kyle said he saw her coming in from the clearing north of here," Stuart said. Stuart, yes that was the voice. I knew him. He was a friend.

"She can't have gone far," Katie said. Oh, sweet Katie.

"Sarah!" Stuart called, and I turned.

The world spun out of sync with my turn, and I moved faster, trying to keep up. I stumbled to the side, falling over a large pile of stones. The rocks dug into my left shoulder and pain lanced through me, clearing the fog for a moment. I lay on a large pile of stones, jagged and unweathered. These shattered remains had once been an ogre.

Something was wrong with my right arm, I realized. Something fairly serious. I couldn't feel it, and the shoulder quaked with pain.

"She's here," Stuart called, closer to me. "Over near the giants."

"I can't see you," Katie called back. "Hold up your axe."

Strong hands gripped me, pulled me off the rocks, and rolled me onto my back. Without a word, I rose into the air, lifted by someone who cared for me. I know I was carried because I felt arms under my shoulders and legs.

"It's going to be okay," Stuart said. He turned his head and yelled. "I have her. Get a stretcher."

He lay me on the soft grass, pulling Gram around to the side. I scrabbled with my left hand, desperate for the sword, mewling as I tried.

"Here," he said, twisting the harness enough that the sheathed sword lay across my chest. With my hand on her hilt, I could breathe. Her presence was a comfort and a curse. She was powerful, and demanding. I both loved and feared her—this sword of the one-eyed god. She slept for the moment, but fitfully. Rest would come as it could in future days, I felt through her. The war had begun. This was but a taste—a hint of the horror to come. Had the dragons not known about Gram? Had they forgotten it in their arrogance? What would happen now that its presence had been revealed?

War indeed. Is that what Black Briar was about? Did they know about these things all along? Jimmy had answers, I knew, but did he understand how big all this was?

And dear, sweet, monstrous Frederick. He'd honestly never done a thing to me, nor mine, but he was captive to his true nature. Was he afraid now? Did the dragons somehow know that one of their own had fallen to one of us? How would Nidhogg, the Corpse Gnawer, react?

Had I doomed us all?

And where was Odin in all this? What of the others? Thor? Freya? Heimdall? Wasn't this their war? And if so, where the hell were they?

"Oh, gods," Katie said, dropping to her knees beside

me and touching my face. "Jesus, Stuart, what's wrong with her arm?"

"Hush," he said, standing.

I watched him as he cupped his hands around his mouth and bellowed.

"We need a goddamned stretcher over here." He stomped away, then back, waving his hands in the air. "Come on, people," he growled.

"Go," Katie said, draping a jacket over me. "Go get help, I'll sit with her."

He hesitated, watching me for a moment, and I smiled. "Hey Stuart," I whispered. "It's real good to see you."

"Right," he said, dragging his hand across his face. Was he crying?

"Hurry," Katie said, stroking my scalp. "Please hurry."

He nodded and turned. "You'd better not die," he said. I assumed he meant me.

"We've been worried sick," Katie said when Stuart left. "Qindra wouldn't tell us what happened, but help's coming."

I reached up with my left hand and captured hers, holding it to my cheek. "I'm sorry," I said, but my face hurt, so I released her hand and closed my eyes. "So tired."

"You're going to be okay," she said, going back to stroking my forehead. "When you are better, you can tell me all about your adventure."

"Just pain," I said. "Nothing worth telling." I didn't open my eyes, but I pictured her face in my mind. Though the light of the day was bright, I could not see past the fog.

"Did you kill him?" she asked, her whisper a mixture of anger and pain.

I pictured him, broken and twisted on the shores of Lost Lake. "Yes."

She let out a single sob, and bent over me, kissing my forehead. "Thank you."

I let her chatter then, not having the strength to offer more. It was peaceful, lying there with her, feeling her touch.

I could smell her, if you believe it. Not a body odor type of thing, more like pheromones. It was the cellular level connection I felt with her, that primal connection that drove most animals. No wonder she scared me.

Stuart returned with Melanie and a few others. I couldn't really make them out. Melanie barked at Stuart, made him wait until she had an IV in me before she'd let them move me.

Where did she get an IV?

Even before they pulled me over onto the stretcher, I could feel the drugs she put in the IV. Everything still hurt like hell, but whatever she put in me had a blissful overlay to the world. I hurt, but I didn't care.

"Can you save her?" Katie asked as they stood, lifting me from the ground.

"Hush, now," Melanie said. "Let us work."

The blue of the sky swam in haze. Not sure when all that would burn off, but the afternoon would likely be warm and sunny. A beautiful day in Washington.

I loved days like this. Days where you could lie in the grass and watch the deep blue of the sky through the rich greens of the trees. That contrast always gave me hope. That stark beauty filled me with contentment.

That's what I wanted the day to be like. Not this murky light that diffused and blurred everything.

Faces swam into view as we moved past the barn.

Qindra paused on her cell phone call long enough to bend over me and touch my forehead. "Yes," she said into the phone. "She lives." Then she had turned away, out of my vision, and we were moving again.

"Put her on that table next to Deidre," Melanie said, directing my litter bearers. "Careful. Don't drop her."

There was a bit of jostling as someone made room for

me, but when things were finally worked out, I found myself glancing at Jimmy's back.

He sat, hunched over, facing Deidre. She also had an IV delivering fluids to her. "How's Dee?" I asked.

Jimmy turned to me, his face haggard but determined. "Fair," he said, not looking at me, but looking at Katie.

Katie must have given him a look, because his face softened and he reached over to squeeze my left hand. "She'll live," he said. "As will you, tough as you are."

"Thanks, boss," I said, thinking I should go to sleep soon. The medicine was making everything even more fuzzy.

"Let Melanie get her stable," Katie said from in front of my head.

I couldn't see her, but her hand rested on my left shoulder.

Jimmy leaned across the open space, putting his face in my view. "Did you kill the bastard?"

"Yes," Katie said, shooing him away. I could see her hand, pushing him. "That's done. Let her rest."

Jimmy moved out of my vision. "Fair enough," he said. "We can get details later."

The warble of emergency vehicles began to sing in the distance.

"Here comes the cavalry," Stuart said from somewhere to my right. "About damn time."

"Help me get this off her," Jimmy said, motioning across me.

Stuart appeared, and began undoing the harness that held Gram to me.

"What, wait," I mumbled.

"Need to get this into hiding," Jimmy said.

When they had the sword and sheath freed from me, Jimmy handed it to Stuart. "Wait, take this, too," he said, turning.

When he turned back, he handed another sword to Stuart. I recognized the sheath as one he wore when we went to battles with the SCA, but I'd never seen the sword. Why was he hiding them?

"Don't forget that axe of yours," Jimmy called.

"And Gunther's claymore," Stuart called back. "I'll take care of them."

More questions, more secrets.

I just wanted to sleep.

Melanie appeared at my side, did something to my right arm that hurt bad enough to cut through the drugs. Apparently I screamed.

"Her circulation is for shit," she said, grumbling. "Katie, help me get her shoulder back into the socket."

"What can I do?" Katie asked.

"Hold her, here." Melanie moved around to my other side. "Press your hip into her left shoulder like this. I'll push from the other side."

"Ready," Katie said.

"On three. One . . . two . . . three."

The drugs allowed me to observe, hear the wet pop as my right shoulder was forced back into its socket. I'm not sure I screamed as much as blacked out.

"Don't panic, she's breathing," Melanie said the next time I could understand anything through the haze of pain.

"Is she going to lose the arm?" Katie asked, squeezing my left shoulder.

"Maybe below the elbow," Melanie said, listening to my chest with a stethoscope. "Her vitals are good, circulation is back in full swing. She'll likely get most of the shoulder motion back."

"At least it's her right arm," Katie said.

"I'm still here," I reminded them.

Both women looked down at me. Katie cried, her face streaked with tears and dirt. Melanie smiled grimly and patted my chest. "We can talk after I get you into a nice hospital bed, young lady."

"I'm flattered," I said. "But shouldn't we wait until Katie leaves?"

Katie barked out a laugh, and took my left hand, pulling it to her lips. "She's not a bad choice," she said, wiping tears from her face with her right hand. "But I'm a better choice."

The ambulances started arriving, a string of six or seven, I lost count.

I refused to go in the first ambulance—insisting I had to speak with Qindra first. I needed some clarity.

Melanie patted Katie on the hand and picked up a clipboard. "Don't let her sleep," she said. "I want a CT scan and some more information."

"Okay," Katie said, scootching closer to my side.

"How many dead?" I asked.

"Too many," Katie said. "More wounded. Let's get them seen to first, eh?"

Dena and her crew were first on the scene and loaded Deidre before the rest even made the turnoff to the house. Jimmy refused to leave her side, so he squeezed in behind the stretcher while they loaded a second person.

Katie gave me the play-by-play.

Melanie kissed her hurriedly, accepting a box of supplies from the truck before they took off.

"Gunther, damn it," I heard Stuart yelling.

I rolled my head to the side, and watched the bear of a man hobbling across the grass to where I lay. He had a crutch under one arm, and held his leg at an odd angle. I could see the splint.

"Let 'em take one of the others," Gunther snarled. "I'm fine."

"Stubborn ass," Stuart said, throwing his hands up into the air.

Gunther sort of hopped the last few feet and leaned

against my table, gasping for breath. Fresh sweat broke out on his face, and I could see he was in considerable pain.

"Hey, Gunther," I whispered. It felt like anything else would break something inside me.

He reached for my right hand and paused, his eyes wide and his mouth agape. Stuart nudged him, and he reached over me. Katie moved my left hand onto my stomach and he placed his hand over mine and bowed his head for a moment. When he looked up, tears streamed down his face. "They better take good care of you," he said, his voice thick.

"She'll be fine," Katie said. I could just see the smile on her face, as she used her best kindergarten voice.

"Yeah, well . . ." Gunther trailed off.

Stuart came up and put an arm around his shoulder.

Gunther glanced over his shoulder, saw who it was, and didn't shrug him off. "Just . . . well . . ." He paused, taking a deep breath. "Thank you for saving me back there," he said finally. "I'd be a battlefield burrito if you hadn't jumped in."

Stuart winced, but didn't say anything.

I turned my left hand, grasping his fingers, and squeezed. "World wouldn't be right without you in it," I said.

He turned his head to the side and Stuart smiled. "Can we please get you to the hospital now?" he asked. "They really need to get that leg set, and make sure you won't lose that hip."

"Yes, mother," Gunther said. He leaned over, pulling my hand up, and kissed it. He looked at Katie and smiled. "Take care of her, huh?"

"Of course," Katie said.

Stuart helped Gunther up and over to an ambulance. I heard him cussing up until they shut the door and drove off.

"Remind me of *The Odd Couple*," Katie said. "When I was little, I thought they were gay."

"Aye," I agreed. "But they're not."

"Makes you wonder," she said.

Stuart returned when there was only one ambulance left. "Can she go now?" he said.

"I don't think so," I said. "I still need to speak with Qindra first."

Katie sighed heavily behind me and stood. "Watch her," she said. "I'll go get the witch."

He waited until she was out of earshot before he sat down, placing his hand on mine. "Kyle recovered one of your hammers," he said. "Pulled it out of one of the choppers."

"Morbid," I said.

"He was looking for survivors," he said, turning his face. "Even among the enemy."

I didn't bring up his own journey through the carnage of the battlefield. It was a moment we had shared and did not need to be discussed.

"Tell him thanks."

"Sure," he said, clearing his throat. "I'm proud of you."

I turned my head, studied his face. He had me by about fifteen years. Not quite old enough to be my father, but old enough. I'd never figured why neither he nor Gunther had married, but they were content with their lives. I'd grown to love them over the few years here at Black Briar, learned to trust their instincts and their wisdom.

"Thank you," I said. "That means a lot."

We sat in silence for a while, just letting the day settle over us, waiting.

Soon enough, Qindra appeared at my side, obviously not completely happy.

"Smith," she said, nodding at me.

Smith again. Warrior, smith . . . "How about Sarah?" I asked.

She looked at me, her face passive.

"Yeah, okay. Whatever," I said. "I'm too damn tired for games."

"You asked for me," she said. "What is it you wish of my mistress?"

Of her mistress. Did she have no life of her own?

"She knows, then. About Jean-Paul?"

"My mistress knows many things," she said. "There was a grave mistake made this evening. Certain things got out of control."

"Out of control?" Katie said, her voice cold and thin. "People died here."

Qindra waved a single manicured hand. "Don't be a child. People die every day."

"Not like this, they don't," Katie said. "This was a slaughter."

Stuart barked out a laugh. "Slaughter indeed." His voice was angry, but his face was too calm. "For every one of us that fell, we took two of theirs. Not just lowly humans, either." I could feel his pulse racing through his hand.

"Yours fought valiantly," Qindra acknowledged. "But this should not have happened."

"This is not our fault," I said. "We didn't ask for this."

Qindra looked from Katie, to me, to Stuart. "Your seneschal is not unknown to my mistress. Neither are his activities here and elsewhere."

I tilted my head, looking over at Stuart. "What?"

He shook his head, as equally confused. "She's a nutter," he said finally.

"How droll," Qindra said, a smile touching the edges of her lips. "Is it possible you have no knowledge of what exactly is going on around you?"

There was something. Jimmy had mentioned a secret

late yesterday, before I drove out to confront Frederick. "You serve them," I said, letting some anger slip into my voice. "You live your life in their service." She did not flinch, did not even raise an eyebrow. "And Jimmy, somehow, opposes you."

"We have suspected him," she said. "Though he has not proven to be a threat. Until now."

"We didn't ask for this," Katie said. "That bastard attacked us."

Qindra nodded. "This is also known to my mistress. And it is why we will fix this."

Stuart coughed. "Fix?" He stood up, laying my hand gently on my stomach, and turned toward her. "Will it fix Susan or Maggie?"

"Let it go," Katie said.

"No," he barked, stepping away, waving his arms. "We lost good people here, friends and family." He stalked up to Qindra and looked up into her face. She had a full head on him, but he was not beneath her in any way. "Will that make Deidre wake up? Or fix Sarah's arm?"

I looked down. My arm was wrapped in a blanket, strapped to my abdomen. "What's wrong with my arm?"

"My mistress is not unjust," Qindra said, drawing a thin willow wand from inside her cloak. The tip glowed with a pearlescent blue light. "I am not without power of my own."

She stepped forward and Stuart stepped in front of her.

"Your kind have caused enough pain and suffering," he said, his voice barely above a growl. "I watched you put Yvonne to sleep."

Qindra sighed. "She was beyond restoring. I stopped her pain."

"You killed her," he barked, his voice suddenly loud.

She paused, staring into his face. "And you showed a similar mercy to those fallen on the field."

His back stiffened but he did not budge.

"I have a bit of leeway here," she said, her voice softening with each word. "She does not begrudge me a few acts of independence."

"Let her pass," Katie said. "You promise to help her, right?"

There had been several moments when she had helped us. She dispelled the illusion of the enemy, showed us their true forms. And she stilled the berserker in me. Gave me some control of that killing fury.

"Stuart," Katie said, placing her hand on his shoulder, "if she can help save her arm."

"If you hurt her any more than she has already suffered," he said, "I'll kill you myself."

Qindra did not smile, nor mock him in any way. She just nodded. "You have my word."

He relented, finally, stepping aside like a door opening, allowing her to pass.

Katie pulled the blanket back, and I looked down at my arm. I'd held the shield with this arm, kept the dragon fire from turning me into toast.

The hand was a twisted claw, the skin a mottle of black and red. Bone showed through at the wrist. It was not until the elbow did I see anything remotely like healthy flesh.

I lifted my arm, the pain in my shoulder a small price to pay. My arm looked like something from a zombie movie. "Oh . . ." I gulped as the urge to vomit swept through me. ". . . oh, God."

"Dragon fire," Qindra said, touching the tip of the wand to my forehead.

The nausea vanished, and a peace radiated outward from that touch. I laid my head back, taking in long, even breaths.

The wand traced down my neck, over my shoulder, down to my elbow, and stopped.

Qindra staggered, nearly falling if not for Katie.

"This is worse than I thought," she whispered. "I need whiskey."

"Right," Stuart said. He sprinted into the house and returned with a bottle of Jimmy's favorite Kentucky bourbon.

She took the bottle and tilted it to my lips, just barely letting the brown liquid wet them. The taste was strong and burned its way down my throat.

"I'm not so sure that's a good idea, with all the painkillers she's on," Katie said.

Qindra shrugged. "Whiskey is life." She took a swig, bent over, and puffed out her cheeks. A thin stream of whiskey sprayed from her mouth, down the blackened parts of my arm. Deadened nerves erupted to life, overloading my brain with conflicting signals. The whiskey rolled down my arm like fire.

The wand followed behind, touching each spot where the whiskey touched, changing the burning to a spot of cold that spread out in concentric circles. Three times she drank, and three times she used the whiskey and the wand to change my arm.

In the end, she handed the bottle back to Stuart and turned away, vomiting into the yard. "Bring water here," she said, pointing to the smoking, putrid mess that lay on the ground at her feet. "Wash this into the earth, before it begins to burn." She turned back, wiping a cloth across her lips and dropping it as it burst into flame. "That is all I can do."

Katie cried, and Stuart just stared at my arm. Pink flesh shone from elbow to wrist. I couldn't see the bone. The last two fingers were fused together, but I knew I wouldn't lose the hand.

"Thank you," I said as Qindra walked away. Whether she heard me or not, I couldn't know.

When Melanie returned, she nearly fainted. Katie pulled her aside and talked to her in hushed tones as the ambulance crew began to load me in their truck.

"Where are we going?" I asked the EMT.

He didn't answer right away, but checked my vitals and changed out my IV. When he was done, he pulled an oxygen mask over my face.

"Burn unit over at Harborview," he said. "They got the best docs there."

I let my head fall back, breathing in the clean, antiseptic smell of the oxygen mask. "I think Melanie Danvers is pretty damn good."

He shrugged. "ER docs are aces in my book," he said. "Doesn't hurt she's a hottie."

Yes, I thought as I drifted. Hottie.

"Helluva accident," he said. "Dena said a gas line blew. That how you got the burns?"

I blinked at him, feeling the onrush of exhaustion.

"Crying shame," he said. "I didn't even know they were doing a movie shoot out here. Bet this jacks the insurance rates."

Movie shoot? Is that what they were told? What about Jean-Paul? His body is nowhere near some pretend gas main explosion.

Qindra concocted that story, no doubt. Another in a list of calm, calculated cover-ups. I bet the fire at the smithy will be classified the same. Earthquake just last week. Bad lines all over the place.

I slipped off, letting the beeping of the heart monitor lull me to sleep.

Sixty-five

THE MOSAIC OF lights hung below Frederick as he soared over Portland. It had been a long time since he'd shifted so completely. Decades since he'd felt the wind flowing along his body, pushed along by the beat of his mighty wings.

Moments like these brought back the rush of his younger days in the motherland—times when man lived in scattered villages and there was no need to watch for airliners and news copters.

He missed the olden days before man had risen so high. Maybe his kind were to blame, allowing them to progress so far and so fast. But he loved it as well. He had more money, more power than any of his kind in the old country. While they squabbled over scraps, he had his own kingdom here in this new country.

There were those who clung to the old ways, but not he. He'd embraced the burgeoning civilization, rode it like a lover until he reigned supreme.

Nidhogg might object, but he saw her frailty as weakness that would not long survive. Once he solidified his base with Seattle and Vancouver, he would have the largest holdings in the world.

Jean-Paul's death was a fluke, brought on by his inability to control the beast. Frederick did not lose his senses in their true form. He even retained the ability to speak. Jean-Paul fell to the fury and rage, and good riddance to him.

He rode the thermals for a bit, breathing in the dreams of his people. They had such hope here in this city of green. Nothing was impossible to the children of the west.

That smith intrigued him, titillated him in ways he'd not been thrilled in years. Here was an adversary worthy of his time. If Jean-Paul had not been so arrogant, so foolhardy, he'd be alive today, crushing Vancouver under his tainted claws. Now his world was ripe for Frederick to take.

The girl, this smith . . . he would watch her and wait. Let her be a thorn in the side of Nidhogg a while longer. It made no never mind to him. The wheel turned, the fires burned. Let the dead lie and the living bring him the tribute worthy of his greatness.

Frederick climbed higher to where the wind buffeted his body—cold and strong. He turned toward Mount Hood, craving the frigid stillness that reminded him of his early years.

Sixty-six

KATIE DIDN'T NORMALLY snore, but that's what woke me. I cracked my eyes open, like opening a vault, and the dim light of the hospital room pierced my brain. I had no idea how long I'd been unconscious, but I know I was not tired. Sore, yes. God, I hurt everywhere.

The soft beep of the heart monitor and the ambient smell of disinfectant were beginning to be familiar. Not sure I liked that.

I watched her for a long time. She sat in one of those square padded chairs with the little kick-out foot rest that the hospitals provided for loved ones. You could sleep in it, if you loved visiting your chiropractor on a regular basis.

Her lap was full of pictures, finger paintings mostly, and some line drawings. They were from her class. The splash of primary colors contrasted well with the earth tones of her skirt.

I didn't mean to wake her. She looked wiped out. My body said it was time to be awake, regardless. Of course, I couldn't see a clock. But I wanted to sit up and I wanted to get some of the tubes and such removed. I couldn't see the catheter but I could feel it. Not the most pleasant experience, let me tell you.

On the table beside my bed was a tray with a water pitcher and small plastic cups. Just looking at it made me so thirsty I coughed.

Katie sat bolt upright, scattering pictures across the floor. "Sarah?" she said, not really awake.

"Sor . . ." I tried to clear my throat. "Sorry," I managed.

She stood up, leaning against the chair, and rubbed her face. "You're awake?"

Not like her, that's for sure. I grinned and the skin on my face felt too tight.

I brought my left hand up, exploring my face with light touches. "What time is it?"

"Tuesday."

"Oh. Wait . . . What happened to Sunday?"

"Let me get the nurse," she said, scampering out of the room.

The nurse gave me the once-over, and okayed me for a glass of water. Katie chattered about the three days I'd been in and out of consciousness while she picked up the papers. Her voice was strained from more than sleep deprivation.

"How is everyone?" I asked when the nurse left.

She shrugged, dropping her hands in front of her waist. "Gunther is in a cast from hip to knee. He's grumpy as hell." She smiled at this. "Stuart had some stitches and is already back to work."

"And the others?"

"Bad." She sat down on the side of the bed, putting the pictures on the tray table. "They've got Deidre in a medically induced coma."

"Jimmy doing okay?"

"Ha." She croaked. "Spends his time blaming himself, you, and damn near everyone else."

I sighed, lifted my left arm carefully so as not to tangle the IV. I couldn't reach her, but I tried. She leaned forward and took my hand. "He loves her."

"Melanie says there's a good chance she'll never walk again."

Crap. I let go of her hand. "I didn't mean for this to happen."

She looked at me sternly. "You are not to blame here," she said.

"I'm sorry this got out of hand," I said, holding my hand out to stop her protest. "How could any rational person believe in dragons and dwarves?"

She half smiled. "Thanks."

Oy, stepped into that one.

"Okay, besides you."

"My father told me stories," she said with a shrug. "It always bugged Jimmy that I believed all of it. Up until the time they were killed. Jimmy found some things, did some snooping."

They knew? "Dragons and witches?"

"Is it any harder to believe than neuroscience or quantum physics?"

Ha . . . I was an English major. It wasn't exactly gibberish, but I had nowhere near enough math. "Apples and oranges," I said.

The thing was, they'd always been open about things. Jimmy had offered me a place in his group on the condition I'd be willing to fight when the need arose. I'd always assumed he meant the SCA skirmishes and wars they playacted in every year. How was I to know he meant it for real. And there was something funny about the way he took the weapons, after all that.

"Where's Gram?" I asked. Suddenly the sword's whereabouts was the most important thing in my life. Maybe more important than breathing.

"Stuart put them in the vault," she said. "Where Jimmy keeps the relics and talismans."

What relics? Talismans? How old was Black Briar? Where did they get these items? Nothing made sense in any way I'd thought of the world before. It was like a fairy tale, only instead of a knight in shining armor you got a blacksmith who needed therapy.

Why had Gram come to me? I was nobody. Hell, I couldn't keep a job, or a relationship. How was I supposed to fight dragons? Okay, the one seemed to have worked out, but the cost was too damn high.

"How many did we lose?"

She winced. "Twenty-seven."

Holy crap. We only had sixty in Black Briar. "How many mustered?"

"Everyone."

Everyone? Sixty-plus people in the battle, and we lost twenty-seven. Mother of God. "Did they cover it up?"

She showed me a two-day-old copy of the paper. The headline read TRAGEDY AT MOVIE SHOOT.

She cleared her throat and began to read.

Director Carl Tuttle could not be reached for questioning, but Frederick Sawyer, a partner in Flight Test, Ltd., released a statement regretting the deaths among the cast and crew. "It's tragedies on this scale that make us appreciate those closest to us," the philanthropist from Portland, Oregon, said. Puget Gas and Electric are investigating the gas leak that caused the explosion.

The movie *Odin's Ghost* is about a fictional battle between humans and the giants and trolls of mythic lore. Many of those killed were extras. "It's a crying shame," said Bjorn Mitchell, a spokesman for the Nordic Cultural Committee of Ballard, Washington. "They had the mythology totally buggered," he said. "No way giants and trolls would be landing in choppers. This is a movie of fantastical imagination."

Among the dead were Susan and Maggie Hirsch. This married couple from Seattle were heralded as trailblazers both within the Seattle police force and in the community at large. "We're the first same-sex married couple on the force and we've been given the highest levels of support," Susan Hirsch was quoted in a 2008 interview.

The names of other deceased have been withheld pending notification of next of kin.

Deidre Cornett, wife of Jimmy Cornett, the seneschal (leader) of the local SCA house, was severely wounded in the accident. She is best known for the computer games *Sisters of Steel* and *Barbarian Bunnies*. She sold Protoplasm Studios in 2004 for 78 million dollars.

"Enough," I said, closing my eyes. "That's enough."

She folded the paper and dropped it on the bed. I didn't have the strength to hear more.

"What about Julie?"

"More fiction," Katie said. "Recovering from an explosion at the smithy, likely a result of another gas leak."

Of course. "Puget Gas and Electric are going to take a real beating for this."

Katie just shrugged.

On the other hand, it's not like people would stop buying gas and electricity. They would weather the storm. Earthquake gave them ample coverage.

"How did they justify the giants and trolls?"

"People will believe what they are told," Katie said. "That's one of the things my father taught us. If you give them a reasonable explanation for an event, they will accept it over the truth."

Truth? What a concept. "So, Nidhogg performed the big cover-up and everyone buys it?"

"Up until this," she waved her hands, "would you have believed it otherwise?"

Good point.

"Funny that insurance for the mythical movie shoot appeared, along with some permits that had been filed but misplaced," she said, standing up. "Qindra thought of everything."

"I guess."

"Well, everything but this." She walked over and grabbed her teacher satchel from the back of the seat she'd been sleeping in. From inside she pulled out a copy of *The Vancouver Sun* and showed me an article on page six of section B.

LOCAL CLUB OWNER FOUND DEAD AT CAMPGROUND. Vancouver entrepreneur and club owner Jean-Paul Duchamp was found mauled to death at a campground in western Washington. Mr. Duchamp has been suspected of drug trafficking in a 2003 court case where he was acquitted when the only witness was found burned to death. The details surrounding Mr. Duchamp's untimely death are still being investigated, but local authorities think nature got the best of the often violent man.

"This guy was running a meth lab out of some of the cabins here on the lake," Sherriff Jeremy Stubbs said. "Seems he wandered into the woods, to take a leak or something, and got surprised by a black bear. They are normally gentle creatures, but we have evidence he ran into a mother and her cubs."

"Killed by a bear?" I asked.

"The burned cabins were empty," Katie said. "He didn't hurt anyone else after he left the farm." She paused, her face hard with emotion. "Besides you."

"I'm alive," I said. My right arm was covered in bandages from elbow to fingertip. I gingerly lifted the arm. "And I didn't lose this." I could remember the way my arm had been cooked down to the bone. Dragons were nasty beasts. "I owe Qindra for saving this."

"Careful who you owe," she said. "They just might decide to collect."

She had a point. "Can I get something to eat?"

"Let me get the nurse." She walked from the room, trailing her hand over my feet as she passed the end of the bed.

I still loved watching her walk in that skirt. Hell, any skirt. But I was so tired.

Maybe I should tell her about the dream. I had never thought about children of my own before, but I'd be damned if I was going to let a dragon force me to *mate* with Gunther or Stuart. Not that they weren't great guys, but come on. It could've been a stress dream, but in light of everything else that had gone on recently, I had a hard time ignoring it.

Qindra served Nidhogg, but she had moments where she seemed approachable. Not that I could trust her as far as I could spit.

And Katie . . . did I want to raise a child with her? Yikes. I can't figure out how to have a grown-up relationship with her. I sure as hell ain't ready to be a mommy. And even if I was, I wouldn't be handing my children off to an ancient dragon for her amusement.

The nurse declared I'd survive and ordered me apple juice and lime gelatin. Soon I'd be on a bulk-up diet, she assured me. So much for my figure.

Since I was going to live, Katie took time to go home and shower, get a change of clothes and a few books for me. The doctors and nurses treated me like a hero. Seems the word had been spread that I had pulled some folks from the burning barn, saving lives and getting burned in the process.

Losing my hair was not too significant; it was growing back. But that, combined with the burn treatments, really made me cranky. I wasn't feeling up to dealing with anyone. I turned away all visitors, except for Katie. I just couldn't face them. To see the pain in their faces, the horror at what I'd done. It was too much to even think about. I isolated myself to avoid the emotion. Cut myself off from what could cause me more pain.

Katie disapproved, but didn't argue with me. The pain of it was clear in her eyes, but I can be pretty darn stubborn.

Sixty-seven

OVER THE NEXT three weeks I had two skin grafts using this new artificial skin Harborview had in trials. The delicate work around my hands was painful and required three surgeries, the first just to separate the ring and pinkie fingers. In the end, while I wouldn't have fingerprints on that hand, with physical therapy I'd use it again. You took what blessings you could.

One night I woke to find Qindra bending over me, the blue glow of her wand and feather necklace lighting the room. She stroked my forehead; I could feel her fingertips tracing the runes in my hairline.

When I turned over, she slipped away. I guess I could've dreamed it. The pain in my shoulder was better the next morning, though, and the doctors were pleased with the way my face was healing.

Sixty-eight

QINDRA SLIPPED INTO her room, peeling off layers of clothing as she went. This was the sixth night she'd gone to the hospital to tend to the blacksmith and she was exhausted. She draped her cloak over her bed and sat at the dressing table, pulling the cover from the mirror.

For several minutes she daubed cream on her face, then she began stripping the polish off her nails. Each movement precise and practiced. One cotton ball per nail, each placed carefully in a small wooden box. Magic was a dangerous thing to work with. The air sparkled as the remnants of stored magic diffused into the air.

Once she was done, she closed the box, walked over, and placed it into the fireplace. She whispered a quiet word, and it burst into flames, sending multicolored flames into the flue.

The smith would be whole, she was sure of it. But she still did not understand the compulsion she felt to help her. She'd killed Jean-Paul, and Nidhogg was deeply hurt. He had been the last of her brood. What did this mean for their world? Nidhogg would surely never spawn another, not at her age.

Was the power shifting? Qindra had only heard of the great wyrms falling in bedtime stories and nightmare tales whispered by her mother. Her mother had told her, when she was very young, that the dragons feared the return of the ancient gods. Feared the end times, and the loss of power they had accumulated over the centuries.

She sat back at the dressing table and began to brush her hair, long even strokes to help soothe her spirit as much as anything.

Was that why she felt compelled to help heal the smith?

Did she see the beginning of the fable her mother had impressed upon her as a young child? Did she harbor hope for her kind?

She touched the mirror and the image shifted to Nidhogg's room. Her mistress, ancient and frail, lay on her great bed, asleep. Jai Li, the surviving twin, slept curled at Nidhogg's feet.

How many generations of girls had this most ancient of dragons used for her own pleasure and needs? How had she been so closed to the depredations?

Qindra covered her mirror and crawled into bed. Sleep would not come for many hours.

Sixty-nine

THE NURSE BROUGHT in a vase of flowers from Stuart just before lunch one afternoon and Katie showed back up after school with a new stack of pictures to stick up on the walls, and an envelope with the Flight Test, Ltd. logo on the front.

Inside was a check from Carl for back pay, and a nice letter inquiring about my health. I suspect it was written by Jennifer, but the dinner invitation at the bottom was definitely Carl's.

"They started shooting again after the state investigated the set," Katie told me when she saw the invitation. "Sawyer filed an insurance claim for the choppers and everything. Flight Line will get a pretty nice check out of their insurance company. Never guess who the major stockholder of said insurance company is."

"Nidhogg, right?"

Katie nodded.

It was a puzzle, a twisty maze of connections and loyalties. How deep did these things go?

"As for Sawyer," she said, wincing, "he's paid all of your medical bills."

"What?" I struggled to sit up, anger flaring in me, but it was weak. "Are you sure?"

She smiled. "A nice note appeared from a nonprofit in Portland. They've declared you are a hero and want to present you with a plaque after you're better."

I nearly choked. "Like I'd go to Portland ever again."

We both laughed briefly. It felt good, honest. "Be careful who you owe," I said. "I think I remember hearing that somewhere."

The look on her face told me there was more. She looked pained, almost embarrassed. What could be worse than having a dragon pay your medical bills after you'd killed one of his kind?

"There's something else," Katie said, finally. "Julie has asked to see you. I had a call from her on my machine. She doesn't know what has happened to you, but wanted to see if the two of you could talk."

Yikes. Was I really up to that? On one hand, I had always considered her a mentor and a friend. But, the thing with Jack and Steve, no matter how awful and stupid it was, didn't deserve the response she gave. Right, I mean, come on. They'd gone out a few times, and slept together once, I think.

I was an asshole, and totally out of control, but . . .

"Sure," I said with a little trepidation. "I'd love to see her. How's her leg?"

Katie took a deep breath, and tilted her head back, closing her eyes. She did that sometimes when she had bad news.

I clenched my teeth and drew in a sharp breath. "Oh, God. Bad?"

"No, no," she said, looking at me and waving a hand. "It's not that."

That was a relief. I let my shoulders sag and un-clenched my teeth. "Her leg was pretty bad."

"Melanie got her stabilized early. It looked uglier than it really was."

I shuddered at the memory. "I can't imagine . . ." And I stopped. Okay, I could imagine. "Well, with the bone exposed like that. That's a horrible break."

"Femur breaks are always bad, but she'll walk again." She was holding something back.

"If she's going to be okay," I asked, "then what's the problem?"

She sat on the bed beside me and took my left hand in hers, holding it in her lap. It was a tender moment, quiet.

"It's been almost a month," she said in a near whisper. "When are you going to stop being so goddamned cheerful? I haven't seen you cry once."

If she would've slapped me, I'd have been less shocked. I was handling things fine, better than fine. Heck, I was getting out of the hospital soon and I was going to be great.

"You've been so cold." She touched my cheek with the back of her hand.

Her eyes were haunted, brimming with tears. She cupped my cheek and leaned forward, gently touching my lips with hers.

I leaned into that kiss, hungry for it after so long.

My heart stopped for the briefest of moments and I tasted her again for the first time. Whatever I had built around me, whatever had kept me together through all this, finally faded.

As it left, I had clarity. It was Qindra on the battle-field, that first moment where I'd been able to set the fury aside, to think rationally despite the overwhelming need to smash things. She'd given me the means to isolate that passion, that unbridled fury. And in the process, I'd tamped it all down, deep into a secret place that had succumbed to the ice.

Katie's kiss, the need in it, the urgent passion that rose in me, were too much for the ice. For a moment, a rush of emotion overwhelmed me and my eyes started to burn.

Without warning, the terror and sorrow burst upward from my chest, erupting into the world as an anguished moan.

"It's okay," she said, quietly, kissing my cheeks. "Crying will help."

Was I crying?

She wrapped her arms around me and held me against her while grief and pain welled out of me in uncontrollable sobs. I held on to her like I had been drowning and she'd just pulled me up to where I could taste the sweet air.

After a while, I settled down and she slowly let me go.

"Sorry," I said, wiping my face. "That was awkward."

She picked up the box of tissues from the bedside table and plucked out two, handing them to me. "Sarah." She looked at me, searching my eyes. "That was human."

"As opposed to what?"

She glanced away and shrugged. "As opposed to who you've been lately," she said.

"Ever since I reforged . . ."

"I think it's the runes," she said, running her hand down my leg and massaging my left shin.

That's a big duh. "Qindra did something at the farm, too. Did something to quiet the rage."

"Maybe," she said, looking away.

We sat there, quietly sharing each other's company for a very long time.

Seventy

KATIE WHEELED ME down to the third floor, to where Julie was recovering. She stopped at the nurses' station to double-check it was okay to go in, and I watched the floor. Nurses hustled about, and the soft double-bing of the elevator opening cut through the heavy stillness that pervaded the floor. Convalescence required quiet. That was the clear message. It seemed that there was a deadening agent of some source at work. The footfalls and voices fell quietly without traveling down the hallway.

I felt fairly helpless, which sucked. If I tried, I could move the left wheel on the chair, but not the right. My right arm was in a sling hugged against my chest. So I could run in circles if I was really inclined to run.

No metaphor there, nope.

Katie smiled and laughed with the nurse, almost flirting, before coming back to me. I watched her with some level of relief. She glowed under the fluorescent lighting, like porcelain.

"Three seventeen," she said, pushing me around in a large looping turn. "They moved her last night."

We arrived at 317 and Katie knocked on the door—three quick raps before pushing the door open and wheeling me in.

"Company," she sang, pulling the curtain aside far enough to wheel me forward. "Hope you're decent."

Julie was sitting up, the head of the bed raised. She turned from staring out the window, and her face beamed. "About damn time," she said.

"Hey boss," I said, feeling sheepish.

She looked at me shrewdly, evaluating. "Okay, I'll accept that."

We stared at one another for a long silent moment. A large yellowing bruise still dusted the left side of her face, and her right leg was in traction. Pulleys and lines held her leg just off the bed, with a handle at the other end that allowed her to pull herself up a bit, to reposition, without moving that leg too awful much.

Three weeks of that. God, I'd be stir crazy.

"So," Katie said. "Joan, the head nurse . . ." She twisted, motioning out toward the nurses' station. "She said I could go get us some drinks from the machine. I'll just be gone a minute."

Julie smirked at me, raising her left eyebrow in that creepy way she had. "Sure," she said. "Drinks. Sounds lovely. I'll have bourbon."

I couldn't help it. I choked out a laugh, as sudden as the moan earlier.

"Yeah, okay," Katie said, pushing me to the side of the bed, near the foot, facing the head. "You have a nice chat, I'll see what I can find."

"Thanks," I said, letting the smile blossom over my face. It felt good.

Katie disappeared and Julie eyed me like she did when I was working with a new horse. "Heard you had some pretty bad burns."

I held up my right arm, not taking it from the sling. "Won't need any conditioner for a bit." I rubbed my scalp. "But doc says it will all grow back again."

She nodded. "Good, good. Shame to lose hair that pretty."

Pretty? Wow. Not a comment I thought I'd ever hear from her. "What about you?" I asked. "Leg doing okay?"

"Pain in the rear," she said, lying back and putting one hand behind her head. "Got another eight weeks, but they don't seem to be in any hurry to kick me out."

"Look, I'm sorry . . . ," I started.

"I was an ass," she said at the same time.

We both stopped and laughed, that nervous laugh you do when you are embarrassed.

"I . . . ," I started again, and she held up her hands.

"Let me," she said. "I've been lucid longer."

Couldn't argue with that.

"I've been talking with Katie for a few days," she said. "Oh?"

She shrugged. "Shared trauma, and all that." She waved her hands, as if to make it all go away. "Anywho . . . We were comparing notes, checking facts, that sort of thing."

I watched her, curious and worried all at the same time.

"And, I'd had several long conversations with Rolph, when he stayed at the smithy."

"Ah," I said, nodding.

"Yeah, so . . ." She scrubbed her face with both hands and sighed. "I know about the dragon, both the live one and the dead one, and I suspect more."

"Yeah, there's another I know about."

"Great." She shuddered. "Anyway. I figured some things out about the sword and you. You know, mood swings, anger management. Drunken, self-destructive behavior."

I knew it was coming to that. How could it not? Still, I blushed, the heat running up my neck to my earlobes if I was reacting true to form.

"So, Jack's an ass, and his buddy's no better," she said. "Not your fault." She made a point of pausing, looking me directly in the face. "Been a long time since I let some dangly bits get between me and a friend."

Friend. That was sounding better with every word.

"I'm sorry I became unglued," she said finally. "Total bitch factor, there."

I kept it together, though I thought I'd start crying again. Hope that wasn't broken now. "Julie." I reached over and took her hand. "I never wanted to do anything to hurt you."

She squeezed my hand. "Of course not. I know that

now. Especially after . . ." She turned and looked out the window, her voice going flat. "Katie told me you killed him."

"Yes."

"Good."

We sat there, watching an air ambulance landing on the helipad across the way. The low pulse of the blades echoed in my chest, echoed the pulse in her wrist.

"I would've died if not for you," she said. "He was going to give me to them, to play with."

"Hush," I said. "It's over. He'll never hurt anyone ever again."

She squeezed my hand one more time, then wiped her eyes.

"I'd say you should come back to work for me." She laughed through her tears. "But I don't have a smithy to work at. Nor a home to return to."

She was all alone, I realized. Everything she'd built, her home, her livelihood, her dignity and pride. Each of those had been taken from her.

All because of . . . Okay, I didn't cause it. Katie was right. But I was at the epicenter. I had to fix this somehow.

"When I get out, I'll visit the regular customers. Assure them things are going to be fine," I said, believing it with each word. "You can use the phone, right?"

She didn't look at me, just stared out the window until the chopper lifted off again. Then she turned to me and shrugged. "Yeah, sure."

"Good," I said. "I'll find us a place to work. A temporary shop. You call some of your cronies and get us some loaner gear."

She laughed at that. "Cronies? Like my secret blacksmith guild?"

"Exactly," I said, perking up. "That's exactly what I mean."

The way she pursed her lips made me smile. She was thinking.

"Rolph had it right," I said before she could speak. "Fire and iron, hammer and tongs. It's in the blood. It's who we are."

"I miss the forge," she said wistfully.

I had her then. We were going to win this. "Call Rodriguez over in Cle Elum. Let him know what's happened. He'll spread the word through the community."

"Frank Rodriguez talks more than any man I've ever met."

"See, that's what I mean. Remember when Chloe Tonks got kicked by that horse over in Sultan? Hell, Frank arranged to get her customers taken care of, while working his own folks."

Hope colored her cheeks and a small smile touched her lips. "He does owe me for that one," she said.

"Done deal then." I felt better. Lord, I think for a fleeting moment there I was content. Something to watch out for.

We chatted then, about who to call, and what customers to tell what. It was like it was before the sword, exciting.

By the time Katie came back with two cans of apple juice and some sort of lemon-lime soda, we were talking about the cute doctors and nurses.

Small victories were often better than the big ones.

Later, after Katie left, and I was alone in my room, I called down to Julie, just to thank her for everything. She told me I was being sappy and to go to sleep. Soon she'd be a total curmudgeon. Made me smile.

Didn't stop me from waking up in tears around two in the morning. I seriously considered calling Katie, but she was exhausted. Instead I tried to work out where Rolph stood in all this. I was surprised no one had found him, or he hadn't called if he were alive. The battle had been chaotic. There's no telling what had happened to him.

I must've dreamt about him, because the next morning, as they were finally sending me home, I realized I didn't hate him. He was preserving the sword. The look in his eyes when he finally decided to take the sword from me was a cross between anguish and madness. He'd been driven by this whole thing much longer than I had. Who was I to judge him?

Seventy-one

KATIE PICKED ME up in a rental. With hers destroyed in the fire, she hadn't gotten around to getting a new one.

"Not sure if I can drive the hatchback," I told her as we pulled out onto Broadway. "With this right arm less than one hundred percent, I'm not sure I can operate a stick."

"About that," she said, hunching her shoulders like I was gonna hit her. "Um, the hatchback was pretty old, right?"

"Yeah?" I half asked. "Paid off and does what I need. I love that car, why? What's wrong with my car?"

This was serious—damnation. Not my car.

"Several vehicles were smashed in the battle," she said.

I laid my head back against the headrest and closed my eyes. Fun and harrowing times flashed through my mind. Kissing Katie for the first time, drive-in movies, hauling away auction finds, getting run off the road, racing to find Katie . . . maybe a new vehicle wouldn't be a bad idea.

"Jimmy said Rolph's truck is at the farm."

"Where's Rolph?"

She didn't answer right away.

"Was he killed?"

"No one's seen him since that night," she said. "Jimmy figures he died somewhere we haven't found yet. Not too many places overlooked out at Black Briar." She turned to me. "Had a helluva time keeping Qindra from snooping too far and wide. She knows there's something there we don't want her to know about."

I watched the slower traffic on the right as we sped along, thank God for carpool lanes. "I need to clarify a few things with you folks when Deidre gets out of the hospital," I said. "I need to know all the details. What are these artifacts and weapons Jimmy is hiding?"

"Yeah. Jimmy said it was time to bring you into the inner circle."

Inner circle? "Well, I killed several giants, some trolls, and one big-assed dragon. Think I've passed initiation?" I was starting to get angry. "Jesus, why'd you keep that from me? I thought we had trust."

"I tried," she said, her voice barely above a whisper. "You even told Jimmy about how flaky I was from time to time."

Ouch! Maybe I was more like my da than I liked to admit. I reached over and put my left hand on her leg, squeezing it briefly. "I'm sorry."

"You weren't ready," she said, patting my hand. "Besides, the fates had other things in store for you, it seems."

"At least."

We rode a while in silence.

"I should have listened to you. Respected you enough to try and understand what you were saying."

She glanced at me, furtively, trying to see my face and watch the road at the same time. "You are a stubborn ass."

I laughed. What else could I do? She was right, of course. I'm sure Julie would agree on many levels. "Guilty as charged."

"Are we witnessing a changed woman?" she asked, a smile flirting with her face.

"Definitely," I agreed. "Through the fire, and all that."

Her face grew serious again. "No sarcasm now," she said. "If we are going to make a go of this again, I need more honest emotion and less witty repartee."

"I'll try." And that must have been good enough for her, because the rest of the drive was peaceful and full of hope. She practically glowed. Damn, she was so beautiful. I had to keep that in my mind at all times. Not just that she was sexy as hell, but she had a real spirit in her, a goodness that changed the world around her.

Rolph's pickup was sitting near the house. I climbed in the driver's side, totally unlocked, and poked around. The keys were under the visor. I leaned over and opened the glove box. The insurance card was there, said it was paid up for the next four months, full coverage. I don't know if he had any payments left to make, but I just needed a ride for the next few weeks.

Under the owner's manual, I found a familiar envelope. "Look at this."

Katie opened the passenger side door and took the envelope from me. "Looks like the one Frederick gave you," she said.

The seal had been broken, so she tipped it up, dropping three papers on the seat.

It was a near copy of the deal I had. Partial ownership in Flight Test, Ltd., some returned family heirlooms, and a cashier's check for one hundred thousand dollars.

"Crikey," she said. "These checks are free money. At this point, you have one hundred fifty thousand dollars."

I took the check from her, thinking about everything

I could do with it: house, smithy, new car. And after every-thing that we had all been through, I thought that taking the money and not giving the sword to Frederick was just about fair and wouldn't make a dent in my idea of honor. "Give it to Jimmy," I said. "Tell him to use it for those who have fallen."

She looked at me a moment and smiled. "Good plan," she said, leaning into the truck and kissing me.

Totally worth it.

Seventy-two

I DROVE UP to Everett. The only bandages left were the ones on my wrist, where the bone had shown through at one point. Not a bad deal.

My grip in my right hand was still pretty weak, but I'd get back most of it. Just hard work. The doctors sug-gested guitar, piano, and knitting. I'd do the exercises and figure something out.

I pulled into the little Mexican place Jennifer preferred and saw her sedan. I parked around the side, where the truck could not be seen from the street, and got out. My reflection didn't suck. My hair was about two inches long—not bad, considering.

I grabbed the envelopes from the dash, climbed out, and closed the door. Jennifer would be very interested in the two agreements I was bringing her. Something I bet they had not been aware of.

The waitress showed me to a booth out on the deck. Jennifer sat in the sun, her shades hiding her eyes.

"Hi," I said, scanning her face. Not a fair conversa-tion there, keeping her eyes covered in mirrors. "I'm sorry, but with all that has gone on, could we sit inside, where we aren't in the direct sun?"

"Oh, I'm sorry," she said, standing quickly. "I didn't think . . . what a moron . . . I'm so . . . ," she stammered, and nearly fell over her chair trying to rise.

I reached out and grabbed her shoulder with my left hand. "It's okay," I said.

She took off her glasses and looked at me sheepishly. "You look pretty good, all things considering."

The waitress took us back inside and gave us a small table near the window. Soon we had chips and salsa, as well as a pitcher of water. My kind of service.

"How are you?" Jennifer asked as I crunched into a chip.

I held up my right arm. "Recovering well enough."

She watched me, unsure of how to proceed. "How come you didn't tell me there was another shoot?"

There it was. It didn't take us long to get right down to it. She was out of the loop. Only, there was no loop. Not before Nidhogg.

I shrugged. "Long story."

"I see," she said, bringing her water glass to her lips.

"These will add to the mystery," I said, laying the papers on the table for her. "Not only was he dealing a second movie on the side"—I hated perpetuating the lie—"he was also trying to sell a greater share of the business than he owned."

She looked through the papers, her brow furrowing. "For a sword?" she asked. "The black one we used in *Elvis Versus the Goblins*?"

I nodded.

"What a bizarre little man."

"Bizarre?"

Her eyes narrowed and she leaned forward. "Looks fair, feels foul."

I laughed. She was such a movie nerd.

She wasn't mad at me. She didn't like Sawyer.

And that was it.

I had chicken flautas and she had pollo de crème. It was lovely. We chatted about the movie, Carl, and how JJ was being so pissy about all of it.

"Frederick has him convinced he's the next Matt Damon," she said, scooping up refried beans with a tortilla chip. "Honestly. The man is insufferable."

"What about the bimbette?" I said, holding my hands in front of my breasts like cupping watermelons.

Jennifer giggled. "Carl believes Frederick when he tells him the movie will sell twenty percent better with enough breast shots, but . . ." She leaned over her dish and whispered. "I told him he could see my breasts if it helped."

"Oh my God! You did not." I loved this woman.

She blushed, but did not lose the smile. "You should've seen him. Like a kid on Christmas morning."

I raised my eyebrows. "TMI, but, you know . . . did you?"

She shrugged. "We made out a little, but that's it . . . so far."

I could tell she had this thing under control. "Good for you."

She was quite pleased with herself. "But, this movie thing, the sex scenes and all . . . He's ashamed to tell his parents."

I laughed. "He's how old?"

"Thirty-three," she said, rolling her eyes. "Yes, I know."

"Besides embarrassing his mother, what does he think about the intrusion?"

She grew serious. "Frederick flusters him. Keeps him off balance."

Not a surprise. I'd hate to have his attention directed at me ever again. "I'm sure JJ likes the whole sex aspect of everything."

"Between you and me," she said, shaking her head, "Juanita, one of JJ's girls, disappeared several weeks ago. He's been despondent."

That made no sense. "He was just using her for sex," I said. "She wanted to get married so she could get her green card and he wasn't interested."

"Well, Babs told me she ran off with Rolph."

I choked, spitting water down the front of me.

Hope no one recognized the truck in the lot. "Thought he died in the fire," I said.

She shrugged. "No idea. Wasn't listed in the papers and the insurance guy was pretty thorough. By the way, local union is pissed Frederick hired folks from Vancouver for the shoot. Why didn't you tell me about it?"

As I watched her, the unease and concern on her face, I realized I had no interest in keeping the dragon's lies. I liked her too much for that.

"Jennifer . . ." I took a deep breath, steeling myself. "I can't play this game. Not with you."

She looked even more confused, but didn't say anything, letting me get it out.

"There was no movie shoot," I said. "You know what happened in part. That bastard Duchamp had snatched Julie and Katie."

"Yes, I remember," she said, watching my face. "I was going to get around to that mess."

So, I told her the whole story. I didn't have anything to lose. Either she believed me, or she wrote me off as crazy.

In the end, it was a little of both. But, I'm not sure I could blame her.

"I heard that phone call," she said. "Everyone there heard it. That's the part that makes all this"—she waved her hand around the room—"movie shoot thing fall apart."

"People believe what they are told, for the most part,"

I said, echoing Katie. "If the explanation is more reasonable than the truth, we accept it."

"That's what we are all about, the illusion of life," she said.

That was the connection. The dragons lived with illusion. Qindra countered it at the battle. And here, the movies were all about illusion and glamour. No wonder Frederick was drawn to it.

More grist for the mill. Katie would have an insight, I'm sure.

The rest of lunch was delightful.

As we walked out, we paused at Jennifer's car. She hugged me with warmth, not like those fake hugs strangers give. It was pleasant, friendly.

"You know," she said as she unlocked her car, not looking at me, "we did say a few weeks."

"What?"

"Your vacation and all," she said, turning her head to the side to see me. "You could come back to work when you are ready."

And there you have it, folks. Honest to goodness joy. It just burst all over me like an . . . well, like a warm sudsy bath, actually, which is what I wanted after weeks of hospital sponge baths.

I hugged her again. "I'll come back next week, if that's okay?"

"Absolutely," she said. "Carl will be very pleased."

I grinned at her. "And we want Carl pleased."

She laughed. "I have most of that covered." She patted my arm. "You just come back to us. You're family."

"What about Sawyer?"

She looked at me, waving the envelopes in her hand. "Our lawyers will be talking to his lawyers. I'm sure conversations of breach of contract and unethical business transactions will keep him tangled up for a while."

I smiled. "Man, you can be a stone-cold bitch, when you want to be."

"Glad you approve."

We laughed and hugged again before she walked to her car.

I stood on the sidewalk there, watching her pull out of the parking lot. She waved at the last minute, and I waved back. Though I have walked through the valley of the shadow of death, I will fear no evil for I have people who love me. I skipped back to the truck. Next stop, home and dead houseplants.

Seventy-three

WHEN I GOT back to my place, I found someone had been busy. All my houseplants were alive and there were three goldfish in the tank. I distinctly remembered one dying before this mess all happened, so one was a miracle. Or Katie had gone to the pet store for me.

I opened the fridge to find it stocked with good food, veggies, milk, cheese, my favorite diet soda, and three bottles of mead. Lovely.

I turned on the stereo, loudly, and began undressing as I walked to the bathroom. I'd pick up the clothes later. Besides, I might need the trail to find my way back to the kitchen later.

The bath was heavenly. I'd passed over the cassia bath beads—not in the mood for cinnamon—and opted for the grapefruit. I wanted something reviving and clear. I stepped into the hot water while Jethro Tull rocked the living room. Once the bubbles were up to my chin, I closed my eyes and just soaked.

After an hour, I showered and dressed in the pink sweats. I switched the music to Pink Floyd and poured myself a glass of mead.

I sat on the couch with my laptop and began taking notes.

I started with dragons and cities, then put in names: Qindra, Rolph, Katie, Mr. Philips.

Somewhere there was a greater pattern.

My phone rang. I set the laptop on the couch and trundled to the kitchen to grab my cell off the counter. I almost didn't answer it, since it was a blocked call, but I was feeling good for the first time in a long time, so I risked it.

"Smith?" the deep male voice said.

I sat down, right in the middle of the floor, my legs just giving up the fight. "Rolph?"

"You have done well," he said. "I owe you an apology."

My heart was pounding. "I thought you were dead."

He chuckled. "I nearly was. If it weren't for the fair Juanita, I would be."

Wait . . . Juanita? "Someone told me you left with her, but I didn't see how."

"It was Babs," he said. "Juanita overheard her. She was working for the dragon Duchamp."

"That was how he knew to call the set," I said. "How he knew about Frederick and things."

"Yes, many things were known to him. I am ashamed," he admitted. His voice trembled—shame, sorrow, fatigue, I couldn't tell.

"Where are you now?" I asked. "I have your truck."

"That is one reason I have called. I need the truck, and some things from my place, if I could impose upon your kindness."

"Well, you did try to kill me," I said.

"Wound," he said. "I could not let you give him the

sword. It would give them more power than they already wield."

"I forgive you," I said, meaning it. "After facing him, seeing what he was, I understand your anger and drive."

"It is a shame you were exposed to this. I meant it when I said you are a talented smith."

"Rolph, you are a master. Julie says so. I can tell it by your knowledge, the little details about smithing."

He barked a bitter, mournful laugh. "I was once, yes," he said. "But something I had in addition to decades at the forge was hubris."

I was lost. "Hubris?"

"Have you not discerned the truth yet?" he asked. "The smith who reforged Gram and failed was cursed. Frederick came to my village demanding sacrifices and treasure. Against the wishes of my father, I attempted to reforge the sword, to hope to slay the beast."

I didn't interrupt. I knew too many details.

"So, I failed in the mending. I was not pure enough," he said, his voice trailing to a whisper. "He laughed at me when I confronted him," he said. "The sword did not sing to me, did not call forth the blood and fire."

He fell silent. After a minute, I thought I could hear him crying.

"He took my sister and my mother, then," he continued. "Blinded my father and left me unharmed."

"Oh, Rolph. I'm so sorry." How many years had he lived with his failure? How many decades, centuries of self-loathing.

"I lost track of the sword after he raided my home. Someone from the village must have spirited it away. I have searched for it ever since.

"So you see, fair smith. The gift you gave me, allowing me to see the sword reforged. That I will always carry in my heart."

I couldn't help it. I was crying. Bastards. All of them. "Okay, Rolph. I'll get you your stuff."

"I am in your debt, Smith Beauhall. Today and forever."

We talked for another twenty minutes. In the end, he wanted several cases of heirlooms and some personal effects, along with his banking information, passport, and a few photos and such.

And he wanted to see the sword again. Not to keep it, but to see how it had survived after the battle. Legend had it Odin shattered it after Fafnir was slain.

I was to meet him in Surrey, British Columbia, in three weeks. He said he'd e-mail me details for the meet. This would give him enough time to work out a few loose ends, and allow time for me to get to his place before the rent was due.

In the meantime, I had to get the word out that Babs was a mole. Jennifer would take care of things, I was fairly sure. If nothing else, let Babs know we knew, so Frederick didn't kill her. I can't imagine she was getting much out of the deal. Nothing worth dying over. Stupid woman.

I finished the mead and took a few more notes before deciding I needed to sleep.

My bed felt wonderful after the hospital. I slid into clean sheets and a toasty warm comforter. The pillows were what I missed most, frankly.

For a moment, I wished Katie was here with me, but the luxury of sleep was too much and I drifted down to oblivion.

Seventy-four

THE SOUND OF crows slipped into my dreams followed by the howling of a lone wolf. I flew across the city, toward the mountains, seeking someone. I needed to warn someone, stop something horrible from happening.

In a clearing at the edge of the snowline I saw a black tree, its limbs reaching toward a stormy heaven. There on the tree hung a haggard man, flowing and matted gray hair and beard, his body twisted in pain. He had been crucified, nailed to the tree for some crime.

"Come to me," he whispered.

In the distance lightning shattered against the mountain peaks.

"I'm afraid," I said to the wind.

The old man cocked his head to the side like a bird. I could see he had only one eye. At the foot of the tree lay his shredded clothes, a broken staff, and a pizza box, open with crusts scattered among the stones.

"Joe?" I asked.

He cackled then, throwing his head back against the bark of the tree. Blood flowed from the already encrusted wounds as his body shook.

"Find me, smith."

I looked around. "Where are you, Joe? Where have you gone?"

"I am lost in the madness of age," he cried against the rising wind. "Find the golden apple. Raise the Æsir. Save the horn blower, call the fallen from their resting place."

I hovered in front of his broken and naked body. "I do not understand."

"I swear to you, warrior-smith. I will spare the blade

this time. That is my payment to you for your deeds. You have slain one of the usurpers, the kin-slayers. No amount of wergild can compensate for the slaughter of our people. The battle is coming, the Midgard Serpent begins to wake."

A word echoed in my head then, a grinding sound of boulders and snow . . . an avalanche roared down the mountain and I could not move from where I hovered.

"We serve the wheel," he shouted above the roaring of the mountain. "The cycle must renew. Promise me, smith. You are the key!"

A wall of ice and stone swallowed him and the tree where he'd hung, choking the world in frigid destruction. The anger and power of it finally loosed me from my tether and I pinwheeled, shrieking across the night sky.

Seventy-five

DEIDRE CAME OUT of the hospital almost five weeks later. Black Briar was having a barn-raising and celebration. This would be the first time we'd all be together since the battle—since so many perished.

Jimmy made sure I was invited, though he hadn't spoken to me himself. Katie and I were working back to some sort of relationship, but this one was deeper, more emotional and spiritual. The physical would return in time, I'm sure. I wasn't feeling any pressure and she wasn't pushing anything.

I planned to crash at Black Briar the night, camping out in the field with Katie. There would be much drinking after the barn-raising and, perhaps, something else.

Rolph's gear was loaded in the pickup, covered with a

tarp and tied down. I was going to Surrey the next day. But today, we were raising a barn. Building back the heart of our community, beginning the healing process.

I pulled into the drive with a bit of trepidation. Maybe we'd all be okay, in some way. I know I had hope.

Turn the page for a preview of

𝕳𝖔𝖓𝖊𝖞𝖊𝖉 𝖂𝖔𝖗𝖉𝖘

J. A. Pitts

Available in July 2011
from Tom Doherty Associates

TOR®

ISBN 978-0-7653-2907-3
(PAPERBACK)

ISBN 978-0-7653-2468-9
(HARDCOVER)

One

JIMMY CORNETT, THE leader of Black Briar, paced the length of the room, eleven long strides before turning and making the return trip. In his left hand he carried a high-ball glass with three fingers of Glenlivet single-malt scotch, but had not taken the first sip.

His world had gotten a helluva lot more complicated these last six months. Running the farm and Black Briar was full-time work. He loved the reenactment and the swordplay, but until this spring, that's what it had been: play. When the dragon attacked the farm with choppers full of trolls and giants, the thin veneer of it all slid right off the cracker.

His sister, Katie, had a better handle on it all. He'd always discounted her beliefs, nodding and patting her on the head. But they were definitely the children of their parents, and the secret world of dragons and myth should not have come as such a surprise to him. Of course, they had been rather vague on the whole "dragons will attack your farm in helicopters" aspect of it all.

He felt a tightening in his chest as he thought back to the battle just a few months earlier. Black Briar had been prepared, sort of. They'd trained for the various reenactment wars around the country. They were good, a well-considered mercenary house on the fringes of the stalwart Society kingdoms. While the Society of Creative Anachronism did things right, down to the linen shirts and hand-sewn boots, real steel weapons and man-to-man combat, nothing prepared them for fifteen-feet-tall giants, hordes of trolls, and a fucking dragon.

They may have come through okay, if not for that damn drake. Killed his best riders: Susan and Maggie. Mangled Maggie and burned Susan to the ground. So many fallen that long black night.

His wife, Deidre, still wasn't home from the rehab center where she'd been recovering from the injuries she'd sustained. There was a damn good chance she'd never walk again.

Sarah had kept the dragon busy, let him rescue Deidre after the giants had broken through their defenses. But part of him blamed Sarah for all of this going down the way it had. Sure, she didn't really understand the sword that she had reforged was the legendary Gram. Hell, only Katie had thought it possible, and even he'd laughed at her. It wasn't until the dragon had kidnapped his baby sister, along with Sarah's blacksmith master, Julie Hendrickson, that Jimmy had accepted the truth. All the crazy shit his parents had told him. All the history and stories were really true.

Didn't mean he had to like it.

And he wasn't alone. He had friends—friends who knew the truth about the world.

Stuart and Gunther sat on either side of a small table, each ensconced in a large leather wingback chair. They hadn't waited and were sipping their scotch while Jimmy gathered his thoughts.

The room was filled with cabinets and display cases, bookshelves and weapons racks, which held a smattering of items: swords, tomes, scrolls, cups, necklaces, and trinkets. The northern wall was dominated by a huge world map.

Jimmy's grandparents had commissioned the map from dwarven artisans in the early twentieth century, but it was based on a much older one, only known by rumor and hearsay. Each continent was laid out in meticulous detail. Political demarcations were absent, but geographical locations were noted in abundance. Remarkable about the map were the tiny lights that glowed from spots on every continent. Most were major cities; they'd figured those out early on. Some were obviously deep in ancient mountain ranges, and two were mysteriously in the middle of an ocean—one in the Atlantic and one in what is now called the Sea of Japan.

These lights, these pinpoints glowing in the shadows of the room, represented the dragons that ruled the world. Jimmy had first seen the map when he was nine. He remembered that day like many children remember the day they learn Santa Claus isn't real, or that their parents were human and fallible. He didn't understand the ramifications of this knowledge at first, not even after his parents had disappeared. It took Sarah, Gram, and that damn dragon, Jean-Paul Duchamp, for the truth of the world to finally become clear.

He'd been in his room in a tent made from blankets, pillows, and a couple of ski poles. He had his flashlight and was reading comic books way past his bedtime. It was late, close to midnight, when he heard a commotion outside. An odd warbling sound echoed through the house. Jimmy scrambled out of the tent and jerked the bedroom door open. Katie was screaming, and his father was rushing toward the front door, pulling a leather harness across his shoulders and settling a long sword into the attached sheath.

"Dad?" Jimmy called. His father paused at the door, his face grim. "Go help your mother," he said, then turned without even waiting to see if he complied. The front screen slammed with a bang that startled him.

He turned to the sounds of Katie's cries. His mother came down the hallway carrying his screaming two-year-old sister in her arms.

"Come on, Jim. Hurry." She waved at him, cradling Katie to her chest.

At the end, near the library, there was an open panel, one he'd never noticed before. She sat Katie on the ground. "Take her hand," she said to him, holding out her own. Katie loved Jimmy, and leaned into him, quieting.

"Don't make any noise," his mother said before kissing him quickly on the forehead. "I'll come get you when it's safe. Go down the stairs. We won't be able to hear Katie there."

"But, Mom. What's going on?" He was horrified. They'd never acted like this. "Where's Dad going?"

She knelt down and cupped her hand against his cheek. "He's going to protect us," she said. "I need to go help him. Can you be strong for me, James?"

When she called him James, he knew it was serious. He swallowed hard and nodded. "I'll keep Katie safe."

She smiled at him, which filled him with warmth. "You are brave and strong."

"Me, too," Katie piped up.

Their mother smiled worriedly and kissed her on the cheek. "Yes, popkin. You are brave and true. Now, go." She shooed them onto the dark landing. "Just go to the first bend. It's seventy-three steps. You'll be safe there."

The door shut with a quiet click. Jimmy pulled the penlight from his pocket and strained to see down into the void.

"Come on," he whispered.

"It's dark," Katie whined. "I don't like it."

"We'll be safe." He squeezed her hand as they crept down into the unknown.

He counted the seventy-three steps and stopped at the first bend. He sat down, his back against the wall, and pulled Katie into his lap. She snuggled up against him and whimpered quietly.

"I'm gonna turn the light off," he said, stroking her hair. "Save the batteries."

"I want Momma."

"She'll be back soon," he said and clicked off the light.

As his eyes adjusted, he could make out a glow coming from below.

"Pretty," Katie said, slipping from his lap.

"Katie, wait." She scooted down the stairs on her bottom, one riser at a time, and he followed, holding his breath. Where the stairs ended they found a room full of treasures, lit by the glowing dragon lights.

He'd found out later that a group of refugees from Vancouver had stumbled onto the farm, harried and wounded, triggering some sort of alarm. His father had come to the strangers' aid, helping fight off a giant and getting mostly dwarves, along with a few humans, into the barn before the sun rose.

It was later, days after this incident, that his father had accompanied him down to the bunker and explained to his son the meaning of the map.

It held hundreds of lights. Some glowed brightly, while others flickered and waned. Only one had grown dark in recent memory. Jimmy pulled his thoughts back to the present and paused in his pacing. He dragged his finger along the bottom frame of the map and stared upward. The map rose from just three feet off the ground to near the ceiling, putting the light for Vancouver out of his reach.

Gunther and Stuart had the best view of the map, sitting a dozen feet away, against the opposite wall. The first time they'd seen the map, three days after Jimmy received the news of his parents' disappearance, they had commented how much the map reminded them of the night sky.

"So damn many," Stuart growled when no one had

spoken. "The bastards feed off us like maggots. It's about time we began to do something about it."

Gunther winced and sipped his scotch.

Jimmy turned, his face flushed with anger. "And what do you propose?" he said, sweeping his right arm to encompass the entire map. "Do you honestly think they'd sit idly by while we . . ." He paused, struggling to keep his anger in check. "We can't just hunt them down. This isn't the Middle Ages. They're practically immortal, have learned to adapt in ways we can only guess at. They don't even look like dragons most of the time. They control multinational corporations and some entire countries, for god's sake. Hell, I wouldn't put it past one of them to use nukes if push came to shove." He looked between the two men, feeling the desperation crawling in his belly. "Most of us don't even know they exist. Can you imagine what the common man would think if he learned we weren't at the top of the food chain?"

Gunther sat his glass on the table, took up his cane, and struggled to his feet. They watched him, saying nothing. The vivid memory of Gunther being smashed to the ground by a giant's cudgel was still too fresh in their minds.

"You overestimate their power," Gunther said, stepping toward the map and pointing at Vancouver with the head of his cane. "They've ruled us for so long that we've forgotten ourselves."

"Amen," Stuart said from his seat. He'd worn his anger on his vest since the spring. Since they'd lost so many friends in the battle with the dragon, Duchamp, and his minions.

Gunther nodded. "We were part of an event that has not happened in written history. Not since St. George have we even heard rumors of a human destroying one of them. Now one of our very own has stepped into legend."

Jimmy flicked his hand toward Gunther and barked, "Bah. We were lucky."

"Were we?" Stuart yelped. "We lost twenty-seven good people. You think that's lucky?"

Gunther leaned on his cane with both hands firmly covering the worked bull's-head handle. "I grieve as you do," he said, turning to his friend. "But this is nothing compared to the wholesale slaughter in the Dark Ages. Entire villages wasted, broad swathes of countryside slaughtered in the great migration."

Stuart growled low in his throat. "So says your order," he finally voiced. "There's proof of the Black Plague, you know."

Gunther sighed and glanced at Jimmy.

"Plague, famine, war, and worse," Jimmy said, his voice even. "My father explained it to me as well. One does not discount the existence of the other."

"We've read all the notes Jim's parents left us and have researched on our own over the last thirteen years," Gunther offered. "Nothing prepared us for Sarah."

They fell silent at that.

TOR

Award-winning authors
Compelling stories

Please join us at the website
below for more information
about this author and other great
Tor selections, and to sign up for
our monthly newsletter!